DAUNTLESS

A NOVEL OF THE GULF WAR

W.D. SULLIVAN

PUBLISHED BY

Escrire

A FICTION IMPRINT FROM ADDUCENT
www.AdducentInc.com
TITLES DISTRIBUTED IN
North America
United Kingdom
Western Europe
South America
Australia
China
India

DAUNTLESS: A NOVEL OF THE GULF WAR

BY W.D. SULLIVAN

HARDBACK ISBN: 9781937592769
PAPERBACK ISBN: 9781937592776

PUBLISHED BY ADDUCENT, INC. UNDER ITS ESCRIRE FICTION IMPRINT
JACKSONVILLE, FLORIDA
WWW.ADDUCENTINC.COM
PUBLISHED IN THE UNITED STATES OF AMERICA

DAUNTLESS

A Novel of the Gulf War

W.D. Sullivan

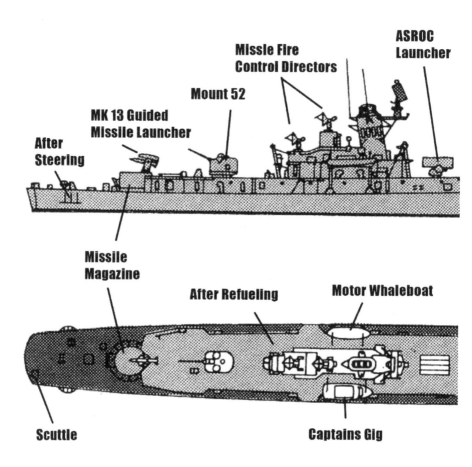

ASROC Launcher

Missile Fire Control Directors

Mount 52

MK 13 Guided Missile Launcher

After Steering

Missile Magazine

After Refueling

Motor Whaleboat

Scuttle

Captains Gig

Stern

USS DAUNTLESS DDG-25

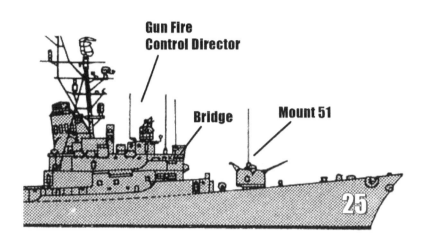

Gun Fire
Control Director

Bridge

Mount 51

25

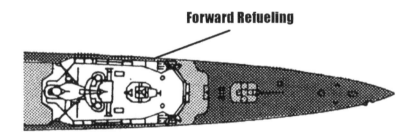

Forward Refueling

Bow

DEDICATION

To the men and women of the United States Navy who quietly go about the perilous business of defending our nation's interests on the high seas across the globe.

And to Iris.

ACKNOWLEDGEMENTS

I am indebted to my wife, Iris, who supported me throughout a 37-year Navy career, raised our two wonderful children in my absence, and held down the fort on the home front while I was out at sea. Her grace and style masked my own shortcomings and kept me on a safe course.

I am also indebted to Dennis Lowery, president of Adducent, without whose guidance, support, and encouragement this book could not have been published. An accomplished author in his own right, Dennis was invaluable in suggesting improvements, catching mistakes, and shepherding me through the process of taking my story from concept to completion. Dennis is a real pro and a pleasure to work with.

I am forever grateful to the thousands of officers and sailors with whom I served during my Navy career who were the inspiration for the characters and events in this novel.

Finally, I want to acknowledge the bravery and sacrifices quietly made every day by the men and women of the United States Navy. Life at sea is tough and dangerous, even in peacetime. As a country, we are fortunate that the best of our youth continues to volunteer, raise their right hand and swear an oath, and then go down to the sea in ships to do our nation's bidding.

W. D. Sullivan
February 2018

FOREWORD

This is a work of fiction based loosely on Operation Desert Shield, the run-up to the first Gulf War, Operation Desert Storm. All of the characters are fictional, and there is no *Adams*-class guided-missile destroyer named *USS Dauntless*. Any resemblance to persons living or dead is purely coincidental.

However, the *USS Saratoga* Battle Group did leave the U.S. east coast on August 7, 1990, five days after Iraq invaded Kuwait. The ships *USS Philippine Sea, USS Spruance, USS Biddle, USS Elmer Montgomery,* and *USS Detroit* were actual U.S. Navy ships making up part of that battle group. The ships of the *Saratoga* Battle Group did take up station in the northern Red Sea and conducted maritime interception operations enforcing the United Nations imposed embargo on Iraq. The events in this story are all fictional.

For purposes of the story, I have altered the timelines of when additional United States and other nation's ship arrived on station to take up the mission of maritime interdiction. In fact, when the *Saratoga* group arrived in the Red Sea, there were already several U.S. and other nation ships on station and enforcing the mission of stopping, boarding, and searching ships entering and leaving the Gulf of Aqaba. *Saratoga* replaced the *USS Eisenhower,* the first aircraft carrier on station. *Eisenhower* had been in the Mediterranean Sea preparing to return to her homeport of Norfolk, Virginia when she was sent through the Suez Canal in response to the Iraqi invasion. *Saratoga* was to have been *Eisenhower*'s replacement in the Mediterranean for a routine peacetime deployment. All of that changed on the fly with the Iraqi invasion and the U.S.-led response.

To my knowledge, little has been written about the work these ships did during Operation Desert Shield in the Red Sea.

Similar operations were taking place in the Persian Gulf. When Operation Desert Storm began with the air war in March of 1991, aircraft from *USS Saratoga, USS John F Kennedy,* and *USS America* in the Red Sea flew combat sorties in support of the removal of Iraqi forces from Kuwait.

I hope this novel will give the reader a sense of the work done by the U.S. Navy in the Red Sea during Operation Desert Shield. Although no combat occurred in the Red Sea during this period, our Navy's sailors and Coast Guardsmen carried out dangerous operations day and night to accomplish the mission. Enjoy!

W.D. Sullivan

PROLOGUE

Philadelphia Naval Shipyard

Two men wearing white hard hats stood on the west quay wall of the inactive ship basin in the Philadelphia Naval Shipyard. Dressed in dungarees and denim work shirts, each wore steel-toed safety boots and bright yellow vests. Across the body of dirty water separating them from the east side of the basin were nested a dozen old, rusted hulks of Gearing and Adams-class destroyers in nests three ships deep. Behind them on the other side of the finger pier loomed two older World War II-era heavy cruisers, *USS Newport News (CA-148)* and *USS Salem (CA-139)*, their large eight-inch gun turrets dwarfing the smaller five-inch gun mounts on the destroyers across the basin. The *Newport News* was noticeably missing the center barrel of the three-gun Number Two Turret, the result of an in-bore explosion off the coast of Vietnam in 1972 which had killed twenty sailors. All of the ships in this area of the shipyard had been placed in lay-up, or "mothball," status, kept in reserve if the world situation required the United States Navy to surge to a higher number of ships. With the Soviet Union on the verge of collapse, that prospect seemed increasingly unlikely. Along the pier to their right and left, lounged a half-dozen men in dirty coveralls and blue hard hats. Shipyard line handlers, standing ready to tie up the newcomer.

The older of the two men shook his head sadly as he looked at the once proud warships arrayed in front of him. He had served in destroyers during both the Korean War and the Vietnam war. It saddened him to see these once proud fighting ships now lifeless. Their haze gray hulls faded and streaked with rust. Gun mounts, if not removed, angled downward, as if in shame. In all likelihood, these former 'greyhounds of the sea' were headed for the scrap yards to be dismantled and recycled. Dead metal, he shook his head again, the only value. Their HY-80 steel had many uses.

A single loud "toot" was heard beyond the channel leading to the basin from out in the Delaware River. Two answering toots responded. Tugboats signaling each other as they maneuvered yet another carcass into the basin.

"Here she comes," he muttered, half to himself and half to the other man, "a real fighting ship."

The younger man, a naval architect recently graduated from college who had never worn a military uniform, looked down at his clipboard. "Ex-*USS Dauntless*," he said, glancing up at his partner and pushing his glasses up on his nose, "Says here, battle damaged."

The older man merely nodded, his eyes focused on the channel entrance. The older, nested ships blocked his view of the approaching tugboats and their charge.

A gray Navy tug boat trailing a wire hawser at short stay emerged around the corner marking the end of the channel and the beginning of the basin. Within seconds the gray bow of an *Adams*-class guided-missile destroyer, the DDG, slid into view, the number twenty-five painted on the side, just behind the starboard anchor, which was 'at the dip,' hanging a few feet out of the hawse pipe, ready to be dropped if necessary.

As the rest of the starboard side of the DDG emerged, a second tug appeared, just aft of midships. A power make-up of two wire hawsers glued it to the side of *Dauntless*, ready to assist in twisting the ship to starboard and bringing it gently alongside the pier. The older man knew that a third tug was similarly made up to the port side of the destroyer.

As the stern of the destroyer cleared the end of the opposite pier wall and the nest of three other destroyers, the tugs began to twist her around to bring her alongside the quay wall, signaling their movements and intentions with a series of whistle signals neither man understood.

As the ship was turned right ninety degrees, men in coveralls on the main deck removed the wires connecting the port side tug to the ship, and that tug backed quickly away, exposing the entire hull that would soon rest against the large "Yokohama" fenders arrayed along the quay wall.

As the tug cleared the side, both men could see the damage noted on the clipboard. Just below where the missile launcher once sat, a rough patch approximately ten feet by ten feet was crudely welded to the hull. Much of the hull and the deckhouse above the main deck was fire-scarred. Black smudge showed through a quick touch-up paint job, applied no doubt to make the ship presentable for its decommissioning ceremony. The missile launcher had been removed, but the cylindrical magazine remained. It looked naked without the launcher rail on top. The deck on top of the magazine and the O-1 level deck forward was buckled, apparently from the force of a massive explosion. The after five-inch gun mount was also missing, a large steel plate covering the hole in the O-1 level where the gun mount once sat. That patch too, was uneven, not flat, evidence of the warped deck on which it had been welded.

"Wow, what happened?" asked the younger man.

The older man looked at him, lowering his glasses, "You don't know?" he asked, the creases in his lined face deepening.

The younger man blushed slightly, glancing down at the clipboard, "Not really, just what it says here."

As the ship was nudged gently alongside the pier, men on deck tossed down small diameter heaving lines which were connected to the five-inch nylon mooring lines lying faked out on the destroyer's main deck. The two men watched as the men on the pier slid the eye of each line over a massive steel bollard on the pier and quickly secured the destroyer in place. With tooting whistles, the three tugs eased away from the old ship's side and headed out of the basin for the next job. *Dauntless* would have only one more voyage, that to a scrap yard someplace, probably somewhere on the gulf coast.

The old man studied the younger man, then turned to look at the ship. His eyes—a little moist, perhaps smarting from the diesel exhaust coming from the three tugs—scanned the once-upon-a-time destroyer. He shook his head a final time.

"Let's go aboard and sign for the ship, then I'll buy you a cup of coffee and tell you a story."

ONE

Mayport Naval Station, Florida

"Single up all lines."

"Single up all lines, aye," repeated the young Operations Specialist into the voice-activated sound-powered phone set strapped around his neck and connected to the headphones squashing down his Navy-blue *USS Dauntless (DDG-25)* ball cap.

Commander Will Tanner nodded approvingly to himself. Repeat back procedures were good business. They ensured the phone talker had understood the order before he relayed it to the other phone talkers on the 1JV net.

"Forecastle, fantail, bridge, single up all lines."

Tanner couldn't hear the responses but knew they should have repeated back the exact same words so that this young seaman knew that those on the other end had understood. He surreptitiously glanced at the neatly stenciled name over the sailor's right breast. Collins. He made a note to remember the name and the face. Young. Barely shaving. Skinny. Bright blue eyes that seemed to dance with the excitement of leaving port. The same excitement Tanner still felt no matter how many times he had done this.

He looked over the splinter shield on the starboard bridge wing to the forecastle below. Another young seaman, black, stocky and solid looking, said something into his sound-powered phone set and then into the ear of the boatswain mate, also black and wearing the three chevrons of a petty officer first class, an E-6 in the military rank system, standing next to him.

"Single up all lines!" bellowed the boatswain mate.

1

The eighteen sailors on deck leaped into action, rapidly uncoiling the figure-eight round turns on the bitts securing lines one, two, and three to the heavy-duty bollards on the pier. Working quickly, they reduced the coils until only three turns remained over the bitts. One section of the doubled up five-inch circumference nylon mooring lines were expertly slacked as they led down to the pier.

Tanner looked down to the berth next to the bow as three sailors from another ship lifted one eye of each of the three lines which had been "dipped" through the other eye and tossed them in the water. Tanner looked on approvingly as the forecastle line handlers quickly hauled in the lines hand over hand through the chocks and began neatly faking them down on deck. Looking aft, Tanner saw the same thing happening three hundred feet behind him as the fantail line handlers singled up lines four, five and six. So far, so good. Now only a single strand of each of his five-inch nylon mooring lines connected *Dauntless* to terra firma.

Turning into the pilothouse, he said, "Stand by to answer all bells." Again, his order to the engineers four decks below in the Main Engineroom was repeated back before the phone talker relayed the order.

With a quick glance up at the signal halyards above and behind him, Tanner saw that a slight breeze was coming off the land, blowing the international call-sign flags November, Delta, Alpha, Uniform toward the ship's port side. *Piece of cake,* he thought, offsetting wind, calm water in the basin. There was a ship tied up astern, *USS Luce (DDG-38)*, but he had made a point of walking along the pier that morning, assessing how much room he had astern. There was enough to twist the stern clear before backing out.

Seaman Jeremy Collins studied his new captain. Nineteen years old and a veteran of fourteen months in the United States Navy, Jeremy Collins had been aboard Dauntless for six months.

For the entire time, he had been the sea detail 1JV talker on the bridge. At General Quarters, he was the JA talker relaying the captain's orders if he was present on the bridge and not in the Combat Information Center twenty feet aft. The sailor staying next to the captain to relay his orders to the other stations on the ship monitoring the IJV circuit. His new captain was of medium height, slight of build, probably a runner. Dark hair sprinkled with gray around the temples showed under the *USS Dauntless* ball cap. Its gold "scrambled eggs" on the bill, denoted his status as a senior officer, a Navy commander. Captain Tanner seemed like a pretty cool customer, nothing like Old Man Schwartz, his predecessor. Schwartz was a screamer, always sweating the load and chewing people's asses when things didn't go just right. A real asshole. Well, it was early yet, *let's see how Tanner does when somebody fucks up, and things turn to shit.*

Tanner took a last look at the starboard side of *Dauntless.* Two large, black 'Yokohama' fenders held *Dauntless* away from the seawall, providing about five feet of separation between the ship and the pier. No lines stretched between the ship and the dock except the six mooring lines. Turning to Seaman Collins, he said, "Take in lines three, four, five and six. Check lines one and two."

Collins repeated the order and then again into his sound-powered phone set. The boatswain mate on the forecastle could be heard giving the order. The line handlers on the pier and the forecastle sprang into action, the sailors on the pier tossing line three off the bollard and into the water. Looking aft, Tanner could see that all three lines securing the after-part of the ship were snaking their way through the chocks and up onto the fantail deck. Now only line one, running through the bullnose on the bow perpendicular to the ship, and line two, tending aft to a bollard on the pier almost directly under the bridge, connected the ship to the dock.

Fifteen minutes earlier, *Dauntless'* executive officer, second in command, Lieutenant Commander Ricky McKnight, had given the orders to take in the brow and disconnect the phone lines. This, after checking with the captain in his cabin to be sure he wasn't making a last-minute phone call to the squadron commander up the hill in his office and no doubt watching to see how his newest skipper got his ship underway.

Turning into the pilothouse, Tanner gave the order, "Right full-rudder. All engines stop. Indicate nine, nine, nine." He glanced at the rudder angle indicator located forward on the bridge wing and watched as the indicator swiftly pointed to starboard, stopping on the thirty-degree mark. Out of the corner of his eye, he could see the helmsman rapidly spinning the ship's wheel. The engine order indicators remained steady in the stop position, pointing straight up at twelve o'clock. By ordering '9-9-9', he was telling the engineers in main control that he wanted speed changes in five-knot increments, rather than by precise revolutions per minute. It made for easier engine orders while maneuvering close to the pier and in restricted waters.

"Ready to go XO?" he said to McKnight. "Aye, Captain, all stations ready." Tanner thought that McKnight seemed a little tense. It was understandable, he had only met his new captain a week earlier.

McKnight, in turn, watched his new captain intently, searching for clues to his temperament. Having spent the first year of his all-important executive officer ride working for Commander Steve Schwartz, McKnight was a little gun shy; like a dog that has been beaten and then finds itself in a new home. This was the first time the ship would get underway with her new captain. On top of that, this was day one of an unexpected deployment to the Middle East to respond to Iraq's invasion of its neighbor Kuwait, bordering the Persian Gulf.

The pier was filled with family members saying goodbye to their husbands, fathers, and sons for nobody knew how long. A week earlier *Dauntless* had been sleepily preparing for a quiet fall and winter as the ship wound down operations in preparation for decommissioning. Many family members were crying, and McKnight hoped the scene was not distracting the sailors on deck. Many personal plans had been upset when the United States responded forcefully to the invasion of the tiny nation of Kuwait.

Captain Tanner had said he would take the ship out himself at the sea detail briefing in the wardroom the day before. McKnight knew that Tanner had served on two previous *Adams*-class guided-missile destroyers, but it had been nine years since the last one. He had hoped that Tanner might let him get the ship underway so that he could impress him with his ship handling expertise. *Get off to a good start with the new captain.* At the same time, part of him was glad that the CO had wanted to do it himself. Commander Schwartz had been an impatient and easily irritated supervisor of bridge operations—and everything else—screaming at officers who reacted too slowly or issued an ill-thought-out command. With the CO taking the ship out, McKnight at least had the opportunity to study his new captain and perhaps learn a thing or two about how he did things.

"Port engine ahead one-third, starboard engine back one-third," ordered Tanner. He heard the bells as the lee helmsman moved the arms on the Engine Order Telegraph, sending a signal to the engineers watching the repeaters in main control. Again, the lee helmsman repeated the order he had been given as he moved the levers. Glancing down, Tanner saw the indicators out on the bridge wing move to the appropriate position. He shifted his attention aft, where two-thirds of his ship lay, and where the first visual indications of the effects of his order would appear. A wash of water moved forward up the side of the ship as the thirteen-foot diameter manganese bronze starboard propeller took a bite out of the black water in the Mayport basin. 70,000 shaft horsepower was unleashed by the engineers opening the steam valves in main control, the port shaft in the forward direction, the starboard in a backing direction. Tanner saw the stern start to move away from the pier. Glancing forward he saw the bow move slightly forward and begin to cock in toward the pier. Line one had developed a downward dip as the ship's movement took all the tension off the line.

"Take in line one," he ordered.

Collins relayed the order via the phone talker. Sound-powered phones were as old as the modern Navy, much like a child's waxed string and tin can telephone system. The XO held a walkie-talkie in his hand, as did Ensign Wilton Grimmage, the ship's First Lieutenant, in charge on the forecastle. Neither was used. Captain Schwartz had insisted on using the sound-powered phones with the walkie-talkie only as a back-up. It was the way they had trained twelve months ago during refresher training at Guantanamo Bay, Cuba. That was before the Navy had decided to strike *Dauntless* from the rolls. Too old, too hard to maintain, and ill-equipped to deal with the high-tech threat posed by modern cruise missiles and quiet submarines. Tanner agreed with the sound-powered phone edict, conflicting orders over different circuits only confused things.

As line one snaked aboard through the bullnose, Tanner gauged the tension on line two, now serving to help pivot the ship in place as his engine twist took effect.

"Check line two," he repeated.

That order should have been unnecessary as it had already been given, but he wanted to be sure the line handlers knew he didn't want too much strain on the line. Years ago, Tanner had been a First Lieutenant himself in *USS Sellers (DDG-11)*. He knew full well how dangerous a nylon mooring line under tension could be. He had watched in horror along with hundreds of family members on the pier as *Sellers'* Chief Boatswain Mate had lost both his legs as a line parted under strain and snapped back like a cracked whip. One of the Chief's legs, severed just below the knee, had flown over the side into the water and had to be fished out later by two sailors in a paint punt. He had decided then, that if he ever became a ship captain, he would never give the order to "hold" a mooring line except in the direst of circumstances.

Turning his attention aft again, Tanner saw that the stern had moved away from the pier at about a ten-degree angle and there was daylight visible off *Luce's* port side. Time to back her out.

"Port engine stop. Rudder amidships. Take in line two." Pause for a second as those orders were registered and relayed. The stern continued to swing out, creating more separation from the hull of *Luce*. "All engines back two-thirds."

Scanning his indicators, listening to the repeat backs, and watching line two slide through the chock, Tanner turned his attention aft as the twin propellers dug into the inky water and the ship began to back straight. The offsetting wind was helping, *Luce* would not be a problem.

As soon as line two was dropped off the bollard by the line handlers on the pier, the Officer of the Deck, Lieutenant Commander Andy Morton, the ship's Operations Officer, announced "Underway!"

The Boatswain Mate of the Watch, Petty Officer Third Class Lee Reinhart, keyed the 1MC mic and sounded a two-second blast on the whistle hanging around his neck. On the forecastle two sailors quickly hauled down the blue jack with fifty white stars. Tanner knew that the American flag, or ensign, flying from the flagstaff on the fantail was also coming down. Glancing at the forward mast, he saw the American flag quickly rising on the halyards as *Dauntless* changed status from moored to underway.

"Sound one prolonged blast," he ordered. Morton reached up to the whistle handle suspended from the overhead and pulled it down. A five-second blast of the steam-powered whistle echoed around the Mayport basin as *Dauntless* announced its change in status.

"Three shorts," said Tanner.

Morton pulled the whistle handle three times, holding it for one second each time, announcing that *Dauntless* was backing down.

USS Dauntless (DDG-25) backed smartly into the center of the Mayport basin as the line handlers on the forecastle and back on the fantail fell into ranks near their faked down mooring lines.

* * *

On a small hill overlooking the basin, Captain Douglas Nordstrom, the commander of Destroyer Squadron 12, stood by his large, smoked glass picture window and nodded approvingly. Next to him stood Commander Roy Knudson his Chief Staff Officer.

"*Dauntless* looks sharp. I like that Tanner didn't use tugs and didn't take a pilot."

"Yes sir," said Knudson.

Commander Roy Knudson had recently been in command of *USS Charles F. Adams (DDG-2)*, the first of the *Adams*-class of guided-missile destroyers and a sister ship of *Dauntless*. He had graded out as the number one commanding officer in DESRON 12 and Nordstrom had selected him as his CSO when his command tour was over. Knudson felt a touch of envy as he watched *Dauntless* begin another twist in the middle of the basin and begin to maneuver toward the channel leading to the St. Johns River and the Atlantic Ocean beyond. Tanner stepped into a good deal he thought to himself. *That crazy fucking raghead Saddam Hussein goes and invades Kuwait five days ago and what was supposed to be a dead-end command tour for Tanner turns into what could be a wartime deployment.* So now *Dauntless* sails with the *Saratoga* Battle Group into what might turn into a war. Sure, *Adams* had deployed while Knudson was in command, but there had been no action, just peacetime presence and show the flag port visits. *Shit.*

Roy Knudson had been one year ahead of Will Tanner and a company mate at the Naval Academy. As an upperclassman, he hadn't competed directly against Tanner, but there had been a tension between them. He didn't know exactly what it was, but it was there. Just like getting this command, Tanner had always seemed to step in shit but come up with a clean shoe.

None more so than the collision while he was XO in *USS Wade (DD-999)*. Tanner had escaped censure in that incident, despite being on the bridge when it happened. The investigation found that it wasn't Tanner's fault, at the same time damning him with faint praise. The Navy personnel system had administered its own version of justice, giving Tanner command of *Dauntless*, a ship not scheduled to deploy and headed for the scrap yard.

Doug Nordstrom watched *Dauntless* head fair for the channel and turned his attention to *USS Elmer Montgomery (FF-1082)*, one of the other DESRON 12 ships in the *Saratoga* Battle Group. Along with the Aegis cruiser, *USS Philippine Sea (CG-58)* and the destroyer *USS Spruance (DD-963)*, the *USS Saratoga (CV-60)* would sail to the Mediterranean with this group of Mayport-based ships. They would be joined by the cruiser USS *Biddle (CG-34)* from Norfolk and the oiler USS *Detroit (AOE-4)* from Earle, New Jersey. Nordstrom too felt a pang of envy. In all likelihood, the *Saratoga* group would pass through Mediterranean, transit the Suez Canal, and enter the Middle East area of operations. The president had vowed that the invasion of Kuwait would not stand. The international community was organizing itself to do something. It was too early to know exactly what. What happened with the *Saratoga* group all depended on what ensued on the diplomatic front. If Saddam Hussein blinked and pulled his troops back, war would be averted. If he didn't, well, who knew? *Would Kuwait's sovereignty be important enough to the rest of the world to go to war?*

* * *

On the flag bridge aboard *Saratoga*, three senior officers stood side by side to watch the fleet leave the harbor. Rear Admiral Nicholas "Nick" McCall, a two-star officer, commanded Cruiser-Destroyer Group Eight. Despite flying his flag in Norfolk, McCall had been directed to command the hastily assembled *Saratoga* Battle Group.

The two captains were McCall's Chief of Staff, Captain John Campbell, and the commander of Destroyer Squadron 24, Captain Alexander Vanzant. McCall and Vanzant were surface warfare officers who had grown up in the surface Navy and had commanded ships of their own. McCall had commanded three, a fleet tug as a young lieutenant, an *Adams*-class DDG like *Dauntless*, and a steam-powered cruiser, *USS Halsey (CG-23)*. Vanzant was in his second, major, command; a tactical Destroyer Squadron, DESRON 24. He had commanded the *Spruance*-class destroyer *USS Paul F. Foster (DD-964)*.

John Campell was a naval aviator, an F-14 fighter pilot who had been on track for command of an aircraft carrier until one of his young pilots killed himself and his radar intercept officer while showboating over his parents' home while on a cross-country flight. Campbell could have done nothing to prevent the accident once the pilot left the ground, but the investigating officer had determined that Campbell had fallen short as a leader, failing to instill the proper standards in his squadron officers. The Navy could be unforgiving, holding officers accountable for everything that happened under their command. It was a time-honored tradition and one which every commanding officer accepted as part of the privilege of command.

Captain Alex Vanzant frowned as he watched *Dauntless* move through the harbor. He had resisted having Will Tanner screen for command when he sat on the command screening board that had selected Tanner three years ago. Vanzant felt that Tanner had unjustly dodged a bullet during the *Wade* collision investigation. He was somewhat mollified when Tanner received orders to *Dauntless*, considering that to be a caretaker command tour, shortened by decommissioning, which would virtually guarantee that Tanner did not get promoted and considered for major command. *And now this.* Vanzant was also skeptical about Tanner having taken command only a week before. Before the Iraqi invasion, he wouldn't have cared. But once this battle group was thrown together to support President Bush's proclamation that the Iraqi invasion would not stand, Tanner and *Dauntless* became his problem. He had approached Admiral McCall about having Steve Schwartz extended in command, arguing that Tanner was too new, untested, and had a checkered past. Nick McCall had demurred, saying, "He's the Captain now, let's give him a chance." Vanzant would be Tanner's reporting senior on this cruise and Tanner was starting with a two-strike count.

* * *

Having satisfied himself that he hadn't forgotten how to drive a ship while cooling his heels in a staff job in the Pentagon, Tanner stepped into the pilothouse and announced, "this is the Captain, Lieutenant Jay-Gee Nelson has the conn."

"This is Lieutenant Jay-Gee Nelson, I have the conn."

They had discussed this at the sea detail brief. Lieutenant (junior grade) Paul Nelson, the ship's Anti-Submarine Warfare Officer and sea detail Junior Officer of the Deck, had been watching the captain and waiting his turn to drive the ship out of the channel and into the open ocean. After a short discussion to make sure he knew exactly what orders were in effect, Nelson was ready to take over.

Tanner moved over to his leather-bound chair on the starboard side of the pilothouse and hopped up and in. The chair was his and his only as the captain. A matching chair was on the port side, unofficially the XO's chair. Tanner watched his bridge and navigation team go through the routine of taking the ship safely out of the restricted waters of the harbor, the St Johns River channel, and past the sea buoy to the open sea. On the forecastle, he could see the line handlers still in ranks and Ensign Grimmage watching over the anchor detail, ready to drop it in an emergency.

As the ship turned right into the river and headed east through the jettys, he turned to the XO.

"XO, secure the line handlers."

"Aye, aye, sir!"

The show was over. The families were headed home, some wiping away tears. Some had hopped in their cars and raced down to the beach to climb out on the south jetty for one final goodbye wave.

Tanner watched as the line handlers on the forecastle began striking the mooring lines below deck to ready the ship for the Atlantic crossing. They wouldn't be needed again for nine days until *Dauntless* pulled into the harbor in Naples, Italy. At least that was the plan now. Scanning the bridge, he saw that Lieutenant Commander Morton hovered around Paul Nelson, coaching him when necessary to keep the ship on a safe heading.

Dauntless was the last ship of the *Adams*-class of guided-missile destroyers. Twenty-four had been built for the United States Navy in the 1960s plus another two for Germany and three for Australia. Tanner had served on two previously, *Sellers* as First Lieutenant and *Lynde McCormick* as Weapons Officer. When they were built, the *Adams*-class were the hottest surface combatants in the U.S. Navy. But that was thirty years ago, and they were getting long in the tooth. Newer destroyers were coming off the ways, powered by gas turbine engines instead of steam, and equipped with the most modern offensive and defensive weapons systems.

Even at her age, *Dauntless* sported an impressive array of weapons. For gunnery, she had two five-inch gun mounts, one forward on the forecastle and one on the O-1 level aft. Equipped with the single-armed Mark 13 guided-missile launcher, she carried thirty-five Standard SM-1 surface-to-air guided missiles and four surface-to-surface Harpoon anti-ship missiles in her magazine. The 40-round missile magazine held one inert missile, painted blue, for systems testing. Just under the bridge on the port and starboard sides were triple tube Mark 32 anti-submarine torpedo tubes, loaded with Mark 46 anti-submarine torpedoes. On the O-1 level deck amidships was the Anti-Submarine Rocket (ASROC) launcher, holding eight ASROC for killing submarines. The ASROC was simply a Mark 46 torpedo mounted on the end of a rocket that could fly about seven miles before depositing the torpedo in the water to search for enemy submarines.

Despite the elegant lines of a destroyer and weaponry, Tanner had also taken note of the condition of his new, thirty-year-old command. Her sides showed the effects of three decades at sea, fighting the elements and unforgiving relentlessness of the ocean. Like an old dog, her ribs showed where the continuous pounding of the waves had resulted in "canning," the scalloped look as the ship's sides gave in to the sea between the stringers and steel beams. There were also indications of lack of attention to detail, no doubt the result of an attitude of resignation about the upcoming decommissioning. Running rust below the scuppers and the anchor hawse pipes. Green verdigris on the brass lifeline turnbuckles. Rust poking up through the non-skid on deck in high-traffic areas. The Chief Engineer, Lieutenant Commander Ken Carpenter, had briefed him on the condition of the engineering plant. The snipes were staying ahead of most problems, but the plant was loose, with minor steam leaks that wasted valuable feed water. There were areas in the bilges where the bulkheads had simply rotted away. There was no doubt, she was a tired ship, although still capable in a limited threat environment.

Will Tanner was just happy to get a ship command, even if it was to be a short one. After the collision in *Wade,* he thought he might be a terminal lieutenant commander. Sure, the investigation had determined that he was not at fault, but still, as the senior officer on the bridge when it happened, many of his contemporaries had questioned the decision not to fry him.

Ricky McKnight sidled up to the captain's chair.

"Great job getting the ship underway Captain!" he gushed.

"Thanks, XO."

Tanner thought that McKnight was a little too exuberant. Kissing ass. *Did he just see Lieutenant Commander Morton roll his eyes and exchange a look with Paul Nelson?* McKnight had been extremely accommodating throughout the turnover week between Tanner and Commander Steve Schwartz, his predecessor. So accommodating that it had made Tanner a little uncomfortable. It was as if he had swallowed his loyalty pill the second Tanner stepped aboard, abandoning his current CO for the new guy.

When Tanner and Schwartz had sat in the privacy of the captain's cabin, and Schwartz had talked him through the officers in the wardroom, Tanner had detected a reserved coolness when it came to the XO. His antennae were up, but so far McKnight had struck him as efficient and organized, although somewhat lacking in attention to detail.

Tanner turned to his Operations Officer, Andy Morton.

"What's the plan Ops?"

"*Sara* gets underway in an hour, at high tide. Alpha Sierra will promulgate a screen, and we'll start executing the SOE. We've got a night unrep with *Sara* tonight. *Detroit* doesn't join up until just west of Bermuda."

Tanner had seen the pre-sail message. The Group 8 staff and the tactical DESRON commander, or Alpha Sierra, had generated a planned series of exercises to drill the battle group as it crossed the Atlantic. So far, the situation in Kuwait had not altered the plan from what would be expected during any peacetime transit of the Atlantic. Tanner figured that would change as things developed in Iraq and Kuwait.

As they passed the sea buoy to starboard, the Atlantic swells began to move *Dauntless* in a rhythmic combination of pitching and rolling. Tanner felt that familiar queasiness that came with the first day at sea after an extended time in port. It frequently resulted in a headachy sluggishness until the inner ear adjusted and the body became accustomed to the constant movement. Many of the crew would get seasick on this first day out, even in relatively good weather. It happened every time.

Settling into his chair, he studied the gray-green ocean swells as they rolled in from their thousand-mile journey across the Atlantic. Four to five feet in height, they were nonetheless gentle, with long troughs between each swell. *Dauntless* rode easily into the swells, her hurricane bow digging in slightly before rising to ride easily up and then down as the swells passed along the four-hundred-thirty-seven feet of the ship's hull. If this kept up, it would be a relatively comfortable ride to the Strait of Gibraltar he mused.

"Request permission to secure the special sea and anchor detail," said Andy Morton.

"Permission granted."

With a nod from Morton, Petty Officer Reinhart keyed his 1MC mic, blew the trill for an announcement on his boatswain pipe, and announced, "Now, secure the special sea and anchor detail. Set the normal Condition 3 watch. On deck, watch section one. All hands shift into the working uniform." The crew had worn the summer white uniform for the underway, it being August in Florida.

Tanner stayed in his chair while the oncoming watch team relieved the sea detail team. On the forecastle, he saw the anchor detail securing the anchor for sea and heading below. He awaited the report from the OOD that the anchors were secured for the crossing. As the officers and enlisted conducted their turnover he listened without appearing to, to see what kind of information was passed from watch to watch. The first day out, especially for those with families, often featured sloppy watch turnover. He understood. Six months seemed an eternity when it was only day one. And there was no guarantee how long this deployment might last. It depended on what happened in Kuwait. Things would start happening fast once *Sara* cleared the harbor and the ships were given their screen assignments. Tanner would certainly be on the bridge for that. Right now, he needed to take a piss.

"Ops, I'll be down in my cabin. Give me a call when *Sara* clears the channel."

"Aye, aye, sir."

He had been impressed by Andy "Salty" Morton despite his less than impressive appearance. Andy was tall and rangy, but a little stoop-shouldered. His uniform shirt barely remained tucked in, blousing over his belt in front and back. Tanner had always prided himself on a tight tuck and a straight gig line. Nevertheless, Andy Morton seemed to have a good grasp of the battle group plans and his previous experience on the 6th Fleet staff in Naples bode well for their future Mediterranean operations, even if it was just while passing through.

As he watched the captain descend the ladder to his cabin one deck below, Ricky McKnight turned on Andy Morton.

"Goddamit Ops, when were you going to tell me about the unrep?"

Morton looked stunned at first but gathered himself. The rest of the bridge team studied their instruments. Paul Nelson buried his head in the rubber light shield on the SPA-25 radar repeater, searching for rogue contacts.

"XO, it's in the pre-sail message and in the POD."

McKnight blushed. As the XO, the Plan of the Day, or POD, was his responsibility. He signed it every evening. Morton knew the XO usually blew it off, letting the Chief Yeoman draft it and bring it to him for signature. He often barely glanced at it before signing. As a result, it was full of conflicting information and typos. The Chief Yeoman had a standard list of daily routine events that appeared in every POD regardless of the reality of that day's schedule. It was not uncommon for the POD to announce that the XO's inspection of messing and berthing would occur at 10:00 AM with an announced General Quarters exercise also at 10:00 AM. The two were mutually incompatible, and everyone knew it. As a result, the POD was taken with a grain of salt by the crew.

"Don't give me that shit," spittle flew off the XO's lips, "you have to keep me informed."

Just then Tanner stepped through the pilothouse door. An awkward silence filled the bridge except for BM3 Reinhart announcing, "Captain's on the bridge."

"Forgot my coffee cup," said Tanner as he immediately recognized he had walked in on something.

"Here it is Captain," said the XO, grabbing the mug off the bridge window sill with an artificial casualness and a forced smile on his face. Morton turned his attention to the bridge window to see where the ship was going, the tenseness in his shoulders moving him stiffly to the centerline pelorus.

Tanner gave McKnight a longer than usual look, then, "Thanks, XO, I'll be down in my cabin. Stick your head in when you get a chance." He turned and pushed through the door to head down to his cabin, McKnight close on his heels.

One deck below the bridge, they turned to the starboard side and entered the captain's cabin. Directly opposite the door was the captain's desk, sitting below a porthole looking out the starboard side at the O-1 level torpedo deck. Forward of the desk was the captain's rack—a bed—folded up to become a faux leather covered couch. Forward of the cabin was a door leading to the captain's private head, the bathroom. It was a small living area, barely ten feet by fifteen, but expansive when compared to the junior officer staterooms and the enlisted berthing compartments. Destroyers were built for fighting, not comfort.

"How we doing XO?"

"Great sir, only one unauthorized absentee this morning."

"Who was that?"

"Seaman Rodgers from 1st Division. Frankly, I'm not surprised."

"Troublemaker?"

"Yessir, in and out of trouble, been to Captain's mast more than once."

"OK. Anything for me to look at before *Sara* gets out here and things start happening?"

"Yessir, a couple of messages to release."

"OK, bring them to me on the bridge. I'm going to get out of these whites and head back up. Oh, tell Ops I want to see the plan for cycling the JO's through special evolutions on the bridge. Starting with tonight's unrep."

"And XO," he studied McKnight's face for a second, "I noticed you had the Ops brief in the wardroom scheduled for 1900 tonight. What time do we go alongside *Sara*?"

"Ummm, I think around 1900."

"That won't work, will it?"

"I'll move it earlier."

Tanner dismissed him and began changing into his working khaki uniform. Something wasn't right between the XO and Ops. There had clearly been something going on before he had surprised them on the bridge. Just then the buzzer rang on the growler phone next to his desk.

"Captain."

"Captain, OOD here. *Sara* cleared the sea buoy, and Alpha Sierra's putting out a signal over PRITAC. TAO is breaking it. It'll be the sector screen."

"OK, be up in a minute. What's the range to *Sara*?"

"About 5 miles."

"Roger, up in a minute."

As Tanner entered the bridge, he heard Morton's voice coming over the "bitch box," the 29MC announcing system, "...330 to 005, five to ten thousand." Morton, the Senior Watch Officer, had assigned himself as the section one Tactical Action Officer, or TAO, and had moved to the Combat Information Center, or CIC. Navigator Lieutenant John "Woody" Woodson had assumed the deck watch.

Dauntless had been assigned a screen sector to patrol, three-hundred thirty degrees relative clockwise around to slightly to starboard in front of the center of the screen which would be occupied by *Saratoga*, the guide of the formation. The inner edge of the sector was 5,000 yards from the center, the outer edge 10,000 yards, or five nautical miles.

Just then the PRITAC speaker on the bridge crackled to life. "All units in Sierra, this is Alpha Sierra, Screen Kilo, stand by, execute, Alpha Four Mike, Charlie One Echo, Golf Three Bravo, over."

Waiting his turn, John Woodson answered, "This is Golf Three Bravo, roger, out."

Tanner glanced out the port bridge door and saw *Saratoga* about three miles away, just off the ship's port quarter. It looked like she was coming at a pretty good clip. He looked back into the pilothouse and saw Woodson and the Junior Officer of the Deck, Ensign Pete Gardner, hunched over a small table, rapidly manipulating the parallel rulers, dividers, and pencil on a sheet of maneuvering board paper. "Woody, let's go," he said.

Woodson looked up. "Working the mo-board Captain."

This touched a nerve with Tanner. He had been brought up by old-school commanding officers. Destroyers were supposed to be the greyhounds of the sea. Lots of flash and dash. When a signal was executed the rudder was expected to go over, and the forced draft blowers wind up as the ship went to a full bell and the engineering plant answered the new steam demand. None of that was happening now. "Pete, get over here."

Ensign Pete Gardner had the conn and stepped over to the port bridge wing. "Yessir?"

"Put the rudder over left standard, and ring up 25 knots."

"But..."

"Do it now."

Pete Gardner didn't need to be told twice. "Left standard rudder, all engines ahead flank, indicate turns for 25 knots."

John Woodson looked up sharply from the mo-board table. "Still working the solution," he said.

"Engineroom answers all ahead flank," sang out the lee helmsman.

"My rudder is left standard, no new course given," said the helmsman.

Pete Gardner acknowledged the reports and then gave Tanner a "what now?" look.

"Pete, you know our station is between 5,000 and 10,000 yards off the port bow of *Sara*, right?"

"Yessir."

"Look where we are. Off her starboard bow. So, we know we have to cross her bow and get over there, right?"

The ship was still swinging to port while it picked up speed.

"Put your rudder amidships."

"Rudder amidships," said Pete Gardner.

"OK, now we're headed in the right general direction, right?"

"Yessir."

"OK, what's base course and speed?"

"Uh, zero-nine-zero at 16 knots."

"OK, we're headed in the right direction. Nav can refine the course to station while we're headed there. Get it?"

"Yessir."

"Now, how does this look to you?"

"Well, *Sara* is coming toward us at 20 knots, so I think if we keep going we'll get across her bow and then the range will get closer."

"Like this course?"

"Yessir." The light went on. Tanner could see it. "Steady as she goes," said Pete Gardner.

"Steady as she goes, aye," shouted the helmsman. Then, "Steady course zero-two-five."

Just then, John Woodson shouted from the mo-board table, "I hold course 030 at 25 knots to center of our sector. Time to enter our sector, 4 minutes."

Pete Gardner looked down at his gyro repeater on the bridge wing. "We're on 025 true," he said.

Tanner gave the young ensign a questioning look. Another light went on.

"Come right, steady course 030."

The kid was grinning a little as he realized he was in charge of four-thousand-five-hundred tons of guided-missile destroyer going twenty-five knots.

"Now, what else should we be doing right about now?"

Gardner gave Tanner a blank look.

"How do you know that you're clearing *Saratoga*?"

"Check the radar?" said Gardner.

"Trust your eyes. What kind of bearing drift are you getting?"

Gardner leaned down and shot a bearing to the carrier. It was evident that *Dauntless* would safely pass ahead of *Saratoga*, but Tanner wanted to make a point.

"Seeing left bearing drift," said Gardner.

"Recommend coming right to 035 and slowing to 20 knots. CIC concurs," said Woodson.

As Gardner ordered the course change, Tanner said, "Let's go to the starboard bridge wing for the rest of this."

As they walked through the bridge, John Woodson shouted out a range to the carrier and recommended a slight course change to starboard. When Tanner and Gardner got to the starboard bridge wing, Tanner asked, "When you shot the carrier, what did you shoot?"

"The island," said Gardner.

"Carriers are pretty big," said Tanner, "you can clear one part and still hit another. Always best to shoot those bearings to the last piece of aircraft carrier you have to clear to avoid a collision."

"Show us entering our sector," said Woodson, moving between the SPA-25 repeater and his piece of mo-board paper on the plotting table.

"Report Alpha Station," said Tanner. Alpha station told the screen commander, call-sign Alpha Sierra, that *Dauntless* had reached her assigned sector. None of the other ships had reported reaching their sectors. Tanner looked at his watch team and saw that look of satisfaction that all ship handlers know when a maneuver is smartly executed.

Just then, a loud bang sounded from somewhere behind them. Within seconds the ship began to slow. The Engine Order Telegraph clanged as the pointers, manipulated from down in the engineroom, moved from full to standard. The lee helmsman reported the event and then looked out at the conning officer and captain on the bridge wing, waiting for instructions.

The bitch box crackled to life. "Bridge, main control, lost fires in One Bravo boiler. Cross connecting the plant, max speed available 22 knots." It was Chief Engineer, Lieutenant Commander Ken Carpenter.

Tanner stepped to the bitch box at the foot of his chair. "Cheng, Captain, what happened?"

"Don't know sir, something blew in the forward fire room, and we lost steam pressure on One Bravo boiler. Chief Jenkins is investigating."

"All right, keep me posted."

Tanner took a quick look at *Saratoga*, now off the starboard quarter and climbed into his chair. "Woody, stay at 20 knots and start patrolling our sector."

He sat there worrying. What had happened? He hoped nobody was hurt whatever it was. He stared at the bitch box, willing Kenny Carpenter to give him an update. *Dauntless* was powered by four one-thousand-two-hundred pounds per square inch superheated steam boilers. It was what allowed the ship to generate seventy thousand shaft horsepower and reach speeds up to thirty-two knots with all four boilers on the line. But twelve-hundred-pound steam was deadly. Steam leaks had killed many a sailor over the years. He couldn't imagine the horror of boiling alive in a sudden escape of steam in the fire room. Even a pinhole leak could sever a finger, or worse.

The bitch box clicked on, "Captain, Cheng, looks like the air casing blew out on One Bravo. Nobody was hurt."

"Can we fix it?" Tanner knew the air casing encircled the boiler and contained pressurized air to feed the fire box and keep the boiler fires going.

"I'll be right up. We're lighting fires in One Alpha."

Lieutenant Commander Ken Carpenter walked onto the bridge a few minutes later. A slightly chubby officer, he had nevertheless impressed Tanner during his week of turnover with Steve Schwartz. Technically, Kenny was still a lieutenant. Because the job of Chief Engineer in these difficult twelve-hundred-pound steam plants was so demanding, the Navy had instituted a spot promotion program to encourage good officers to take the job. Kenny had been aboard *Dauntless* for about eight months. Under the rules, an officer received the pay and the authority to wear the gold oak leaves of a lieutenant commander after six months on the job.

"Captain, we had that air casing repaired by *Yosemite* about three months ago." *USS Yosemite (AD-19)* was the destroyer tender, a large repair ship, manned by men and women with special skills and equipment, based in Mayport.

"Is it a job we can do or do we need help?" He knew the answer before Carpenter could give it to him.

"No sir, it's a depot level job. We don't have the metal stock on board either."

"Shit," Tanner thought for few minutes. *Here they were only about six hours into a possible wartime deployment, and already one of his four boilers was out of commission.* The *Saratoga* Battle Group had sailed majestically out of Mayport with the drums of war beating because of the Iraqi invasion of Kuwait. He sure as hell didn't want to turn around and go back to Mayport for repairs. The ship could operate on three boilers, but its readiness was reduced. "All right, I'll call the commodore. Woody, I'm going to CIC to notify the DESRON, keep patrolling our sector."

Walking into the Combat Information Center, he was greeted by Andy Morton, now the Tactical Action Officer. "We've got the admin circuit dialed in here," he said, handing Tanner a red telephone receiver connected to a red painted radio set mounted on a bracket hanging from the overhead.

Tanner took it, keyed the mic and waited for the sound of the two encrypted radio sets to synchronize, "Alpha Sierra this is *Dauntless* Actual for the Commodore, over."

On *Saratoga,* a watch officer answered up, "This is Alpha Sierra, roger, stand by, out."

A few minutes later, Captain Alexander Vanzant, the commander of Destroyer Squadron 24, came on the line. DESRON 24 was the Tactical Destroyer Squadron Commander deploying with the *Saratoga* Battle Group and serving as the admiral's warfare commander for anti-submarine warfare and as screen commander for formation steaming. Vanzant would be Tanner's direct reporting senior throughout the deployment, the officer who would rate Tanner's performance alongside the other commanders in command of ships in the group.

"*Dauntless* this is Alpha Sierra Actual, over."

"Commodore, Will here. We just suffered a casualty to One Bravo boiler. Blew out the air casing. It's out of commission. I'll be sending out a CASREP shortly." Tanner was already mentally wording the casualty report, an official message which reported degraded readiness to the chain of command and requested whatever parts or technical assistance was required to correct the problem.

There was a pause while Vanzant absorbed the news. Among other things, the age of *Dauntless* had been one of his reservations about including her in the battle group. "Roger, what kind of ETR are you looking at?"

"Can't give you an estimate to repair yet, sir, it's a depot level job. At a minimum, we'll need the metal stock to patch it and an HP welder, over."

"OK, fly the CASREP, and we'll look at options." Vanzant paused for a second, thinking. Tanner had been in command for too short a period to place any blame for the apparently shoddy work performed by *Yosemite*. "I'll want a full report on the circumstances of the casualty, who was on watch and how they were qualified, over."

Tanner's head jerked back, and he looked at the handset as if it somehow was responsible for this accusatory comment. "Roger sir will do, over."

"Alpha Sierra, out."

Tanner returned the handset to the cradle and was about to head back to the bridge when the admin circuit speaker again crackled to life.

"*Dauntless* this is Alpha Bravo for Charlie Oscar, over."

Tanner recognized the voice and the casual style of the battle group admiral, Rear Admiral McCall.

"Charlie Oscar here, Admiral," said Tanner.

"Will, what's your assessment?"

Tanner thought quickly. He had met the admiral in Norfolk while going through the pipeline training before reporting to *Dauntless*. He was also aware, through the grapevine, that some on the admiral's staff had questioned the wisdom of allowing him to take command of *Dauntless* a mere five days before a possible wartime deployment. He was an unknown quantity. Added to that was the apparent hostility in the commodore's comments. He was on full alert.

"Sir, we can continue. I've got three good boilers. But we'll need some help to make repairs. Metal stock and an HP welder. I'll have the CASREP out shortly."

"OK, keep me posted, I'll get N4 working on the assistance. Out."

Tanner hung up the handset and turned to his Operations Officer. "Well, that's that. Take a good look at Cheng's CASREP then run it by me. Make sure it has all the right add'ees on it."

Returning to his chair on the bridge Tanner thought through the situation. The admiral had seemed supportive and helpful. Commodore Vanzant, on the other hand, seemed peeved that *Dauntless* was presenting him with a problem so early in the cruise. *What circumstances did he want to know about? Did he think we were speeding or some such shit?*

Forty years old, Commander Will Tanner had negotiated the Navy surface officer career path in a capable but unremarkable manner. The lone blemish on his record was the collision on *Wade* during his XO tour, second in command of that ship. He had thought he might never screen for command, but he had, on his second look, by the board of more senior officers convened to review records and make that all-important selection. Even though he had faced no disciplinary action as a result of the collision, he knew that service reputation was as important in a selection board as anything written on paper about his performance. Ironically, when he had attended the pre-command course at the Surface Warfare Officer's School Command in Newport, Rhode Island, the *Wade* collision had been one of the case studies used in class. Embarrassingly for him, a Navy captain, leading the class, had asked him to describe the circumstances to his fellow classmates. He had done so in as straightforward and unemotional way as possible, but he could see from their expressions that some in the class wondered what he was doing in the pre-command course. After that episode, he had noted a coolness among some of his fellow commanders, as if he were damaged goods, to be avoided lest the bad luck rub off.

Putting that aside, he refocused on the task at hand. However, it had happened, he was now in command of his own ship. He was responsible for everything in the ship, for its operational performance, and for the lives of 350 officers and sailors. He needed to think two steps ahead of everybody else. He was the most experienced officer aboard, and no matter how talented and smart the rest of the officers were, it was to him that everyone would turn when things got dicey. It was a lot of responsibility. He couldn't help having an uneasy feeling about his relationship with the commodore. Before taking command from Steve Schwartz, he had paid a courtesy call on Commodore Vanzant in his office at Mayport Naval Station. The commodore had seemed cool toward him, no words of encouragement or hearty welcome like he would have expected. It was almost as if Tanner had stepped in dog shit and tracked it across his carpet. *Fuck it, all I can do is my job, best I can.* Yet he still wondered, *what in the hell did Vanzant have against him?*

TWO

North Atlantic Ocean

Two levels below the bridge on the main deck level, port side, Lieutenant Commander Ricky McKnight sat at his desk looking at, but not seeing, a stack of papers. His deck, sitting directly above the after-fireroom, was warm to the touch. A hum of blower motors and machinery sounds created a constant background noise that he no longer heard. If it suddenly stopped, that would get his attention. McKnight was second in command of *Dauntless*, responsible for running the ship for his captain. He had been in the Navy for fourteen years, receiving his commission from the Reserve Officer Candidate program at Texas A&M University. In addition to managing the day-to-day operation of the ship, as second in command, he was getting his graduate-level training for his own future command. If things worked out as planned, his next sea assignment would be in command of his own ship. McKnight stood, turned to the small sink in his stateroom and splashed some cold water on his face. He looked in the mirror, doing a self-assessment. He had a full head of hair, almost too much by Navy standards, that he was quite proud of keeping perfectly coiffed. His eyes were a little bloodshot from lack of sleep, and maybe from that third vodka tonic last night before dinner at home. A late dinner, almost nine o'clock, given that he hadn't gotten off the ship until nearly eight.

He thought back to the events of the day, particularly being surprised by the new captain on the bridge. He had fucked up. He could tell by the way the captain had looked at him that he knew something was going on. *Shit, shit, shit*. He had seen this change of command as a chance to make his mark and set himself up for a destroyer command of his own someday. Preferably one of the newer *Spruances* or *Oliver Hazard Perry*-class frigates. Something newer than this old rust bucket.

His executive officer tour under Commander Schwartz had not lived up to his expectations. Schwartz had been a micromanager, constantly in his business and questioning his work. He had never expressed any unhappiness with McKnight's performance, but he had never seemed to fully trust him to do his job. On top of that, he had a short fuse and a well-deserved reputation as a screamer. He had written McKnight a good fitness report when he left the ship, but it didn't shout excellence. As the executive officer, McKnight was in a special category, his one of three ranking and recommendation for early promotion had no real clout. It was what CO's were expected to do for their XO's. He had viewed the arrival of Tanner, mere days before this unexpected deployment, as his chance to shine. He had expected that while the new captain was getting his feet on the ground and learning the ship and the crew, he, Ricky McKnight, would be the indispensable right-hand man. He would run the ship. He would give the new captain sage advice on how to do things. Throughout the week of turnover, he had fallen all over himself to welcome and impress the new captain. But Tanner had proven himself tough to read. He kept his own counsel. He had not asked McKnight a thousand questions about how things worked on *Dauntless* and what the strengths and weaknesses were of his wardroom and Chief's Mess. He had listened intently to the briefings by department heads and division officers but had merely nodded his head with little to say. Even his speech at the change of command ceremony had been short and sweet, with no lofty projections of how he would command the ship.

McKnight's thoughts drifted to his personal life. His relationship with Theresa was unraveling. He actually looked forward to being away from his wife for six months or more. The last week had really sucked. For one thing, the fucking ship had kept him busy well into the evening and on the weekend. There had been so much to do to get the ship ready to sail away without any mission limiting deficiencies. On top of that, he had a change of command ceremony to execute just last Friday. *Whose bright idea was that*, he wondered. It would have been far easier for Tanner to wait a couple of weeks and meet the ship in Naples to take over from Schwartz. When he had left their quarters at Naval Station Mayport that morning at 5:30, their parting had been a cool one. Maybe the vodka tonics had contributed to the chill. Hell, he was going to sea, who knew when he'd have his next drink? At that thought, McKnight subconsciously glanced down to the locker beneath his rack. Theresa had not bothered to come down to the pier before they sailed. Maybe she had walked down to the beach to watch *Dauntless* sail through the jettys and out to sea. He resolved to write her a letter that could be mailed from Naples or flown off from the carrier, maybe try to patch things up.

Now he had had a run-in with Ops in front of the bridge watch team and been ambushed by the captain. It hadn't helped that the captain had brought up the inconsistencies in the POD right after Ops had mentioned it. *That fucking fat ass Chief Yeoman had screwed him again.* How many times had he told him to make sure the POD didn't contain mistakes. Schwartz had never called him on it. He doubted Schwartz had even read it.

A knock on the door interrupted his thoughts. Lieutenant Commander Kenny Carpenter stuck his head in.

"XO, got the One Bravo CASREP here."

"You already run it by Ops?"

"Yessir, he chopped it."

Without another word, McKnight took the draft message out of the Chief Engineer's hand and scribbled his initials in the upper left-hand corner without reading it.

"Thanks, XO."

On the bridge, Will Tanner watched Woodson and Gardner run the ship through its paces as they patrolled their assigned sector. They seemed to be enjoying having something to do besides sailing a straight course. *Saratoga* was not flying her air wing, so the entire formation steamed steadily eastward at sixteen knots. The air wing aircraft, F-14 Tomcats, A-6 Intruders, EA-6B Prowlers, A-7 Corsairs, S-3 Vikings, and E-2 Hawkeyes were due to arrive in a couple of hours. The A-7's first, coming out of Cecil Field near Jacksonville. The rest were coming from their base in Norfolk. The EA-6B's had flown all the way across the country the day before from their base at Whidbey Island, Washington. The complement of helicopters was already aboard. It was just as well, winds were out of the west. Constantly turning away from the Strait of Gibraltar to launch and recover aircraft would make positive progress toward the Mediterranean that much more difficult. The Screen Kilo was in place around the carrier, a holdover from the Cold War days when the screening ships were always on the lookout for Soviet submarines, surface ships, and aircraft. With the Soviet Union falling apart, the Screen Kilo seemed unnecessary. Oh well, he rationalized, it was as good a way as any to cross the Atlantic, and it gave his watch team something to concentrate on besides their families at home.

The Chief Engineer walked through the door at the rear of the pilothouse. "Got the CASREP here sir."

Tanner took it and began reading. He noted the initials of Carpenter, Morton, and McKnight, signifying that, in their minds, the message was ready for transmission. Of course, the captain always had the prerogative of changing happy to glad.

"Cheng, I don't see CTF-63 on the address list."

Carpenter had a perplexed look on his face.

"CTF-63 Cheng, they're the maintenance group in the Med. If we're gonna get any help fixing the boiler, it'll come from them."

"Sorry sir, my bad."

"Need to add *Yosemite* and SIMA Mayport too. Especially *Yosemite*, I'd like to make sure they know their repair work didn't hold up. It's also possible that the HP welder we need might get flown to *Saratoga* from either the tender or SIMA." SIMA was the Shore Intermediate Maintenance Activity in Mayport.

"Yessir, I'll fix it."

The remainder of the message passed muster. Tanner signed it after writing in the new addresses and handed it back to Carpenter. "Make sure you show the changes to Ops and the XO. We need to get everybody's head into Med ops."

"Aye, aye Captain, will do."

The bitch box clicked on, and Andy Morton's voice came over. "Captain, TAO, sending out a flash message that just came in from Group Eight." Cruiser-Destroyer Group Eight was Rear Admiral McCall. His actual command was the cruiser-destroyer group. He was Alpha Bravo under the composite warfare concept while sailing the battle group at sea. Because while crossing the Atlantic they were under the operational control of Commander Second Fleet in Norfolk, McCall was currently commanding Task Group Two Point One. When the group arrived in the Mediterranean, he would assume the mantle of Commander Task Force Sixty or CTF-60. If they went through Suez to the Middle East Force area of operations or AOR, his designation would change again.

A young radioman walked out on the bridge and handed Tanner the naval message on a clipboard. He read:

FLASH
FM CTG 2.1
TO TG 2.1
SECRET//N03000//
SUBJ OPERATION DESERT SHIELD(U)

1. (S) NCA HAS DESIGNATED US RESPONSE TO IRAQ INVASION OF KUWAIT OPERATION DESERT SHIELD. IN SUPPORT OF INTERNATIONAL SHOW OF FORCE, SARA BAT GRU TO SPRINT TO EASTERN MED FOR SUEZ CANAL TRANSIT DATE TBD. SARA AND PHIL SEA WILL DETACH UPON SIGNAL AND MAKE BEST SPEED TO XSIT GIBRALTAR AND CHOP TO C6F. REMAINDER TG 2.1 CONTINUE XSIT AT 18 KT SOA. TG 2.1 SET EMCON A WITHOUT SIGNAL 2300Z7AUG90. MCCALL SENDS.//
DECL 7AUG2000
BT

Tanner initialed the message and handed it back to the radioman. *So much for a summer and fall Med cruise*, he thought. Looks like we're headed to the Mideast. Leaning down to the 29MC he pressed the lever for CIC.

"Ops, any change to the unrep tonight?"

"Not yet Captain, but I bet it gets canceled. *Detroit* joins up tomorrow so we can gas up from her. *Sara* just signaled a base speed change to 18 knots."

"Roger, let Cheng know we're going to be at 18 knots for the next week. Let everyone know about EMCON beginning in," he glanced at his watch, "half an hour." EMCON A meant that no radio or radar transmissions could leave the ship. The task group would communicate by flashing light and signal flag when within visual range and by naval message bounced off the satellite with the shore establishment.

It was almost time for dinner in the wardroom. The XO should give him a ring when the meal was ready, and the officers not on watch were gathered in the wardroom. Tanner sat back in his chair and reflected on what this all meant. Clearly, the United States was gearing up militarily in response to the Iraqi invasion.

Perhaps a show of force would be all that it took to convince Saddam Hussein to withdraw from Kuwait. Perhaps not. The flash message suggested the entire battle group would be passing through the Med and entering the Red Sea via the Suez Canal, maybe going all the way around to the Persian Gulf.

Dauntless heeled to port as the bridge team changed course to continue patrolling the Screen Kilo sector. With the base speed up to eighteen knots, they would need more speed than that when moving forward in the sector. All that would probably change with the departure of *Sara* and *Philippine Sea*, the Aegis cruiser. Whoever was the senior CO would be left in charge of the rest of TG 2.1. Probably the CO of either *Biddle* or *Detroit*, both full captains. It sure as hell wouldn't be Will Tanner, the junior commanding officer in the group. The ship rolled easily in the Atlantic swells, with an occasional wave sending a shower of salt spray above the forecastle, dissipating in the wind.

The phone rang at his chair. It was the XO letting him know dinner was ready in the wardroom.

"Be down in a minute XO, think I better let the crew know what's going on. Word will be all over the ship by now anyway."

Walking over to the quartermaster's table at the rear of the pilothouse he said, "Boats, give me a whistle on the 1MC, I need to make an announcement."

The boatswain pipe trilled and then, "All hands stand by for a word from the Commanding Officer."

Tanner keyed the mike.

"Good evening Bombers, this is the Captain." The ship's name had conjured up memories of the famous Douglas Dauntless dive bomber of World War Two fame. Sometime years ago, the crew of *USS Dauntless* had begun referring to themselves as the Bombers, and the name had stuck, passed down from crew to crew. It was said that when they frequented bars in foreign ports, they became the "Dive Bombers."

"As many of you may have already heard, our mission is evolving in response to the Iraq invasion of Kuwait. We don't have all the details yet, but *Sara* and *Phil Sea* will be sprinting ahead of the rest of the group, crossing the Med, and preparing to transit the Suez Canal. *Dauntless* and the rest of the group will follow, but we have not yet been ordered through Suez." In the background, he heard the TAO on the 29MC telling the OOD that the evening underway replenishment with *Saratoga* had been canceled. He continued, "Tonight's unrep has been canceled, we'll probably go alongside *Detroit* tomorrow to take on fuel. As you all are aware, President Bush has vowed that the Iraqi invasion of Kuwait would not be permitted to stand. We'll stay on top of things as they develop and keep you all posted. I want to congratulate you all on a smooth underway this morning and congratulate the engineers on the professional way they handled our boiler casualty this afternoon. I also want to congratulate each of you for the professional way you have all responded to get the ship ready to deploy on short notice. Well done. That is all."

He stepped out on the starboard bridge wing for one last glance at the aircraft carrier and headed down to dinner.

"OOD, give me a call if we get any new instructions or if *Sara* and *Phil Sea* start their sprint."

As Tanner stepped into the wardroom, the officers all stood and moved to their chairs around the table. The XO clenched his hands together and said, "Great announcement sir, the crew really likes to be kept informed."

"Don't we all," he replied.

As they sat down, he looked around the table and realized that this was his first meal underway as captain of the ship. As a rule, he thought mealtime in the wardroom should not be where the officers got grilled on how things were going in their divisions or departments. The meal should be enjoyable, maybe share some sea stories or talk about sports. But the change in plans had everyone excited about unknown adventures that possibly lay in wait. The Chief Engineer started it.

"The plant's running good Captain. We'll rotate the two boilers aft but will keep the plant split and One Alpha on the line up forward."

"Sounds good, Cheng. We got anyone on board qualified to weld the patch when we get the right metal stock?"

"HT2 Taylor, sir. He's had the training."

"Good."

The Weapons Officer, Lieutenant Commander Vince DeVito, was next. "Captain, I've got the guys grooming the five-inch and the missile system, we'll be ready. Gonna run some drills on the way over. Harpoon too, although I don't think the Iraqi's have much of a Navy."

Tanner smiled to himself, the boys were excited about the possibilities. No one wanted a war, but hell, if there was one and you were in uniform you damned sure wanted to be part of it.

The Operations Officer, Andy Morton walked into the wardroom. "Captain, I've been relieved as TAO by Lieutenant Lewis. Request permission to join the mess."

Morton sat down next to the XO, his usual seat. Tanner watched out of the corner of his eye as he ladled his split pea soup to see if there were any telltale signs of animosity.

With a clear effort at lightness in his voice, the XO said, "How's the weather looking for the transit Ops?"

"You know that low that was just off the coast of Africa over the weekend? Well, the weather-guessers are saying its beginning to strengthen and move west, northwest. Not a tropical storm yet, but it is a depression."

"Well it is technically hurricane season," said the XO, glancing at Tanner as he spoke.

"If it becomes a hurricane it'll be the first one of the season," said Ops, "most don't happen until September or October."

Dinner passed, and the ship's pitching and rolling were slight as they crossed the Gulf Stream steaming further into the Atlantic on the great circle route to Gibraltar. They felt the ship heel from time to time as the bridge team continued to maneuver to patrol their sector. Every now and then there was a shudder as the ship hit a wave at just the right angle. Tanner enjoyed the sensation of the ship moving through the sea, instinctively curving one hand around his soup bowl to protect against spills as the ship gently rolled. Once in a while, a shot of salt spray splashed against the portholes on the forward bulkhead.

As they finished their coffee, Tanner sensed that the officers were waiting for him to leave, too polite to get up before he was finished. He realized that they didn't have the luxury he did to relax over coffee after dinner. They all had jobs to do while also standing their watches. Some would be on the midwatch tonight and no doubt hoping for an hour or two of sleep beforehand. The younger officers would also have to work on their qualifications. Nobody got too much sleep on a destroyer at sea.

"Well, I think I'll go back to the bridge and see how things are going. XO, come by the cabin after 8 o'clock reports, if I'm not there, I'll be on the bridge."

Chairs scraped as the officers leaped to their feet as Tanner got up and walked out.

Plopping into his chair on the bridge, Tanner was both pleased and melancholy. Hell, this is what he had worked eighteen years for, to command a U.S. Navy warship, possibly even going to war. He should be sporting a permanent hard-on. The scene in the wardroom, however, reminded him that he was the captain, not one of the guys. The officers, the chiefs, the crew, would never act perfectly normal and relaxed around him. It was just a fact of life.

He walked out on the starboard bridge wing and looked over at *Saratoga*. It was twilight, the sun would set in a few minutes. Inside the pilothouse, the SPA-25 radar repeater was dark. Total EMCON was in effect. He glanced up at the SPS-10 surface search radar on the forward mast above him. It was rotating, but not radiating. Shifting his gaze back to the SPS-39 three-dimensional air search radar he saw that it was center-lined, not rotating at all. The two-dimensional SPS-40 air search radar, like the 10, was turning, but not radiating. Except for the human eye, the ship was blind. Above him on the flying bridge, a young black seaman from First Division stood forward lookout watch. He was looking over the rail at his new captain.

"What's your name, sailor?"

"Moncrief, suh," said the sailor.

"Well, Seaman Moncrief, keep a sharp eye tonight. We've got no radar, so we're all counting on you."

"Yes, suh Cap'n."

"Especially keep an eye on that bird farm over there."

He saw a flash of white teeth in the fading light. "You know I will Cap'n."

Tanner left the bridge and headed down to his cabin to tackle the never-ending in-box.

Around 7:45 the XO knocked on his door and stepped in. "Got 8 o'clock reports here sir. Couple of messages to release."

"Thanks, XO, pull up a chair. How we lookin?"

"Other than One Bravo boiler, no real problems. Weps has the FC's working on some oscillations in Director Three." Director Three was the second of two SPG-51 missile fire control radars, the system that enabled his Standard SM-1 surface-to-air missiles to semi-actively home on a target.

"Did Cheng show you the One Bravo CASREP?"

McKnight blushed slightly, "Yessir, Ops should have known to put CTF-63 on there."

Tanner studied his XO for a second before responding.

"XO, when you and the department heads put your initials on a message, you're telling me that it's ready for prime time. That if you were the Captain, you would release it and send it off the ship."

Tanner had served on a battle group staff as the Flag Secretary before his XO ride. He knew that ships were judged as much by how they came across in official message traffic as they were in any other category. Sometimes more.

"Someday you're gonna have a ship of your own, and there won't be anybody looking over your shoulder to make sure these things are right. Start thinking that way now."

McKnight looked chagrined but nodded his acknowledgment of the counseling session.

"Roger sir, I'll take a round turn."

Having made his point, Tanner turned to the other business at hand and then excused the XO to go take care of his own overflowing in-box.

Finishing up the paperwork, including a short letter to Karen and the kids, Tanner glanced at the clock mounted on the bulkhead over his desk. 22:30. *Think I'll make a pass through CIC and the Bridge and then hit the sack.*

He walked into CIC where Kenny Carpenter had assumed the 20:00 to 24:00 watch. He would get relieved at midnight and probably make his own pass through the engineering spaces before turning in for the night. Seated in the TAO chair, Carpenter looked up from a stack of messages, "Evening Captain."

"Evening Cheng, how's it going?"

"Pretty quiet sir, in total EMCON there's not much to do in here. Bridge is patrolling the sector using mark one mod zero eyeball."

"OK, I'm headed out there myself, then to the rack. Don't hesitate to spend some time out there yourself, give 'em a hand."

"Aye, Captain, will do."

Tanner walked out into the darkened pilothouse. The interior red lights below decks and in CIC had helped with his night-vision, but it still took his eyes a minute to adjust.

He walked out on the starboard bridge wing, took a routine report from the OOD, Lieutenant Don Evans, and studied the lights of *Saratoga*, some three miles distant off the starboard quarter. Satisfied, he climbed into his chair.

It was a clear night, bright with the light of a million stars and a three-quarter moon rising in the east. He thought of a quote he had read from the 19th Century French author Alexandre Dumas:

"...and what solitude is at the same time so complete and so poetic as that of a vessel floating isolated on the sea; in the darkness of night; in the silence of immensity; and under the eye of heaven..."

That certainly applied tonight, except for the solitude part. And unlike the sailing ships of which Dumas wrote, *Dauntless* hummed under his feet with the steady background noise of a modern warship powering through the ocean. He headed down to his cabin to get some sleep; tomorrow would be another busy day.

THREE

North Atlantic Ocean

"Bzzzzt!" The growler phone buzzer next to Tanner's rack jolted him out of a deep sleep. The sleep of exhaustion was enhanced by the gentle movement of the ship as it rolled through the calm seas of the Atlantic.

"Captain."

"Captain, Lieutenant Wilson sir, OOD. Getting flashing light from *Sara* indicating she's starting her sprint. Guide is changed to *Spruance*. We're working a course to station now. Signalmen are breaking it as it comes in."

Lieutenant Walter Wilson was the ship's Electronic Material Officer, a prior enlisted sailor who had been selected to serve as a Limited Duty Officer.

"OK, where's *Sara*?"

"Just off our starboard quarter, looks like she's picked up speed." It would be hard to tell without radar.

"I'm going to ease over to the far-right side of our sector and let her go by."

"OK, call me when we get our new station." He glanced at the luminous dial of his watch, it was one-thirty in the morning. Wilson had the midwatch.

Tanner rolled over to go back to sleep. As he was about to drift off, the geometry of what Wilson had just proposed clicked into his head. *Shit!*

Leaping out of bed, Tanner pulled on his khaki trousers and his boots and sprinted to the bridge in his undershirt. Arriving on the bridge, he was thankful for a good moon, his eyes would not have to adjust to a pitch-black night. Lieutenant Wilson and his JOOD were on the starboard bridge wing looking aft. He heard the signalmen shouting down from the signal bridge as they broke the flashing light.

Stepping to the starboard bridge wing, he saw *Saratoga* looming large just off the starboard quarter, signal light flashing madly at *Dauntless*.

"This is the Captain, I have the conn," he shouted. "Left full-rudder, all engines ahead flank for twenty-five knots!"

The helmsman and lee helmsman responded immediately. Walter Wilson and the JOOD, Ensign Grimmage, looked wild-eyed at Tanner. *Dauntless* heeled sharply to starboard as the twin rudders dug in and the ship began to accelerate. A light mist of salt spray hit Tanner in the face as *Dauntless* turned broadside to the rolling swells, the ship heeling to starboard in the full-rudder turn.

"Steady course zero-zero-zero," said Tanner. As the helmsman eased his rudder to meet the new course, *Saratoga* passed directly astern of *Dauntless* at no more than three hundred yards, signal lights still flashing wildly.

From the signal bridge came, "Stand clear, course zero-nine-zero speed three zero." The signalmen had finished breaking the flashing light signal.

Tanner turned to Ensign Grimmage. "Wilt, take the conn, slow to twenty and come back to zero-nine-zero."

Just then the junior signalmen climbed down the ladder and handed Lieutenant Wilson a message form on a clipboard. "Here's the new screen, sir."

Wilson handed it to Ensign Grimmage and told him to plot it on the mo-board. He then turned expectantly to Tanner.

"Walt, what were you thinking cutting across the bow of the carrier?" They were alone on the starboard bridge wing as *Dauntless* turned back to the east and *Saratoga* opened up ahead. *Philippine Sea*, her shotgun, was keeping pace off *Sara*'s starboard side. Ensign Grimmage was comparing notes on the new screen with the TAO in CIC.

"Sir, I didn't want to get out of our sector."

Tanner collected himself before continuing. "Walt, the sector was not important with *Sara* sprinting ahead. Do you realize how close we came to getting run over by the carrier?"

"I'm sorry Captain, it was hard to judge the distance in the dark with no radar."

"Walt, when you're the OOD the safety of every man on this ship is your responsibility. I'll never chew your ass for being out of station if there is a question of safety. Now get in there and help Wilt sort out the new station."

"Aye, aye Captain, sorry, it won't happen again."

Tanner hopped into his chair. No getting back to sleep now, too much adrenalin. He'd almost lost his ship the first night underway. Besides, he had lost a certain level of confidence in Lieutenant Wilson. *Probably not a bad idea to sit here until we get to the new station.*

His left leg began shaking as he sat in the chair with his foot up on the bridge windowsill. Memories of that night on *Wade* came flooding back. The darkness, his eyes not adjusted to the night, the confusion of the bridge watch team, the lights of the other ship filling the bridge windows, the voice on the bridge-to-bridge radio, a strange accent, "My rudder is left full!"

Tanner squeezed his eyes shut and tried to clear the images from his mind.

The TAO, Weapons Officer Lieutenant Commander Vinny DeVito came out to the bridge. With no radars, there wasn't much to look at in CIC.

"Evening Captain, I've got the new screen plotted. *Spruance* is the guide, we're just supposed to cover the north side, *Monty* will cover the south side. No closer than five thousand yards. We'll just have to guess the range until daylight. There will be a new screen when *Detroit* and *Biddle* join up tomorrow. CO

Spruance is the temporary screen commander. Got the night intentions message right here."

"This just come in?"

"Yessir."

Night intentions at two in the morning, thought Tanner. Obviously, the staff on the carrier was shaking out the cobwebs just like everyone else. *Probably a lot going on over there with this Operation Desert Shield thing shaping up.*

Just then Ensign Grimmage came over to the captain's chair. "Sir, we're more or less in station now, I'm just going to slow and drop back on *Spruance*'s beam."

"OK Wilt, go ahead. Tell Sigs to send Alpha Station to *Spruance*." *Spruance*'s CO, Commander Chris Winters, was the new screen commander as the senior officer among the three remaining ships. He was also an acquaintance of Tanner's, and even though he was a peer, Tanner wanted to make sure his own ship was smartly operated. Even friends judged each other's performance at sea.

Tanner liked Ensign Wilton "Wilt the Stilt" Grimmage. Grimmage was five feet seven inches tall, but solidly built as a former Naval Academy fullback; the "Wilt the Stilt" nickname was tongue in cheek, but he liked it. It made him one of the guys. The wardroom's lone black officer, he had a ready smile and a positive attitude. From Atlanta, he'd been a back-up running back at the Naval Academy. Now he was the First Lieutenant. Tanner reflected on that for a moment. Probably the highest percentage of black sailors in any division on the ship were in First Division. Had Schwartz and the XO had that in mind when they made Grimmage the First Lieutenant? Tanner had a soft spot in his heart for the boatswain mates. They had a tough job. Responsible for all the seamanship, small boats, underway replenishment, helicopter operations, and keeping the ship looking good. They stood all the bridge and lookout watches too. Being in the Deck

Division was not high-tech, but it was important. Most non-rated sailors in First Division had their hearts set on striking for a rating other than boatswain mate and eventually moving to another division.

Vinny DeVito strolled back to the captain's chair.

"Sir, you saw that we unrep from *Detroit* tomorrow afternoon. We go alongside after *Spruance*, starboard side to."

"I did Weps. Who does Ops have driving?" Andy Morton was the Senior Watch Officer and Training Officer responsible for keeping track of which junior officers needed to drive the ship for special evolutions as part of their surface warfare qualifications.

"It's the Commo's turn. Lieutenant (jg) Satterlee." Tanner pictured Satterlee in his mind. Another baby-faced JO. When Satterlee had briefed him on his Communications Officer duties, Tanner had been favorably impressed. The kid seemed to have a good handle on the communications plans and especially important, the COMSEC. COMSEC or Communications Security Material was all the tightly controlled crypto material that was required to conduct secure, encrypted communications. A screw-up in the COMSEC could not only make it impossible to communicate, but it could also get the Commo and the Captain fired. Also, anyone else snagged by the investigation. There were a million ways for a ship captain to go down in flames, most of them out of his control.

With things settled out, Tanner got out of his chair to get some rack time before reveille, a mere three and a half hours away. He motioned DeVito out to the starboard bridge wing.

"Vinny, with the ship in EMCON there's not much going on in CIC, spend some time tonight out here on the bridge. Keep an eye on things."

DeVito nodded his understanding, "Got it, sir."

Tanner re-entered the pilothouse and addressed his OOD, "All right Walt, I'm hitting the sack. Call me if anything changes."

"Aye, aye sir," said a still chastened Lieutenant Walt Wilson.

* * *

"Bzzzt," the buzzer jarred Tanner out of deep sleep. Instinctively he reached for the growler phone.

"Captain, OOD, it's oh-six hundred sir." Tanner recognized the voice of Lieutenant Chris Palmer, the ship's Fire Control Officer.

"Mornin' Chris, what's the latest?"

"Mornin' Captain. Sir, we're patrolling our sector on base course zero-six-zero, base speed eighteen. *Spruance* is the guide. The ship is at Condition Three and EMCON Alpha. The plant is split with One Alpha and Two Alpha boilers on the line, max speed available is 27 knots. We should rendezvous with *Detroit* and *Biddle* later this morning but do not yet hold a visual. We've got no contacts visible other than *Spruance* and *Montgomery*."

"OK Chris, thanks."

Tanner lay in his rack a few minutes before rolling out and hitting the deck for a few pushups. It had been a short night. By the time he had hit the rack after the close call with *Saratoga,* it had been after two. Twice during the night, he had been called when the lights of another ship had been sighted, merchants headed west toward the U.S. east coast. Without radar, the watch officers were guessing at ranges and using bearing drift to determine whether or not a risk of collision existed. Neither of the reports had generated enough concern for him to go to the bridge himself to take a look, but his sleep had been interrupted nonetheless.

Pulling on a fresh set of khaki's he went to the bridge to look over the tactical situation, the navigation track, and to let everyone know he was up and about. As he climbed into his chair, the Boatswain Mate of the Watch came over.

"Cup of coffee Captain?"

"Thanks, Boats, that'd be great." He glanced at the first class petty officer. He was the one giving orders on the forecastle during sea detail yesterday. Big guy, black, looked squared away in his uniform. The neatly stenciled nametag said BUTT.

"Want me to send the messenger to the wardroom?" he asked.

"No, thanks, I'll take whatever they've got brewing in CIC."

"You sure, Cap'n? That's midwatch coffee with powdered creamer."

Tanner gave BM1 Octavious Butt an appraising look.

"On second thought Petty Officer Butt, I'll go with a cup of that fancy wardroom coffee with real creamer. Good call, thanks."

A few minutes later the XO appeared on the bridge with a stack of papers in one hand and a cup of coffee in the other.

"Mornin, Captain, got your message traffic here."

"Thanks, XO, anything hot?"

"Uh, haven't had a chance to go through it yet. Ops told me that the unrep with *Detroit* will go as soon as they join up. We'll go alongside after *Spruance*, starboard side to."

"OK, thanks. Anything new on that storm?"

"I'll check sir."

Just then Lieutenant Commander Morton, the Ops Officer, walked out on the bridge.

"Mornin' Captain, got the replenishment plan here and the latest on that storm, it's now officially a named tropical depression, Anita."

"Thanks, Ops, any change in the unrep plan?

"Yessir, we're now second alongside *Detroit* but port side to. I've told Weps; he's got the deck apes re-rigging for port side to."

At this news, McKnight gave Morton an icy stare but didn't say anything. Tanner knew that once again the XO was behind the power curve. He tried not to act concerned.

"Figures, things are always in flux out here. What's the storm track look like?"

"Too early for a good guess, but it looks like it will definitely curve north. Hopefully, we'll get across the track, and it will pass west of us."

"XO, let's make sure we know what to do to rig for foul weather, talk to everybody about making certain that we've got things tied down. Just in case."

"Got it, sir, will do."

Tanner got out of his chair and headed to his cabin to go through the message traffic. On the way, he grabbed the day's POD off the chart table.

McKnight turned to Morton. Pointing a finger at him, he signaled him to follow him out to the starboard bridge wing. A stiff wind was blowing, enhanced by the ship's speed.

"Ops, when were you gonna tell me about the change in unrep plans?"

"XO, it was in the morning traffic. When I went to radio, I saw that you had already picked yours up."

"I'm busy Ops, I don't have the luxury of sitting around sipping coffee and reading every bullshit message that we get. I need you to make sure I know what's going on as soon as you know it."

Taking a deep breath, Morton looked over at *Spruance* some three miles away and then looked back at the XO. "Got it," he said.

Although they were both lieutenant commanders, Ricky McKnight was four years senior to Andy Morton. McKnight had already been a department head twice, once in an *Oliver Hazard Perry*-class frigate, and then aboard an amphibious ship, an LSD.

McKnight would be up for promotion to commander in a little over a year and then would be looked at for command screening. His performance as executive officer in *Dauntless* was critical to his future in the Navy. His excitement at having the opportunity to make a new start with a new CO seemed to be slipping through his fingers. For one thing, he was being upstaged by Ops, who appeared to have all the answers.

For his part, Andy Morton was finding the XO a difficult man to work for. He insisted on a lot but didn't put in the effort to keep himself on top of things. The Plan of the Day was a joke. Eight o'clock Reports was almost as bad. The XO seemed to have no curiosity when one of his department heads reported an equipment casualty or some other issue that needed to be dealt with.

McKnight left the bridge wing, and Morton headed into the chart room to work with the quartermasters and navigator to plot tropical depression Anita and her many potential tracks.

Shortly after lunch, the OOD called Tanner in his cabin to report sighting *Biddle* and *Detroit* on the northern horizon.

Tanner put down the letter he was writing to Karen. Karen was living in the Navy Lodge with Mikey and Susan, waiting for the base housing office to let her know when their government quarters at Mayport Naval Station would be ready for them to move in. Before this dust-up in the Middle East, Will would have been home to help. But now, he was sailing east across the Atlantic and, when it was time, Karen would have to do everything associated with the move in. It wouldn't be the first time. At least it was August and school hadn't started yet. The kids would be there to help.

Arriving on the bridge, he could see the watch team bustling about getting ready to set the underway replenishment detail. Forty-five degrees to port he saw the telltale masts of a Navy warship coming over the horizon. That would be *Biddle*, a steam-powered *Leahy* class cruiser. To the left of *Biddle* were the easily recognized kingposts of *Detroit*, a large AOE, ammunition, oiler, and stores ship. *Detroit* would be the battle group's gas station, Winn-Dixie, and Home Depot for the duration of this cruise.

As the ships drew nearer and went from hull down on the horizon to fully silhouetted against the eastern sky, the signal lamps on *Biddle* began flashing in their direction. That would be CO of *Biddle* taking tactical command thought Tanner to himself. *Biddle*'s CO was a full captain, on his second, major, command tour. He must be senior to *Detroit*'s CO thought Tanner, or maybe Admiral McCall just wants a surface officer in charge of the group. Tanner had looked both officers up in the 'blue book' before sailing and knew the CO of *Detroit* was a naval aviator earning his deep draft ship qualifications in hopes of someday commanding an aircraft carrier.

He heard the OOD, on the port bridge wing shout up to the signal bridge to make sure the signalmen saw the flashing light.

Terry McKnight came out on the bridge and stood next to Tanner's chair.

"How far in advance do you set unrep detail XO?"

"Usually about a half an hour sir. Make sure everything's checked out, and we're ready to go."

"How much do we need, I haven't seen the fuel report yet."

"I'll check with Cheng."

McKnight leaned over to the 21MC, selected the lever for main control and depressed the switch.

"Main Control, Bridge, how much fuel do we need?"

Kenny Carpenter's voice came over, "About 200,000 gallons XO."

That sounded like a lot for the second day at sea, but then Tanner remembered that Atlantic Fleet headquarters had sharply curtailed in port refueling out of concern for fuel spills in the harbor. The environmentalists were vicious when it came to the

U.S. Navy polluting the environment. They didn't like smoke, they didn't like dirty wastewater, and sewage and fuel oil were worst of all. A captain could lose his command over that too. All it took was an inattentive sailor opening the wrong valve or not paying attention when the tanks got full. It was frowned upon in the open ocean as well, but out here, Mother Nature could absorb a little oil in the water. Nobody would say that out loud, too politically incorrect, but it was true.

As the morning wore on, the gaggle of five ships gradually became an organized formation with everybody taking station on *Detroit*. It was a ballet that never got boring. Now five ships would be operating near each other, and a loss of focus could get dangerous in a surprisingly short period of time. Tanner watched his crew go through their paces, and he felt a burst of pride and satisfaction. *His crew*, he thought to himself. In his previous seagoing assignments, there was always someone else higher up the food chain who bore ultimate responsibility for the ship. Now it was him. *Nobody to turn to for help if things turned to shit.* Everybody would be looking at him for the answer in a tight situation.

Dauntless fell in 500 yards astern of *Spruance*, slightly to starboard of *Detroit*'s wake. *Biddle* was in position on the other side of the wake. *Detroit* would refuel both ship's together, one on each side. Sitting in his port bridge wing chair sipping his fourth cup of coffee for the day, Tanner looked across to see *Elmer Montgomery* 500 yards astern of *Biddle*, also in waiting station. *Spruance* and *Biddle* had the red and yellow "Romeo" flag at the dip, not hauled all the way up on the yardarms. *Detroit* had Romeo dipped to both sides. The day was warming, bright and cloudless, it was going to be a beautiful day at sea. Certainly, no sign of tropical storm Anita a thousand miles away to the south-east. Tanner wished he had thought to put some sunblock on his face before coming to the bridge. The sun reflecting off the water nailed you in the face even if you wore a protective ball cap. Glancing at the water rushing between the ships he watched as flying fish zipped along, wing-like fins extended and only their tails tracing a wake in the water. There was a swell running from east to west, maybe five feet, but no white caps. A beautiful morning for an unrep.

Snapped out of his reverie, Tanner realized that this would be his first time 125 feet alongside an oiler while in command. He decided to talk things over with LT(jg) Shelby Satterlee, the Communications Officer, who would have the conn for the approach and alongside. Satterlee was at the centerline pelorus with the stadimeter in his hands checking his distance from *Spruance* up ahead.

"Shelby, come on out to the bridge wing and let's talk this over."

Satterlee came out to the bridge wing, looking a little nervous.

"Tell me how you plan to do this."

"What do you mean, sir?"

"Walk me through the sequence of events, how you plan to make the approach. Is this your first time?"

"Umm, no sir, I did it once before with Captain Schwartz. So, when *Spruance* goes alongside, we'll move up to 500 yards behind her. When *Spruance* is done, and *Detroit* is ready for us, I'll go to eighteen knots and move into position."

"Okay."

The OOD, LT Wilson came out to listen.

"How will you know when *Detroit* is ready?", said Tanner.

"They'll close up Romeo, and we'll close up Romeo, and I'll order up eighteen knots and close in. I'll keep shooting bearings to the side of the oiler and use the radian rule to figure out if I'm too close or too far out. I want to be at 150 feet when we're in position.

I'll cut speed to thirteen knots when our bow crosses *Detroit*'s stern."

Tanner looked at Wilson. "That sound about right, Walt?"

"Yessir, standard way we've always done it."

"OK, a couple of things I want to do differently. First of all, we'll approach at 25 knots. And Shelby, don't get hung up on the radian rule. It's useful, but keep your head up and use your judgment on spacing. Look over at *Detroit*'s wake and use that to decide whether to open up or close in. Too easy to lose the big picture if you're peering through the alidade eyepiece shooting bearings."

Turning to Wilson, he said, "When do we close up Romeo?"

"As soon as we bring up the speed to move in."

"Use the stadimeter and close up Romeo at three hundred yards. Know why?"

"No sir, we always just closed it up when we rang up the full bell."

"I'll explain. When we do REFTRA at Gitmo, the instructors grade you based on the time when Romeo was closed up to when the first messenger from the oiler was in hand. ATP-1A says waiting station is three to five hundred yards astern. So, if we start our move from five hundred yards but don't close up Romeo until three hundred, we've got a head start on the problem and can shave over a minute off the time."

Both officers nodded their heads. Made sense.

Just about then *Detroit* closed up the Romeo flags on both her port and starboard yardarms. Immediately, both *Biddle* and *Spruance* began the run into station.

Tanner watched his team in action as *Dauntless* moved into station five hundred yards astern of *Spruance* and held position while *Spruance* topped off her tanks. He was enjoying his afternoon on the bridge wing. Looking over the splinter shield, he saw the refueling team at the forward station just below on the torpedo deck and the phone and distance line team standing easy on the forecastle, awaiting their turn. He noted that BM1 Octavious Butt, he of the wardroom coffee recommendation, was the rig captain forward, wearing the yellow helmet.

After an hour he saw the spanwire slack and *Spruance* begin to send the hoses back to *Detroit*. It wouldn't be long now. *Biddle* was still taking on fuel on *Detroit*'s port side. When the last line was over the side and in the water, *Spruance* hauled down the Bravo flag, broke some kind of unit flag, he couldn't see what it was from back here, and a surge of whitewater billowed up from the stern. He knew that Chris Winters had ordered flank three on *Spruance*. Powered by four LM-2500 gas turbine engines and equipped with controllable reversible pitch propellers, the *Spruance*-class destroyers could get up and go. These were jet engines, and the acceleration was noticeable, far more responsive than the steam-powered ships. Tanner was briefly disappointed. Like almost every other officer screened for command, he had wanted a newer, more modern *Spruance* or even a *Perry*-class frigate. Nobody had ever told him, but he suspected that the *Wade* collision had knocked him out of the running for command of a newer ship. His consolation prize had been *Dauntless*, scheduled for very little operational time and then decommissioning.

Satterlee was at the forward edge of the bridge wing where he could shout orders through the open door of the pilothouse, see his engine order and rudder indicators, and best judge his approach on the oiler. He was shifting his weight from foot to foot, like an athlete waiting for the starting gun.

He didn't have long to wait. *Spruance* was tearing around to starboard to take station a thousand yards astern of *Detroit* and be the lifeguard ship, ready to pick up any sailor unfortunate enough to fall overboard during the replenishment. The Romeo flag fluttered its way to the top of the yardarm on *Detroit*'s starboard side. Satterlee looked expectantly at Tanner. Tanner nodded.

"All engines ahead flank, indicate turns for twenty-five knots," shouted Satterlee through the pilothouse door. The Engine Order Telegraph bells rang, the indicators answered, and BM3 Reinhart announced over the 1MC, "All hands fall in to port, the ship is beginning its approach."

Tanner heard the forced draft blowers wind up as the engineering plant adjusted for the increased steam demand. *Dauntless* surged forward.

"Four hundred yards," said LT Wilson, looking down at the stadimeter dial.

"Close up Romeo?" said the signalman above Tanner's head on the signal bridge.

"Not yet," said Wilson. He took another look through the stadimeter, twisting the dial to bring the image of *Detroit*'s mast down to the image of the waterline in the side by side glass.

"Close up Romeo," he shouted. Tanner knew they had reached three hundred yards. The wind over the deck picked up as the ship gained speed and the bow dug into an oncoming swell. A shower of salt water flew into the air and curled over the deck, lightly spraying the phone and distance line crew on the forecastle. They ducked their heads and hunched shoulders but didn't move.

Satterlee was watching *Detroit* get closer and closer. He bent his head down to the alidade and began to shoot a bearing to the tangent of *Detroit*'s starboard side. Tanner leaned forward and tapped him on the shoulder. Pointing at *Detroit*'s wake, he said, "Shel, how does this look? Imagine *Detroit* is right there. Too close or not close enough?"

Satterlee took a look. "Too close I think."

"OK," said Tanner, "use your best judgment."

"Come right, steer zero six two," said Satterlee.

Dauntless' bow was now almost to the stern of *Detroit*.

Satterlee looked at Tanner, questioning. Tanner nodded.

"All engines ahead standard, indicate turns for thirteen knots. Come left steer zero six one."

Tanner was grinning inwardly. The kid was doing a good job. He seemed to be gaining confidence with each decision. *Dauntless* moved smoothly up *Detroit*'s side, the speed coming off as the ship began to match *Detroit*'s speed. Tanner heard two tweets of the bosun's whistle, and heard Reinhart announce, "Attention to port." A pause. Nothing back from *Detroit*. *Aviators*, thought Tanner to himself. Then a single tweet came from all the way across *Detroit* - from *Biddle*. Close enough thought Tanner. He nodded to the XO inside the pilothouse. A single tweet, answered by *Biddle*, and then two tweets from *Biddle*, followed by two tweets from *Dauntless;* the carry-on signal. The ritual of rendering passing honors to the senior ship having been more or less successfully accomplished, the rig crew on *Detroit* fired the messenger line over to *Dauntless,* and the process of bringing successively larger diameter lines across the angry expanse of water between the two ships began. Finally, the one-inch diameter spanwire was across at both the forward and after refueling stations, the wire put under tension by the oiler, and the heavy black six-inch diameter refueling hoses began to cross between the two ships. Each hose was fitted with a large probe, resembling a penis, which would seat into the receiving horns on *Dauntless*. Once all was in place, *Detroit* would begin pumping life-giving fuel into *Dauntless*' tanks. With each station guzzling hundreds of gallons a minute, they'd be topped off in less than two hours.

Throughout this process Lt(jg) Satterlee continued to make minute course and speed changes to keep the two ships parallel and at the proper distance. The phone and distance line was passed from *Dauntless* to *Detroit* with the green-red-yellow-blue-white-green flags spaced every twenty feet. That same line contained a sound-powered phone line and once hooked up at either end, Tanner could talk to Captain Mel Andrews, *Detroit*'s CO. He grinned inwardly as he thought back to his early days and how they taught the sequence of the phone and distance line to young officers: green-red-yellow-blue-white-green. Go-rub-your-balls-with-grease. He wondered what the new mantra was now that women officers were being assigned to ships. Boobs instead of balls? Not likely.

"Nice approach," said Mel Andrews once the phone and distance line had been connected and tested.

"Thanks," Tanner replied, "got one of the JO's on the conn. What are you hearing?"

"I was just on the line with Roger Welsh on *Biddle*. He's been told to take this group straight to the eastern Med once we chop to Sixth Fleet. After that, who knows?"

So, no stop in Naples. Well, that figured, they wouldn't have thrown together this little task force only to do business as usual in the Med. Saddam Hussein had to be shown that President Bush was serious. He knew from the message traffic that ships from the west coast were steaming west across the Pacific toward the Strait of Hormuz.

"Whoops, gotta go, *Biddle* is about done." Welsh was gone. No chance to go over emergency breakaway procedures and the standard safety brief. There'd be time for that later.

After an hour alongside, Lt(jg) Satterlee surrendered the conn to Ensign Grimmage so that he could get some alongside experience.

"Good job Shelby," said Tanner. "Any questions?"

"No sir, thanks for the opportunity." Satterlee hung around to watch Wilt Grimmage, beaming with pride.

Lieutenant Commander Andy Morton stepped out on the bridge wing, and Tanner waved him over, keeping one eye on Ensign Grimmage, the line-up, the phone and distance line, and the horizon.

"Sir, we've got a planning message in hand. Once the unrep is complete *Biddle* will promulgate a screen around *Detroit,* and we'll head for Gibraltar - continue on the great circle route. Nav is plotting the track now."

"Okay Ops, keep me posted, I think things are going to remain in flux while this whole Desert Shield thing gets organized."

"Yeah, looks like Naples is out, we've been given a ModLoc in the eastern Med."

Tanner looked at the latitude and longitude written on the notepad Morton held in his hand. It marked the point they would maneuver around while awaiting further orders. "Heard that from *Detroit*'s CO."

"Also, the weather center is projecting Anita to curve north. This Bermuda high is bending her track."

"OK, let's talk storm evasion and preps in the wardroom tonight at Ops-Intel."

After an hour and fifty minutes alongside *Detroit*, Kenny Carpenter reported the tanks full and pumping was secured.

Tanner leaned into Ensign Grimmage. "Wilt, we'll ring up twenty-five for breakaway. We're also going to do an emergency breakaway drill, but that doesn't concern you too much, it's for the rig crews. You drive the ship. We don't have a station yet so just clear *Detroit* and then veer about forty-five degrees off base course and take station five thousand yards on *Detroit*'s bow. Maybe *Biddle* will get the hint."

"Aye, aye, Captain."

With pumping stopped, *Detroit* initiated the emergency breakaway drill. Five short blasts, the danger signal, sounded from her whistle. *Dauntless* answered with five short blasts of her own. Immediately both rig crews and the phone and distance line team sprang into action, hurriedly going through the steps to disconnect the rigs, send them back to *Detroit*, and break the connection between the two ships. On the forecastle, the connection with *Detroit* was already broken, and the team was hauling in the phone and distance line hand over hand as fast as they could.

Tanner said to Grimmage, "Wilt, what do you think we should be doing?"

"I guess it depends on the reason for the emergency breakaway."

"Right you are, but as a general rule, we want to gradually open the distance from *Detroit*, give ourselves a little better margin for error until the rigs are clear."

"Aye, aye sir, helmsman, come right steer zero six three."

Suddenly a panicked shout rang out from the forward refueling station on the torpedo deck, just below the bridge wing. Tanner sprang out of his chair and leaned over the splinter shield to see what was happening. In their haste, the rig crew had lost control of the inch and a half manila inhaul/outhaul line which was attached to the spanwire, now in the water and bouncing along between the ships. As the line was madly whipping through the snatch block on deck, no one could grab it to get it under control. One of the seamen had two turns of the messenger wrapped around his ankle and was being dragged toward the block. Two sailors grabbed him by his kapok life jacket, but the pull of the spanwire in the water was too great. All three men were being pulled toward the block. The seaman could lose his foot once it made contact with the block and the thousands of pounds of pressure of the rig bouncing through the water between the two ships would sever his leg at the ankle.

Quick like a striking snake, BM1 Butt grabbed the wooden signal paddle out of the hands of the rig signalman and jammed the handle into the block, pinching the line in place. Everything held. With the line no longer paying out, they quickly untangled the unfortunate seaman and regained control of the rig. When everyone was ready, Butt smashed the wooden handle of the signal paddle with a mallet, and the crew began paying out the line again under control.

When all lines were clear, Tanner gave Grimmage a nod, and the ship surged ahead out of station. Once the stern was clear of *Detroit*'s bow, Grimmage applied rudder, and the ship headed at speed to the position Tanner had chosen.

The XO came to the bridge. "Who got hurt down there on the forward rig," asked Tanner. He hadn't been aboard long enough to know everybody's name.

"Seaman Tice, First Division," said the XO. "Corpsman said he's gonna have a bad bruise, but he'll be OK."

"Butt saved his leg," said Tanner. "Quick thinking, I wanna write him up for a NAM."

"Got it, sir, I'll get Weps on it." A NAM was a Navy Achievement Medal, the lowest level personal award and one which Tanner, as the ship's commanding officer, had limited authority to award on his own.

Tanner looked over the bridge wing at the forward refueling station. BM1 Butt was supervising clean up. Tanner caught his eye and gave him a thumb's up. Butt looked at him, made an exaggerated gesture of wiping his brow and shook his head.

FOUR

North Atlantic Ocean

"Attention on Deck!"

"Carry on, seats everybody," said Tanner as he entered the wardroom for the nightly Ops-Intel briefing.

Andy Morton stood at the head of the wardroom table in front of a collapsible screen. An overhead projector sat on the wardroom table next to Lt(jg) William 'Willy' Kim, the ship's CIC Officer. Willy was a second-generation Korean-American and Naval Academy graduate. Tanner had been favorably impressed during Willy's in-brief on operations in CIC.

The XO sat across the table from Tanner, a stack of papers in front of him.

"Nice job on the unrep today everybody," said Tanner, "what have you got Ops?"

"Evening sir. On the screen, you can see our track through Gibraltar and across the Med to our ModLoc point. Just north of Port Said, Egypt. I'm assuming we get sent through the canal, but that has not been announced yet. *Sara* and *Phil Sea* are four hundred miles ahead of us, still going at twenty-five knots. They don't yet have a canal transit date or even confirmation that they'll go through. They could keep them in the East Med where *Phil Sea* could launch Tomahawks, and the *Sara* airwing could hit targets in Iraq flying over Syria or Turkey, probably Turkey. But it would be easier from the Red Sea where they could fly over Saudi Arabia who we are helping defend."

He paused to look at his notes.

"On the diplomatic front, the UN has put out a couple of resolutions condemning the invasion and demanding that Iraq remove its troops from Kuwait."

Out of the corner of his eye, Tanner saw some of the officers exchanging glances and making masturbation motions with their hands. He ignored it.

"Another resolution imposes an embargo on Iraq, prohibiting any cargo that could have military use from entering Iraqi ports. Also, preventing any illicit cargo from leaving Iraqi ports. There's really only one, in the northern Persian Gulf, but cargo also goes into and out of Aqaba, Jordan and then overland to Iraq."

Tanner held up his hand to stop Morton. "XO, let's take a look at our prize crew bill. Make sure it's up to date. If this drags on, we could end up doing some maritime interdiction."

"Got it, Sir." The XO scribbled in his green wheel book.

Morton nodded at Willy Kim who put a new transparency on the overhead projector. This one showed the Atlantic, the task group track, and tropical storm Anita, sitting off the coast of Africa. A number of potential storm tracks were plotted. Four had the storm curving north and east, two had it taking a southerly path across the Atlantic.

"We got this from the weather center in Norfolk. Current barometric pressure at the center is 28.50, winds sustained at fifty-five knots. The center is about eight hundred miles southeast of our current position."

Tanner frowned. If it curved north, it would cross their intended track.

Carnes continued, "We're sitting under a Bermuda high, that's why our weather is so good. That's the good news. The bad news is that this high is going to push the storm one way or the other. If it's the northern track, we could have some rough weather ahead."

Again, Tanner looked at the XO, "XO, let's have everyone make rounds of the ship, make sure things are tied down. Weps, if it looks like bad weather be prepared to rig the storm lines on deck, tighten down the boat gripes, all that. You know what to do."

Turning to Morton, "When's the next unrep scheduled?"

"Three days sir."

"All right, let's keep a close weather eye out and make sure we're ready. Hopefully, this thing will stay south."

Tanner thought to himself that he might want to inquire from Captain Welsh on *Biddle* if they were thinking about a storm evasion plan, just in case. But he was the junior CO and brand-new to boot. Best to keep quiet and not come across as a Nervous Nellie, let the more experienced officers figure things out for themselves.

"Anything else, Ops?"

"Yessir, *Biddle* put out an SOE for the transit, here it is."

Kim put another flimsy on the projector, and they spent the next fifteen minutes discussing the events scheduled for the next several days and what needed to be done to prepare. The imposition of total EMCON, still in effect, meant all the coordination would be done by message traffic and locally by flashing light or flag hoist. Old time Navy stuff.

On the subject of EMCON, Lieutenant Wilson asked the obvious question – *why?*

Tanner agreed, EMCON seemed pointless given the circumstances. But he didn't want to undermine the wisdom and authority of the chain of command; that would be unprofessional. He was certain the idea was not Admiral McCall's, but came from higher up, maybe even Washington.

"Well Walt, I agree that given everything's on CNN it's no secret we're on the way. Perhaps the intent is to be able to mislead the Iraqi's as to which forces are on station or when they will arrive. Ours is not to reason why," he said with a smile he didn't believe in.

When the meeting adjourned, McKnight followed Tanner up to his cabin to go over several outgoing messages that needed to be released and talk about the material condition of the ship; what equipment was out of order, what the plan was for repairs, and any personnel issues requiring his attention.

Pushing open his cabin door, Tanner saw that the duty yeoman had shoved tomorrow's POD under the door; the standard means of delivery if a knock went unanswered. He picked it up, glanced at it, and frowned. Flipping it over he saw that it had been signed by the XO.

"Sit down XO."

He held up the POD. "This doesn't have any of the SOE events for tomorrow we just talked about. In fact, it looks like the only things scheduled tomorrow are reveille, breakfast, messing and berthing, sweepers, lunch, dinner, the evening movie, and taps."

He gave the XO an exasperated look.

McKnight looked flustered. "Sorry sir, I hadn't seen the SOE, and I had to get to Ops-Intel."

"XO, if the Plan of the Day is meaningless we might as well not have one. Ops had time to put the SOE on a view graph for Ops-Intel."

Inwardly McKnight fumed. *Fucking Ops keeping things to himself again - knowledge is power. And Chief Dougherty, that fat turd. Takes no initiative to help me out.*

"Sorry Captain, I just didn't have time to get through all the message traffic today with the unrep and all. I'll take a round turn on it."

"XO, I need to count on you to run the ship; to coordinate the efforts of the department heads and to stay on top of things. If I know you're on top of things, I can focus on operations. Someday you're going to be sitting in my chair. You'll need to know you can count on your second in command."

They spent the next fifteen minutes going over the outgoing messages, reviewing the status of support for repairing One Bravo boiler and discussing other minor repairs throughout the ship. Things regularly broke on a thirty-year-old ship, keeping the crew busy doing both preventive and corrective maintenance. They also talked about what might lie in store for *Dauntless* based on developments in the Middle East. Each outgoing message required Tanner to add a new addressee or correct a misspelled word. He sighed inwardly but didn't say anything as McKnight watched him make the corrections. Hopefully, he was learning by watching, another verbal rebuke not necessary - yet.

When the XO left, Tanner leaned back in his chair and rubbed his eyes. Steve Schwartz had not warned him about any of this. Maybe he had different standards.

Getting up, Tanner stretched and then headed for the bridge. He stopped in CIC, but there was little activity with the radars shut down. A full Condition Three watch was in place, but all the consoles were dark except the electronic warfare sensing system, the SLQ-32. At Condition 3 the ship was ready to defend itself from attack, as unlikely as that was in the middle of the Atlantic. If a threat was detected, people had to be on station to bring up the radars, the fire control system, and all the associated support systems to fight the ship.

Stepping out on the bridge, Tanner took the obligatory report from the OOD.

"Evening Captain, we're on station, course zero-seven-five, speed one eight. *Detroit* is the guide, we're in diamond formation with *Detroit* in the center five thousand yards to our port, *Biddle* in the van, *Spruance* five thousand yards to *Detroit*'s port side and *Montgomery* bringing up the rear. Had one surface contact about an hour ago headed west, pretty far out to the south."

"Thanks, Walt, how's the weather looking?"

"Barometer's been dropping, and the winds and seas have picked up a little. Last time I checked, it was 29.40."

Tanner stepped out to the starboard bridge wing. The wind and seas had picked up since the morning. He tried to remember the rule. *Let's see, face the wind and stick your right arm out a little past ninety degrees, that's where the storm center is.* Of course, at eighteen knots that wouldn't work, the ship was generating its own wind.

"Walt, what's true wind?"

Wilson had Ensign Grimmage work a quick wind problem on the mo-board. Good training for the young officer.

Grimmage straightened up from the chart table. "Sir, true wind is zero-four-zero at twenty knots."

Tanner did some mental calculations. Sounded about right based on the chart Ops had shown. He sat in his chair for a while, enjoying being at sea. The sky was clear, but the ship was pitching and rolling more than it had earlier in the day. As his eyes adjusted to the dark, he could see the figures of the bridge team quietly going about their duties. The silence was broken only by the occasional report from a sound-powered phone talker or an order to the helm or lee helm as Ensign Grimmage maneuvered to stay on station. Once in a while he and Lieutenant Wilson conferring in low voices. Of course, with the captain on the bridge, everybody was on their toes. He recalled a fair amount of midwatch grab-assing during his JO days and smiled to himself. He looked over at the helmsman, intently staring at the gyro compass and making minute movements of the wheel. It was hard to see in the dark who it was, but he knew he was just a kid. Probably nineteen, maybe twenty, maybe younger. Deck division of course. Worked his ass off yesterday rigging for unrep on the starboard side, then this morning tearing it down and re-rigging to port. Then working on one of the rigs while the fuel came over. Now standing watch from twenty hundred to midnight. Back at it again tomorrow. Could he be one of the ones who jumped on Seaman Tice, trying to save him from being dragged into the block by the runaway messenger line?

Tanner had gone down to sickbay to see Tice once the unrep was over. He had a bad rope burn on his ankle but no real damage. The 'Doc,' Hospital Corpsman First Class Tyrone Williams, said he'd give him a no duty chit for twenty-four hours but after that, he'd be OK, just sore for a while. Butt had really saved the day.

A dark shape loomed next to his chair, one hand out feeling his way, eyes not yet adjusted to the dark.

"Captain?" said a deep voice.

Tanner recognized the Command Master Chief, the senior enlisted sailor in the crew, Damage Controlman Master Chief Derwood King.

"Right here Master Chief, what's up?"

"Sorry sir, eyes aren't adjusted yet."

Tanner saw that King was holding a porcelain coffee mug, probably his twentieth of the day.

"No worries, Master Chief, how's everybody doing?"

"All's well Cap'n. Crew is kinda excited about everything going on. A few are worried about what might happen, but most are excited."

"Any family issues with our unexpected departure?"

"Nothing to worry about Cap'n, no more than usual."

"Master Chief, I'd like you to keep your finger on the pulse, know you will, but don't hesitate to come see me if there is anything I should know. The chiefs doing okay?"

"Chief's Mess is fine sir, don't need to worry about them."

Master Chief King hesitated, then, "Sir, mind we step out on the bridge wing for a second?"

Tanner's antenna went to full alert. King's responsibility as Command Master Chief was to be the commanding officer's principal enlisted advisor, the man with his finger on the pulse of the crew, privy to information that the ship's officers were simply not in a position to know.

"Sure, let's go out on the port bridge wing, less wind there."

Once on the bridge wing, King reached into his pocket and withdrew two fat cigars. "Mind if I light up sir? Got one for you if you want it."

Tanner was not a smoker, but accepting the offer felt right. Both men ducked their heads out of the wind as King took a minute to light both cigars.

"What's on your mind Master Chief?"

King hesitated, then plunged in, "It's the XO sir. Not my business to worry about the officers, but he's riding them pretty hard. Seems pissed off most of the time, pardon my French."

Tanner took this news in. McKnight was sweetness and light whenever Tanner was around, but that could just be an act. He had seen some tension between the XO and Ops.

"How about the crew? The chiefs?"

King studied the ash on his cigar, "Doesn't have much to say to the crew. Deals with the officers. Does messing and berthing in about twenty minutes. Not much to say."

Tanner knew a good messing and berthing inspection on a ship like *Dauntless,* done properly, should take at least an hour, usually more.

"This being talked about in the mess?" he asked.

"Yessir, some. Believe it or not, the chiefs are feeling sorry for the officers. The pressure kinda rolls downhill, know what I mean?"

"I do Master Chief. Thanks. Any other good news?"

King smiled in the glow of the ship's running lights and cigar tips. He had been in the Navy twenty-nine years and seen his share of ship captains and executive officers come and go. So far Tanner seemed like a straight shooter.

"You've made a good first impression with the crew sir, if I may say so."

"Thanks, Master Chief, nice to hear. Keep an ear out for me and you know I'm always available for a chat. I appreciate your concern."

"Good night Cap'n, don't forget to get some sleep yourself."

With that, King opened the pilothouse door and stepped through the bridge to the ladder. Tanner remained on the bridge wing, thinking about what he had just been told about the XO. He threw the rest of his cigar over the side and stepped inside. "Walt, I'll be down in the cabin, call me if anything changes."

"Aye, aye, Captain, g'night."

"Captain's off the bridge," barked the Boatswain Mate of the Watch. The Quartermaster of the Watch made a log entry so noting. The ship's log was a legal document and whether or not the captain was present on the bridge when something bad happened mattered a lot. Like that night on *Wade*, thought Tanner as he went down the ladder. When his captain had not been on the bridge.

* * *

Tanner awoke with a start, something had changed. He looked at the luminous dial of his watch; 0437. Without doing so consciously, he did a sensory inventory. All the typical noises of a ship at sea, the hum of blowers and fan motors and general equipment sounds that were a constant backdrop. It was when they went silent that an experienced sailor would be jolted awake. Dark, nothing to see. Then the inner ear registered movement. Pitching and rolling. The ship was working through a heavier sea than when he'd gone to bed five hours earlier. A creaking noise as the ship's hull worked through the seas, putting torque on the hull. Then the shudder as the ship crested a wave and moved down the trough. Occasionally a corkscrewing motion as they crested a larger than normal roller. Familiar sounds and feelings all.

The weather had apparently worsened, but nobody had called him. The night orders specified that the captain be called if the barometer dropped .10 in a six-hour period or the wind and seas increased noticeably.

Bzzt! Just then the growler buzzer rang next to his head. He felt the ship shudder again as he picked it up.

"Captain, OOD here sir. You probably felt it, but the wind and seas picked up a lot just in the last few minutes."

Tanner recognized the voice, Lieutenant John Woodson, the navigator.

"OK Woody, yeah, it woke me up. What's the barometer say?"

"29.20. Seas are up too. Taking one over the bow every now and then. Came up kind of fast."

"All right, I'll be up in few minutes."

He wasn't going to be able to sleep anyway. Tanner got out of his rack and got down to do his morning push up routine. With the ship moving like this, it became a lot harder. On one pushup he would practically fly up like he was on the moon. The next one was like being on Jupiter; he felt like he weighed four hundred pounds. Giving up, he hopped in the shower, grabbing the hand bar to steady himself as he took a Navy shower; water on, water off, soap, rinse, done. Conserving fresh water on a Navy ship was everyone's responsibility, even the captain's.

As he made his way up to the bridge, he could feel the movement of the ship. The higher he went, the more pronounced the movement. Like with the pushups, one step on the ladder strained his thigh muscles, then he practically floated up the next step.

Arriving on the bridge, he took John Woodson's standard report while holding on to the guy wire stretched across the overhead from port to starboard; installed just for that purpose. The sun was not yet up, but there was a faint lightening of the sky ahead, the first indication of coming daylight. An event looked forward to by every sailor who ever stood a four to eight watch. In the glow of the masthead light, he could see the spray rise over the bow as the ship dug into the next wave. At eighteen knots the effects of the waves were greatly exacerbated. If it got much worse, Roger Welsh would have to slow the formation, or the ships would begin to suffer some damage. He looked left and saw the green starboard running light and white masthead and range light of *Detroit*. Looking forward of *Detroit* he could barely make out the single white stern light on *Biddle*. He knew he'd see *Montgomery*'s lights if he went to the port bridge wing, but had no desire to go out in the weather. *Spruance* was hidden by Detroit.

Moving to his chair, he hopped up and settled in. "Woody, call down to radio and have them bring up my traffic."

The Boatswain Mate of Watch, BM3 Reinhart, came over. "Coffee Captain?"

"Yeah, thanks, Boats. CIC is fine, stuff in the wardroom is probably worse this time of day. Two powdered creamers."

Reinhart grinned, "Coming right up Cap'n."

The 21MC clicked and then, "Captain, TAO here, just got a message from *Biddle* about the storm. Says we're going to try to get ahead of it, go a little further north. I'll bring it out." Vince DeVito was on watch as TAO. He knew the captain was on the bridge because the status board phone talker had relayed the word as soon as Tanner stepped through the door. DeVito came out to the bridge holding a red lens flashlight and moved next to Tanner.

"Morning Weps," said Tanner.

Taking the message while DeVito held the flashlight, Tanner read the plan.

"Well, given where we are, this is about all we could do. If we try to run for the safe semicircle and the storm stays south, we'd run right toward it. But this calls for us to run into the dangerous semicircle. If the storm curves north and east we're screwed."

"Looks like that's what it's doing Captain. Here's the latest from Norfolk."

The Weather Center message showed the storm gaining strength and moving to the north.

"Have you plotted this?"

"Quartermaster is doing it now."

Tanner climbed out of his chair, and they went to the chart table inside the chart room where the light wouldn't affect the bridge team's night-vision. Quartermaster Third Class Benito Aquilino had just finished plotting the storm's position.

"Thanks, QM-three," said Tanner and picked up the dividers. Four hundred miles southeast of their current position. Still tracking northwest but now more north.

"I don't like how this looks," said Tanner. "What's *Biddle*'s message say about the evasion course?"

"Zero four five," said DeVito.

We might be better off going due east, mused Tanner. *Get across the front of the storm faster. If this son of a bitch keeps curving north and then east it could chase us all the way into the English Channel.* He kept his thoughts to himself.

"All right, when you call the XO and wake him up, brief him on what's going on and let him know I'm on the bridge."

Tanner returned to the bitch box in front of his chair. "Main Control, Bridge, this is the Captain."

"Main aye, Captain, Cheng here," responded Kenny Carpenter. *Good Cheng*, thought Tanner to himself, *always working*.

73

"Cheng, better light fires in Two Bravo boiler, we're gonna need more speed."

* * *

Three decks below and halfway aft the length of the ship, Lieutenant Commander Ricky McKnight tossed and turned in his rack. He felt the growing movement of the ship, but it was not as pronounced lower and more to the center as it was up on the bridge. His tossing and turning had as much to do with his failing marriage, and his thus far piss-poor performance in front of the new captain as it did the weather. The son of a retired Navy captain who had commanded a destroyer during the Korean War and a cruiser after that, he wanted desperately to make his father proud. First, he had the misfortune of working for that flaming asshole Schwartz. Nothing he did or said was met with praise, only sarcastic criticism. Tanner wasn't like that, he was even-keeled and patient. But he had a way of looking at you and talking to you that let you know he was disappointed. He didn't yell and scream like Schwartz, but in some ways, his style was worse. McKnight felt guilty when Tanner got that disappointed look on his face. There were so many demands on his time as XO that he couldn't do everything. Knowing the schedule, writing the POD, staying on top of repairs and personnel issues, inspecting the crew berthing compartments and the mess decks, galley, and wardroom pantry, running the planning board for training; shit, it was too much. It didn't help that Ops kept showing him up either. Sure, he knew what was in the message traffic, that was his fucking job. He sat in CIC as TAO with nothing going on and had time to make fancy view graphs for the Ops-Intel brief. He needed to have a come-around with Ops and let him know that he needed to keep his XO informed *before* he went running to the captain.

Knock, knock. The door cracked open an inch. "XO, Messenger of the Watch, it's zero five thirty, sir."

"OK, thanks."

"TAO wants you to call him in CIC."

"Got it, thanks."

McKnight rubbed his eyes. *Five fucking thirty already?* He felt like he hadn't slept a wink. Groggily, he reached for the growler phone next to his rack, dialed up the TAO, and gave the handle a sharp crank.

"TAO."

"Who's this," said McKnight.

"Weps, XO. Good morning."

"If you say so."

"Sir, just wanted you to know the weather has gotten worse and *Biddle* is planning some changes for storm evasion. Captain has been on the bridge for about an hour."

Just fucking great, he thought. *I suppose I should've felt the ship start moving more and run up to the Bridge myself to make sure everything was OK. Fuck me.*

"OK, I'll be up shortly."

"Captain wants to see you on the bridge when you get up."

"Roger."

He hung up, climbed out of his rack, splashed some water on his face from the stateroom sink, and put on his khaki uniform. As he moved forward up the centerline passageway, he continued all the way forward to the wardroom on the main deck level. He heard the duty MS and the messcook banging around in the wardroom pantry, getting ready for breakfast. A splash of seawater hit the porthole glass on the forward bulkhead. Up here he could really feel the ship moving. He poured himself a cup of black coffee in a styrofoam cup and headed for Radio Central on his way to the bridge to pick up his morning message traffic.

Climbing the last ladder to the pilothouse, the ship took a hard roll and, hot coffee splashed on one hand. He dropped the stack of messages trying to grab the ladder rail. "Motherfucker!"

The shout could be heard through the pilothouse door. BM3 Reinhart went to the door to chew somebody's ass; nobody disrupted the decorum of his bridge watch.

"Oh, XO... is everything all right?"

"No Boats it's not. I dropped all my message traffic. How about giving me a hand." Looking through the open pilothouse door with his head at deck level he saw the captain in his chair, looking at him.

With Reinhart's help, McKnight gathered up all the paper message traffic and went to the bridge.

"Morning Captain, sorry about that, bad night."

"Morning XO. Afraid the rest of the day may not be much better. Weather is turning lousy."

"Yessir, Weps briefed me. What do you think?"

"*Biddle* wants to run northeast and try to get past the storm. I believe we're in for a pretty rough ride. Take a look at today's schedule and get back to me with what we can and can't do. I don't want anyone getting hurt. Get with the department heads this morning and make sure we're secured for heavy weather."

"Roger sir, will do."

When the XO left the bridge, Tanner went back to the chart room and studied the chart some more. The more he looked at it, the more he thought the smart thing to do would be to run due east at best safe speed and get across the storm's path. But how to convey this to Welsh over on *Biddle* without sounding like he was questioning his judgment? Welsh was in tactical command of this five-ship group - it was his call.

From out in the pilothouse, he heard Woodson on the bitch box. "Sigs, bridge, flashing light from *Biddle*."

"We got it, sir."

Tanner returned to his chair to see what was coming. After a two-minute series of flashing lights, the signalman entered the pilothouse with a hand-written message on a small clipboard, handing it to the OOD who initialed it and gave it to Tanner.

"Execute to follow sir, new base course zero four five, base speed twenty-five."

More flashing light from *Biddle* followed. When that message was broken and delivered it tightened up the diamond formation to two thousand yards spacing. Made sense, thought Tanner, easier to communicate on flashing light or signal flag. They were still in total EMCON for some reason Tanner didn't understand. EMCON was there to fool the Soviets and their electronic surveillance satellites or high-frequency direction finding systems. The Soviet Union was in the process of collapsing, and they were actually being courted by the Bush administration to join the coalition against Saddam Hussein. They were going to be on our team. Iraq didn't have ELINT or photo satellite capability. And so what if they did, wasn't the purpose of this show of force to convince Saddam to leave Kuwait? The more he knew about what was being assembled against him, the better. EMCON made no sense to Tanner.

Over the bitch box came, "Bridge, Sigs, standby, execute, over."

"Roger up," said Woodson.

The JOOD had worked the mo-board and figured a course and speed to station on Detroit's starboard beam at two thousand yards. It was going take everything they had with three boilers on the line, twenty-nine knots. And it was going to be a rough ride.

"Be a while before we get there Captain," said Woodson, "it was a turn signal, so we'll be way aft of station and only gaining with four knots excess speed. If we can even make twenty-nine knots in these seas."

Tanner decided to wait on breakfast and see how the ship rode at twenty-nine knots. The course to station was left of the base course of zero four five, so the seas would be off the starboard bow, almost the beam. He stood centerline and watched as the ship dug in and accelerated. Each wave sent a geyser of white foam up through the hawse pipes and onto the fo'csle. When the timing was just right, the ship nosed into a wave and green water washed across the forecastle deck. Saltwater and foam mixed with rain splashed against the bridge windows. The steady whomp-whomp of the windshield wipers kept up a continuous beat.

"John, pass the word that the weather decks are secured." The smokers would have to go without.

Tanner growled the wardroom, and the XO picked up.

"XO, ask Cookie to make me a fried egg sandwich and send it up to the bridge."

All that day the formation steamed northeast at twenty-five knots. The weather continued to worsen, and much of the crew was down with seasickness. Tanner stayed on the bridge, occasionally directing the conning officer to steer into the seas when he saw an unusually large roller coming their way. The seas had a pattern to them. About every six or seventh roller was bigger than the rest, often pushing green water over the bow. The course had the ship rolling sharply, sometimes fifteen or twenty degrees. Bridge watch-standers had to hang on to the overhead cable to remain upright, and the helmsman fought the helm continuously. The direction of the seas convinced Tanner even more that an easterly course would be better, it would point the bow more directly into the seas. The speed was another matter, they were damned if they did and damned if they didn't. The ship was taking a pounding at twenty-five knots, but the speed was required to cross the T and get past the storm track. Well past it.

The Fleet Numerical Weather Center in Norfolk was well aware of the task force position and began sending hourly reports. At 10:00 Anita was upgraded to a category one hurricane with sustained winds of 80 miles per hour. The track continued to bend more and more toward the north.

Just before noon the radioman brought Tanner a P4 message from Commodore Vanzant, embarked in *Saratoga* with Admiral McCall, some 900 miles further east, just now entering the Mediterranean Sea through the Strait of Gibraltar.

```
FM: COMDESRON TWO FOUR
TO: BIDDLE
DETROIT
SPRUANCE
ELMER MONTGOMERY
DAUNTLESS
INFO COMCRUDESGRU EIGHT
UNCLAS/PERSONAL FOR COMMANDING OFFICERS
FROM VANZANT
SUBJ: HURRICANE ANITA//
BT
1. CAPTAINS, CTG2.1 IS FOLLOWING YOUR SITUATION
CLOSELY. USE BEST JUDGMENT TO MINIMIZE
STORM DAMAGE WHILE CONTINUING EAST. CO
BIDDLE PROVIDE HOURLY REPORTS AND
RECOMMENDED COA. GOOD LUCK. VANZANT
SENDS.//
BT
```

Tanner thought the message conveyed a blinding flash of the obvious. He also wondered how it was received in *Biddle*. Welsh and Vanzant were contemporaries, the same year group, although Vanzant was Naval Academy and Welsh was ROTC, so Vanzant was probably senior. It was his position as battle group screen commander under the composite warfare commander concept that gave him his authority even though he was almost a thousand miles away. The message had a condescending tone to it, and Roger Welsh had probably balled it up and thrown it overboard.

By mid-afternoon, reports from the weather center indicated that the storm had appeared to steady on a north by northwest track. If it continued, they would be across the track sometime later that evening. The downside was that they would remain in the dangerous semicircle while the eye of the storm continued north behind them.

Tanner looked at the plot again. Now it seemed more than ever that a turn to zero-nine-zero would be beneficial. It would put them into the seas, it would hasten their move to the east, and it would accelerate the relative movement of the storm to the north. He wrestled with what to do.

At 21:00 the bridge-to-bridge VHF radio crackled to life on channel 16, required to be monitored by all ships at sea for safety.

"All ships in TG 2.1.1, this is *Biddle* Charlie Oscar, meet me channel seven-three."

About time, thought Tanner, *this EMCON business is bullshit*. Waiting his turn, he rogered up and dialed in channel seventy-three.

When all four ships had responded, Captain Roger Welsh came over channel seventy-three.

"Gents, it looks like we're in for a rough next twenty-four hours. I intend to continue to try run away from the storm on this course. As you saw from Alpha Sierra's P-four, he wants hourly reports. I'd like to get a feel for how each of you is doing and fuel state. Break, *Detroit, Spruance, Montgomery, Dauntless*, over."

Each commanding officer, in turn, reported his fuel state and indicated the condition of his ship. No one questioned the evasion course that Welsh had chosen.

When it was his turn, Tanner took a deep breath, figured *what the hell* to himself, and made his report.

"*Biddle* this is *Dauntless* Charlie Oscar, current fuel state is seven zero percent, no significant damage, ship is rolling twenty degrees and corkscrewing on this course, over."

"This is *Biddle*, roger all, break, will pass same to Alpha Sierra, continue to monitor channel seven-three, out."

Tanner looked over at McKnight, standing next to his chair. "Here goes," he said.

"*Biddle*, this is *Dauntless*, have we considered a more easterly course to ride more directly into the seas and increase the separation from the projected storm track, over."

For thirty seconds there was no response. Tanner looked at McKnight. "You think he heard me?" he questioned.

Then the VHF crackled, "*Dauntless*, this is *Biddle*, your recommendation is noted. As CO you have authority to maneuver your ship as you think best to minimize damage. Formation course will remain zero four five until further notice, out."

Tanner returned the handset to its cradle. He said nothing, pondering the implications of Welsh's reply. It felt like a slap in the face. *Thank you for your interest in national security.* McKnight said nothing. Just then a large roller slammed into *Dauntless,* rolling the ship hard to port. Blackwater came over the bow and washed over the forecastle. As the ship struggled up the face of the wave, it shuddered noticeably. Cresting the wave, the bow nosed down the opposite side while the ship remained listing to port. Everyone on the bridge hung on, the swish, swish of the bridge windshield wipers the only sound. The helmsman struggled with the wheel to stay on course. Tanner glanced at the inclinometer as the ship struggled to return to an even keel. Twenty-five degrees. To the south, a large bolt of lightning traced a jagged course to the ocean surface.

Hitting the bitch box switch, he said, "TAO, Captain, you monitor channel sixteen, bridge will stay on seven-three."

He turned to the OOD, Lieutenant Don Evans, the Main Propulsion Assistant, or MPA, "Don, come right to zero-six-five, let's see how she rides. Use five degrees rudder."

McKnight leaned into Tanner and whispered, "Sir, are you going to tell *Biddle*?"

"Not yet, nobody knows how far out of station we are in this weather and with no radars. Let's see if this helps."

Once steady on the new course, the ship continued to take large waves on the starboard bow, rolling heavily and corkscrewing into the troughs. For fifteen minutes they held the course, gradually opening the distance to *Detroit*. *Not good enough*, thought Tanner to himself.

"Don, same thing, let's try zero-seven-five."

As *Dauntless* fought its way through the seas to the new course, the seas gradually moved more directly on the bow, and the rolls decreased. Blackwater still flowed over the forecastle, and the ship pitched severely, but the ride was better. In the glow of the masthead light, Tanner watched as two geysers of seawater shot up through the hawse pipes. The turtleback on the starboard hawse pipe ripped out of its dogging bolts and slid across the forecastle toward the port side.

Once again, he turned to his OOD, "Don, come right to zero-eight-five."

The new course put the seas slightly more toward directly in front. Still, the ship pitched and rolled violently at twenty-five knots.

"Don, let's hold this and see how we do."

Tanner did some rough geometry in his head. If he slowed the ship, it would reduce the pounding, but he needed the speed, both to keep up with the rest of the formation and to get away from the storm.

"TAO, Captain, DR the rest of the formation so we have an idea where they are in the morning. We're going to hold this course until conditions improve, probably all night." DR was dead reckoning, a method for calculating position based on the ordered course and speed. It would not be accurate but would provide a ballpark location for the other ships.

"TAO aye," responded Vinny DeVito over the 21MC.

"Don't you think you better tell *Biddle*?" said McKnight.

"You heard him, I have authority to maneuver as necessary to minimize damage. That's what I'm doing."

Tanner looked at McKnight. He was hard to read in the dark, but he apparently thought Tanner was making a mistake. *Good*, thought Tanner, *I don't need to be surrounded by yes-men.* But McKnight didn't push it.

"I'll take my chances with Welsh," said Tanner, "And I'm gonna stay on the bridge for a while to watch the ride. Why don't you get some sack time, I may need you up here when I crash."

McKnight beamed inwardly. *Finally*, he thought. *An indication of trust.*

"All right, sir, call me if you need me."

Tanner stayed on the bridge until after midnight. Gradually the lights of the other ships faded from view in the rain and sea spray as they moved further apart on diverging courses. With no radar, *Biddle* would have no idea where Dauntless was, probably attributing the lack of her lights to reduced visibility in the storm. That would change when the sun came up. The ship still pounded heavily into the seas, but the rolls and corkscrewing were far less violent. Twenty-five knots rung up probably only gave them twenty knots over the ground in these seas, maybe less. The weather was too bad for celestial navigation, but they were still receiving the periodic signals from Omega and once in a while Loran. He was confident he could rejoin the group the next day.

* * *

Tanner was jolted awake by a rogue wave that disrupted the steady rhythmic pounding into the seas. He had fallen asleep in his chair. He glanced at his watch – 04:10. When had he gone under? Straining his eyes to get a look at the watch team he realized that Don Evans had been relieved as OOD by Walt Wilson. They had changed the watch, realized he was asleep, and not bothered to wake him. He wondered how much he had snored.

It was still pitch dark outside, but the howl of the wind seemed to have abated. He looked at the wind-bird dial - sixty knots. It had died down a little. Rousing himself, he said, "Walt, what's the latest true wind?"

"Oh, morning Captain. We just figured it, two-zero-zero at seventy."

So, the wind was veering around to the southwest. The eye of the storm was behind them. True wind was more than relative wind because of the ship's speed. All good signs.

He keyed the bitch box, "TAO, Captain, what's your DR show for the *Biddle* group relative to us?"

"Should be about thirty nautical miles at about three-five-zero," said Andy Morton, the new TAO.

"Been anything on bridge-to-bridge?" asked Tanner. It would have probably woken him up if there had been.

"Nothing on seventy-three and nothing on sixteen," said Morton, "we might be out of range."

"OK, let's hold this course and speed until daylight and then figure our next move." He looked over at Wilson to make sure he understood.

"I'm going to get a few winks horizontal," he said, "call me if anything changes, especially if we hear from the other ships. And a wake-up at six."

* * *

Tanner awoke to the growler at 06:00. He had slept fitfully, the ship pitching and rolling, but not as violently as it had been nine hours earlier. He decided to forgo the pushups, the shower, and the shave and go to the bridge.

Arriving on the bridge, he noted that the sun was up although not visible through the cloud cover. The rain had stopped. The seas were still angry, and wisps of foam flew off the wave crests in the wind. The seas had also worked around to the south and were no longer dead ahead, but slightly off the starboard bow. No other ships were in sight. He hopped into his chair, asked the Boatswain Mate of the Watch for a cup of coffee from CIC and called Radio Central on the growler phone for his message traffic.

Andy Morton walked through the pilothouse door with some message traffic in his hand and sidled up to the chair.

"Mornin' Captain, got *Biddle*'s reports from last night here. Sounds like *Montgomery* and *Spruance* took some damage last night. *Montgomery* lost her motor whaleboat, and *Spruance* lost some life rafts and the accommodation ladder."

"Any mention of us?" he asked.

"Not yet, but bet the next one does."

Just then the bridge-to-bridge radio gave a static-filled burst that was indecipherable.

"That'll be *Biddle* now," said Tanner, "wondering where we are."

"They may report us sunk," laughed Morton.

Morton picked up the handset, looked at Tanner, got a nod, and keyed the mike, "Station calling, this is *Dauntless*, over."

They were rewarded with more static but thought they could make out the word *Biddle*.

Several tries were no more successful at either end.

"Well, at least they know we're out here," said Morton.

The duty radioman came to the Bridge with Tanner's message traffic, followed closely by the XO.

"Captain, good morning, this just came in," he said, waving a message in the air. "It's *Biddle*'s latest report to Alpha Sierra and Alpha Bravo. Says they changed course around zero two-hundred to zero-nine-zero to minimize damage. Also, reports that we departed the formation sometime during the night."

Tanner felt a surge of satisfaction at the course change news. Welsh had decided to follow his recommendation after all, but probably not before *Spruance* and *Montgomery* were damaged. It also meant they weren't as far away as the DR indicated. His satisfaction was short-lived.

"Bridge, Radio, is the Captain still there? Got a P-four from *Biddle* for him."

The same radioman came to the bridge with the P4, a 'personal for' message, used to privately communicate between senior officers and commanding officers.

PRIORITY
FM USS BIDDLE
TO USS DAUNTLESS
INFO COMDESRON TWO FOUR
CONFIDENTIAL PERSONAL FOR CO FROM CO//
SUBJ STATUS?(U)
1.(C) REQ ADVISE POSITION SOONEST AND INTENTIONS TO REJOIN FORMATION. WHEN WEATHER PERMITS, SPR HELO WILL ARRIVE YOUR DECK FOR PICK UP AND TRANSFER TO BID. EXPLANATION FOR ACTIONS ANTICIPATED. WELSH SENDS//
DECL AUG 2000//
BT

Tanner read it twice then handed it to the XO. McKnight gave it a quick read and looked at Tanner, eyes wide. "Shit," he said.

"Sounds pissed doesn't he," said Tanner. "Nice of him to info the commodore."

"What are you gonna do, Captain?"

"What can I do, I'll fly over there and tell him why I did what I did. Make rounds this morning and determine what, if any damage we sustained last night. Might help make my case if we're OK."

As the day wore on the seas gradually abated and the wind died to thirty knots. Patches of reluctant sunlight poked through the thick cloud cover. By late afternoon Tanner adjusted *Dauntless'* course to the northeast to intercept the track of the rest of the formation. Just before 1600 the kingposts on *Detroit* poked above the horizon and Tanner watched as his bridge team maneuvered into station two thousand yards on *Detroit*'s beam. He picked up the bridge-to-bridge radio handset, thought to himself, *what the fuck*, keyed the mike and said, "*Biddle* this is *Dauntless*, alfa station."

"What time is sunset QM3?" he called across the pilothouse.

"2005," sir.

Shit, plenty of daylight, he thought. *Dauntless* had no helicopter deck, only a vertical replenishment deck on the fantail. The ship was not certified for nighttime helicopter operations. The ship was still pitching and rolling although conditions were markedly improved.

"Are we within limits for a helo transfer," he asked the OOD.

"Barely sir, but yes."

Bridge-to-Bridge crackled, "*Dauntless* this is *Biddle* Charlie Oscar for your Charlie Oscar, over."

Tanner grabbed the handset, "This is *Dauntless* Charlie Oscar, over."

"*Spruance* helo will be overhead in fifteen mikes, have a green deck, out."

* * *

Dressed out in a white float-coat with CO stenciled on the back, white cranial helmet, and goggles, Will Tanner stood on the starboard side of the missile magazine and watched *Spruance*'s LAMPS SH-2 Seasprite helicopter approach the ship. Out on the flight deck stood BM1 Butt, the Landing Signal Enlisted, or LSE, in yellow float-coat, yellow cranial helmet, and goggles, holding two yellow wooden paddles to signal the pilots in the helicopter. Next to Tanner was BM3 Reinhart, dressed out like Butt, only in blue. *These guys are everywhere* thought Tanner to himself. He was leaving McKnight in temporary command for his little pow-pow with Welsh.

Butt signaled the helo into a hover twenty feet above the deck, and a yellow horse-collar snaked down on a wire, blowing wildly in the wind. Reinhart ran out, clipped the grounding glove into a padeye on deck and got control of the horse-collar. Tanner knew that a static electricity charge built up in the wire as it dangled under the helicopter and grabbing it without the glove could result in a nasty shock. Reinhart signaled to Tanner, and he ran out, slipped the horse-collar around his back, under his armpits, and folded his arms in front. Reinhart gave him a quick once-over and nodded to the crewman crouching in the door of the helicopter. Immediately, the winch started pulling Tanner up into the hovering helicopter with Reinhart steadying his feet until he was out of reach. He heard the 1MC announce, "*Ding, ding, ding, ding, Dauntless* departing!" He spun a couple of times on the way up, then felt the crewman grab the back of his float-coat and drag him to a sitting position in the door of the helicopter. He scrambled in and felt the Seasprite bank away for the mile and a half ride to *Biddle*.

On *Dauntless*' bridge, Terry McKnight climbed into the chair on the port side and leaned back to watch the helicopter head for *Biddle*. Even though he was temporarily in command, he wasn't going to push it by sitting in Tanner's chair on the starboard side. Somebody would probably rat him out to the captain. He sensed that he was not very popular with the crew. *Fuck it*, he said to himself, *I'm not here to be popular*.

He wasn't sure how he felt about this meeting between Welsh and Tanner. On the one hand, he thought Tanner was a pretty decent guy, based on a little over one week's experience. And Tanner had made the right call last night, heading the ship into the seas. On the other hand, if Welsh turned this into a major stink, they might fire him. McKnight would have to step up and take command until they found a replacement. *Yikes, they could bring Schwartz back*; no thanks on that. Still, that would be pretty cool, even if it was only for a month or so. Early command of a guided-missile destroyer headed to a war zone. Every XO's dream. Shit hot.

"What's range and bearing to the guide," he asked the bridge at large, savoring his new authority. Ensign Wilton Grimmage said, "Two-seven-zero relative, two thousand yards by radar."

"Good, keep it there," replied McKnight.

The emission control status had changed in the morning with radars now authorized.

***

The *Spruance* helicopter landed on *Biddle*'s flight deck, and Tanner hopped out and jogged toward the helo hangar forward of the flight deck. He heard the four bells and announcement of his arrival as soon as his foot hit the deck. *Cruiser Navy*, he thought to himself. He didn't know Captain Roger Welsh, but that was about to change.

Biddle's XO met him in the hangar where *Biddle*'s SH-2 Seasprite helicopter sat, blades folded.

"Welcome aboard, Captain, I'm Joe Bankert, XO."

"Thanks, XO. How's the ship doing after last night?"

"We're OK, a couple of bent stanchions and the boat boom and two life rafts washed away sometime early this morning. Nobody got much sleep. How about you?"

"No real damage, but like you, not much sleep and a lot of puke on the bridge wings."

"Roger that. Well, the skipper's waiting for you in the cabin. I'll walk you up."

Tanner followed Bankert through the ship and up to the captain's cabin. He noted how clean the passageways were despite all the bad weather. *Sign of a squared away ship.*

The XO knocked on the captain's door, opened it and announced Tanner's arrival.

Captain Roger Welsh sat at his desk, reading glasses perched on his nose and a stack of papers in front of him. He was a large man, heavy in the middle but with powerful looking shoulders and beefy arms. He was bald on top with a Friar Tuck batch of strawberry blonde hair. He did not look up.

Tanner stepped forward and extended his hand. "Captain Welsh, Will Tanner, pleasure to meet you, sir."

Welsh slowly turned in his chair and did not take Tanner's hand.

"That was quite the stunt you pulled last night Commander. Leaving station without signal, not reporting your intent." His eyes bored into Tanner.

"Sir," Tanner began. Welsh stopped him with a raised hand.

"That was the most unprofessional act I've ever witnessed at sea. Insubordinate might be a better description. Unprofessional *and* insubordinate. What were you thinking?"

"Sir, I took you at your word that I had authority to maneuver to save my ship."

"Save your ship? That storm was nothing. You owed me, as the officer in tactical command, the courtesy of announcing your intentions. Why didn't you? Instead, you quietly faded over the horizon. What kind of bullshit is that?"

Tanner stood his ground. "Sir, *Dauntless* was riding very poorly on zero four five. I thought we'd do better riding into the seas. I tried zero-six-five for a while. Then zero-seven-five, finally zero-eight-five. That worked better. We had no damage last night." *Unlike you and the other ships*, he thought but didn't say.

Welsh glared at him. "You listen to me Commander. As long as your ship is under my tactical command, you will obey my orders. If you think you have a better idea you ask me first. And if you still don't like the answer then you inform me of what you intend to do and why. Is that clear?"

"Yessir," said Tanner.

Welsh paused, looking Tanner up and down. "I'm going to give Commodore Vanzant and Admiral McCall a detailed report on everything that happened last night, including one of my screen ships disappearing over the horizon. Is that understood?"

"Of course, sir."

"Now, this cruise could last two months, or it could last a year. We have to work together as a team. We could be going into combat for all I know. I need to know that I can count on *Dauntless* to do her part. No maverick shit."

"Got it, sir, you can count on us."

"All right, you'll be info on my report."

Welsh grabbed the growler phone and spun the handle. "Bridge, Captain. Set flight quarters, CO *Dauntless* is leaving the ship."

"Thank you, sir," said Tanner, spinning on his heel and opening the door. Lieutenant Commander Bankert was standing in the passageway looking a little sheepish. "Ready sir?" he asked.

"More than ready," said Tanner, taking his float-coat and cranial from the XO, "Appreciate the hospitality."

Bankert just smiled as they headed aft.

FIVE

Central Mediterranean Sea

Dauntless cruised easily through an oily calm sea in the central Mediterranean. The previous five days had been filled with activity as the United States and the rest of the world organized to react to the Iraqi invasion of Kuwait. President George H. W. Bush had managed to orchestrate a coalition opposed to Iraq's invasion and occupation, the likes of which had never before been seen. In addition to the usual reliable allies from NATO, Australia, Japan and Korea, the Russians and most Arab nations had pledged allegiance to the effort to force Saddam out of Kuwait. Although Japan's pacifist constitution would not permit a military deployment, Japan would contribute funding to offset the costs of other nation's deployments.

Passing through the Mediterranean Sea brought back fond memories of past summertime deployments to this charming part of the world. Port visits in Spain, Italy, France, and Greece were always enjoyable. In August, the coastal resort towns would be bustling with tourists, many of them Brits and Germans on holiday and enjoying the laid-back lifestyle of the southern European countries bordering the Med. *Not this year for the U.S. Navy* mused Tanner from his seat on the bridge, all attention was focused on the building crisis in the Persian Gulf.

For the ships of the *Saratoga* Battle Group, countless guidance messages had been received from higher headquarters, outlining procedures and rules of engagement for enforcing the United Nations sanctions on Iraq. Along with the rest of the battle group, *Dauntless* had fired her five-inch guns every other day, organized boarding teams to conduct maritime interception operations, and pored over the numerous directives flooding the

93

airwaves. All combat systems were being groomed to ensure peak performance. As the group sailed south of Italy, *Detroit* received a CH-53 Sea Stallion helicopter from the naval air station at Sigonella, Sicily carrying metal stock to repair One Bravo boiler along with a high-pressure welding certified hull technician to assist HT2 Taylor with repairs to the boiler air casing. All of this was transferred to *Dauntless* by highline during refueling which occurred every third day. The day that the repair materials were delivered to *Dauntless*, *Saratoga* and *Philippine Sea* passed through the Suez Canal and entered the Red Sea. There, Admiral McCall assumed responsibility for the multi-national coalition of ships enforcing the embargo on Iraq, stopping and boarding all ships entering and exiting the Gulf of Aqaba. That coalition was still being assembled, so for the immediate future, it consisted of only *Saratoga* and *Philippine Sea*.

The geographical separation between *Saratoga* and the ships under Roger Welsh's tactical command had spared Will Tanner a face to face with Commodore Alexander Vanzant. True to his word, however, Captain Welsh had sent a message report to Vanzant outlining the events surrounding the encounter with Hurricane Anita. Much to Tanner's relief, his actions were lumped in with an account of the damage suffered by the other ships. Dealing with that damage consumed the attention of the battle group staff, especially the need to repair *Elmer Montgomery*'s davit and find her a new motor whaleboat. With maritime interdiction the primary function of the Red Sea task force, the motor whaleboat would be *Montgomery*'s main battery. While the rest of the group continued straight through the Mediterranean, *Montgomery* diverted to Naples for the davit repairs and a new boat.

Sitting in his cabin, Tanner reread Welsh's report for the umpteenth time.

CONFIDENTIAL
FM USS BIDDLE
TO COMDESRON TWO FOUR
INFO COMCRUDESGRU EIGHT
     USS SARATOGA
     USS PHILIPPINE SEA
     USS DETROIT
     USS SPRUANCE
     USS ELMER MONTGOMERY
     USS DAUNTLESS
     CTF SIX THREE
     COMDESRON TWELVE
     COMLOGRON TWO
SUBJ HURRICANE ANITA AAR (U)//
1. (U) UNDER CTG 2.1 TACON, TG 2.1.1 EVADED HURRICANE ANITA WITH CPA NIGHT OF 12 AUG. MAX OBSERVABLE WINDS WERE 95 KNOTS, BAROMETER 27.9, SEA STATE 9/10 AS STORM PASSED WEST OF FORMATION.
2. (C) MOST SIGNIFICANT DAMAGE WAS LOSS OF MON MWB AND RESULTANT DAMAGE TO PORT DAVIT. RECOMMEND DIVERT MON TO NAPLES FOR REPAIRS AND REPLACEMENT MWB. SPR LOST TWO LIFERAFTS, AND ACCOMMODATION LADDER AND BID LOST BOAT BOOM AND TWO LIFERAFTS. DET AND DAU SUFFERED NO SIGNIFICANT DAMAGE.
3. (C) TG 2.1.1 INTEGRITY SUFFERED WHEN DAU DETACHED WITHOUT SIGNAL TO PURSUE A MORE EASTERLY CSE NIGHT OF 12 AUG. DUE EMCON, DAU ABSENCE NOT DETECTED UNTIL MORNING 13 AUG. DAU REJOINED PM 13 AUG. DAU CO HAS BEEN COUNSELED APPROPRIATELY.//
DECL AUG 2000

BT

Tanner winced each time he read the line about being counseled. He knew this was polite record traffic speak for "*I chewed his ass.*" He imagined that Vanzant would want additional details and that Welsh would gladly describe their meeting when he and Vanzant were face to face. He also noted with dismay that Captain Welsh had seen fit to info Commodore Nordstrom at DESRON 12 on his message. *Great, put him on report to his administrative commander back in Mayport. Shit, why not info the CNO while he's at it.*

Throughout this time, Will Tanner had been getting to know his ship and his people. As he convened the nightly war council in the wardroom, he gained an appreciation for the competence of his line department heads. Andy Morton in Ops, Vince DeVito as Weapons Officer, and Ken Carpenter, the Chief Engineer, all impressed him with their drive, intellect, and enthusiasm for their jobs. XO Ricky McKnight however, was proving problematic. His performance in routine administrative tasks continued to frustrate Tanner. There continued to be an undercurrent of bad blood between McKnight and Morton, and he had sensed additional tension between the XO and the other department heads. Around Tanner, McKnight was all smiles and bubbly praise. On two occasions since the bridge encounter with Ops on the day they left Mayport, Tanner had unexpectedly walked into, once the wardroom and another time CIC, and interrupted what appeared to be a heated confrontation. Each time there was an awkward silence, followed quickly by a suddenly smiling McKnight effusively greeting the captain while everyone else looked at their shoes.

"Attention on deck."

"At ease, seats," said Tanner as he entered the wardroom for the nightly Ops-Intel brief. As usual, Lieutenant Commander

Andy Morton stood next to the movie screen. The ship was south-southwest of the island of Cyprus enroute to Port Said, Egypt.

"Go Ops."

"Evening Captain, on the screen is our track to Port Said. We go through Suez day after tomorrow. Sequence will be *Biddle*, *Spruance*, *Detroit*, and *Dauntless*. Our group will be at the front of the convoy. Tomorrow night after anchoring we'll do the nav brief for the canal transit."

Seaman Collins flipped the next overhead onto the projector. Tanner had gotten to know Collins as he was the 1JV and JA talker for special evolutions. They had spent a lot of time together on the bridge during underway replenishment. Lt(jg) Kim was relieved of projector duty so that he could focus on his division officer and watchstander duties. Collins had impressed everybody. He also seemed to enjoy sitting in the wardroom at Ops-Intel and absorbing all the scuttlebutt from the officers and chiefs in attendance. He was becoming very popular in operations department berthing and on the mess decks, always having the latest word.

This slide showed the northern Red Sea and the Gulf of Aqaba. "Sir," Ops continued, "these are the 'gate guard' stations in the north Red Sea. We'll be assigned to patrol along with the rest of the Cru-Des. There are also British, French, Greek, and Italian destroyers and frigates on the way to assist with the patrolling. *Saratoga* and her shotgun will be about a hundred miles south, down here," pointing with his pointer.

"The gate guard ships stay south of the Strait of Tiran. Every ship entering or exiting the Gulf of Aqaba is to be stopped and boarded to search for illicit cargo - no exceptions."

"Been any problems so far?" asked Tanner.

"No sir, not that I'm aware of. But with only *Sara* and *Phil Sea* on station, they haven't been able to cover the entire area. *Sara* is flying both CAP and triple-S-C." SSSC was surface-subsurface surveillance by aircraft. "You've all seen the procedures. Every boarding will be supported either by a helo or CAP from *Sara*."

"CAP?" asked Tanner. CAP was combat air patrol, typically armed fighter jets prepared to engage enemy aircraft. SUCAP was a surface CAP, loaded out with weapons appropriate for engaging an enemy ship.

"Yessir, does two things, let's the master of the ship know we're serious, and gives you eyes in the sky to detect any suspicious activity on deck that we can't see from over here. *Sara* is also flying routine CAP to protect *Sara* and the rest of the battle group."

Tanner thought about that. The odds of the Iraqi Air Force successfully attacking ships in the Red Sea were pretty slim. He made a mental note to have a discussion with Ops and Weps about that possibility.

Ops continued, "The plan is for *Detroit* to top everybody off in the next couple of days and then head south to go around to the Persian Gulf."

"What do we do for gas?"

"Sir, it'll be *Sara*. Unless an oiler is coming through on the way to the gulf. Maybe we'll get *Detroit* back once all the ships get assembled in the gulf. The Op Task says *Phil Sea* will normally be the shotgun, but when *Biddle* and *Dauntless* go south for gas, we may be tasked as shotgun." The carrier shotgun had to be a guided-missile ship, capable of shooting down enemy aircraft. *Spruance* was loaded out with Tomahawk land attack missiles but had no surface-to-air capability besides her guns. *Montgomery* was designed primarily for anti-submarine warfare and likewise had no surface-to-air missile system. There was no submarine threat in the Red Sea to speak of so *Montgomery* would be busy doing board and search once she rejoined with a new motor whaleboat.

"OK, continue."

"On the diplomatic front, Iraq has been threatened that if Saddam doesn't leave Kuwait military action could follow, but the forces are still being assembled. We're actually the first carrier battle group in theater, although the *Indy* group from Japan is about to enter the gulf."

"They're going through Hormuz?"

"That's the plan. Iraq is too far away to keep the carrier outside the gulf."

This was a change. The Navy had never deployed aircraft carriers inside the Persian Gulf. The waters were considered too restrictive, and the possibility of an attack by unfriendly Iran was found to be too high a risk with little warning time if a surface-to-surface missile were launched from the coast. Throughout the 1979 to 1981 Iranian hostage crisis, a carrier battle group had operated in the Indian Ocean as a deterrent to Iran. From there, targets at Bandar Abbas and Cha Bahar could be attacked, and the Strait of Hormuz kept open if necessary. Now, most of the deterrent presence in the Persian Gulf was done by U.S. Navy cruisers, destroyers, and frigates assigned to the Middle East Force. Only occasionally was an aircraft carrier available for Indian Ocean or North Arabian Sea patrols.

Ops continued, "For now the focus is on protecting Saudi Arabia from Iraq continuing on to the Saudi oil fields. The Air Force is deploying to Saudi Arabia, and the Army and Marine Corps are on the way."

Seaman Collins flipped another transparent slide onto the projector showing the schedule of events for the next day. Tanner gave it a quick scan.

"What's this abandon ship drill?" he asked.

"It's required Captain," said Andy Morton, "we're supposed to do one every six months and report it in our monthly training report."

"Cancel it," said Tanner.

"Sir..." began Morton.

Tanner raised a hand to stop him.

Addressing the room, he said, "We're not doing abandon ship drills in *Dauntless*. It's a loser's drill. Does anyone think that if we sustain enough damage that the ship is in danger of sinking that we'll be conducting an orderly muster at life raft stations?"

Tanner looked around the room and saw heads nodding in agreement. Turning back to Morton he said, "Put it in the report, but we're not going to waste time doing it."

Andy Morton and Ricky McKnight exchanged glances. This would be falsifying an official report, known in the Navy as 'gundecking.'

Satisfied that he had made his point, and also sent a signal to his crew about pointless requirements directed from on high, Tanner continued, "OK, good update Ops." Addressing the room again he said, "Focus tomorrow is on continuing to train for our mission in the Red Sea. Day after tomorrow we get ready for the canal transit; it'll be a long night when we do. We'll go over everything at the nav brief after we anchor at Port Said. XO I want to continue to drill the boarding teams and review the requirements. This is something the Navy hasn't really done since Market Time during Vietnam. Ops, Weps, let's talk about the Iraqi air threat. It seems a long shot that they could get to the Red Sea, but we need to think it through. If we're going to shotgun *Sara,* we need to be up to speed on Red Crown procedures and make sure our air controllers are ready to work with the air wing and the carrier. Weps, let's also continue to drill the procedures for firing warning shots and disabling fire against an uncooperative merchant once we get down to the Red Sea. I thought the tactic we tried yesterday worked pretty well. Any questions?"

Nobody had a question, so Tanner got up to leave. "Come on up XO."

"Be right up sir, gotta put out a little word."

Tanner passed through CIC before heading for his cabin. After they had evaded the hurricane, transited the Strait of Gibraltar and entered the Mediterranean Sea, the emission control restrictions had been lifted. All the radar scopes were alive with the displays of electronic beams painting the returns of air and surface contacts for miles around the ships. Somebody had finally decided it made no sense to try and hide the location of the Navy ships headed to the theater of operations. News of the mobilization and movement of dozens of naval assets in support of what was now officially named *Operation Desert Shield* was everywhere on CNN and the major news networks. The Air Force was flying combat air patrol missions over Saudi Arabia, and the Navy would be doing the same in the Persian Gulf and the Red Sea. Army forces were streaming into Saudi Arabia to meet up with heavy equipment being delivered by maritime pre-positioning ships and ready reserve force ships hauling gear from the United States and Europe. A Marine amphibious group had entered the Persian Gulf and was busy drilling holes in the ocean, ready in case the two thousand embarked Marines were needed ashore.

Tanner took a quick update from the TAO and headed to his cabin. It was time for another chat with Ricky McKnight.

* * *

In the wardroom, McKnight took his time with the department heads before heading to the CO's cabin. He dreaded these one-on-one sit-downs with the captain. Tanner always asked a question or inquired on a status for which McKnight had no answer. The Plan of the Day was his favorite prop for discussing the next day's activities until McKnight wised up and had Chief Dougherty hold the POD for a final review until after his evening meeting with Tanner. *One less piece of ammunition for their discussion* thought

McKnight. Of course, that meant it sometimes didn't get distributed until after taps, when only the watch-standers were likely to read it.

Knocking on Tanner's door, McKnight stuck his head in, "Evening, Captain, got a couple of messages here for release. Got the CASREP on One Alpha Lube Oil Purifier."

"Come on in XO."

As the XO walked through his items for the CO, Tanner studied his XO, only half listening to what was said. McKnight looked terrible. It looked like he had lost weight, he needed a haircut, and his hands were visibly shaking as he gave Tanner the pieces of paper for review.

Finally, he said, "XO, are you all right? Getting enough sleep?"

"I'm fine sir, just a lot going on; lots of balls in the air."

"How are the department heads doing? A lot on their plate with running their departments, prepping for the upcoming ops, and standing watches. At least you and I aren't on the watch bill."

"They seem to be doing fine, sir. The TAO's have time on the midwatch to plow through the message traffic and get organized. Cheng has enough to do just keeping the plant running. Looks like repairs to One Bravo are about done."

Tanner got to the point, "How are you and Ops getting along?"

McKnight sat back, "What do you mean, sir?"

Tanner studied McKnight for a few seconds before responding, "I've sensed a little tension between you two. Anything going on?"

"No sir," McKnight protested, "Sometimes he tells you things before he tells me, but that's not a problem."

"It's not?" Tanner paused. "My guidance to the department heads is to keep you informed. You're second in command. But it doesn't mean they have to tell you before they can tell me. Don't take it personally."

"I'm not sir, it's just that..." McKnight paused, then plunged ahead, "Sometimes it seems he holds out on me so he can roll out big news to you..." His voice trailed off, never quite completing the thought.

"Like I said XO, don't take it personally. Everybody's busy. We need to work together to get the mission done and not worry about who gets the credit. That reminds me, I'd like for you, me, Ops and Weps to sit down and talk through some of the potential threats down there in the Red Sea. Take a look at what we should be doing in the event the unexpected happens."

"Right sir, I'll set it up."

When McKnight left, Tanner went back to CIC. Ops was on watch as TAO. Tanner took a look at the surface plot, saw the formation steaming toward Port Said, now just four ships with *Montgomery* in Naples for repairs. He noted that surface traffic had picked up as they approached the Suez Canal. He had been taking more and more contact reports from the OOD's as they closed on Port Said.

"Pretty quiet Captain," said Ops. "Just got this in from DESRON 24, updated ROE, further outlines the procedures for ships that refuse to stop."

"What's the bottom line?" he asked.

"Warning shots, call for the SEALS from *Sara*, disabling fire as a last resort."

"OK, lots to talk about. Let's have a detailed discussion at Ops-Intel. Go over the ROE. Talk about how we'd do warning shots and disabling fire. I've already spoken to Weps about continuing the drills. I also want to look at the Iraqi air threat, however unlikely."

"Got it, sir."

Tanner headed for the bridge.

As he walked through the pilothouse door and paused to let his eyes adjust to the dark, he heard the sound of the growler phone handle being spun. He saw the shape of somebody silhouetted against the ambient light from the clear, star-filled night of the eastern Mediterranean.

"Captain, just trying to call you," said the OOD, Lieutenant (junior grade) Paul Nelson.

"What's up?"

"Got three skunks with fairly close CPA's, traffic coming out of Suez."

"OK, what do you recommend?"

"Looks like the first one will pass north of us at about a thousand yards, Skunk November in about fifteen minutes. If he doesn't change course, he'll go between *Detroit* and us. Got a visual, looks like standard merchant configuration, port running light, slight left bearing drift."

Hopping into his chair, Tanner grabbed his binoculars and took a look. "All right, keep an eye on him. Maintain course and speed unless he changes course. How about the other two?"

"Oscar is about the same as November, but I just watched Skunk Papa come left, now got a starboard running light. Working CPA now."

Meat in the sandwich, thought Tanner to himself. Funny how often in this great big ocean two ships could end up in the same spot at the same time. Happened more often than one would think. The big merchants easily recognized a warship's running lights at night and knew that it would always be the Navy that maneuvered to avoid, no matter what the rules of the road said. No biggie, he thought, a destroyer was powerful and maneuverable, much easier for him to maneuver than a two-hundred-thousand-ton tanker.

Tanner sat in his chair and watched Nelson run the watch, coordinating with CIC to figure out the best way to avoid a collision and keeping Tanner advised of his intentions. Doing a good job, Tanner thought to himself. He reflected on what he knew about Nelson. Commissioned through officer candidate school after graduating from college - somewhere in the Midwest. Purdue, he thought. Fraternity boy. Probably about twenty-four, twenty-five years old. Single. *Wonder what his frat brothers were doing tonight*, he thought. Bet none of them had as much responsibility as Nelson did, the lives of three-hundred fifty men in his hands, responsibility for a multi-million-dollar warship. Serving his country.

His thoughts turned to his own career, especially that night in *Wade*. The circumstances were eerily similar. Except that time, he had not been the captain, although in a way he was. *Wade*'s CO was Commander Fred 'The Hammer' Williamson. Commander Williamson was notoriously hard to wake up in the middle of the night. Suffering from arthritis, the only way he could get to sleep was to take aspirin at night, lots of aspirin. *Wade* had left Subic Bay and was in the South China Sea, on the way to the Strait of Malacca. When it became clear to the *Wade* watch-standers that Williamson was hard to wake up, or didn't seem to grasp what he was being told, Tanner had quietly put out the word that, as XO, he should be called if the OOD or TAO didn't think Williamson was getting it. That's what had happened that night. It was around two in the morning, and *Wade* was encountering heavy merchant traffic either headed east after passing through Malacca or west toward the strait. The CIC Officer, Lieutenant Pete Lewis had the watch as OOD.

Pete was dealing with numerous surface contacts and, in the course of calculating his maneuvers, figuring out what the other ships were doing, and calling the captain, he confused a slower ship with one that had overtaken and passed it headed his way. By the time he realized that he had lost the bubble, the ships were very close. When Williamson had been unresponsive, Lewis called Tanner and asked him to come to the bridge.

Rubbing his still not night-vision ready eyes, Tanner had stepped onto *Wade*'s bridge only to see the shape and lights of a massive ship filling the bridge windows and to hear the frantic blaring of a ship's whistle sounding the danger signal: five short blasts. In the one second, he had to process what he was seeing, Tanner realized he was watching a starboard, green, running light, racing left to right just off *Wade*'s starboard bow. "This is the XO, I have the conn!" he shouted. "Hard-left rudder, all engines back emergency!"

When he gave the order, he had no idea what orders were already in effect. His instincts told him the geometry was all wrong. Two ships on opposite courses were supposed to pass port to port except in unusual circumstances. Had *Wade* begun a turn to starboard at the same time the other ship turned port?

It didn't matter, the other ship filled his field of view, and it was clearly crossing his bow from port to starboard. He watched, still standing in the back of the pilot house, behind the helmsman, as the helmsman spun the wheel and the lee helmsman jerked the pilothouse throttles all the way to the emergency back position.

The ship began to respond to the rudder as the bow began to swing left although it was hard to judge exactly what was happening. The collision seemed to happen in slow motion, but then again, not. The bow was not moving fast enough. There was nothing but the steep, black sides of the other ship, looming over *Wade*. The hard-left rudder was enough to almost, *almost*, swing the bow clear. *Wade* struck the starboard side of the other ship, later determined to be a one-hundred and fifty-thousand-ton container ship, a glancing blow and then scraped along the side for five hundred feet. Anything protruding from *Wade*'s starboard side was ripped away: lifelines, the captain's gig splintered, life rafts, the screw guard, everything. The sound was a horrible screeching, metal on metal that seemed to go on forever. *Wade* rolled hard to port at impact but then straightened out as she continued to scrape down the side.

When it was all over, Captain Fred Williamson was relieved of command, and Lieutenant Pete Wilson and the CIC watch officer were found negligent. They were punished at a formal hearing, their budding careers over. Tanner was issued a letter of caution but exonerated by the board of inquiry. His split-second decision to put the rudder over hard-left and reverse engines was deemed to have prevented a much more serious collision. Miraculously, nobody on either ship was seriously hurt.

Tanner felt himself shaking in his chair as he thought about that night. What else could he have done? *Stayed in his rack*, he mused. Although exonerated, it was common knowledge in the fleet that he had the conn when the collision occurred. Never mind that he had taken it less than twenty seconds before impact.

Clearing his thoughts, Tanner turned his attention to the upcoming Suez Canal transit and the operations in the northern Red Sea. *Much to think about in the coming days.*

SIX

Southeastern Iraq

Twenty thousand feet above the Iraq desert and one-hundred miles southeast of Baghdad, Major Abdul Tikriti banked his Dassault Mirage F-1EQ fighter jet to the east-northeast and steadied up on a twenty-mile leg that would take him toward the border with Iran. Glancing over his left shoulder, he saw the blinking lights of his wingman following his lead. He scanned his instruments for any air traffic ahead. Nothing. This would be a short leg before turning north to reposition for another run to the south, toward the border with Saudi Arabia. There he knew his Cyrano IV radar would detect multiple contacts, just as it had on the previous leg. The American Air Force was up over Saudi Arabia this night just as they had been every day and night for the last week. F-15's and F-16's performing a mission similar to his own. His jet was loaded for air-to-air combat, two AIM-9 Sidewinder missiles, and two 30-millimeter cannons, each loaded out with 150 rounds of ammunition. His wingman was similarly armed, except instead of the Sidewinder, he had two radar-guided 530F air-to-air missiles.

Tikriti was confident that if the Americans were foolish enough to push over the border into Iraq, they would go down in a ball of fire at his hands. They were relative nuggets compared to Tikriti. A veteran of the eight-year war with Iran, Tikriti was an ace, having downed six Iranian jets during that war. Two F-14 Tomcats and four F-4 Phantom jets, flown by Iranian pilots trained in America. The Americans across the border had no combat experience. It was doubtful that any of them were old enough to have flown in Vietnam. When else since then had America engaged in air-to-air combat? Sure, American pilots were supposed to be the best, they trained hard, and the wealthy Americans had enough money to give them each many training hours per month. But playing war was not waging war. Tikriti had been in actual air-to-air combat and won.

Tikriti secretly hoped that he would get the chance to prove his mettle against the Americans. They were building their forces in Saudi Arabia and at sea, but would they have the will to try force his great leader, General Saddam Hussein, to give up Kuwait? He doubted the Americans would send their boys to die in the desert for some corrupt Arab monarchy in tiny Kuwait. Kuwait was, after all, legitimately part of Iraq - the 19th Province. Kuwait was not a real country. It was an arbitrary creation of the British and French, and the Americans, at the end of World War I. The great General Saddam Hussein had merely righted a wrong by re-taking Kuwait. He had been provoked by the Kuwaiti's at any rate. They were demanding to be repaid debts owed from the war with Iran. And it was reported that they were slant drilling under the border. Stealing Iraqi oil thousands of feet under the surface and selling it as their own. They had also conspired with the Saudis to keep the price of oil low, costing Iraq millions in potential sales. He had been briefed on all of this by the Mukhabarat officer assigned to his wing before the invasion.

The powerful Atar 9K-50 turbojet engine pushed his jet north at a comfortable 300 knots as he calculated his next turn to continue his racetrack patrol pattern. 300 knots was really loafing. In full afterburner, he could accelerate to Mach 2.2 in seconds. He wondered what would happen in the days ahead. "*Allahu Akbar*," he said to himself. *God is great*. Allah will guide Saddam, and when the time comes, Allah will guide his own hands to spill American blood. He could only hope.

Glancing at his fuel gauge, he calculated his remaining time on station. About another hour. If nothing happened, he would be met by another section of Iraqi Mirage jets and then he would head to Al-Asad Air Base, west of Baghdad, to turn his jet over to the mechanics to make her ready for the next mission. He would sleep until sunrise, then get up, do his prayers, and prepare for his next CAP mission, this one in daylight. He preferred daytime. He was not afraid to fly at night, but it was harder to see your enemy, and he had been told that the Americans had special devices that allowed them to see in the dark. He doubted that this was true, but perhaps. Whatever, he preferred daylight. These were his skies, and he would have the advantage in any fight over Iraq.

An hour later, Tikriti flared the nose of his jet and gently settled on the runway at Al-Asad. As his nose wheel touched the pavement, he popped his drogue chute to assist in slowing the aircraft. Taxiing to the hardened revetments that lined the taxiway, he followed the signals of his chief mechanic, shutting down his engine on signal. Silhouetted in the revetment under the yellow haze of the sodium lights, he recognized the bulky shape of his squadron intelligence officer, Lieutenant Colonel Muhammed Ali Muhammed.

Climbing out of the cockpit he briefly exchanged notes with the mechanic, briefing him on his perception of the condition of his aircraft, and then strode under the revetment overhang.

"Brother Muhammed, what brings you out at this hour?"

"Greetings Abdul, I trust you had a good flight."

"Only better if I had sent an American to his death."

"Well," said Muhammed, you may yet get your chance. Come with me to see the colonel."

"At this hour? What is going on?"

"You will see."

Together the two Iraqi officers walked to the operations hut. Tikriti was thin and wiry, not tall, but fit. Muhammed carried the extra weight of a staff officer. Too much time sitting behind a desk sipping tea and munching on dates. There was nothing like pulling g's in a high-performance aircraft to keep the body in shape.

Entering the hut, Tikriti saw that only two men awaited their arrival. Despite the around the clock combat air patrol missions, no one else was present at two-thirty in the morning.

"Ah, Major Tikriti, Allah be with you," said Tikriti's commanding officer, Colonel Bashir Mohamed. Tikriti rendered an unenthusiastic salute, and then the two men kissed both cheeks as was the Arab custom. He was tired and wanted only to sleep. To rest up for tomorrow's mission.

Colonel Mohamed wasted no time, "That was your last combat air patrol, I have a new task."

Tikriti raised an eyebrow, glanced at Muhammed, but said nothing.

"You will begin training for a special mission. We will have a surprise for the arrogant Americans who think they can operate with impunity in our backyard."

Leaning over a chart of the entire region, Colonel Mohamed began explaining the special mission to Tikriti.

"As you can see, the infidel's Air Force is building up in Saudi Arabia. Those cowardly traitors to the south have allowed the Americans free access to their bases. Along with the Air Force, the Navy is moving aircraft carriers to the region along with missile-firing ships. Some have the Tomahawk missile which can attack targets on land. An amphibious group has entered the gulf with two thousand Marines on board. The American Army is also coming to Saudi Arabia. Giant ships are on the way carrying tanks, artillery, helicopters, and other equipment."

Tikriti, wrinkled his nose and looked up at Colonel Mohamed, "Do we really think they will fight over Kuwait?"

"The great general, Saddam, does not think so. It is a bluff. The Americans have grown soft. After Vietnam, they no longer want to fight overseas. They are bluffing."

"It is an expensive bluff, moving all of these forces across the ocean."

"They are rich, they can afford it. Their President, this Bush, he will not spill American blood over some rich Arabs 7,000 miles away."

Tikriti looked skeptical but kept silent. The colonel was right, after Vietnam, the Americans had no stomach for sending their boys overseas to fight. They had been bloodied by the Syrians, losing a jet over the Bekaa Valley during the Lebanese civil war. Their only successes had been in their own hemisphere, invading a tiny island to rescue students and invading Panama to arrest a drug-dealing dictator. They would stand little chance against the highly trained and battle-hardened Iraqi army that had overwhelmed tiny Kuwait and fought a bloody eight-year war with Iran.

"So, what brings you out at this time of night? You said you have a mission for me. No more combat air patrol."

"It is not I. The great General Saddam Hussein has a mission for you."

Tikriti said nothing, waiting patiently for the punch-line.

"Brother Abdul, be patient, and I will explain. General Saddam has personally chosen you to deliver a crushing blow to the Americans. One that will destroy their morale and cause their people to demand a full withdrawal. They care nothing about Kuwait, most don't know where it is."

Tikriti waited expectantly. Savoring the moment, Colonel Mohamed let him wait. Finally, he could contain himself no longer.

"Brother Abdul, you are going to sink one of their aircraft carriers."

Tikriti and Muhammed said nothing, staring at the map with the laydown of American forces. Finally, Tikriti spoke, "Their carrier in the gulf will be heavily defended. Already it is impossible to leave Iraq's airspace without being intercepted."

"You are quite right brother, it is no doubt why you are an ace. You will not attack the carrier in the gulf."

Tikriti looked confused and then studied the map further.

"The Mediterranean?" he asked. Syria had a coastline bordering the Mediterranean Sea. Aircraft carriers planning to transit the Suez Canal would be vulnerable in the Mediterranean. And they would not be expecting an attack. But, it was rumored that the Syrians were against Iraq and considering joining the American-led coalition.

"No," replied Mohamed, "although it has been considered. You will hit them in the Red Sea." Mohamed stabbed the chart with his pointer.

"The Red Sea?" he asked.

"Yes, my brother, the Americans will not expect such an attack."

"I am willing, but it is many miles from here to the northern Red Sea, how will we accomplish this bold strike?"

"General Saddam has thought of everything. We will be assisted by the Syrians."

"But Syria has sided with the Americans."

"Do not worry brother, they have done that only to avoid difficulty in the United Nations. Secretly they support our just re-taking of what rightfully belongs to Iraq. They have their own eyes on Lebanon. Brother Saddam has spoken with President Assad, all is arranged."

With a questioning look, Tikriti said, "Please explain."

"You will fly to Damascus, loaded with two Exocet missiles. We will announce that one of our pilots, a known coward, has defected to Syria rather than fight the mighty Americans."

Tikriti's eyes flashed and his back stiffened as he glared at his commanding officer.

"Do not worry brother Abdul, we will not use your real name," said a smiling Mohamed, secretly pleased at Tikriti's reaction.

Continuing with his pointer indicating the route, he said, "The Syrians will announce your arrest and the confiscation of your jet. You will remain in Damascus until your 'defection' has been forgotten by the Americans. When the time is right, you will leave Damascus and skirt the Jordanian border crossing into Saudi airspace far from the American CAP. You will stay close to the mountains at low altitude, masking your approach to the Red Sea, flying west of Al Jowf and Tabuk. The Americans in the Red Sea believe they are safe from air attack. Exiting north of Duba, you will launch your Exocets before the Americans know you are there."

Tikriti traced the route on the map, mentally calculating the distances. Straightening, he looked Mohamed directly in the eye.

"This will be a one-way flight."

"Yes brother, praise be to Allah, you will strike the greatest blow against the infidel Americans since Pearl Harbor. You will be forever lionized in the Arab world. Even those pretending support for the Americans will rejoice at your victory."

Again, Tikriti was silent, thinking.

"Excellency, my jet can only carry two missiles, even given the impact of the missile itself, that is unlikely to sink an aircraft carrier."

The French-made Exocet missile was feared throughout the world. Carrying a 365-pound warhead, it flew 10 feet above the water at Mach.092, or 700 miles per hour, making it a tough target to defend against. At 4.7 meters in length and weighing 670 kilograms, the missile itself, containing unexpended fuel, would do significant damage even without a warhead.

"You are right, my brother," said Colonel Mohamed, "for that reason you will not be alone. This will be a three-ship attack, led by you."

Tikriti nodded, that improved the odds, "You have chosen the other pilots?"

"We are leaving that to you. Pick the very best. I guarantee that they will volunteer," said Mohamed with a knowing smile.

"When do I go?" he asked.

"It will be soon," replied Mohamed, "we must strike before the Americans have built up their forces in the Red Sea."

Tikriti paused, then snapped to attention as he saluted Mohamed.

"Allahu Ahkbar, it will be my honor."

SEVEN

Eastern Mediterranean Sea

"Attention on Deck," shouted the XO as Tanner entered the wardroom for the nightly Ops-Intel briefing. *Dauntless* was 150 miles west of Port Said, Egypt, the northern entrance to the Suez Canal.

"Seats everybody, evening," said the Captain as he plopped down in his chair. He looked around the wardroom at the eager faces. For many, tomorrow night's transit of Suez would be their first. Once through they would steam south through the Gulf of Suez and enter the northern Red Sea to begin enforcing the United Nations sanctions on Iraq.

Andy Morton began, "Evening Captain. As you can see from the chart, we'll arrive off Port Said tomorrow afternoon and anchor in the approaches to the canal. It looks like *Biddle* will be the lead ship tomorrow night and will moor to a buoy inside the harbor, downtown Port Said. All that could change, depending on the Egyptians."

Seaman Collins changed view graphs and put a map of the northern Persian Gulf showing Iraq, Kuwait, northern Saudi Arabia and western Iran.

Morton continued, "The Air Force and ground force build-up in Saudi Arabia continues. We now have more air assets in the region than Saddam. The Air Force continues to flow air-to-air F-15s, air to ground F-15s, F-16s, A-10s, AWACS, and other support aircraft including search and rescue helos. *Independence* is in the Indian Ocean and scheduled to transit Hormuz in five days. As you know, that will be a first. Middle East Force surface ships are positioned in the central Persian Gulf and have already begun maritime interception ops. When we get into the northern Red

Sea, Iraq will have no sea approaches that aren't subject to stop, board, and search."

Morton paused to see if there were any questions or comments.

There being none, he continued.

"For now, they are keeping the Persian Gulf ships well south of the Iraq-Kuwait coast. Obviously, after *Stark*, there is concern that the Iraqi's might attack with Exocets as the embargo starts to take effect."

Three years earlier, the frigate *USS Stark (FFG-31)* had been mistakenly targeted by an Iraqi Mirage thinking it was attacking an Iranian oil tanker at night during the Iran-Iraq war. Thirty-seven U.S. sailors had been killed when two missiles plowed into *Stark*.

"The trouble with that is that there is too much ocean to cover with too few ships. Eventually, they'll have to move em' in closer. Once we get some Aegis ships up there to provide air defense, they'll probably move em' up."

Tanner nodded his acknowledgment but didn't interrupt. Ops was on a roll. The Aegis cruisers, like *Philippine Sea*, had the most sophisticated combat system in the world and were the best equipped to deal with the sub-sonic, low-flying Exocet. He knew the Exocet was a near impossible target for the antiquated combat system in *Dauntless*.

"We won't have the same problem in the Red Sea. It's too far for the Iraqi's to reach us and they'd get waxed by the Air Force on the way down."

Ops began to wrap up the brief with a chart of the eastern Mediterranean approaches to Port Suez and the Suez Canal.

"Captain, when we get to Port Said, we'll just have to find an open spot to anchor as close to the canal entrance as we can get. There will probably be a hundred merchants at anchor waiting their turn to go through. Once we anchor, I recommend we..."

The XO cut him off, "I got it Ops." Turning to the Captain, McKnight continued, "Sir, I recommend we anchor and hold the nav brief for the canal as soon as we get settled."

Wondering why this announcement necessitated interrupting the Operations Officer, Tanner paused, then said, "Okaaaay, makes sense. Remind me, what's the sequence for the transit after *Biddle*?"

"I don't know, but I'll find out," said McKnight.

Still standing at the head of the wardroom table, Morton nodded to Seaman Collins.

Collins flipped a view graph onto the projector showing that the entire convoy of almost fifty ships would be led by *Biddle*, followed by *Spruance*, *Detroit*, and *Dauntless*, in that order. All of the merchant ships would follow behind the warships.

McKnight shot daggers at Morton but said nothing.

"OK, got it," said Tanner, "makes sense they'd put a destroyer both in front of and behind the oiler. *Detroit* still going on around?"

Morton deliberately looked at the XO, giving him the opportunity to answer the captain's question, but inwardly knowing he wouldn't - or couldn't.

Tanner turned a questioning look toward McKnight. McKnight just stared back. Deer in the headlights.

Ops jumped in, "Yes sir, she's going around to the Persian Gulf. She'll top everybody off in the Red Sea and then head south. Our gas will come from *Sara*."

Tanner turned to his Weapons Officer, Vinny DeVito, "Weps, good drill today on the disabling fire. We'll practice it again once we get into the Red Sea."

That afternoon they had thrown an empty oil drum over the side, brought the ship up to about 300 yards, and had Mount 51 fire a round at it in local control.

"How does Mount 51's gun crew feel about it?" he asked.

"Sir, they're really pumped. Case is pissed that they missed, wants to try again."

Gunners Mate Second Class Ray Case was the mount captain.

"Tell Case not to worry, he was close enough. Be a lot easier into the rudder of a merchant ship."

"All right, thanks, everybody," said Tanner. "XO, I like the idea of doing the nav brief after we anchor. Everybody who can, should try to get some sleep before we enter the canal. Most of us will be up all night."

Gotta bail the XO out a little, he thought to himself, *he looked like an ass back there.*

Getting up, as chairs scraped away from the table and the whole room rose, he said, "Carry on everybody, XO, I'll either be in my cabin or on the bridge."

Will Tanner headed to the bridge. Surface traffic would pick up as they got closer to the canal and it would just be easier to be up there rather than down in his cabin taking phone reports from the OODs. The fifty or so ships which had transited north that day would be flowing into the eastern Med and heading off to whatever ports were on the schedule. It would be a busy night. Roger Welsh's little task group was still in the rigid diamond formation which resulted in a two-mile-wide gaggle of ships heading toward Port Said. Tanner thought the smart thing would be to release everybody to proceed independently to allow more freedom to avoid commercial shipping.

As he settled into his chair and watched as dusk settled over the ocean, his thoughts turned to the XO. Had this bad blood with Ops existed under Steve Schwartz? Schwartz never mentioned any problems between the XO and the department heads. Morton was very competent and good at his job. The XO should love him for that; makes his job easier. Ops didn't appear to be deliberately showing up the XO. The maneuver with the slide showing the sequence of ships was a little snarky, but the XO had it coming for cutting him off and trying to take over the brief. Tanner's thoughts were interrupted by the OOD approaching his chair. It was Lieutenant (junior grade) Satterlee, the Commo.

"Captain, we've got seven skunks starting to paint on the 10. We'll work up the CPAs. Just wanted you to know in case you wanted to stay up here."

"Thanks, Shelby, think I will. Keep the night-vision going. How about calling radio and having my traffic sent up."

"Aye sir, will do."

The XO came to the bridge a minute later.

"Captain, got 8 o'clock Reports here. Want to go below?"

"No XO, I'm going to stay up here for a while, the shipping is picking up. Anything hot that can't wait?"

"Weps is chasing some oscillations in Director 3, everything else is about the same as before. Cheng says the repairs to One Bravo boiler should be complete before we anchor tomorrow. The lube oil purifier is back up after we got new seals during the unrep."

"Taylor do the welding?"

"I think so, I'll double-check with Cheng."

"Let's write him up for a NAM; that's really great work if it holds."

"Yes, sir."

"XO, I know you're going to be busy tomorrow, but I want you to get some sleep after we anchor and during the transit. I may need you up here the next night when we go through the Gulf of Suez."

Ricky McKnight beamed. "Yes sir, I'll try. If there's nothing else I'll head below, I've got a stack of E-6 evals in my in-box."

"Never ends, does it? OK, good night XO, get some sleep."

As the XO felt his way to the pilothouse door, Tanner thought more about the odd behavior of Ricky McKnight. He must have performed well in earlier assignments, or he wouldn't have screened for XO. He thought to himself, if this keeps up I have two choices: I can shoot him in the face and relieve him. Ask the Bureau for a new XO. Ops could fleet up in the meantime. Or I could try to salvage him. Hell, I've only been in command for three weeks, can't shit-can him yet. A plan began to form in his mind. It would entail some risk, but if he could, he would rehabilitate Ricky McKnight. Ricky needed a confidence boost.

But that was only part of the problem, he mused. The XO's shortcomings in staying on top of things were annoying. Worse was the friction in the wardroom that he seemed to be causing. This grated on Tanner more than anything. He had always hoped to get command, and now that he had it he wanted that command to be a happy command. Squared away and professional to be sure, but happy too. He felt that he created the conditions for good morale by the way he conducted himself. To have his number two upset things could not be allowed to continue.

As the night wore on, Tanner stayed on the bridge. Shipping picked up, and the Bridge and CIC team was kept busy sorting through all the radar contacts, figuring out which ones would pass close to *Dauntless*, and make recommendations to Tanner if maneuvers were necessary to avoid a collision. Having the captain on the bridge was a relief to the watch-standers. He was in on each situation from the beginning, making their reporting requirements that much simpler. Often, he would tell them to stop worrying about one contact, which in his judgment no longer posed a danger, and focus on others that did.

Finally, just after midnight, the tactical circuit crackled to life, and the signal came from *Biddle* authorizing all ships to leave their diamond formation stations and proceed independently to Port Said. Tanner thought to himself that Roger Welsh must have gotten tired of taking reports from his watch officers every time a ship in the formation had to leave station to avoid other shipping. He was probably trying to get some sleep himself.

He called out to Lieutenant John Woodson, the midwatch OOD, "Woody, use this as base course, but do what you have to do to avoid shipping. Try to keep *Detroit* in sight. Since we're following her in the canal, I want to try anchor close to her tomorrow. I'm going below. Call me for any contacts with a CPA of 1,000 yards or less."

"Aye, aye Captain. Regular wake-up call?"

"Sure, but tell your relief to call the XO first and bring him up to speed."

Entering his cabin through the night-vision enabling red light passageway, he noted the 8 o'clock Reports sitting in his in-basket where the XO had left them. At his feet was the next day's Plan of the Day, the POD, slid under his door by the duty yeoman. Grimacing, he scooped up the POD and gave it a quick look, hoping against hope that it bore some semblance to the way events were likely to play out the next day. Actually, today, he corrected himself.

Fuck it, he thought. *I'm hitting the rack. I need sleep too.* He tossed the POD on top of the 8 o'clock Reports. He'd read it in the morning.

* * *

It was a tired Will Tanner that rolled out of the rack at 0600 the next morning. He had taken numerous calls from the OODs throughout the night reporting the proximity of other ships. He had only gone to the bridge once when a particularly challenging situation developed with a much faster container ship overtaking a tanker while both ships were calculated to pass close aboard *Dauntless*, one to port and the other to starboard. It brought back memories of *Wade*. Quickly sizing up the situation he had the

OOD increase speed and cut across the bow of the slower tanker at a safe distance, leaving both ships to port.

The eastern Med was flat calm, so he knocked out fifty pushups on the deck before entering his head for a Navy shower and shave. Fresh water was a valuable commodity on a Navy ship, especially a steamship, and not to be wasted with what was known as a 'Hollywood shower.' Not even for the captain. *Especially not the captain*, he thought to himself.

Picking up the POD while toweling off, he noted that anchoring at Port Said was planned for 1600 with the navigation brief at 1700 followed shortly after that by the evening meal. No mention was made of a late-night sea detail and Suez Canal transit. He sighed, the rest of the day's events looked reasonable. No one was really sure when they would be called on bridge-to-bridge radio and told to weigh anchor and form up the convoy. That was up to the Egyptian Suez Canal authorities and was a moving target. Much depended on when the next day's northbound convoy was due to leave Port Suez at the southern end of the canal. The southbound convoy would anchor in the Great Bitter Lake around noon the next day to allow the northbound convoy to pass by. Except for the Great Bitter Lake, the Suez Canal was a one-way street.

At two o'clock that afternoon, Tanner was called in his cabin by John Woodson, the navigator.

"Captain, we're painting landfall on the 10, trying to get a radar fix. Land's pretty flat here, so it's tough. Looks like lots of ships at anchor off Port Said."

"OK Nav, I'll be up in a minute. Let the XO know."

Tanner went to the bridge and took a look at the radar picture, burying his face in the rubber hood of the SPA-25 radar repeater. Fifteen miles ahead was the coast of Egypt and lying just offshore were too many surface contacts to count. He looked out the bridge window to see a yellow, hazy sky with no clear horizon.

"What do you think the visibility is?" he asked the OOD, Lieutenant (junior grade) Nelson.

"Sir, we've got *Detroit* just off the port bow at about two miles, but she's been getting harder and harder to see."

"How about *Biddle* and *Spruance*?"

"We're tracking *Biddle* about a mile ahead of *Detroit* and just to port and *Spruance* at two miles on *Detroit*'s beam. Can't see either one visually."

Tanner climbed into his chair and picked up his binoculars. The haze was pretty thick, and it seemed to be getting thicker. Seeing whitecaps on the sea surface, he glanced up at the wind-bird indicator above the bridge window. Thirty-five knots, coming off the coast.

"What's true wind?"

"We just worked it. 145 at 25."

"OK, let's tuck in about 1,000 yards behind *Detroit*. We'll try anchor near her so she can run interference for us tonight into the canal."

Nelson gave some orders, and Tanner watched quietly as *Dauntless* increased speed and began to close *Detroit*. The bridge-to-bridge radio was non-stop babble as merchant ships, and Suez Canal authorities discussed anchor locations and other administrative details on channel 16. Tanner waited for an opening to call Captain Mel Andrews on *Detroit*.

When he got it, he transmitted, "*Detroit*, *Dauntless* CO for CO channel one-six."

"*Detroit* Charlie Oscar, roger, switch to channel seven-three."

Andrews was on the bridge too, as he knew he would be.

"*Detroit* this is *Dauntless* actual channel seven-three."

"Go ahead, *Dauntless*, over."

"Captain, good afternoon. I plan to follow in your wake and anchor near you until we get underway tonight. Would appreciate a heads up when you think you've found your spot, over."

"Roger, will do, looks like a real goat-rope up there."

"Roger, thanks, sir, standing by seven-three, out."

Tanner grinned as he replaced the handset. Andrews, the F-14 pilot, was getting a taste of the surface Navy. His wardroom would be manned by surface warriors, and his XO would be a SWO. This was Andrew's training tour for eventual carrier command. He had no doubt that Andrews had had many hairy carrier landings at night and in lousy weather, but handling an 800-foot 55,000-ton ship in tight quarters was no picnic. *Detroit* was no fighter jet.

He pressed TAO on the bitch box, "TAO Captain, guard channel 16 for us, I'm going to stay on seven-three to talk to *Detroit*."

"TAO, aye."

Tanner liked what he heard from his TAOs and OODs on both internal communications and the tactical radio circuits. No wasted words. Brevity and clarity were critical when the action got hot and heavy.

Re-focusing on the approach to the anchorage he noticed the visibility continuing to drop. This was more than haze. He stepped out on the starboard bridge wing and felt the sand sting his face. Sand. The wind was kicking up the sand of the Egyptian desert and blowing it out to sea. *Detroit* was barely visible only a half mile ahead. *Shit*, this was supposed to be an easy anchorage. Just pick an open spot and drop the hook. Make sure you had enough room to swing around at anchor and not hit anybody else.

Because the Navy ships would lead the convoy, it would be advantageous to anchor in a location closer to the canal entrance, thereby avoiding a midnight adventure winding through the ships already anchored helter-skelter in the approaches. As they began to encounter a denser concentration of anchored merchant shipping of all sizes, the visibility continued to drop as the sand blew. The steady patter of sand crystals hitting the bridge windows provided an annoying backdrop to the sounds of the bridge team navigating the ship. Finally, *Detroit* disappeared completely from view 1,000 yards ahead.

The Bridge and CIC sea detail watch team had been trying to keep track of all of the contacts and had reached the saturation point. The last report he had heard identified skunk "Charlie November." They'd been through the alphabet three and a half times since midnight. Most were anchored, but a few were underway looking for their own spots. The anchor detail on the forecastle was fighting the sandstorm, hunched over with their backs to the wind.

Tanner decided to get more involved.

"Paul," he said to OOD Paul Nelson, "cease trying to track skunks, we'll have to pick our way through the anchorage using radar and eyeball. Keep close track of *Detroit*. Tell the anchor detail to come back into the break and get out of the sand. We'll run em' back out there when it's time to anchor." Glancing at the fathometer, he saw they had 60 feet of water under the keel. He'd have to keep an eye on that as well. The conditions made piloting by radar or visual navigation impossible.

A shape loomed ahead out of the yellowish gloom created by the sand.

"Paul, left full-rudder," said Tanner. At five knots they slowly moved left and then back in the direction of *Detroit* as a large container ship at anchor passed down the starboard side, probably only 200 yards away.

They continued dodging anchored ships and tracking *Detroit* for the next hour as they followed her closer to the canal entrance. The sandstorm continued in intensity and as dusk began to fall visibility became worse. No lights were visible except on anchored ships as they passed by.

"*Dauntless, Detroit*, channel seven-three. Had enough, I'm anchoring here, over."

"*Dauntless*, roger, out."

"Paul, let's try anchor about 500 yards from *Detroit*, should be open if we stay behind her."

Tanner oversaw the anchoring of *Dauntless* and checked his watch. 1800. So much for anchoring at 1600, doing the navigation brief and then having dinner and a nap. The whole schedule was out of whack because of the sandstorm.

At 1900 they gathered the entire wardroom, most of the Chief's Mess, and several senior petty officers in the wardroom to brief the Suez Canal transit and the next day's events. Throughout, the CDO kept being summoned to the quarterdeck to deal with various Egyptian authorities bringing paperwork to be signed or requesting information about the ship.

Morton assumed his briefing position next to the movie screen, and Seaman Collins sat next to the projector with a stack of view graphs.

"Captain, gentlemen, we can expect to set sea detail tonight any time after 23:00. We won't know until we get the actual convoy start time from the Egyptians over bridge-to-bridge. Bridge watch will have to keep a sharp ear, there's constant chatter on channel 16, and that's what the Egyptians use."

"Captain, Weps has set up the watch rotation for the bridge, forecastle, fantail and motor whaleboat."

A ready boat had to be available for launch on short notice in case of emergency. Likewise, line handlers had to be on station in case the mooring lines were needed for any reason. A pilot ladder was rigged to the starboard side fantail for the Egyptian pilots who would board by boat.

"We'll get one pilot at the entrance to Port Said harbor who will ride us through the city. He'll be replaced by another pilot for the run down to Ismailia which takes about six hours. In Ismailia, he gets off, and we get a third pilot from there to Port Suez, including while we anchor in the Great Bitter Lake around noon tomorrow."

Using a pointer, Ops traced the canal route south as he went.

"The whole convoy will anchor in the Great Bitter Lake until the northbound convoy passes. There are no designated anchor spots, so Captain, I recommend we haul ass to the southern end of the lake, so we're in good position to continue south when we get moving again. Like tonight, we should stay close to *Detroit*. Suppo the pilot will eat lunch with us in the wardroom. Need to make sure we feed him right, no pork, no ham. Fish is the safest bet."

"Suppo" was the Supply Officer, Lieutenant Larry Logan.

The captain turned to Logan, "Suppo, I'm going to need a carton of Marlboro's and a ball cap and lighter for each pilot. Put it on my tab."

It was expected that each pilot be rewarded with a ball cap, cigarettes, and a lighter with the ship's crest for the excellent job they did, at great taxpayer expense, in guiding the ships through the canal. Ship captains were not given any funds to pay for these gifts.

Ops continued, "Pilot number three rides us to Port Suez, and we get another pilot to take us through the city and into the Gulf of Suez. After that, we're on our own. We should be through Port Suez by 19:00 or 20:00 tomorrow. Any questions?"

There were none. Tanner turned to McKnight, "XO, any word to put out?"

"No sir, I think that covers it."

Ops spoke up, "Captain, I had planned to have a briefing on our MIO procedures tomorrow night after we've cleared the canal. Get the boarding teams, TAO's, OOD's, really all the watch-standers, and review the procedures and ROE one more time. We'll be put to work as soon as we enter the Red Sea." MIO was shorthand for Maritime Interception Operations.

"All right Ops, let's see. We may be able to wait until the morning after. We're going to be pretty busy the next 36 hours, and I want everyone paying attention."

Just then the duty yeoman entered the wardroom with a stack of PODs for the next day. The XO blanched, he had been busy and had not looked at it carefully when he signed it as he was walking to the navigation brief.

Tanner took a copy and glanced at it while McKnight looked on nervously. He noted the schedule. It was pure boiler plate, right out of what the ship's instruction on inport daily routine called for:

0600 Reveille, Breakfast for the Crew
0745 Officer's Call
0800 Quarters
1000 XO Inspection of Messing and Berthing
1100 Sweepers
1130 Lunch for the Crew
1300 Planning Board For Training in the Wardroom
1300 ESWS Lecture on the Messdecks - OBAs
1600 Knock Off Ship's Work
1730 Dinner for the Crew
1830 8 O'Clock Reports on the Quarterdeck
1900 Movie Call
2200 Taps

Tanner did not look up and simply dropped the worthless POD on the wardroom table. Gathering himself, he began, "OK everybody, long couple of days ahead. Those that can try to catch a few Z's between now and sea detail. When you're off watch tomorrow, do what you need to do but get some rest too. I need everybody sharp for the canal transit and ready to go to work when we hit the Red Sea and start MIO. Good brief Ops. XO, come on up with me."

Instead of his cabin, Tanner went to the bridge with the XO in trail. Stopping first to look at the chart, survey the anchorage, and take a quick report from the OOD, he signaled McKnight to follow him out to the starboard bridge wing. The wind had died, the sand was gone, and it was a bright starry night in the Middle East. A petty officer was on the starboard bridge wing, at the pelorus and wearing sound-powered headphones to take navigation bearings. The lights of Port Said glowed brightly just a couple of miles away, as well as the lights of the hundred-plus ships at anchor.

He signaled McKnight to continue aft to the signal bridge.

"Captain I'm sorry about the POD. Chief Dougherty wrote it, and I didn't have time to fix it before the nav brief."

"XO, I don't know what to say. I need to count on you for as long as this thing lasts. We're going to be busy, and I need to know you've got things under control when I'm too busy to worry about adminis-trivia. That schedule bears no resemblance to reality. Yet, you signed it. Why?"

"I'm sorry, I know, I was in a hurry. It won't happen again, I promise."

"XO, listen... when your tour is up, I have to write a report on your fitness for command. You'll go ashore from here. This is your last chance at sea before the command board meets. Right now, I don't think you're ready. I don't know what kind of tickets you got from Captain Schwartz. And I don't want to know. I've got to make my own judgment, and right now I'm not impressed."

The XO looked at his feet, totally chagrined.

"Sir, I promise I'll do better, I'll take a round turn."

"It's not just the POD, XO. That's just a symptom. I've been watching you interact with the department heads, and I don't like what I see. Especially Ops. I want your leadership style to reflect mine. I do not subscribe to the theory that the XO has to play bad cop so the CO can play good cop. I want this crew to *want* to work for us, not *have* to."

"Yessir."

"Now get below and get horizontal for a while. I want you on the bridge as we move into the canal and through the city. After that, rest when you can. I need you rested tomorrow night for the trip down the Gulf of Suez. I'll have been up a long time by then, and I plan to let you run things and take reports while I sleep. You up for that?"

McKnight brightened, "Yessir, I won't let you down, Captain."

When the XO left, Tanner climbed into his chair. Too spun up to sleep, it was already 2200, he might as well stay up here and keep his night-vision and situational awareness. The cacophony on bridge-to-bridge radio never let up. How was anyone going to know what to do, most of it was unintelligible.

Forty minutes later, OOD Lieutenant John Woodson, nudged Tanner awake in his chair. "Captain, just got the call on bridge-to-bridge, convoy underway at 23:30. Recommend we set sea detail at 23:00."

"OK Woody, make it so." He had not heard the call, nor realized he had dozed off. Time to get focused. He went over to the chart table and studied the chart for the approach and then looked over at *Detroit*. He'd simply follow in her wake and leave it to Captain Mel Andrews to fall in behind *Spruance*.

Woodson's walkie-talkie crackled and a voice said, "Bridge, Fantail, we've got a small boat approaching, could be the pilot."

"Roger, if it is, he's early, let me know."

Two minutes later the walkie-talkie squawked again, "Bridge, Fantail, it's the pilot, and he says it's time for us to move."

"OK, bring him up."

Tanner heard all this, "Set sea detail Woody, looks like we're going early."

A petty officer brought the Egyptian pilot to the bridge. He appeared agitated as he babbled in Arabic into his own walkie-talkie. He was burly, slightly overweight, and sported a bushy black mustache. A heavy odor of flowery cologne wafted throughout the bridge. He wore a short-sleeve khaki shirt and olive drab trousers.

Tanner stepped forward and extended his hand to welcome him aboard, but before he could get a word out the pilot exclaimed in a loud voice in English, "Let's go! We move now. Convoy leaves."

Tanner withdrew his hand and said, "We'll go when we're ready. We were told 23:30."

"No, go now. Must move!"

The sea detail team for the first leg was in the process of turning over with the anchor watch. Tanner took the walkie-talkie from Woodson, ignoring the pilot who began pacing back and forth behind the bridge windows.

"Fo'c'sle, bridge, this is the Captain. Ensign Grimmage up there?"

"Aye, Captain, I'm here."

"Wilt, as soon as you have enough people, start hauling up the anchor. We're going early."

"OOD, tell main control to stand by to answer all bells."

Dauntless set a new record for getting underway from anchor and quickly had the anchor at short stay, ready to be lifted off the bottom. Tanner saw that *Detroit* had secured anchor lights and energized navigation lights. They were underway. He turned to the new OOD, Lieutenant Commander Andy Morton, "Let's go, Andy, raise the anchor and follow *Detroit*."

Dauntless moved forward and fell in 500 yards astern of *Detroit*. The Egyptian pilot had little to say to the bridge team, devoting most of his time to speaking Arabic into his walkie-talkie, presumably coordinating with the other pilots as the convoy formed up astern of *Dauntless* in some sort of order.

As they entered the Port Said inner harbor, it became almost as bright as day. The city was garishly lit but without modern, office-style buildings. Numerous minarets dotted the skyline along with ornate stone buildings which lined the water's edge. They passed a nest of Russian made *Osa* patrol boats which had been exported to Egypt by the Soviets. As they approached the southern end of the city, another small boat motored out from the west bank, and pilot number two was escorted to the bridge to replace pilot number one. Number One had been aboard for all of forty-five minutes, but Tanner gave him his gifts and shook his hand as he left. Pilot number two and Tanner exchanged pleasantries, and then he moved to the starboard bridge wing to light a cigarette. Tanner winked at Morton and said, "Just as well, he'll let us know if he wants us to do anything different."

Leaving the lights of Port Said behind, the convoy moved into the Egyptian desert at 12 knots, approaching the long due south leg of the canal which would take them to the city of Ismailia some forty miles further south. As Tanner looked to his left, he saw an eerie sight. There, seemingly sailing through the desert was the superstructure of a large oil tanker, also moving south and keeping pace with *Dauntless*. A few years earlier the Egyptians had dug a branch off the canal which ran nine miles south of the Mediterranean before it joined the main channel. It allowed the very largest super-tankers to enter the canal without passing through the tight quarters of the city. Tanner pointed to the tanker to bring it to the pilot's attention. He nodded and said something in Arabic into his walkie-talkie. "Will go behind," he said. Tanner nodded but continued to watch the bearing drift which did not appear to be changing. The tanker began to get closer as the two channels converged. Still directly abeam, no drift.

As the channel convergence appeared ahead, Tanner turned to Woodson.

"Woody, go to 20 knots."

The pilot whipped his head around, wild-eyed. "No, too fast," he shouted.

Tanner just pointed at the looming tanker and shook his head. The pilot relaxed as *Dauntless* began to outpace the tanker. When it was evident that the tanker would enter the main channel safely astern, *Dauntless* returned to 12 knots.

Tanner remained on the bridge all night as the watch-standers rotated positions. As the sun began to rise over the desert, the sheer nothingness on both sides of the canal became clear. It was quite an engineering feat thought Tanner as he watched their position in the channel and the distances to *Detroit* ahead and the super tanker astern.

At mid-morning they reached Ismailia, and pilot number two was replaced by pilot number three, pilot number two leaving with his gifts from Tanner. Pilot number three was entirely different than his predecessors, like them, paying little attention to navigating the ship, but garrulous and talkative. He told Tanner that he loved American television.

"What's your favorite show?"

"Beverly Hills 90210."

Tanner laughed.

At noon they entered the Great Bitter Lake and anchored the ship near the south end. Having been up for 36 hours, Tanner went to his cabin for a power nap while McKnight entertained the pilot over lunch in the wardroom. Early that afternoon they watched from the bridge as the northbound convoy, some sixty ships, sailed past on their way to the Mediterranean. Once past, the anchor was raised, and the southbound convoy resumed its voyage.

As it grew dark, they arrived at the southern end of the canal at Port Suez, some 200 miles north of the Red Sea, and traded pilots for the final, brief run past the city. Ricky McKnight was on the Bridge with Tanner as *Dauntless'* boatswain mates secured the anchor for sea. Tanner was visibly tired having spent most of the past two days on the bridge.

"Gonna hit the rack, Captain?"

"I am. Did you get some sleep?"

"Yessir."

"Alright, after dinner I'd like you to stay here through the night. There's going to be a lot of shipping, those from our convoy heading south and those on the way north for tomorrow's. Don't call me unless you really need to. You can sit, but try not to fall asleep. I'll make it clear in the night orders that you are to take all reports."

"Got it, sir."

That night Ricky McKnight stayed on the bridge to cover for the captain. There were a few minor course changes to safely clear other shipping but no major problems. He didn't call the captain once.

Sitting in the chair and savoring the responsibility of command, he had a lot of time to think. The ass chewing last night really hurt. Yet, the captain had entrusted him with the safety of the ship tonight. He was hard to read. I've got to do better, he thought to himself.

His thoughts turned to home. The last mail call had been during the last unrep with *Detroit* in the Med. *Detroit* had received a CH-53E helicopter from Sigonella as they passed south of Italy and had distributed mail to each ship as they came alongside for fuel. There had been nothing from Theresa. What had gone wrong he wondered? They had no children, marrying late, and Theresa had not adapted well to Navy life. She thought the wardroom was stuffy and that everybody walked on eggshells around the captain. Of course, that was Screamin' Schwartz. She hardly knew Tanner. Met him once at the hail and farewell party in their quarters on base. He sensed that they were drifting apart and he didn't know what to do about it. And now, here he was stuck on this ship on a deployment that nobody knew when would end. Hell, they might be going to war with Iraq. He considered his options. The captain sure hadn't said anything encouraging about his prospects for command. Maybe he should cut his losses and get out now. Try patch things up with Theresa and start a new life on the outside. On the other hand, this deployment might be just what his career needed. If they went to war, he'd be one of the few of his year group to do so. That had to count for something. Besides, he couldn't just quit now. Well, he could. But he wouldn't. That would be cowardly and leave the ship short-handed. No, he'd stick it out and do his job. After the cruise, he'd hash it out with Theresa and make a decision. He decided to put this in a letter home, tell her he loved her and wanted to make things right.

EIGHT

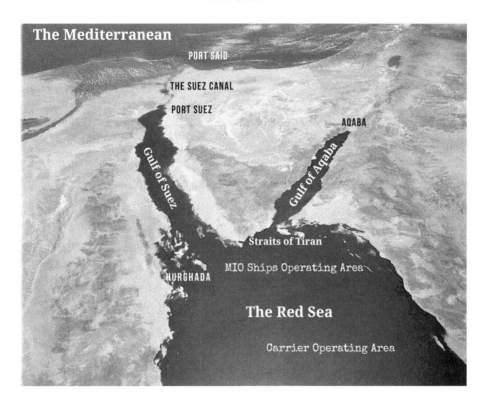

Southern Gulf of Suez

"Bzzt." The growler phone rang on the bridge next to the CO's chair. Will Tanner set down his coffee mug and grabbed the handset.

"Captain."

"Captain, XO here. We're all set in the wardroom for the MIO brief."

"All right XO, I'll be right down."

Tanner hopped down from his chair and walked to the chart table. *Dauntless* was twenty miles north of the southern end of the Gulf of Suez, just north of the entrance to the Red Sea. To the left was the Sinai Peninsula, light brown, dusty, with darker low-lying mountain ranges and hillsides. To the right was the Egyptian mainland, at the corner of the continent of Africa, flat and dusty. It was 09:00 and Tanner had slept the sleep of the dead the previous night. In his dreams, or so he thought, he felt the ship move in a light sea or heel as the rudder was put over to change course. He was aware in some distant corner of his brain when the pitch of the forced draft blowers changed in response to a change in steam demand as the ship slowed or accelerated. But he had slept soundly. No one had called all night for the first time since he had taken the ship to sea over three weeks earlier.

Glancing out the bridge window, he saw *Detroit* 2,000 yards ahead. Captain Welsh in *Biddle* had put his charges in a loose column formation at 2,000 yards spacing, in the same order in which they had exited the canal. Tanner had approved. The signal to maneuver as necessary to avoid shipping was always in the air. The ships that had made up their convoy the day prior had spread out through the night, and now none were in close enough proximity to be a concern.

He turned to Lieutenant Chris Palmer, the OOD, "Chris, I'll be in the wardroom, call me if anything changes or if we have a close CPA."

"Aye, aye, Captain."

Entering the wardroom, he waved everybody back into their seats as he sat down. It was standing room only. All officers not on watch, all hands involved in boarding operations, and all the chiefs not on watch were present. He wanted all of the chiefs to know what was going on, even those that would not be directly involved in the boarding operations.

He looked at the XO. He looked a little haggard from his full night on the bridge, but he also looked energized. He took a moment to scan the room, making eye contact with the two lieutenants and one lieutenant (junior grade) who would lead the boarding teams. He then sized up the enlisted crew who would operate the motor whaleboat and who would scale the sides of ships, take control of the crew, and thoroughly search each ship. They had chosen well. The officers were Main Propulsion Assistant Lieutenant Don Evans, CIC Officer Lieutenant (junior grade) Willy Kim, and Repair Division Officer Lieutenant Jimmy Nicholson. Kim was the junior man. The boarding teams, each consisting of eleven petty officers and seamen or firemen had been chosen for their physical size and proven common sense. This was a job for those who would keep their cool and not go "cowboy."

"XO, thanks for holding down the fort last night - got some much-needed sleep." *Might as well throw the XO a bone in front of the crew. Jack him up a little.*

Ops was in his usual position as was Seaman Collins.

"Morning Captain, this chart shows the gate guard stations in the northern Red Sea just south of the Strait of Tiran which provides access to the Gulf of Aqaba. Alpha Sierra has promulgated boxes stretching across the entrance to the Gulf of Aqaba named after pro baseball stadiums. We've been assigned Fenway here in the middle. *Spruance* will be further south in Three Rivers, and *Biddle* will be to our west in Yankee. *Montgomery* has her new motor whaleboat and will transit Suez in three days, taking up station in Dodger. *Sara* is 100 miles south flying combat air patrol and air support for the MIO ships. *Phil Sea* will stay with her for shotgun. *Detroit* is headed for a spot about 20 miles south of *Spruance* and will refuel all the MIO ships in turn and then *Saratoga* before going around the Arabian Peninsula to the gulf. We don't yet have the unrep plan. COMDESRON 24, Alpha Sierra, will remain embarked in *Saratoga* and manage the whole MIO op from there. Any questions so far?"

Chief Engineer Kenny Carpenter spoke up, "Captain, since we will have to take fuel from *Sara* until another oiler shows up, I can go to one boiler, cross-connect ops, to save fuel. Would limit our speed to 22 knots."

Tanner thought for a second, "Cheng, let's see how the ops go before we do that. I'd like to keep two boilers on line, and the plant split for both speed and redundancy until we get a feel for how this all plays out. With One Bravo fixed, we can afford to stay on two." Petty Officer Taylor had completed the weld job on One Bravo boiler with the help of a high-pressure welder provided by CTF-63 out of Naples. That petty officer had been sent over to *Saratoga* by helicopter where he would eventually be flown back to Italy.

Ops continued as Collins put up another view graph, "Here are the basic rules for MIO. Every ship entering or departing the Strait of Tiran is to be stopped and searched. The port of Aqaba, Jordan is the only way for the Iraqi's to get goods delivered by sea other than their own ports in the Persian Gulf, either in Iraq or now, Kuwait. We have a list of prohibited cargoes, mainly military equipment, and we're supposed to look for contraband being smuggled out of Kuwait through Aqaba."

"What if the ships don't want to stop?" asked Don Evans.

"Coming to that. Several courses of action are permitted. All subject to clearance by Alpha Sierra, and probably Alpha Bravo too, maybe higher. MIO ships can fire warning shots to convince them to stop. In extreme cases disabling fire could be authorized. The preferred method to stop a ship determined to break through is to helo over a SEAL team from *Sara* and let them fast-rope down and take over the ship. We could also be ordered to board a non-compliant ship from our motor whaleboat if it meets the right conditions, mainly a low enough freeboard so that these guys can climb over the side."

Tanner thought about that option. *Not good.* The MIO ships had left port without loading any special equipment for these kinds of operations. The boarding team would be wearing bulky kapok lifejackets, steel helmets, and carrying M-14 rifles; .45 caliber pistols for the officers. It was less than ideal. Besides, the motor whaleboat was not designed for speed, any cargo ship could outrun it.

Ops went on, "For each boarding, a helicopter will be assigned to fly cover, report any suspicious activity, and count the crew on deck. If no helo is available, *Sara* will send over a fixed wing to do the same thing."

Willy Kim piped up, "How do we know what to look for?"

"Like I said, there's a list of prohibited items. I've also got instructions on how to read a ship's manifest and compare it to what you find. If they don't match, it's a violation, and we turn em' around. You guys will have laminated cheat sheets to take with you."

Another officer asked, "What do you mean turn them around?"

"If they are trying to get into Aqaba, we send them back where they came from or to another port where they can offload any prohibited cargo. If they are on the way out, we send them back to Aqaba to do the same thing."

"Finally," said Ops, "here's the bad news. If we get a container ship, every single container has to be opened and inspected. Every one. Unless they are impossible to get to. Then we have to report that so they can be inspected in port."

Willy Kim spoke up again, "Why don't we just put a ship up the gulf near Aqaba where nobody can get by?"

It was a good question, thought Tanner. With only three ships now, four when *Montgomery* showed up, there was a lot of ocean to cover before the entrance to the Gulf of Aqaba.

Morton answered, "Coupla reasons, Willy. First, the Gulf of Aqaba is about 100 miles long. Putting a ship up there puts them too far away from the rest of the group, makes it harder to come south and get fuel, harder to provide mutual support, and so forth.

Second, that would be an affront to the Jordanians. Us patrolling in their back yard."

Tanner nodded and added, "Good question Willy. I think you make a good point about the area we have to cover. Ops, I'll want us to position *Dauntless* at the northern end of our box, closest to the strait. We'll be the goalie. The closer we are, the harder it will be for someone to get by undetected."

Tanner waited a beat to see if there were any more questions. "Ops, what are the threats that the intel weenies have come up with for the Red Sea group?"

"Sir, the main threat is an ambush by crewmembers as our guys climb up the side and over the rail. We do not expect that from foreign flagged ships, but word is that Saddam has threatened to hang the master of any Iraqi flagged ship that cooperates with the MIO forces. No way of knowing how true that is."

"What else?"

"That's all they've given us so far sir. There will be no Iraqi naval forces getting out of the gulf, and nobody thinks aircraft could get down here from Iraq. It's too far, and they'd be intercepted going over Saudi Arabia by our guys. The ships in the Persian Gulf have to worry about the Exocet, like got *Stark*. Swedge is supposed to be issuing some Exocet guidance for all the ships."

"Swedge," or SWDG, was the Surface Warfare Development Group in Norfolk. They were supposed to develop and assess tactics for Navy ships to meet various threats.

Tanner was worried about the ambush potential. The first man sticking his head over the rail would be vulnerable. They would be climbing single file up accommodation ladders or pilot ladders. Perhaps even rope ladders. The helicopter or airplane flying cover would be critical to protecting his guys from that possibility.

Everyone looked expectantly at the captain.

"Okay Ops, good brief. Folks this is unlike anything we've done before and unlike anything we've trained for. I'm proud of all of you and grateful that you have volunteered to take on this dangerous mission. And it *is* dangerous, even if the ships cooperate fully. Getting from the motor whaleboat to the ladder and up the side of the ship with your gear will be the most dangerous part. Same with getting off the ship. This mission is important, but not as important as your safety. Boarding officers, you are responsible. If you think a situation is too dangerous, call me and tell me. We'll talk it over. I don't want anyone getting hurt. If we have to sit and wait until the seas abate, or direct the ship to move into calmer water, we will."

He looked carefully around the room to make sure everyone knew he was serious. The truth was, they had far more volunteers to be on the boarding teams than they could use. Everybody wanted to get in on the action.

Tanner turned to McKnight, "XO, anything further to add?"

Flattered that he was given a chance to pitch in, McKnight hesitated, unprepared to contribute, then, "No sir, I think that covers it. Obviously, we'll vary the daily routine to accommodate what's happening operationally." He looked expectantly at Tanner, hoping that he'd said the right thing.

Tanner nodded, "Master Chief, anything to add?"

Command Master Chief Derwood King, coffee mug welded to his left hand, looked pointedly at the enlisted boarding teams.

"The Captain is counting on you guys to accomplish this mission and to do it right. Have each other's backs, and support these officers leading the teams. You guys are the main battery for this. Make us proud."

Tanner nodded his approval, "OK, let's go to work, we'll be on station in a few hours. No telling how quickly we'll be put to work. Ops, Weps, XO, we'll stay at Condition III ready for anything. Weps, I want to pac-fire the guns when we can and let's review our procedures for warning shots and disabling fire. I'll want to practice that some more too."

With that, everyone clambered to their feet as Tanner left the wardroom and headed back to the bridge.

"Ops, Weps, Cheng, Suppo; stay behind," said McKnight.

Exchanging glances, the four department heads stayed back while the rest of the crew filed out of the wardroom. When they were alone, Lieutenant Commander Carpenter asked, "What's up XO?"

"The Captain is pretty tired," McKnight began, "I want you guys to call me first on anything you have for the Captain. I'll decide whether or not to bother him with it. He's going to be focused on our operations. I'll handle all the administrative stuff, casualty reports, personnel issues, so on."

The three officers exchanged glances and looked uncomfortable. Morton broke the silence, "XO, you know the Captain wants that kind of stuff ASAP. He told us to keep you informed, but not delay getting him the word."

McKnight fixed the Operations Officer with a hard stare.

"Ops, I don't need you fighting me at every turn. I'm second in command of this ship. When I give an order, I expect it to be followed."

Morton looked up at the overhead, a frown on his face, but made no reply.

"Is there a problem, Ops?" persisted McKnight.

"No sir."

"All right then, carry on."

McKnight walked out of the wardroom and headed aft to his stateroom.

Morton looked at his fellow department heads.

"I don't know about you guys, but I'm not doing anything different until the Captain tells me. This is bullshit. What is that guy's fucking problem anyway?"

Nobody responded, each thinking through their own reaction to the XO's dictum. Nobody was smiling, the tension between the Operations Officer and the Executive Officer had the potential to bleed over into their own departments.

On the bridge, Will Tanner watched the navigation team as *Dauntless* cleared the southern mouth of the Gulf of Suez and rounded the Sinai Peninsula to take up station fifteen miles due south of the Strait of Tiran in MIO station Fenway. The status board showed him the bearing and range to each of the other MIO ships as well as to the three surface contacts close enough to show up on the surface search radar, the SPS-10. All three appeared to be heading north into the Gulf of Suez, not toward the Strait of Tiran.

"TAO, Captain," he said into the bitch box, "let me known when *Biddle* and *Spruance* arrive in their assigned boxes. What's our ETA?"

"Aye Captain," came the response, "at this speed, we'll enter Fenway at 1400. I'll report in to Alpha Sierra when we do."

"OK, I'm going to walk around the ship. Find me if anything happens."

With some time on his hands, Tanner set out on one of his favorite activities - walking around the ship and talking to his crew going about their duties. It was a good way to start learning who was who and it showed the crew that he was interested in what they were doing. He knew the OOD and the TAO would be keeping track of his movements as every space he entered would find a way to get the word back to the bridge or CIC.

He decided to start in the forward boiler room. He saw Operations department, Weapons department, and Supply department people, all day long, but the snipes lived in a different world. Besides, he wanted to have a look at the One Bravo boiler repairs. Climbing down the vertical ladder into the forward fire room, he entered a different world. He was immediately engulfed in hot, humid air, smelling of steam, fuel oil, and sweat. He began sweating immediately. Stepping onto the upper level, he was confronted by a dizzying array of piping going in all directions and the noise of blower motors and fans, pumps, and the constant howl of a boiler firing away at 975 degrees Fahrenheit. A startled sailor almost ran into him, head down studying a preventive maintenance card and carrying a flashlight and a handful of rags. He was wearing grimy dungarees, a dirty white, loose fitting, tee shirt, and paint splattered boon-docker boots.

"Oh, uh, sorry sir." For a second he looked like he was wondering who this officer was, then recognition set in. "Captain. Can I help you?"

"Just looking around," he shouted over the deafening noise in the space, "how's One Bravo holding up?"

"It's on line now sir, working like a champ."

Noting that the petty officer was wearing a set of "Mickey Mouse" hearing protection, he looked around for the box of soft foam ear plugs that was supposed to be nearby the foot of the ladder. Seeing it, he grabbed a pair, rolled them and stuck one in each ear.

Tanner stayed in the forward fire room for about ten minutes, chatting with the Boiler Tender of the Watch and getting to know some of the crew he had only briefly encountered. He needed to do this more often, the demands of topside operations had kept him spending almost all his time on the bridge or in CIC. He climbed the ladder and headed aft to main control where the Engineering Officer of the Watch and the machinist mates plied their trade.

He was turning to leave main control when the phone talker said, "Captain, bridge just called, OOD wants to talk to you."

Tanner knew that the second that he had come down the ladder and been recognized, that same phone talker had said into the 1JV circuit to the bridge, "Captain's in main control."

He went to the bitch box and pressed the lever marked "pilothouse," "OOD, Captain, what's up?"

"Sir, Lieutenant Jay-gee Nelson here, looks like we've got our first customer, *Spruance* is closest and is challenging them now on bridge-to-bridge."

"Got a visual?"

"Not yet, sir, they're still about fifteen miles away if it's the contact I think it is."

"OK, head for the northern end of Fenway, I'll be up in a minute."

Tanner decided to stop in CIC where Lieutenant Commander Vinny DeVito was standing watch as TAO. DeVito had the VHF bridge-to-bridge radio tuned to channel 16. Tanner heard Commander Chris Winters' voice come over.

"Container ship south of my position at five nautical miles on course three-four five, this is U.S. Navy destroyer niner-six-three, channel one-six, over."

There was no response.

"How long's this been going on?" Tanner asked DeVito

"That's about the sixth call with no answer. They tried channel 13 too. We've got the tactical circuit up over here. *Spruance* is launching her helo and reporting back to Alpha Sierra."

All ships at sea were required by international law to monitor channel 16 for safety. Channel 13 was an alternate, often used in harbors to keep 16 clear for emergencies.

Tanner went to the DRT, the Dead Reckoning Tracer, on which a plot of the surface picture was being kept. His own ship was indicated by a light projecting upward and moving with the actual course and speed of the ship. Transparent paper, like freezer paper, was laid across the glass top of the DRT, and the other ship's positions plotted based on radar range and bearing from *Dauntless*. Every three minutes an Operations Specialist drew a dot on the paper directly over the moving light. It was a handy device for providing a god's-eye view of what was happening on the ocean's surface. He saw at a glance that *Spruance* was not yet in her Three Rivers box and that the ship in question was coming from the eastern side of the Red Sea at twenty knots. *Spruance* was slightly out of position for an intercept without a high-speed chase.

He pressed OOD on the CIC bitch box, "OOD, Captain, set a course for the mouth of the Strait of Tiran and come up to 25 knots."

He turned to DeVito, "Tell *Spruance* and Alpha Sierra that we are moving into a blocking position between this contact and the strait. I'll be on the bridge."

CIC was ten feet behind the bridge on the same level, Tanner was out in a matter of seconds as the OOD ordered course 025 at 25 knots. The bells on the Engine Order Telegraph dinged as main control answered the new speed and the helmsman reported, "Steady course zero-two-five."

He grabbed his binoculars and looked south. *Spruance* was just visible, ten miles south, only her upper works visible above the horizon. He scanned east looking for the uncooperative merchant ship. Still not visible. He checked the radar picture on the SPA-25. He was looking too far south. The contact of interest was almost due east of *Spruance*, about 15 miles from *Dauntless*.

DeVito called out from the bridge on the 21MC, "Captain, TAO, *Spruance*'s helo is circling the ship. Says it's a medium-sized container ship, flying no flag. Won't answer the helo on bridge-to-bridge either, but they know they see them. They flew right over the bridge. *Spruance* is at 30 knots on an intercept course. The helo can't see a name anywhere."

"Captain, aye, we're going to get further north, try to get between this guy and the strait. Tell *Spruance* what we're doing."

Tanner thought for a second. With her four LM2500 gas turbine engines *Spruance* could reach speeds more than 30 knots. They should be able to outrun this guy no problem.

"TAO, Captain, call away the SCAT team and man the .50 Cal."

The SCAT team, or Small Arms Combat Action Team, was designed to deal with small boat threats when the ship's five-inch main gun mounts were either of little use or too much for the situation. When they had practiced the warning shot scenario before entering the Red Sea, he had told Vince DeVito to have the port and starboard side .50 caliber machine guns prepared with a belt of all tracer ammo. A ship seeing a stream of all tracer rounds flying across his path forward of the bow could not deny that it had been warned.

Tanner decided to tell the crew what was going on. This might be their first action, and he wanted everybody up to speed. He signaled the Boatswain Mate of the Watch and pointed to the 1MC, the ship's general announcing system.

"Bombers, this is the Captain speaking. We've arrived on station in the Red Sea, and we are positioning the ship to intercept a merchant ship which is being chased by *Spruance*. He does not appear to be cooperating. We've called away the SCAT team in case we need to fire warning shots, but this is *Spruance*'s target now; we are in support. Boarding Team Alpha should be prepared just in case, but I am going to hold off manning up until the situation develops further. That is all for now. Stay on your toes. This is why we are here."

As Tanner turned his attention to the developing situation, he could now clearly see *Spruance* racing northeastward at high-speed. Hull down on the horizon to the southeast he saw the white superstructure and multi-colored containers of the unidentified merchant ship headed for the Strait of Tiran.

"Brad, what kind of bearing drift are you getting on him?"

"Steady. Radar shows CBDR, sir."

Constant Bearing Decreasing Range. Good, the intercept course was working, but he needed to stay out of *Spruance*'s way.

"Let's come left to 015," he said. Lead him a little more, give *Spruance* some room. *Spruance* had just about completed the intercept. He could hear Commander Chris Winters on bridge-to-bridge continuing to try to raise the merchant ship.

"Captain, TAO, *Sara* is getting ready to launch an SH-3 with the SEALS if this guy won't stop. *Spruance* is getting all kinds of advice from Alpha Sierra," he chuckled.

Tanner had no doubt. This was the *Sara* group's first day on station and the first day that any naval forces had been able to patrol the approaches to the Gulf of Aqaba. *Philippine Sea* had been required to stay south and ride shotgun on *Sara*. Middle East Force ships had been conducting MIO in the Persian Gulf for two weeks. To his knowledge, nobody had gotten through without being boarded. Admiral McCall would not want his team to be the first to fail.

The XO came to the bridge.

"What's your plan Captain?"

"We're closing in on the Strait of Tiran and trying to stay out ahead of *Spruance* and this guy, whoever he is."

"Think he's Iraqi?" he asked.

"Could be I suppose. No flag, no name visible on the stern from the helo. Maybe they thought they could get some ships through before the MIO forces were in place. If it had been yesterday, nobody would be here to stop him."

"XO, how about staying in CIC, work with Vinny, keep me informed. I'm staying out here where I can see what's going on.

We might have to do some close-in ship handling before this is over."

"Aye, sir." McKnight left the bridge.

Spruance had completed the intercept of the container ship and was now riding alongside at 20 knots, 300 yards off her port side. The merchant remained silent on bridge-to-bridge radio.

"Captain, XO, *Spruance* is requesting authority from Alpha Sierra for warning shots. They got a wait-out."

"Any word on the SEALS?"

"Supposed to launch in five mikes."

Tanner stepped over to the chart and looked at the geometry. They were now ten miles south of the Strait of Tiran. *Spruance* and the merchant were five miles to their south-east, coming fast.

He turned to Petty Officer Aquilino, the Quartermaster of the Watch, "Let me see the Strait of Tiran chart."

He wanted a larger scale look at the strait. He knew it was narrow and surrounded on both sides by treacherous reefs. He also knew that the hulks of ships sunk during the 1973 Yom Kippur War littered the waters on both sides. Looking at the chart with Aquilino he saw that the strait itself was not very long before it opened out into the Gulf of Aqaba, but it was quite narrow, maybe a half mile at the narrowest point. Things could get real crowded if this chase kept going.

Andy Morton came to the bridge to spectate. Tanner turned to him, "Ops, what does our guidance say about entering the Gulf of Aqaba?"

"It's not real clear, sir. All the patrol areas are outside. The strait is controlled by Egypt. There are two Egyptian islands between the channel and the Saudi mainland, so the strait is Egyptian territorial water. Under international law, we can go through there under the provision for transit passage, or innocent passage. But if you're doing that, you're not supposed to be conducting military operations."

The bitch box crackled again, "Captain, XO, *Sara* launched the SEALs, and the helo had to return to the deck. Chip light."

Shit, thought Tanner. A chip light was an indicator light in the cockpit of a helicopter that warned the pilots of some kind of mechanical malfunction. How many chip lights turned out to be nothing more than a faulty indicator light? But you couldn't risk the lives of thirteen people by guessing that it was a false alarm. He took one more look at the chart and then at *Spruance* and the merchant ship, still coming fast.

"Paul," he said, head straight for the entrance to the strait. Ring up 27 knots. We're going to try and block the entrance."

Nelson's eyes widened as he acknowledged the order and came up in speed. Consulting with Aquilino, Nelson said, "Recommend zero-zero-five, Captain."

Just then, Andy Morton shouted, "Holy shit! He's trying to ram 'em!"

They watched from the starboard bridge wing as the merchant ship slowly turned to port, in the direction of *Spruance* running alongside at about 300 yards. For a few moments, *Spruance* held her course, testing the determination of the merchant ship master, whoever he was.

As the gap began to quickly narrow, *Spruance* turned hard to port and put on a burst of speed. *Probably went to Flank 3* thought Tanner to himself as he watched through the binoculars. Flank 3 was maximum available power. Pedal to the metal.

As *Spruance* appeared to accelerate quickly away to the west, the merchant ship adjusted course back to starboard. Back toward *Dauntless*. With 27 knots rung up, Dauntless was gradually opening the distance on the merchant, but also closing the Strait of Tiran at the rate of almost a mile and a half every three minutes.

"Think it was just a feint, Captain?" said Andy Morton.

"Maybe, but he bought some time. *Spruance* will take a few minutes to get back alongside."

"Captain, TAO, *Spruance* reported the ramming attempt to Alpha Sierra and got permission for warning shots."

Things were really getting interesting. Tanner looked at the chart again and then up at the coastline. Rocky, low peaks on both sides of the strait, now only five miles ahead.

"TAO, Captain, prep Mount 51 for disabling fire as we practiced in the Med. Load, one round, B, L and P." At Condition III, one gun mount was manned day and night.

"TAO, Aye."

As they transited the Mediterranean while the rules of engagement for MIO operations were flowing in, they had thought about how to disable an uncooperative merchant ship without doing too much damage. The.50 caliber machine guns were too small, and the five-inch gun mounts were almost too big. They had come up with a plan to fire one round of BL&P into the rudder area of an uncooperative ship at close range. BL&P was a training round without an explosive warhead. BL&P stood for blind loaded and plugged. Each round weighed 70 pounds just like the explosive rounds and was often used to test fire the guns so as not to waste real ammunition. Because of the close range anticipated, it was decided to let the mount captain optically train the mount and fire the round in local control, sighting down the barrel like a hunter. They had thrown an empty 50-gallon oil drum in the water, drove the ship up to about 300 yards, and watched Gunners Mate Second Class Ray Case, depress the barrel, fire, and almost hit the oil drum. Close enough. If nothing else it would convince the master that they were serious, and it was unlikely to kill anybody. Nobody was more thrilled with this plan than Case.

That test had been under ideal conditions, with the ship coming to a stop close to the oil drum. It would be a different story with a ship moving at 20 knots in restricted waters and maneuvering aggressively.

Still steaming north at 27 knots, they watched astern as *Spruance* regained position on the container ship and sent a volley of .50 caliber machine gun rounds across the bow of the ship. At this range, they could not see the rounds, every fifth a tracer, but they heard *Spruance* report the firing on the tactical circuit.

The reaction of the merchant captain was to once again turn toward *Spruance* without slowing down. Once again *Spruance* veered away to port to avoid a collision and again the container ship adjusted course back toward the strait.

Tanner watched this situation play out astern of *Dauntless* while keeping an eye on the navigation as they approached the restricted waters of the entrance to the Strait of Tiran. It would not do to run his ship on the rocks while trying to help *Spruance* in blocking this ship from entering the strait. He decided to slow the ship and drop back in a position to possibly herd this ship away from the strait while also remaining clear of *Spruance* as she fired warning shots.

"Brad, slow to fifteen knots and continue on this course. Let's get closer to the action while still closing the strait."

Tanner picked up the handset for the secure tactical circuit which was patched into the bridge, "Golf-November-Bravo, this is Whiskey-Alfa-Whiskey, Charlie Oscar for Charlie Oscar, over."

"Whiskey-Alfa-Whiskey, this is Golf-November-Bravo, roger, wait, out."

A minute later, the voice of Commander Chris Winters, came over the encrypted UHF radio circuit, "Whiskey-Alfa-Whiskey, this is Golf-November-Bravo actual, over."

They reverted to informal language, "Chris, Will here. Looks like you got your hands full. What can I do to help? over."

"Roger Will, thanks. Yep, he's determined to get by. We think he's Iraqi, some painted over name on the stern, helo can't make it out, over."

"Kind of what we figured. Some reporting on threats to Iraqi ship masters for cooperating from Saddam, over."

"His freeboard is too high for a non-cooperative boarding. You heard the SEALs had to abort for a chip light. I'm going to try and crowd him to the east and prevent him getting to the entrance. Not sure it will work, you saw him try to ram me twice. Law of gross tonnage, over."

"Roger. Where do you want me? over."

"How about falling in astern, if he gets by me you could follow him through the strait. I'll brief Alpha Sierra. They're monitoring on the coordination net, over."

"Roger, WILCO, out."

Tanner turned to Paul Nelson, "Paul, I'm going to take the conn, easier that way."

"Aye, aye sir, attention in the pilothouse, this is Lieutenant jay-gee Nelson, the Captain has the conn."

"This is the Captain, I have the conn, belay your reports."

The helmsman, lee helmsman and Boatswain Mate of the Watch all rogered up while the Quartermaster of the Watch made an entry in the ship's log.

Tanner stepped out to the starboard bridge wing where he could see *Spruance* and the container ship just off the starboard quarter, coming fast about two miles astern.

"Right full-rudder, belay your headings."

Tanner maneuvered *Dauntless* across the bows of the two ships and headed south on a reciprocal course which would take them past the container ship at about 500 yards. As he passed the container ship, he ordered twenty knots and swung around to starboard to assume position in the ship's wake at 500 yards. The 'snoopy detail,' the ship's intelligence collection team, was in

155

position on the signal bridge and snapping away with their high-powered cameras as the two ships passed on opposite courses. Nobody was visible on the decks of the ship. One man stood on the starboard bridge wing watching *Dauntless* as she passed by. Incredibly, he waved.

Falling in astern, Tanner watched as *Spruance* tried to crowd the ship to the east, away from the strait entrance and toward shoal water on the coast of Saudi Arabia. Once again, the container ship put his rudder left and chased *Spruance* away. Chris Winters was not going to risk a collision which would likely do more damage to the 9,000-ton *Spruance* than the approximately 40,000-ton container ship. All three ships were now only three miles south of the strait. At twenty knots they had nine minutes left. If they continued through, it would be single file as the channel was too narrow for safely transiting alongside the container ship. A turn toward *Spruance* in the strait would either result in a collision or *Spruance* running up on the rocks.

Tanner hit TAO on the bitch box, "TAO, Captain, request disabling fire from Alpha Sierra."

Hearing the request, Chris Winters came over the tactical circuit, "What's your intention Will? I'm going to have to peel off in a minute." Radio discipline had dissipated in the heat of the moment.

Tanner was multi-tasking.

"All engines ahead flank, indicate turns for 25 knots."

"Chris, I'm going to close up and put a round of BLP into his running gear."

There was silence on the net.

"Captain, TAO, wait, out from Alpha Sierra."

At 25 knots, Dauntless rapidly closed the distance to the container ship as Tanner maneuvered to a position about 200 yards outside the wake on the starboard quarter and matched speed.

"TAO, Captain, have Mount 51 load, one round, BLP, train out in local control. Target is the rudder. Hold fire. What's the word on disabling fire from Alpha Sierra?"

"Still got a wait-out, Captain, want me to pimp em'?"

"Negative, patch the coordination net out here."

In seconds the handset on the bridge was re-patched to the Surface Coordination Net.

"Alpha Sierra, this is *Dauntless* Actual for the Commodore, over."

"*Dauntless*, Vanzant here, over."

Tanner took a breath, he knew he was viewed skeptically by the commodore, both for the *Wade* incident and his independent actions during the storm. Chris Winters was the senior officer on the scene. Was he usurping his authority? He plowed ahead.

"Commodore, Will Tanner here sir, we're about two miles south of the strait and closing fast. *Spruance* is going to have to maneuver clear. I'm in position to put a round of BL and P into his rudder if granted authority, over."

The ensuing silence felt an eternity but was actually less than thirty seconds.

"How do you plan to do that?" Again, radio discipline was out the window.

"Sir, we practiced it in the Med. Mount 51 in local control. One round of BLP. Aim at the rudder. Might also damage the screw."

"*Spruance*, Alpha Sierra, what's your recommendation?"

"Sir, I've hauled out to port and am swinging around. This guy was going to scrape me off on the rocks or hit me. No choice. I think it's the only way to stop him before he gets into the gulf, over."

A prolonged silence as the two ships continued toward the strait. Now only a mile. *Spruance* was racing around on a reciprocal course to come in behind *Dauntless*. There was about to be a parade of ships through the Strait of Tiran.

"*Dauntless*, Alpha Sierra, permission granted. Film everything, over."

With *Spruance* out of the way on his port side, the container ship began shifting his rudder left and right, steering a winding course toward the strait. Tanner could see the same individual standing on the starboard bridge wing and looking aft at *Dauntless*. He could no doubt see the gun mount trained out to port with the barrel depressed, pointing at his ship's stern.

Tanner moved out to the port bridge wing and eye-balled the lay of the gun. *Looks about right*, he thought to himself.

"Ops, give TAO batteries released. One round, BLP, Mount 51."

There was a twenty second delay, the word being passed to Petty Officer Case in Mount 51. Case no doubt checking his aim one more time. Then, BLAM!

Tanner watched a large splash just astern and to the port side of the container ship. *Shit, missed.* Gas ejection air pushed a puff of gray smoke out of the gun barrel, and the empty powder canister was ejected from the mount below the barrel. It hit the deck with a clang and began rolling around on the forecastle.

Tanner didn't hesitate, "Ops, pass to TAO, reload, one round BLP, Mount 51, local control."

He watched as Mount 51 swung centerline, and the barrel went to the ready surface position for reloading. Just then, Andy Morton, shouted, "Captain, he's slowing. And turning."

Tanner turned his attention to the container ship, now visibly taking off speed and turning to port, to the west. He maneuvered *Dauntless* to starboard to open the distance and dropped his speed while following him around in the turn.

Over bridge-to-bridge channel 16 in a heavily accented voice came, "Navy ship nine six three, this is motor vessel *Nisa Batu*, I am stopping."

Spruance took over, "Motor vessel *Nisa Batu*, this is United States Navy destroyer niner-six-three, I intend to board you in accordance with United Nations Resolution six-six-one. Assemble your crew on the forecastle and stop your engines. State your port of departure and port of destination. What is your flag? Over."

"I am Iraqi. From Port Sudan. Going to Aqaba. I am stopping engines," came the reply.

Over the coordination net, Alpha Sierra directed *Spruance* to board *Nisa Batu* and directed *Dauntless* to return to MIO station Fenway. There was no acknowledgment of *Dauntless'* role in stopping the ship.

Tanner turned the conn back to Paul Nelson and turned to Ops, "Well, it worked, even if we missed," he said with a wry grin.

The XO's voice came over the bitch box, "Sir, Case says he's sorry he missed. He'll do better next time."

"Tell Case it might be just as well. It worked anyway. Well done."

Tanner went to his chair as *Dauntless* cleared the area. Looking through his binoculars, he saw that the *Nisa Batu* had just about coasted to a stop and *Spruance* was in the process of lowering its rigid-hulled inflatable boat, or RHIB, with the boat crew. The boarding party was assembled on the fantail. He was still keyed up from the action. *So, this guy was an Iraqi flag after all.* Maybe there was something to the report about Saddam threatening his ship masters. After all, they cooperated in the end. Maybe he felt he'd done just enough to avoid hanging.

NINE

Al-Asad Airbase, Iraq

Major Abdul Tikriti closed the last folder and sat back with his cigarette to consider his decisions. As the smoke wafted up and into the blades of the slowly rotating ceiling fan, he reflected on the past two days. Following his late-night meeting with his commanding officer, Colonel Bashir Mohamed, he had turned his jet over to the mechanics for a thorough overhaul. He had since flown two check flights, but no combat air patrols. Colonel Mohamed had made available the personnel files of every Mirage pilot in the Iraqi Air Force. Tikriti knew most of them personally and had already formed an opinion as to who would be one of his wingmen on the carrier attack mission.

He had flown combat missions with Major Dawud El-Amin and knew him to be a combat-tested and resourceful pilot. El-Amin had been his wingman on two of his successful engagements against Iranian Air Force opponents. El-Amin himself could claim two kills of his own. He knew El-Amin to be a devout Muslim and fiercely loyal to their exalted leader, General Saddam Hussein. El-Amin was his first choice for the mission. Nothing in his personnel file gave Tikriti any reason not to choose him.

Finding the second wingman had proven more complicated. After poring through the records, he had found one who stood out. A young captain who had seen limited combat during the war with Iran, but who had received glowing praise for his airmanship and for his skill and tenacity in the limited training flights permitted by the Iraqi Air Force. Tikriti did not know Captain Falah Al-Taweek personally, but he had heard of him. He studied the picture. He was slender, almost slight, but wiry. What caught Tikriti's attention were the eyes. They stared back at the camera over his bushy mustache with hawk-like intensity. The eyes of a bird of prey. *That's what they would be*, he mused, *birds of prey, streaking out of the sky and delivering death to the hated Americans*. The thought captured his imagination. "Birds of Prey" would be a fitting code name for this mission.

All that was left was to interview both pilots. He wanted to look into their eyes and be assured that they shared his hatred of the Americans; his dedication to the mission. To the side of his desk lay four more file folders. His next alternate choices in the event neither El-Amin or Al-Tawfeek were deemed suitable for the mission. He picked up the phone and dialed the number of Colonel Mohamed's aide-de-camp.

Two hours later the two selectees stood in front of his desk. He and Major El-Amin embraced and kissed each other twice on the cheek. They were old friends and squadron mates.

"Praise be to Allah brother Abdul," exclaimed El-Amin, "it is good to see you."

"And you brother Dawud," replied Tikriti as Captain Al-Tawfeek stood awkwardly to the side.

Turning to Al-Tawfeek, Tikriti extended his hand, "Captain Al-Tawfeek, thank you for coming. I suspect both of you wonder the purpose of this meeting, especially you."

Al-Tawfeek did not respond, merely nodded as he shifted his eyes between the two more senior pilots. He knew of Tikriti's status as an ace and the most admired pilot in the Iraqi Air Force. He had no idea why he had been summoned to Al-Asad for this meeting.

"Come, I will explain."

Tikriti led both men to a table at the side of the room which was covered by an ornate blanket. Grabbing a corner, he whipped it off and to the floor in one swift motion, revealing a map of the northern Persian Gulf, Iraq, Kuwait, Syria, Jordan, northern Saudi Arabia and the northern Red Sea. Labels affixed to the map identified Al-Asad Air Base and Damascus International Airport. Other labels identified the American combat air patrol stations and the American AWACS orbits over Saudi Arabia. Over the Persian Gulf, a label indicated the nominal position of the American fleet, including one aircraft carrier. In the Red Sea, another label identified the positions of American destroyer-type ships and that of a second aircraft carrier. A line connected Al-Asad Air Base to Damascus International Airport. A second set of lines mapped a route from Damascus due east to the border with Iraq, just north of the Jordanian border. From that point the line ran south-southeast, paralleling the border between Jordan and Iraq. Just east of the point where the borders of Iraq, Jordan, and Saudi Arabia came together, the line turned almost due south, crossing the empty wastelands of the Saudi desert, close to a low mountain range and west of the town of Al Jowf. It continued southwest to the Saudi coastline and continued straight over the water until it ended at the label annotated "American Aircraft Carrier."

Tikriti paused to let the two pilots absorb the implications of the map. Both quickly grasped its significance and turned questioning eyes toward Tikriti.

"This, my brothers, is Operation Birds of Prey. You have been hand-selected for the glory of striking a crippling blow to the infidel Americans."

He waited expectantly for the questions to begin.

Despite his youth and relative inexperience, Al-Tawfeek spoke first, "It is a long flight. We cannot return to Damascus or Al-Asad."

"That is correct," replied Tikriti, "we are exploring options, to include continuing into Egypt, or even Sudan, although Sudan appears too far. We have also considered a drop tank in place of one missile. That idea was discarded as diminishing probability of success by 50%. The engineers are drawing up plans for a centerline drop tank to enable each jet to carry two missiles."

The two pilots nodded, understanding. To sink an American aircraft carrier was a prize to be worth whatever sacrifice it required.

Exchanging glances, they both turned to Tikriti and said, almost in unison, "We are with you brother, all glory be to Allah."

Tikriti went on, "It is remotely possible that we can continue across the Red Sea and land at the airport in Hurghada, Egypt. We will turn off our transponders and just declare an emergency. They will have no choice but to let us land. Word of the attack on the American aircraft carrier will take time, they will be unaware. Even without clearance, we will simply land. Hurghada is not a busy airport, but it has a 4,000-meter runway to handle flights from Europe bringing tourists."

Both men nodded their understanding.

"When will we go?" said El-Amin.

"The aircraft are being prepared now. We fly to Damascus tomorrow night. We will await the launch order as guests of our Syrian brothers. There will be a cover story reporting our defection and arrest by the Syrians. Our real names will not be used."

With that, Tikriti led them back to his desk and handed each a folder. "Study this carefully. It contains everything you will need to know for this mission. We will preflight in squadron operations tomorrow night after prayers and launch when we are ready."

Dungunab, Sudan

Special Agent Mahmoud Da'Woud stood on the pier in the Sudanese port of Dungunab, on the Red Sea coast one-hundred and twenty miles north of the central Sudanese port of Port Sudan. He shook his head as he looked over the small fishing vessel tied to the pier. The motor vessel *Basra* was a sixty-foot trawler designed to drag the ocean bottom while streaming a large net from two twenty-foot outrigger booms located on either gunwale of the wooden boat. The hull was painted a dark blue with a white superstructure to ward off the heat. Inside the small pilothouse placed forward on the bow of the small ship, the owner was nervously checking his gauges as he prepared to start the twin diesel engines of the dilapidated vessel. Akram Najaf was an Iraqi fisherman who had the misfortune of being located in the Red Sea when the invasion of Kuwait had occurred, and the United Nations embargo on Iraq had been announced. Najaf looked nervously at the intense man on the pier who looked disdainfully at the *Basra*. He feared for his life and with good reason. Mahmoud Da'wud was Iraqi Mukhabarat, Directorate 4; the most feared arm of Saddam Hussein's intelligence organization. Yesterday Najaf had been minding his own business, tending to his fishing boat and preparing to venture into the Red Sea to continue fishing when Da'wud had appeared and informed him that his boat was now government property and he was being enlisted into the service of their great leader, President Saddam Hussein. Da'wud had made it clear that Najaf's complete cooperation was expected. In not so veiled terms, Da'wud had suggested that Najaf's wife and three young children would remain safe in Basra as long as he cooperated fully. Najaf had been forced to release the two Sudanese deck hands he had hired in Dungunab. No great loss really, they were barely capable as deck hands, high on qat most of the day. He had paid them a small amount of money, augmented by some fish to help feed their families. His first mate, another Iraqi, had been retained; he had explained that it would be impossible to operate *M/V Basra* all by himself and Da'wud had agreed.

Da'wud flinched as the first diesel coughed to life with a belch of black, oily smoke from the small stack atop the pilothouse. With a rumble, the diesel idled unevenly as the engine warmed up. A second belch of smoke announced the start of the second diesel. He peered through the open pilothouse door and watched as Najaf studied his gauges and advanced his throttles to speed the engine warm-up. After several minutes, Najaf looked nervously at Da'wud, nodded his head, and announced, "We are ready."

Da'wud proceeded to the aft end of the small vessel and threw the frayed mooring line off the bollard on the pier. As he did so, he took one last look at the transom. The name *Basra* had been painted over, and although the fresh blue paint did not quite match, it was good enough, not detectable from any distance. He moved forward and then did the same with the forward line. Again, he took note of the fresh white paint on the bulkhead of the pilothouse, also covering the boat's name. It had taken several coats of white to cover the blue lettering. He made a note to dirty up all three locations with oil or grease to hide the new paint. He stepped aboard as Najaf and his first mate rapidly coiled the lines on deck and rushed back to the pilothouse to begin maneuvering the *Najaf* away from the pier.

As Najaf negotiated the winding channel connecting the tiny fishing village of Dungunab to the Red Sea he looked nervously at his unwelcome passenger.

"What is our destination sir?"

"Make best speed to the Strait of Tiran. How long?"

Najaf consulted his charts, laid out on a table next to the helm, "About four hundred and fifty kilometers. Just over a day once we reach the open ocean."

With a last look at the chart, Da'wud announced, "I am going below to report. Proceed."

Northeastern Saudi Arabia

At 20,000 feet above the Saudi desert, Air Force Major Paul 'Bwana' Breedlove studied his display aboard the Boeing 707 variant E-3A Sentry AWACS aircraft, call-sign 'Winston.' Rotating above the fuselage was the 30-foot diameter radome hosting the AN/APY-1 electronically scanned radar. At altitude, the radar gave him eyes out to almost 400 miles. As mission commander, Breedlove was in direct contact with four sections of U.S. Air Force F-15C Eagle fighters patrolling the skies above Saudi Arabia. To the west, he watched as two sections of Iraqi F-1 Mirage aircraft performed the same mission over Iraq. Four hours into his six-hour mission, Breedlove was bored. They had been flying missions day and night since arriving in theater. So far nothing significant had happened. With diplomatic efforts underway to convince Iraq to abandon Kuwait and the force build-up in the region continuing, neither side was yet ready for decisive action. The Iraqis, however, gave no indication that they intended to leave Kuwait. Perhaps that would change over time as the balance of forces swung heavily in favor of the coalition. The U.S. led coalition was just coming together with air, naval, and ground forces deploying into theater.

About time for that section of Iraqi CAP to be relieved he thought to himself. He turned his attention to the skies around Al-Asad Airbase. Still nothing. *Wait, here they come* he said to himself as the display showed first one, and then three aircraft climbing out of Al-Asad.

"Eagle, Winston," he broadcast over the fighter control net, "Single Group, Heavy, Medium, Bull 300, 150, bogies."

As each section of CAP acknowledged his report, Breedlove tracked the new contacts as they climbed out and headed east toward the CAP station just inside the Iraq border. He assigned each a track number that would be electronically shared with the fighters, ensuring that each aircraft had the same picture, the same situational awareness. As he watched the aircraft climb through 10,000 feet, he wondered why there were only three planes. *Perhaps the Iraqi's were having trouble keeping their two CAP stations filled with a two-ship section. Maintenance problems, probably.*

He leaned forward as the three aircraft executed a slow turn to the south and then due west, away from the Saudi border toward Syria. *Must be a training flight* he thought, *not the CAP reliefs after all.* Unusual at night. His radar picture was digitally passed to each of the fighters comprising Eagle Flight by the Link-16 tactical data link. There was no need to keep a running narrative going. Two more hours, he thought, then back to Riyadh and some sleep.

He turned his attention back to the two sections of Iraqi CAP, lazily boring holes in the night sky. Nothing new there. Shifting his scan, he watched the section of three aircraft increase speed dramatically and head straight for the Syrian border. Hooking the targets with his cursor, his readout told him the three aircraft were travelling over 1,000 miles per hour and descending in altitude. Highly unusual. Would they keep going he wondered? Syria had joined other Arab nations in deploring the Iraqi annexation of Kuwait. *Could this be a hostile action against Syria?* None of the intelligence reporting had suggested such a possibility.

Switching channels on his radio he contacted the Combined Air Operations Center, or CAOC, at Prince Sultan Air Base in Al-Kharj, Saudi Arabia.

"Chariot, Winston, New Group, flank west out of Al-Asad, fast, probable F-1."

"Winston, Chariot, roger, we see them in the link. Continue to track and report."

Breedlove brought up the political map overlay on his display screen which showed borders and major cities. This feature was normally disabled as it created too much clutter on the screen. The three jets continued due west at 1,000 miles per hour, rapidly approaching the border with Syria. They would soon be beyond radar range. He continued to track and report all friendly and enemy aircraft via Link-16. Finally, he lost contact on the three westbound jets. They had flown beyond radar range.

Western Iraq

In the lead aircraft, Major Abdul Tikriti checked the position of his two wingmen as he pushed his jet beyond the speed of sound on a course that would take his flight just north of the Jordanian border and then southwest direct into Damascus International Airport. His radar warning gear suddenly emitted a loud buzz. He checked his display and saw that he had been locked up by a ground-based fire control radar. *Probably the Jordanians*, he thought. Hopefully, the Syrian air defenses had been alerted to his flight. It would not do to get shot down by some trigger-happy air defense officer who didn't have the word. He realized that their supersonic approach could easily be mistaken as an attack profile.

Signaling his wingmen, he turned slightly northwest to open the distance between his flight and the border with Jordan. Jordan was part of the American-led coalition and therefore might consider Iraqi jets a threat. Throttling back, he dropped speed to 500 knots as the jets crossed the border into Syria and began a slow descent to 3,000 feet. El-Amin and Al-Tawfeek smoothly followed suit. Manipulating his receiver, he dialed up the Damascus International VOR and adjusted course accordingly.

As he had been briefed by Colonel Mohamed, at twenty miles out, he radioed Damascus Tower and declared an emergency, requesting a straight in approach for his flight of three aircraft. They would land on runway two-zero and then taxi to a series of revetments on the eastern side of the airport, where military aircraft were based.

As the lights of the airport came into sight, Tikriti flashed his lights twice, signaling his wingmen to fall back into trail formation as they had briefed before departure. At one-mile intervals, the other two jets would follow Tikriti straight in, without calling the tower.

Praise be to Allah, he thought, *I hope the Syrians know the plan.*

Tikriti flared his jet and gently settled on the runway, popping his drogue shoot and turning to the east after rolling out. As he taxied toward a series of concrete revetments, he looked left to see El-Amin execute a perfect landing. Scanning the night sky, he saw the lights of Al-Tawfeek's jet on final approach, a mile behind. Looking ahead, he was relieved to see a ground crewman signaling his aircraft with red lens flashlights. The crewman signaled him straight into an empty, poorly lit revetment. He noted two more empty revetments to the right of his in the glow of the yellow sulfur taxiway lights. All seemed in order.

Shutting down his engine, he raised his canopy and noted a fellow Iraqi, Major Muhamed Bandari, approaching through a side door. Bandari, an intelligence officer, had been dispatched to Damascus to coordinate with the Syrians. Walking next to him was a full colonel in the Syrian Air Force.

Tikriti climbed out of his jet, greeted Bandari with a kiss on each cheek and then saluted the Syrian. His nametag identified him as Colonel Asmeh.

"Welcome to Damascus Major, I am Colonel Bashir Asmeh, base commander."

"Praise be to Allah, Colonel. I bring regards from Colonel Mohamed. Thank you for your hospitality."

They turned as El-Amin's jet taxied into the adjacent revetment and shut down. Further out on the airfield, Captain Al-Tawfeek had turned onto the taxiway and was approaching. The first step in the plan had been completed. Operation Birds of Prey was underway.

TEN

Northern Red Sea

Rear Admiral Nick McCall sat at the head of the table in the secure Flag Intelligence Center aboard *USS Saratoga (CV-60)*. To his right sat Chief of Staff, Captain John Campbell, his gold naval aviator wings twinkling in the artificial light cast by the bank of recessed overhead lighting above. To his left sat Captain Alexander Vanzant, Commander, Destroyer Squadron 24, and current Alpha Sierra in the composite warfare commander's organization. Next to Vanzant sat Captain Mike Reasoner, *Saratoga*'s commanding officer and across from Reasoner sat Commander Jim "Shorty" Herlong, the Carrier Air Wing Commander, or CAG. Carrier Air Wing 7 made up the cadre of fighters, attack, and support aircraft as well as the embarked SH-3 Sea King helicopter squadron assigned to *Saratoga*. Next to Herlong was *Saratoga's* Executive Officer, Captain Ben "Saint" Nicholson.

At the front of the room stood Lieutenant Commander Steve Reilly, the Commander, Cruiser-Destroyer Group 8 Intelligence Officer. Around the room, arranged by relative seniority, either sat or stood a dozen other officers representing the admiral's staff, the commodore's staff, and key *Saratoga* ship's company and air wing officers. Reilly had just completed a comprehensive intelligence briefing which covered the situation throughout the theater of operations.

McCall turned to Vanzant, "What's your assessment of what went down today with the *Nisa Batu*?" Vanzant cleared his throat, "Admiral, I think both *Spruance* and *Dauntless* handled it pretty well all things considered. You heard what Commander

Winters reported once the ship stopped. The master was all apologies."

"So, you think he had to resist to avoid punishment by Saddam? Do just enough to save his own skin?"

"That's the way it looks. Given his cargo of weapons from the Sudan, he was probably pretty important to the Iraqi effort."

"Winter's report says he was sure the master fully intended to ram him."

"Yessir, he's the guy on the scene. Hard to second guess him from here."

"How about *Dauntless*, firing at him with the five-inch? That's not in the ROE."

"Nossir it's not. I plan to visit all the MIO ships tomorrow and talk to him about it when I get to *Dauntless*. Disabling fire is listed as an option, but no specific guidance has yet been issued as to caliber."

McCall fixed Vanzant with a longer than necessary look, then continued, "Worked though, didn't it? When you see Commander Tanner, tell him to write-up a lesson learned message on the procedure. I hear they practiced it in the Med?"

"Yessir, fired at an old oil drum."

"Pretty creative when you think about it," mused the admiral. Vanzant just nodded.

Turning to his Operations Officer, McCall said, "Let's flesh out the ROE for disabling fire. Incorporate *Dauntless'* procedures once we get the lessons learned."

Admiral McCall turned his attention to Lieutenant Commander Reilly, patiently watching the exchange between the two senior officers.

"Steve, what's this I read about some Iraqi defectors?"

"Yessir, unconfirmed, but the Air Force AWACS observed a flight of Iraqi fighters, they believe F-1's, apparently cross the border into Syria the other night."

McCall considered this for a moment, "Any other signs of weakening resolve on the part of the Iraqis?"

"Not that we know of sir, could have been a one off. If anybody's getting nervous, I would think it would be the ground forces occupying Kuwait."

McCall turned back to Vanzant, "Make sure we're keeping an eye on *Nisa Batu*, make sure he returns to Port Sudan and offloads."

"We've got triple-SC on him, Admiral, so far he's tracking in the right direction."

"OK, we're still stretched pretty thin up there, it's not inconceivable that somebody could slip by hugging the coast and get through the strait before they can be intercepted."

"Roger sir, we've got *Montgomery* showing up tomorrow. She went through Suez last night. That'll help."

McCall turned to Captain Reasoner, *Saratoga's* CO, "Mike, the experts say there's no way for the Iraqis to get attack aircraft down here without our Air Force intercepting them, but we need to stay on our toes none the less."

"Roger sir, we're on it. The CAP mission is the main effort, but our defensive systems are manned and ready."

He turned to Herlong, "CAG, how's the air wing holding up?"

"Doing fine, sir, the CAP are bored, but the triple-SC and helos are staying busy supporting Alpha Sierra and the MIO boardings. Whenever possible we're also getting some air-to-air and simulated war at sea strike training."

Having another thought, McCall turned back to Commodore Vanzant, "Al, when you bring *Biddle* or *Dauntless* down to fuel are you going to turn over shotgun and send *Phil Sea* up to fill a MIO box?"

"That's the plan sir, we need the hulls up there until we can get more ships involved. Hate to use the Aegis that way, but we're short-handed. Not so sure about *Dauntless* though, she's not as capable as *Biddle* or *Phil Sea*."

McCall noticed a frown on Herlong's face, "Problem CAG?"

Herlong hesitated, then said, "No sir, we'll be fine. It's just that we've gotten all the Red Crown kinks worked out with *Phil Sea*. We'll have to break in the other two." Red Crown was the air control cruiser, the air warfare commander, responsible for air defense of the battle group. Red Crown had to coordinate with the aircraft carrier, the E-2C Hawkeye airborne control aircraft owned by CAG, and the individual aircraft operating around the carrier flying CAP or returning to the carrier from other missions. There was often tension between Red Crown and the air wing as the cruiser insisted on mandated return to force procedures which were designed to ensure aircraft approaching the carrier were the good guys.

"I'm sure it will be fine, we're all on the same team here. It'll be good training for everybody. Anybody else?" said McCall, "if not, we're done."

Chairs scraped as McCall got to his feet to leave the room.

* * *

Will Tanner watched the SH-2 Seasprite helicopter grow larger in his binoculars as it approached *Dauntless* from the east. It was *Elmer Montgomery*'s embarked helicopter, and it had recently lifted off her deck to bring Commodore Alexander Vanzant on his next ship visit, to *Dauntless*.

He turned to Ricky McKnight, "I'm going back to greet the commodore, have a green deck when he gets here."

"Aye, aye, sir."

Tanner headed down the ladder to the ASROC deck, crossed under the captain's gig on the starboard side and then down another ladder aft to the main deck and the MK-13 guided-missile launcher and fantail. Arriving at the starboard side quarterdeck station he tapped Ensign Wilt Grimmage on the shoulder to get his attention. Grimmage was the Landing Signal Officer, responsible for the flight deck crew. He was dressed out in a white cranial helmet with Mickey Mouse ears, and white float-coat with his khaki trousers tucked into his socks. On the flight deck, he saw BM1 Butt dressed in the same gear, only yellow in color, and three of the deck seaman dressed in blue float-coats and cranials. Grimmage lifted one side of his hearing protection so he could hear the captain.

"We all set Wilt?"

"Yessir, bridge just passed green deck."

The helicopter approached from the starboard quarter as Butt began signaling it in with his yellow paddles. Two sailors stood in the center of the flight deck, one wearing a grounding glove connected to a tie-down padeye on deck. The helo would have to hover and lower the commodore to the deck in a horse-collar attached to a winch by a thin wire. Tanner removed his ball cap and stepped behind Grimmage.

As soon as Captain Vanzant's feet touched the deck, the ship's announcing system sounded four bells and, "DESRON Two Four, arriving."

Slipping out of the harness and waving at the air crewman, Vanzant strode toward Tanner, guided by one of the blue-garbed sailors.

Tanner grabbed the commodore's hand for a shake and, shouting above the departing helicopter, said, "Welcome aboard Commodore, follow me."

Once clear of the flight deck, Tanner turned to the commodore, "Where to sir?"

"Let's go to CIC, and you can show me your plot and brief me on what you've been doing."

As they walked, Tanner sized up his boss. Because of the way the battle group had been thrown together after the Iraqi invasion, they had only met once, briefly in the Commodore's office in Mayport. Vanzant was tall, even taller than Tanner, and carried himself with an aristocratic, almost snobbish air. *Future admiral material* thought Tanner to himself.

Except for those manning consoles and wearing sound-powered phones, the CIC watch snapped to attention as Tanner and Vanzant entered the space. Vanzant marveled at how cramped it was compared to *Saratoga* or *Philippine Sea*. Tanner walked him to the DRT, where the surface plot was kept.

"Here you go sir, we're staying to the far north in Fenway to be as close to the strait as possible. So far, we've done two boardings as you know. Both ships were cleared in to Aqaba."

"How are your boarding teams doing, any problems?"

"No sir, other than the difficulty of climbing the sides and working in confined spaces in kapoks and steel helmets. Except for *Nisa Batu*, everybody has cooperated. We ever get a good answer on what *Nisa Batu* was doing?"

"We think he was putting up a token fight to avoid getting in trouble with Saddam."

"He put up a pretty good token fight. *Spruance* could have been hit a couple of times. You know, somebody on the bridge waved as we went by to take up station astern. Maybe he was sending a signal."

Vanzant looked around CIC. "How about your air picture, getting what you need?"

"We're keeping the scan up sir, would be easier if we had Link-11. Sometimes takes a few minutes to correlate the air tracks. We have to rely on IFF and EW, but we're in touch with Alfa Whiskey by voice if we need to sort something out quickly." Alfa Whiskey was *Philippine Sea*, the air warfare commander.

Vanzant nodded, he had forgotten that *Dauntless* was not Link-11 capable. All the newer ships were. Link-11 allowed the ships to share radar data in a common picture which significantly reduced confusion and allowed rapid correlation by two ships holding the same radar contact. Another reason not to let *Dauntless* substitute for *Phil Sea* when she came south for fuel.

"Let's go to your cabin and talk about *Nisa Batu*."

As they entered the CO's cabin, Tanner offered the commodore a cup of coffee or soda. Ricky McKnight had followed them down from CIC. Vanzant turned to McKnight, "XO, why don't you let the CO and I talk alone for a minute."

When McKnight had excused himself and shut the cabin door, Vanzant sat in Tanner's chair and motioned him to sit on the small couch which folded down into a bed.

"Commander, you caught us a little off guard with that stunt with the five-inch yesterday."

Stunt, thought Tanner to himself. *Interesting description.* "How so sir?"

"Well, it had never been promulgated as a course of action in these situations. Had we known of your idea it could have been given more careful consideration. As it was, we had to make a snap decision on the flagship."

Tanner considered this for a second, struggling to keep his expression neutral, "Disabling fire was listed as an option in the ROE. I have nothing between the .50 cal and the five-inch." The newer ships were equipped with a 25-millimeter chain gun which would be more effective than the .50 caliber machine guns but do less damage than a five-inch round.

"We reported the training in our nightly reports," he added.

"Granted, but this is developing into a pattern with *Dauntless*."

"What's that sir?" replied Tanner, this time allowing a quizzical look to cross his face.

"Keeping secrets from your superiors."

Tanner said nothing, willing the commodore to explain.

After a pause, Vanzant continued, "Disappearing from the formation during the storm evasion without notifying CO *Biddle* of your intentions. Yesterday springing this tactic on me in the heat of a tactical situation."

Tanner thought before responding, "Sir, during the hurricane CO *Biddle* had authorized us to maneuver as necessary to minimize damage. I experimented with several course changes before settling on the one that gave us the best ride. As to yesterday, I did not recommend the BL and P tactic specifically beforehand, but I did report that we had practiced disabling fire in my nightly sitrep back in the Med. Yesterday it just seemed that firing a BL and P round was more prudent than HE."

"Oh, it was. In fact, Admiral McCall wants you to write it up as a lesson learned. What concerns me is an apparent tendency to go it alone. That's not healthy."

"All right sir, that wasn't my intent, but I'll be more careful in the future."

Vanzant nodded while fixing Tanner with a look intended to put him on notice that he was skating on thin ice. Shifting gears, he said, "OK, we're working out the plans for refueling all the gate guard ships and keeping enough assets up here to accomplish the MIO mission. We've also got to keep a shotgun on *Sara*. We'll be rotating you and *Biddle* down together to refuel and sending *Phil Sea* up for a couple of days of MIO. *Biddle* will be primary shotgun, but it will shift to you when *Biddle* is alongside."

"Got it sir, any idea when we'll get an oiler?"

"The French are going to send *Durance* up from Djibouti along with a frigate to help with MIO." The French Red Sea Fleet was based in Djibouti just outside the Strait of Bab al Mandeb, the southern entrance to the Red Sea. "They should be along in a week or two. Until then it's *Saratoga*."

Tanner nodded, "Would you like to take a walk around the ship, Commodore?"

"No thanks, have your TAO call *Montgomery* and have the helo sent back, I'm due on *Spruance* next. Like to get Commander Winters' take on yesterday."

* * *

Tanner watched as Vanzant ran under the beating blades of the hovering helicopter and was helped into the horse-collar by one of the deck seamen under the watchful eyes of BM1 Butt. Once his feet left the deck, the 1MC blared, "*Ding, ding, ding, ding, DESRON Two Four, departing.*"

Tanner patted Wilt Grimmage on the shoulder and headed back to the bridge as the helicopter tilted nose-down and headed off the port side toward *Spruance.* As he walked forward on the main deck, he reflected on the conversation in his cabin. Commodore Vanzant had acted very strangely, grudgingly admitting that the five-inch BL and P round had been effective, without ever acknowledging the initiative taken by *Dauntless* to help *Spruance* out in a difficult situation. Yet, he said the admiral wanted a lessons learned message prepared to share the technique with the rest of the ships. And what about the 'go it alone' comment? Sounded like he was off to a bad start with the man who would be writing his fitness report for this cruise.

Arriving on the bridge, he took the regular reports from the OOD and settled in to his chair. He remembered that Vinny DeVito was on watch as TAO. He pressed the lever on the 21MC, "TAO, Captain, Vinny, come out to the bridge for a second."

Two clicks answered and thirty seconds later DeVito stepped onto the bridge. "What's up, Captain?"

"Weps, the admiral wants a lessons learned message on how we did the disabling fire yesterday. How about drafting it up. Include the way we practiced it in the Med."

"Roger sir, will do. Won't help *Phil Sea* and *Spruance* much, they've got the newer, unmanned, five-inch mounts."

"Good point. Write it up in such a way, so that's obvious but without pointing out the obvious if you know what I mean."

DeVito grinned, "Got it, sir, I'll have it to the XO by 8 o'clock Reports."

As DeVito departed the bridge, CIC called in on the 21MC, "Bridge, CIC, we've got a merchant coming north, Skunk November, Alpha Sierra is assigning us to do the query."

"Bridge aye," replied OOD Walt Wilson, looking at the captain as he answered. Tanner nodded. *Let the watch team do their thing* he thought to himself.

"Give me a course to intercept Skunk November, I think I see his superstructure hull down on the horizon," said Wilson.

"That should be him," replied Vinny DeVito, now back in CIC.

As the ship to be boarded closed and became clearly visible, Tanner picked up his binoculars. High freeboard he noted. Strange topside configuration, pilothouse, and superstructure all the way forward, almost over the bow. Behind the superstructure and funnel was a long, flat, rectangular structure, as tall as the superstructure and continuing aft all the way to the fantail. It looked somewhat like a container ship, but those did not look like containers.

Lieutenant Wilson began the scripted query over the bridge-to-bridge radio. Apparently expecting to be contacted, the master, or perhaps the officer of the watch, answered immediately, identifying the ship as the motor vessel *Gedaref*, registered in Cyprus and enroute from Christchurch, New Zealand to Aqaba, Jordan. Wilson continued the litany, telling the *Gedaref* to stand by to be boarded in accordance with United Nations Resolution 661 and to provide a crew count and muster those on deck not required to safely operate the ship. Again, the *Gedaref* acknowledged and indicated an intent to comply.

Wilson called away the boarding team to muster on the fantail and prepared to lower the ship's motor whale boat.

Tanner watched all this with some concern as he noted three to four-foot swells running from the west and saw that the *Gedaref*, like many merchant ships, was steaming with the accommodation ladder rigged on her port side amidships. The ladder was not fully extended, angling up to the main deck at about a sixty-degree angle.

"Who's the boarding officer?" he asked Wilson.

Checking his pass down notes, he replied, "Lieutenant Evans, Team Bravo." Don Evans, the Main Propulsion Assistant, or MPA. *Good*, thought Tanner, *Evans was pretty sharp*.

"Pass the word to the fantail to have Evans come up to the bridge. Wait, never mind, as soon as the boat's in the water I'll go back there. Tell him not to board until I get back there."

As *M/V Gedaref* coasted to a stop and began assembling non- critical crewmembers on the forecastle, the TAO called up on the bitch box, "*Montgomery* helo inbound. He'll look the ship over and give us a crew count on the forecastle."

Tanner took another look through the binoculars as *Dauntless* closed to within 500 yards of *Gedaref*. He saw movement in the strange contraption that constituted almost 500 feet of this 600-foot ship. He realized he was looking at cages with some kind of animals inside.

"Son of a bitch," he said, "it's a sheep carrier." As they closed on the upwind side so that the stopped ship would not drift into *Dauntless*, it became evident that thousands of sheep where being transported to Jordan from New Zealand.

As he left the bridge, he said to Wilson, "Ask him to lower the accommodation ladder so our guys can get aboard."

Tanner headed aft down the starboard side as he saw the motor whale boat hovering off the starboard quarter. Arriving on the fantail, he returned Don Evans salute and looked over the boarding team. Eleven burly sailors outfitted in the orange kapok lifejackets, steel helmets, M-14 rifles and dungaree uniforms, milled about, waiting to climb down the pilot ladder and board the motor whale boat. Don Evans, in his khaki uniform, was similarly outfitted but carrying a .45 pistol strapped to his waist and thigh.

"Don, got the team all here?"

"Yessir Captain, just awaiting the word. Funny looking ship."

"It's a sheep carrier. Not likely he's carrying contraband. Says he came from New Zealand. But you'll have to search below decks to be sure. If there's room, walk among the cages topside to be sure there's nothing there besides sheep."

Tanner looked over at the stopped ship and noted that the accommodation ladder had not been lowered.

"Let me see your walkie-talkie. OOD, Captain, is he lowering the ladder?"

"Sir, he says it's jammed. The winch isn't working. They were going to fix it in port."

Tanner looked across the expanse of choppy water. The bottom rung of the ladder looked like it was about ten feet out of the water. He turned to Evans, "OK Don, this seems a little tricky, I don't want anyone getting hurt. Give me an assessment when you get over there."

As Tanner returned to the bridge, Don Evans and his boarding team climbed one by one down the aluminum pilot ladder and took up position in the motor whaleboat.

Arriving on the bridge, Tanner said to Wilson, "What's the latest?"

"Fourteen-man crew. The Master is alone on the bridge. Two engineers in the engineroom. Helo confirms eleven men on deck on the forecastle. Boarding crew is on the way," pointing to the full motor whaleboat bouncing in the seas between the two ships.

* * *

Lieutenant Don Evans stood next to the boat coxswain on the coxswain flat as the motor whale boat bounced along in the choppy seas. Every now and then a wave sent a shower of salt water curling over the bow and soaking the boarding team. As they approached the *Gedaref*, he began to notice an overpowering smell. He wrinkled his nose and turned to Boatswain Mate Third Class Brian O'Dell, the boat coxswain, "Boats, you smell that?"

"Fuckin-A sir, stinks."

The entire boarding team began shifting in their seats and glancing back at Evans as the stench grew stronger.

Evans turned his attention to the accommodation ladder, now swinging about five feet above the motor whale boat. As a wave carried them up alongside the gently rolling sheep carrier, it came within four feet, when they dropped into a trough, it rose to over six feet. O'Dell struggled to position the motor whale boat under the ladder as he fought the swells.

Evans turned to Electrician's Mate First Class Josiah Washington, the senior enlisted member of the boarding team and Evans' right-hand man on Team Bravo.

"Washington, I'll go first, looks like I'll need a boost. You go last, make sure everybody gets up safely."

Washington nodded, then braced himself with his back to the coxswain console and cupped his large black hands for Evans' foot. They waited, judging the timing of the swells and watching as O'Dell worked the throttle and the wheel, struggling to position the ladder over Washington's head.

Two-hundred yards away, Tanner watched from the starboard bridge wing as the boarding team maneuvered under the ladder. He didn't like the way the motor whale boat was moving beneath the ladder. Wilson kept the ship parallel with small backing and ahead bells as both ships drifted. They were beam to the seas and rolling five degrees.

Timing it with an approaching swell, Evans planted his right foot in Washington's hands and leaped, grabbing the second step of the ladder. The boat dropped out from under him, and he hung for a moment suspended over Washington's head. As the boat rose again, Washington pushed with both hands, and Evans clambered up, gaining a foothold. The hardest part was getting the bulky kapok lifejacket past the bottom rung.

Looking down at the boarding team, he said, "Do it without the M-14's, hand them up to each man once he gets on the ladder."

EM1 Washington helped the remaining ten boarding team members in the same manner. Some were agile and scrambled up the ladder like monkeys, reaching back to grab their M-14 from Washington. Others were not as graceful, larger men who struggled to pull themselves up the ladder. Evans waited at the rail, nervously watching as each man made the climb. He sent the first two to the forecastle to stand watch over the assembled *Gedaref* crew. The *Montgomery* helicopter continually circled the ship, ready to report any suspicious activity.

Finally, only Washington was left. He was a big man, over 200 pounds, and solidly muscled. Evans sized up the boat crew. Both the bow hook, Seaman Michael Tice, and the boat engineer, Engineman Third Class Ricardo Alvarez, were much smaller than Washington.

"Think you can make it?" he shouted down.

Washington nodded, then turned to Tice and Alvarez, "Both of you, give me a boost."

While O'Dell jockeyed the motor whale boat in the swells, both Tice and Alvarez braced their backs against the coxswain console and cupped their hands. Washington set his rifle aside and gazed up at the ladder and then at the approaching waves.

"Now!" he shouted as the boat rose on a swell. He leaped up with his right foot held by both men and reached for the ladder as the boat crested the swell. As the boat dropped underneath him, he struggled mightily to pull himself up, but his kapok lifejacket snagged on the bottom step. Tice and Alvarez lost their grips on his foot and fell sideways as the boat rolled away. They struggled to their feet and on the next swell pushed at Washington's hanging feet. They had no leverage and were unable to help before the boat dropped again.

Tanner watched through his binoculars as Washington lost his grip and fell, striking the gunwale of the boat, and bounced into the water between the motor whaleboat and the ship's hull.

Reacting quickly, O'Dell threw the throttle full reverse and gunned the motor whaleboat back, away from Washington. Tice and Alvarez were thrown forward, falling into the cross bench, Tice banging his head hard. He had removed his helmet to help lift Washington. He lay still in the bottom of the boat, stunned.

The next wave threw the motor whale boat hard against *Gedaref's* hull while also bouncing the floating Washington against the barnacle encrusted hull. Evans looked down helplessly from the main deck, kicking himself for not telling Washington to stay in the boat.

O'Dell began moving the motor whale boat forward to try to pick up Washington. Evans shouted down, "No! He'll get crushed. Throw him a life ring!"

Alvarez grabbed the orange life ring and heaved it forward at Washington who was grimacing in pain and continually being pushed against the ship's hull with each wave. He managed to weakly grasp the life ring.

Evans shouted down, "Pull him away from the ship and see if you can get him into the boat."

O'Dell nodded and began working the wheel and the throttle to back away while Alvarez wrapped the lifeline around a cleat. Tice still lay in the bottom, conscious but dazed.

Tanner called Evans on the walkie-talkie. "Don, what's going on, is Washington OK?"

"He looks hurt Captain. Bounced off the side of the boat and then against the hull. We got a life ring to him, and O'Dell is trying to pull him away from the ship and get him back in the boat, over."

"Did he get caught between the boat and the ship?"

"Don't think so, O'Dell backed the boat away. Probably saved his life, over."

Evans watched as the motor whale boat stopped about thirty yards from the side of the sheep carrier, Washington still clinging to the life ring. O'Dell and Alvarez pulled Washington in and, leaning over the gunwale, tried to haul him aboard. The boat rolled in the swells, throwing them off balance. He saw they couldn't get him over the side. Washington appeared to lack the strength to help, and Tice still lay in the bottom of the boat.

"I don't think they can get him in, Captain," he radioed over to *Dauntless*.

Tanner thought quickly, "OK Don, tell them to pull him further away from the ship. I'll bring in *Montgomery's* helo. They'll put the rescue swimmer in the water and hoist him up, get him to the carrier where he can get proper medical attention."

Tanner went to the bitch box, "TAO, Captain, bring *Montgomery's* helo in for a man overboard pick up. Injured man. We'll need the rescue swimmer. Litter if they've got one." He thought for a second, "Tell the First Lieutenant to get the flotation litter back on the fantail. We'll set flight quarters. Tell *Montgomery* what's going on."

Turning to Walt Wilson, he said, "Walt, set flight quarters, I doubt they'll have a litter in the helo."

186

The bitch box again, "Captain, TAO, no litter in the helo. They know what's going on and the air crewman is a qualified rescue swimmer. They need a little more room away from the ship to safely hover. They might be able to get him up in the horse-collar."

Tanner radioed Evans, "Have the boat crew tow Washington at least 50 yards from the ship. The helo is coming in to pick him up."

He stepped back to the starboard bridge wing as O'Dell slowly maneuvered Washington further from the sheep carrier. Wilson reported flight quarters set, the litter staged on the fantail.

"OK Walt, have everyone stand easy on station, we may not need it."

They watched as the SH-2 Seasprite helicopter hovered into the wind only ten feet above the water. A body, clad in shorts and a tee shirt, wearing a snug fitting inflatable life vest, and carrying flippers and a mask, dropped into the water and swam toward Washington and the motor whale boat. Waving to the helicopter, the swimmer motioned the helo into position over himself and Washington. A yellow horse-collar lowered from the winch swung out on an arm over the open, starboard side helicopter door. Tanner saw what looked like the co-pilot operating the winch. Swinging his binoculars up he saw the right seat was empty. *Figures* he thought, there were only three of them in the crew. *Good on em'*.

Moments later, he watched EM1 Washington being lifted out of the water, spinning slowly as he rose. The winch stopped, and the co-pilot pulled him into the helicopter and laid him on deck. The horse-collar went down again, rising quickly with the swimmer who was pulled into the door.

He heard the TAO on the 21MC, "bridge, TAO, the helo's headed down to *Saratoga* with Washington. They'll get him to the docs, refuel, and return to station. *Sara* and Alpha Sierra have been briefed."

They had unfinished business. Tanner gave Wilson a thumb's up to signify that he'd heard the report and turned his attention back to the boarding.

"Don, Captain here, let's get on with the boarding. Have someone look at the accommodation ladder and see if we can get it lowered."

"Roger sir, smells to high heaven over here, standby, out."

Turning to his boarding team, he gave out the assignments and headed for the pilothouse where he would interview the master, inspect the manifest, and then compare it to what his team found. He doubted it would be much more than the smelly sheep. Before leaving the main deck, he radioed BM3 O'Dell in the motor whale boat, "How's Tice?"

"He's got a big knot on his head and seems a little out of it, over."

"Roger, take him back to the ship and let the Doc look at him. Get a new bow hook and stand off until we're ready to leave, over." Before O'Dell could respond, Evans pressed the transmit button again, "Good work back there. Washington could have been crushed against the hull. How do you think he is? over."

"His leg may be broken, he was in a lot of pain, over."

* * *

Two hours later, the boarding complete, Don Evans gathered his team on the main deck above the accommodation ladder. They were hot, tired, sweat soaked, and stunk something awful. The ship carried nothing but sheep, originally over 5,000. Many had died during the passage from New Zealand, so nobody knew how many remained. Most of the dead sheep had been thrown over the side, but many remained, lying in their cages, adding to the stench as they decomposed in the summer heat. The master and the crew had been cooperative, fully expecting to be boarded. Once the United Nations Resolution became public knowledge, all shipping companies doing business in the Middle East were aware of the requirement and had advised their ship captains to cooperate. It sometimes meant delays in arriving in scheduled ports, and on those occasions when sloppy paperwork resulted in manifests not matching cargoes, it meant a diversion to a port other than Aqaba.

The *Gedaref* first mate, a swarthy Greek, had escorted Evans to the main deck and stood by to see the team off the ship. Those sequestered on the forecastle had been allowed to return to their work stations or off duty quarters. Evans looked at the accommodation ladder rigging. It was suspended from two sets of davits and tended from forward to aft. The forward davit secured the upper platform and the after davit secured the bottom step with two cables, one attached to each side of the bottom step. The ladder was configured so that it could be swung out to rest on a pier, or hung just above the water for use by boats.

He turned to the mate, "What's wrong with this, why can't we lower it?"

The mate pointed to the winch closest to the hull and attached to the bottom step, "Jammed, no move," he said.

"The other winch work?" asked Evans, pointing to the outboard winch and wire.

Rather than answer, the mate stepped to the control box mounted on the ship's life rail. He hit a switch, and the unit began to hum. Manipulating the levers, he first tried to lower the ladder. The outboard cable started to pay out, but the inboard cable did not move. Immediately the ladder became badly cocked at a sharp angle. The mate stopped it.

"Try to raise it," said Evans.

The mate worked the levers again, and the outboard winch began to pick up the cable. As the ladder began to rise, it cocked in the opposite direction, but with the inboard cable under no strain, it hung loosely as the ladder came up to deck level, a big loop in the inboard cable.

Evans examined the connection between the cable and the bottom step. A large u-bolt was fed through a padeye on the lower level, held in place by a cotter pin. He turned to one of the boarding team, Damage Controlman Second Class Richard Arias.

"DC2, see if you can get the pin out."

Arias pulled a pair of needle nose pliers out of his belt, twisted the mousing wire on the pin and pulled the u-bolt free of the step. The wire swung free, slapping against the side of the ship.

Evans turned to the first mate, "Now lower it, all the way down."

Not pleased at the way the Americans were making modifications to his ship, he nonetheless began lowering the ladder by the outboard cable. He stopped when it reached to just above the water.

Evans signaled the motor whale boat in.

"OK, one man at a time, back in the boat."

When everyone else had successfully climbed down the ladder and stepped into the boat bobbing alongside, Evans turned to the mate, handed him the u-bolt and cotter pin, shook his hand, thanked him for his cooperation, and scampered down the ladder and into the boat.

Tanner had watched his team disembark while sitting in his chair on the starboard bridge wing. As the motor whale boat cleared the side, he signaled Walt Wilson to release the *Gedaref*.

Walt Wilson picked up the bridge-to-bridge handset, "Motor vessel *Gedaref*, this is U.S. Navy destroyer two-five, you are cleared to proceed to Aqaba, thank you for your cooperation, have a safe voyage, out."

Tanner went back to the fantail to meet the boarding team. Evans was first up the ladder. He stunk, but not as bad as those that had inspected the ship, particularly those who had walked among the sheep pens.

"Good job Don, how's everyone doing?"

"We're okay Captain, but we could sure use some Hollywood showers. How's Petty Officer Washington?"

"He's in sick bay on *Sara*, looks like he broke his hip. Could have been worse, the kapok may have cushioned his fall."

"The kapok was the reason he couldn't get up the ladder, it got hung up on the bottom step. We need something better, maybe inflatables. How about Tice?"

"He's got a knot on his head, but Doc says he'll be alright." Seaman Tice was having a terrible cruise, first the ankle in the messenger line during the refueling detail and now this.

"BM3 O'Dell saved the day, Captain. If he hadn't backed the boat out, Washington would have been caught in the next wave. Coulda killed him."

Tanner watched as the boarding team began stripping off their dungaree uniforms and throwing them over the side. Ten naked men then began taking turns at a fire station with a gooseneck spray nozzle as they helped each other take a salt water shower.

He turned to Evans, "Get an inventory, the Navy will buy them new uniforms."

As he walked back toward the bridge, climbing the ladder to the gig boat deck and the ASROC deck he thought about how everyone had performed in a tough situation. Don Evans had shown solid leadership skills and had been cool under pressure. He would recommend BM3 O'Dell for a Navy Achievement Medal for his quick actions as boat coxswain. He mentally drafted a P-4 message to Commander Bob Higgins, *Montgomery's* CO, recommending something similar, maybe even the lifesaving medal for his helicopter crew for the way they had responded. It gave him a great sense of satisfaction to realize that these men were his crew, his responsibility. It was also humbling. As their captain, it was his job to lead them, to enable them to do what had to be done to accomplish the ship's mission. The enormity of his responsibilities became suddenly overwhelming in a way that had not registered before. Petty Officer Washington was *his* responsibility. The officers and crew looked to him to make the right decisions and to *lead*. He felt himself choking up and paused before climbing the ladder to the O-2 level, the bridge level. He needed to gather himself before putting on his game face back on the bridge.

ELEVEN

Northern Red Sea

On the main deck level, amidships, port side, Lieutenant Commander Ricky McKnight twisted the crank handle next to his stateroom desk and growled the TAO station in CIC.

"TAO."

"Ops, XO here. Come see me when you get off watch."

An hour later Andy Morton appeared at the XO's door, which was open. The heat in after-officer's country was oppressive. The XO's stateroom sat above the After-Fire Room.

"What's up XO?"

"Ops, we need to do a line of duty investigation on Washington's injury. I want you to do it."

"How about Suppo, sir, he's not standing watches."

McKnight sighed and fixed the Operations Officer with a stare, "I want it done by a line officer and someone not in Washington's chain of command."

"Pretty obvious he was in the line of duty, isn't it?"

"This is for his protection. If the hip is injured bad enough, he could get medically discharged from the Navy. He doesn't have twenty in yet. We need to document this so he can get a disability if it comes to that. As it is he's probably lost to the command. Just do it and don't argue. As you said, it should be a no-brainer."

"Aye, aye sir." Morton started to turn away, then paused and faced McKnight from the doorway. "Can we talk?" Without waiting for an answer, Morton stepped into the stateroom and closed the door behind him. McKnight put down his pen and leaned back in his chair. He didn't invite Morton to sit down on the faux couch.

"What is it, Ops?"

"Sir, how am I doing as Opso?"

"What do you mean?"

"I mean you have been on my case since before the change of command, but since Commander Tanner took over, it seems to have gotten worse. Am I doing something wrong?"

McKnight was taken aback by being so directly challenged. "Ops, you're doing fine. The Captain is happy."

"Well, what's the problem between us?" They were both the same rank, but a significant difference existed in seniority and status in *USS Dauntless*. McKnight had successfully completed two department head level tours. He was now second in command of *Dauntless*. Next for him was shore duty, hopefully followed by command screening and his own ship command. Morton was a full three steps behind McKnight in his own career. *Dauntless* was his first department head assignment. It would likely be followed by a second sea tour as a department head in a newer and more complex ship than *Dauntless*. After that, shore or staff duty somewhere and then his own screening for an XO slot.

McKnight looked uncomfortable. After a moment's reflection he went on, "Ops, we have a brand-new captain. I want to support him in the best way possible and help make him successful. He succeeds, we all succeed. I need him to turn to me when in doubt. You undercut me when you showboat at Ops-Intel or keep me in the dark on things until I hear you telling them to the Captain. You know what I mean, schedule stuff, when's the next unrep, changes to the SOE, all that shit."

Morton was quiet for a moment, then, "Just doing my job XO, I'm not trying to outdo you."

The two officers endured an uncomfortable silence. Just then the 1MC announcing system clicked on, "Planning Board for Training is now being held in the wardroom."

"Fuck," said McKnight, "already?"

Andy Morton grinned, "It's in the POD XO."

McKnight got to his feet, gave a meaningful look at the stack of paperwork in his in-box, and started for the door. Morton blocked his path.

"XO, I get it, I'll try to keep this conversation in mind. I'm not competing with you. You gotta believe me."

McKnight fixed him with a look that bordered on appreciation. "OK, thanks, Andy, let's go to PB for T."

* * *

That evening the usual gathering took place in the wardroom for the nightly Ops-Intel briefing. Tanner started things off.

"Gents, we had a challenging day today, and we lost a good sailor. Looks like EM1 Washington broke his hip pretty bad. They will medevac him off the carrier as soon as he's ready to travel, probably to Landstuhl where he can get good care. Looks like he'll need surgery. Cheng, the XO is working the message to BUPERS, we'll try to get a relief sent out here."

He continued, "The boarding team did a great job despite the difficulty. Don, good work by you and your team. BM3 O'Dell probably saved Washington's life when he backed the boat out. But, what happened today didn't have to happen. I should have called it off when we saw the condition of the acom ladder, maybe moved the sheep ship into calmer waters. The point is, as important as this mission is, it's not worth getting somebody hurt or killed. I want to make it clear to everybody, boarding officers, OODs, TAOs, hell, seaman deuces, if you think we're getting ready to make a mistake, do something dangerous, something stupid, bring it to my attention. Or the XO's attention," he added.

He looked pointedly around the room for emphasis, then turned to Ops.

"Evening Captain, everybody, we'll start with the force laydown." He pointed at the overhead of the northern Red Sea. "Three Rivers is empty while *Spruance* goes south to refuel from

Sara. Our turn comes in four days. Because *Spruance* isn't a SAM ship, *Phil Sea* will stay south. So, we're a little short-handed up here." He paused.

"Ops," said Tanner, the Commodore told me that when we refuel we'll do it in concert with *Biddle* and *Phil Sea* will come north and do some MIO. That what the schedule shows?"

Morton looked at his notes, "Could be Captain, yep, *Biddle* is refueling the same day. Shows *Phil Sea* in Yankee and *Spruance* covering our box in Fenway."

Morton fidgeted then said, "Commodore say why he'd pull two ships off station, sir?"

Tanner decided to shoot straight, "Has to do with shotgun duties and Alpha Whiskey. *Phil Sea* will transfer Alpha Whiskey to *Biddle* while doing MIO up here. Whoever is with the carrier needs to play Alpha Whiskey, mainly because of the return to force procedures for the air wing. The missile ship not alongside for fuel is the shotgun."

Vinny Devito said what they were all thinking, "They don't believe we can do it, be Alpha Whiskey, that it?"

Tanner liked that they were offended. "Vinny, it's about two, maybe three things. Number one is NTDS. Alpha Whiskey has got to be link capable. Second is capability, both cruisers have longer range missiles than we do. Finally, it's about seniority. They're captains, and I'm a commander. Don't anybody take it personally. I'm not."

Morton spoke up, "When I get to the 'swedge' stuff you're going to be even more pissed Weps."

They turned back to the brief as Morton signaled Seaman Collins to throw up the next vu-graph as he continued.

"Sir, this shows the force build-up. *Independence* and her support ships enter the gulf day after tomorrow. The coalition is starting to come together with several nations pledging to send ships to support MIO ops and air and ground forces for combat if it comes to that. First, we'll see here is the French from the Red Sea Fleet down in Djibouti. They're sending the oiler *Durance* and the frigate *Cassard*. *Cassard* is relatively new, and she's SAM capable. Got the same MK-13 launcher we do. The Brits, Italians, and Greeks will also be sending ships to the Red Sea, and they will work for Admiral McCall in *Sara*."

Tanner spoke up, "What do we know about the ship *Montgomery* diverted this morning?"

"Yessir, it was a Liberian registry, motor vessel *Dongola,* coming out of Aqaba and on the way to Sudan. When the boarding team got aboard, they found a bunch of cars and trucks, including some nice Mercedes. They all had what looked like freshly painted license plates. They had an Arabic speaker in the crew and sent him over. He said they were all from the nineteenth province of Iraq. That's what Saddam is calling Kuwait. Sent 'em back to Aqaba to offload."

"OK Ops, what else?"

"Sir, you saw the message from 'swedge' about the Exocet threat. All the TAO's have it, but I thought we should discuss it here since it could have a bearing on your battle orders."

Tanner nodded, "Agree, give us a run down."

"OK, Weps, this is the part you're not going to like. They broke down the guidance by ship class. Aegis ships are considered the only ones with a realistic chance of shooting down an Exocet. For everybody else, it says to turn away and launch chaff. 'See-whiz' ships have a chance if the profile is right."

Chaff were tiny strips of Mylar in a container which was launched from mortar-like tube launchers located on the port and starboard sides of the superstructure behind the signal bridge. At a pre-set height and distance from the ship, the mortar rounds exploded out a cloud of the Mylar strips which slowly floated down to the surface of the ocean. If launched correctly, the cloud of chaff would present a more inviting target to an incoming missile seeker, luring it away from the ship. 'See-wiz' was the vernacular for the close-in-weapons-system, or CIWS, an autonomous twenty-millimeter Gatling gun that could fire 2,000 rounds per minute. The system included an independent detection and tracking radar and could fire automatically at an incoming missile. *Dauntless* did not have CIWS.

"What about engaging with SM-1?" said Weps.

Ops smiled wryly, "You ready? Bottom line, don't even try."

Tanner took over, "Vinny, here's the deal. The whiz kids have decided that by slewing the fifty-ones at the target, we'd increase our radar cross-section by a factor of ten. Negates any value of the chaff. And our chance against a sea skimmer coming over the horizon at 500 miles an hour is pretty low even if we get a lock-on."

Vince DeVito knew his combat system and grudgingly nodded his agreement. Ensign Wilt Grimmage was surprised at this admission by the captain.

"Sir, what do you mean? Why not?"

A good teaching moment, thought Tanner. "Wilt, the seeker in the SM-1, doesn't perform well against a low-flyer. It can get confused by the surface of the ocean and miss. That is if we're even able to launch."

Grimmage still looked confused.

"Wilt, go up to CIC when we're done and talk to the FC's on watch. Ask them how we get a target detected on the air search radar into the fire control system and achieve lock-on with the fifty-ones."

Tanner was referring to the Target Selection and Tracking Console, or TSTC, which was manned by Fire Controlmen. There were two consoles in CIC, one for each SPG-51 missile fire control radar. An air target detected on the air search radar appeared on the scope of the TSTC. The FC then had to manually generate a track by holding a device directly over the radar video and pushing a button as it moved. This created a track in the fire control computer which, in turn, sent a signal to the SPG-51 to slew out and look for the target. It took time, and if the Fire Controlman manually tracking his target on the console was sloppy or unsteady, the fire control director could be looking at the wrong piece of sky. It was 1950s technology.

Tanner took over the briefing again, "Weps, we're not going down without a fight. Here's what I want you and Guns to do. Punch the pubs and take a stab at what elevation setting will cause a five-inch round of RF to fuse on the ocean's surface at about a mile."

RF stood for radio frequency. RF rounds emitted a signal that, when bounced off something, like an airplane, triggered the round to explode. RF ammunition was designed against air targets but could also trigger an air burst when the fuse sensed return from the ocean surface or the ground, on land.

Vinny DeVito's expression brightened. "Got it, sir, thinking about setting up a wall of air bursts down the bearing?"

"Exactly. If we have enough warning time, we can put up a barrage of shrapnel with both mounts in rapid continuous that the missile will have to fly through."

"We'll get right on it, sir."

"Good, I want to test fire tomorrow when you've come up with a recommendation. Experiment with the elevation setting."

* * *

Will Tanner and Vince DeVito stood on the starboard bridge wing the next morning scanning the horizon through binoculars for small boats that might not paint on radar. CIC had declared the area clear of shipping.

Satisfied, Tanner turned to his Weapons Officer, "OK Weps, batteries released, one round, HE-RF, Mount 51, 090 relative."

DeVito spoke into his sound-powered phones, "Gun Plot, Weapons Control, batteries released, one round, HE-RF, Mount 51, 090 relative, set elevation as briefed."

The previous evening, DeVito and Gunnery Officer Ensign Walter Sloan had studied the 5"/54 Mark 42 gun mount publications to estimate the proper barrel elevation to achieve an air burst with a high-explosive, radio frequency five-inch round approximately one mile from the ship. It was mainly guess-work, extrapolating the result from the manual which provided air burst guidance at much longer ranges.

The train warning bell sounded as they watched Mount 51 swing out to starboard and lower its barrel to an almost perfectly horizontal position. They heard the telltale click as the round was rammed into the breech and an instant later a loud boom as the mount fired. Almost simultaneously a second loud explosion and a large airburst bloomed close to *Dauntless*. Tanner's hat blew off his head, and he was pushed back against the bridge bulkhead by the concussion from the blast. DeVito fell backward as well, instinctively ducking behind the splinter shield.

"Shit! That was close!" exclaimed DeVito.

"Cease fire, Mount 51," said Tanner.

They put their heads together as DeVito described the blast to Ensign Sloan in Gun Plot, "Gun Plot, Weapons Control, that one went off about 500 yards from the ship. Adjust the barrel upward a bit, record the setting, and we'll try it again." He looked at Tanner who nodded his agreement.

Tanner looked into the pilothouse and told the OOD, "Pass the word for all hands topside to move inside the skin of the ship or to the port side. Weps, we'll move inside the bridge and shut the door before the next round, that was a little too close."

Once inside the pilothouse, Tanner and DeVito went through the process again after Ensign Sloan and the fire control team in Gun Plot made a slight adjustment to the mount elevation for the next test firing.

Again, Mount 51 trained out to starboard and fired a round. This shot travelled further from the ship before the fuze detected the ocean's surface and detonated, resulting in a large, black air burst just above the water.

"That looked pretty good," said Tanner, "what range from the director?"

"Director Officer reports eighteen hundred yards, sir."

"OK, good, record the setting and we'll revise the battle orders. What else?"

"Sir, Guns and I thought it would be a good idea to load the drums with alternating rounds of HE-RF and HE-VT. Give us a better chance to get the airbursts."

HE-VT was high-explosive-variable time. These rounds were set with a fuze setter as they were loaded into the gun. A specific range for detonation could be set into the shell just before it was fired.

"We set the HE-VT for 2,000 yards and between the RF and VT rounds we should be able to lay down a barrage."

Tanner nodded approvingly, "I like it. Draft it up for me and in the meantime, have the mount crews load the drums."

* * *

Will Tanner sat in his bridge chair studying his message traffic, making notes on some and setting them aside for distribution to his officers, dropping the rest into the burn bag on deck. It was late afternoon, and *Dauntless* was patrolling Fenway at five knots, on the lookout for ships meeting boarding criteria. Lieutenant John Woodson, the Officer of the Deck, walked over and pointed to the north. In the distance, a small boat was moving west to east, south of the Sinai Peninsula and the Strait of Tiran.

"There he is again, sir."

Tanner set down the latest MIO guidance message and picked up his binoculars. Adjusting the focus, he observed a non-descript blue-hulled fishing vessel with a dirty white cabin forward and what appeared to be two booms for handling fishing nets extending up from the fantail.

"What about him?"

"He's not like the other fishing and dive boats we see out here. Never seen him put the nets in the water. Never see any dive activity either."

The area around the Strait of Tiran and the Sinai Peninsula was known for its excellent diving. Numerous commercial dive boats routinely plied the waters, mostly catering to British and German tourists who travelled to Sharm-al-Sheikh on the Sinai Peninsula or Hurghada, to the west, on the Egyptian mainland.

"You think he's watching us?"

"I don't know sir, he's been in that general area for the last four days. Like I said, never seen him doing anything that looks like fishing or diving."

Tanner looked south. No merchant ships were visible approaching the Gulf of Aqaba. He toggled the 21MC, "TAO, Captain, any potential customers on the scope."

"No sir," came the reply from Vince DeVito, "pretty quiet right now. There's somebody headed north 48,000 yards south of here that Alpha Sierra has already assigned to *Montgomery*."

"OK, we're going to head north and take a look at Skunk Alpha."

"We've got him as a fishing boat, sir, not a candidate for boarding. Been there several days."

"Right, we'll go up there anyway and take a look. OK, Woody, let's go."

As *Dauntless* approached the fishing boat, Tanner and Woodson studied it through the binoculars. It was flying no flag. The small boat appeared to have more than the standard complement of radio antennae. As they drew to within a nautical mile, the boat turned to the west, away from *Dauntless*. A figure momentarily appeared in the door to the deckhouse and then disappeared inside.

"No name on the stern, Captain." Signalman Second Class Michael Weinrod was inspecting the boat through the "big eyes," large and very powerful binoculars mounted on a pedestal on the after-section of the bridge wing.

"Take us in to about 500 yards and parallel his course, I'll give him a friendly call on bridge-to-bridge."

As they overtook the small vessel, a figure reappeared in the deckhouse doorway and raised a pair of binoculars to study the approaching U.S. Navy destroyer.

Tanner keyed the mike on the bridge-to-bridge radio, "Fishing vessel on my starboard bow, this is U.S. Navy warship two-five, channel one-six, over."

The man lowered his binoculars and stepped into the deckhouse.

"Ah, yes, Navy two-five, this is, uh, *Aphrodite*, channel one-six," came back in an Arabic sounding accent.

"Yes, good afternoon *Aphrodite*, this is Navy two-five, how is the fishing over?"

There was a pause, and then in halting English, "Yes, thank you, very good."

Tanner and Woodson exchanged skeptical glances.

"What are you catching? We might want to buy fresh fish," said Tanner, winking at Woodson.

There was a long pause, finally, "Ahh, Navy two-five, so sorry, but I am required to bring my catch to market. Very sorry."

Tanner thought for a second, "Thank you, *Aphrodite*. Where is your port and what flag do you fly?"

At this question, there was a prolonged pause. Finally, "Ahh, yes, Navy, we are Egyptian, from Safaga."

Tanner, called the TAO, "TAO, Captain, quietly get the Snoopy Team up and get some pictures of this guy."

"TAO, aye."

Turning back to the bridge-to-bridge radio, Tanner keyed the mike, "*Aphrodite* this is Navy two-five, good luck with the fishing. If you need assistance, we will be in the area guarding channel one-six, over."

Immediately *Aphrodite* responded, "Ahh, thank you Navy, have a safe sailing."

After verifying that the Snoopy Team had captured enough high-resolution pictures, Tanner headed *Dauntless* back to Fenway. He called Vince DeVito out to the bridge. Both DeVito and Morton stepped into the pilothouse. Morton had learned of the Snoopy Detail being called away. As Operations Officer, the Snoopy Detail fell under him.

"Vinny, make it a pass down item for the TAOs to keep a plot of *Aphrodite's* movements, there's something unusual about him. Ops, write-up an intel report for Alpha Sierra and Alpha Bravo. When we go alongside *Sara,* we'll send over the film for them to develop. Put that in the intel report. If they're really interested they'll send up a helo to get the film."

* * *

Aboard the motor vessel *Basra,* Akram Najaf wiped his forehead with a dirty handkerchief and looked questioningly at the figure in the shadows at the rear of the pilothouse.

"Praise be to Allah," he said, "I think we are safe."

Mahmod Da'wud stared back with piercing black eyes, "You are fortunate brother Najaf, if the Americans had decided to board, your lies would have been found out."

Najaf nodded nervously, "I had to think fast if they knew we were Iraqi they would have boarded for sure."

"We will have to be more careful, or they will come back. Can you actually catch fish with this piece of shit?"

"I do not know in these waters. Too deep. I will lower the nets, so we appear to be fishing. Maybe we will catch something."

Da'wud turned to the photographs taped to the rear bulkhead of the pilothouse. They depicted the ships of the *Saratoga* Battle Group, each annotated with the ship name and class of ship. They had been ripped from the pages of an old issue of *Jane's Fighting Ships of the World*. Pointing, he said, "This is the one we want to see, this *Philippine Sea*. When it is near us, the aircraft carrier will be unprotected."

With a menacing look at Najaf, Da'wud turned to leave the pilothouse, "I am going to report this. Keep sailing west. Get the nets in the water."

As Mahmod Da'wud disappeared through the hatchway, Najaf let out a long sigh and wrung his hands. Da'wud scared him to death. He was Mukhabarat, the Iraqi Intelligence Service. Even worse, he was Directorate 4, the most dangerous element. He thought about how he had handled the American destroyer. Looking at the photo, he remembered it was called *Dauntless*. At least he hadn't blown his cover by revealing that he knew the name of the ship. The arrogant Americans were heard every day on the bridge-to-bridge radio, challenging shipping and identifying themselves only by their numbers. Yet the names of each one was painted on the stern for all to see. *Did they think we were stupid?*

He thought about the special radio equipment that Da'wud had brought aboard. It was kept in a hold below decks, but the antenna was clearly visible. A thorough search would find the radio set unless they had time to throw it over the side as the Americans lowered their small boats. He did not think Da'wud would be happy if that were necessary. He cursed his bad luck. It was pure chance that he had been fishing in the Red Sea when all the trouble started. He was sorry that he had agreed to this mission. But he had no choice. If he refused, he would surely die. Probably his family too.

Below decks, Mahmod Da'wud cursed to himself. *That fool,* he thought. *Aphrodite? Where had that come from?* He cursed himself as well. They should have thought this through ahead of time. They had no documentation naming the ship *Aphrodite* or claiming Egyptian registry. They didn't have an Egyptian flag to fly either. The entire mission had been thrown together on short notice when the embargo had been announced, and the Mukhabarat had devised the plan to strike a crippling blow against the American aircraft carrier. It had been a coincidence that Akram Najaf had been in the Sudan so that they could confiscate his piece of shit boat. But it was all they had so they had commandeered him and his boat.

Pecking away at his encrypted transmitter key he began filing his report to Mukhabarat headquarters in Baghdad.

TWELVE

Northern Red Sea

"Now station the underway replenishment detail, the ship expects to go alongside *USS Saratoga* at 11:00, port side to. Now station the lifeguard detail."

Will Tanner lowered his binoculars and turned to Andy Morton. "Who's got the conn for this one, Ops?"

"Ensign Pete Gardner, sir, the DCA. He's been alongside an oiler but never a carrier."

Tanner watched *Biddle*, some 1,000 yards ahead begin to take station 500 yards astern of *Saratoga*, slightly offset from *Sara's* wake on the starboard side of the carrier. Refueling from an aircraft carrier could only be done from her starboard side because of the angled flight deck sticking out to port. *Biddle* would go alongside first as the senior ship while *Dauntless* filled the lifeguard and waiting station 500 yards astern. *Dauntless* would also serve as shotgun in the unlikely event the ships came under attack. *Biddle* would be unable to employ her guns or missiles while alongside the carrier with refueling hoses connecting the two ships. The lifeguard ship was there to rescue anyone that fell overboard during the sometimes-dangerous evolution of passing hoses and wires between the ships and pumping hundreds of thousands of gallons of fuel oil. The previous night, Captain Roger Welsh in *Biddle* had taken tactical command of *Dauntless* and together they had departed the MIO area to join *Saratoga,* one-hundred miles to the south, for refueling both ships. Earlier that morning they had listened as *Philippine Sea* had passed responsibility for air warfare commander, Alpha Whiskey, to *Biddle* and headed north. With *Biddle* and *Dauntless* further south, the MIO station was lightly manned, with only *Montgomery* and *Spruance* on station.

Tanner listened as Ensign Pete Gardner took the briefing from the JOOD, Lieutenant (junior grade) Willy Kim.

"Romeo Corpen is 180 at 13 knots. When *Biddle* gets into waiting station, we'll close in to lifeguard station 500 yards astern. Looks like she's moving up now. Ready?"

"Got it," said Pete.

"In the pilothouse, this is Lieutenant jay-gee Kim, Ensign Gardner has the conn!"

"This is Ensign Gardner, I have the conn, belay your reports."

As the helm, lee helm, Quartermaster of the Watch and Boatswain Mate of the Watch acknowledged this transfer of authority, Willy Kim picked up the stadimeter to begin shooting ranges to *Biddle* up ahead. Pete Gardner stepped out on the port bridge wing, saluted Tanner, and said, "Captain, I have the conn."

Tanner returned the salute and said, "Very well, any questions Pete?"

"How close do you want to make the approach, Captain?"

"Let's start at about 175 feet and then ease into 150 as we get alongside."

"Aye, aye sir."

Willy Kim shouted out from the pilothouse, "*Sara* and *Biddle* have Romeo at the dip!"

Tanner said, "OK Pete, let's close up to 500 yards, just get in *Biddle's* wake."

Tanner hopped into his chair on the port bridge wing and watched as his bridge team coordinated their efforts to bring *Dauntless* into lifeguard station astern of *Biddle*. It was a perfect day for an UNREP. The seas were practically flat calm with only a slight swell running south to north. The sun was bright and high in the sky, and the temperature was a comfortable 85 degrees. He knew ashore in Saudi Arabia to the east and Egypt to the west, the temperatures would be at least 25 degrees higher, and the humidity stifling. It was pleasant to be out on the ocean. He thought about the Army, Air Force, and Marine Corps personnel ashore in Saudi Arabia and Bahrain, sweltering in the oppressive heat in their heavy uniforms and battle gear. *Give me the Navy any day*, he thought to himself. He glanced over the side and watched as a half-a-dozen flying fish skimmed the ocean surface, running away from the bow of his ship as they fled from this giant creature churning through the sea. He noted the offset from *Saratoga's* wake and made a note to watch *Biddle's* approach to get an idea of what that wake looked like when it was time to make their own.

Ricky McKnight walked out to the bridge wing, "All stations report manned and ready, Captain."

Tanner acknowledged and surveyed his XO, "How's everything else going XO?" McKnight had been quiet of late, having little to say during their nightly get together after 8 o'clock Reports and during the nightly Ops-Intel brief in the wardroom. He seemed to be avoiding the captain, only meeting with him when required and staying off the bridge or out of CIC when he knew Tanner was in either place. The day prior, Tanner had been doing his routine walk around the ship and had stuck his head into after-officer's country and found McKnight dozing on top of his rack in the middle of the afternoon with the door open. He had not awakened him, *hell, he'd taken his share of nooners over the years*. Life on a destroyer at sea was tough, everyone was tired. The XO had a busy job and worked well into the night. He had taken note, however, of the large stack of folders and papers in the in-box on McKnight's desk. They had been late on a couple of routine reports recently, and each time, McKnight had blamed it on one of the department heads turning it in late. Now, he had his doubts.

"Everything's fine sir," replied McKnight.

"Anything new on the home front? About time we sent out a family-gram, don't you think?"

McKnight flinched, and an uncomfortable look crossed his face, quickly replaced by a smile. "Got the draft down on my desk," he lied. He had totally forgotten the CO's guidance that they send a family-gram home via the squadron offices in Mayport at least once a month during deployment.

"Everything good at home?" Tanner probed.

"Yessir," replied McKnight vaguely.

"I heard from Karen last mail call. She mentioned that she hadn't seen Theresa around the base lately." Both Tanner and McKnight lived in base housing at Mayport, Karen had moved in by herself just the previous week.

"She's gone to visit her parents while we're gone," replied McKnight, again looking uncomfortable over this third-degree line of questioning.

Tanner accepted this explanation without comment but thought to himself that if that was the case, protocol called for the Executive Officer's wife to notify the commanding officer's wife out of courtesy. Although the wives of ship CO's and XO's had no official duties, they, in fact, had many responsibilities for which there was no compensation and rare official recognition. Most had to do with looking out for the welfare of families left behind.

Just then, Andy Morton stuck his head through the door and announced, "Romeo closed up on *Sara*."

Tanner shifted his attention to the carrier and the cruiser ahead. As soon as the Romeo flag was closed up on *Sara*, the Romeo flag on *Biddle's* port side rose quickly to the top of the yardarm.

A surge of white water churned up behind *Biddle* as the cruiser picked up speed for her run into station alongside *Saratoga*. Tanner saw Pete Gardner looking expectantly at him and nodded. Turning into the pilothouse, Gardner ordered 20 knots and moved up to take *Biddle's* previous position relative to the carrier. Inside, Willy Kim called out ranges using the stadimeter. *Dauntless* slid into position 500 yards directly astern of *Biddle* as the cruiser finished her approach and settled out alongside the carrier. Pete Gardner was doing a good job with the conn and the watch team, under Andy Morton's guidance, was operating smoothly. Tanner decided to sit quietly and watch. *Let them run this themselves.* He realized that in the hectic days following their departure from Mayport, and the hurried transit to the Red Sea, he had not given Ricky McKnight the opportunity to drive the ship. He made a note to himself to have the XO conn during an unrep or man overboard drill. He needed to judge Ricky's ability to handle the ship. If he was going to recommend him for his own command, he needed to assure himself that McKnight had the requisite ship handling skills.

Up ahead, both Romeo flags came fluttering down as the messenger lines were in hand on *Biddle*. They watched the ritual as the span wires slowly made their way across the distance between the two ships, soon followed by the thick, black refueling hoses. *Biddle* was taking fuel at both her forward and after refueling stations, as would *Dauntless*.

Pete Gardner was making minor course and speed adjustments to stay directly in *Biddle's* wake and hold steady at 500 yards astern. So far, so good.

Ninety minutes later, *Biddle* signaled five-minute standby as she lowered the Bravo flag to the dip. She was just about topped off. Minutes later, the flag was hauled down, and Tanner saw the spanwire slack as *Biddle* prepared to unseat the fueling probes and send the rigs back to *Saratoga*. On *Dauntless*, they heard five short blasts of the ship's whistles as an emergency breakaway was executed for training purposes. Finally, with the hoses hanging clear of the water at *Saratoga's* refueling stations, the inhaul-outhaul line was slipped, and again a surge of white water churned up from *Biddle's* stern as she powered out of station to break away. *Biddle* pulled ahead of *Saratoga* and then began a sweeping, high-speed turn around to starboard to take up station astern of *Dauntless*. In a role reversal, *Biddle* would serve as lifeguard ship while *Dauntless* filled her fuel tanks.

After a few minutes, the Romeo flag on *Saratoga's* starboard side fluttered up to the dipped position, halfway up the yardarm. Looking up, Tanner saw Petty Officer Weinrod position the Romeo flag at the dip in response. Within minutes, Romeo was closed up by *Saratoga*. With no oiler in the Red Sea, *Saratoga's* rig crews were gaining proficiency in the art of underway replenishment. Keeping the five ships of the battle group topped off on fuel meant serving as delivery ship on average every other day.

Tanner slid out of his chair and stood next to Pete Gardner, but said nothing. He was disciplining himself not to take over. He'd let the bridge crew manage the approach and only step in if they made a dangerous mistake. Pete Gardner looked a little nervous now that he was about to bring *Dauntless* in alongside the 82,000-ton *Saratoga*.

"Romeo closed up on *Sara*," called out Willy Kim, "range 500 yards." Willy had re-adjusted the stadimeter to configure it to give ranges to the carrier, now that *Biddle* had moved away.

Gardner looked at Tanner for a signal but got none. Recognizing what the captain was doing, Andy Morton said, "OK Pete, let's go, 25 knots." Morton had been on the bridge for each unrep since Tanner took command and he knew what his captain wanted.

"All engines ahead flank, indicate turns for 25 knots," ordered Gardner.

"The ship is commencing its approach, all hands fall in to port," announced Boatswain Mate Third Class Reinhart.

Morton looked up at Weinrod, standing expectantly at the ready on the Romeo flag halyard. Holding up his hand, he signaled, "not yet."

The forced draft blowers wound up as the engineers in main control opened the valves to release more steam to the turbines in response to the flank bell. *Dauntless* surged forward.

"400 yards," called out Willy Kim.

Tanner glanced at *Saratoga's* wake, then back at the carrier. Tapping Gardner on the shoulder, he pointed at the wake. Gardner looked over, understanding Tanner's intent.

"Come left, steer one seven nine."

"300 yards," announced Kim.

Morton signaled a thumb's up to Weinrod and up went the Romeo flag to the top of the halyard.

Things were happening fast now as *Dauntless* gained speed and closed on the much larger aircraft carrier. The bow dipped into a swell, and a spume of spray curled up and over the port bow, soaking the phone and distance line team standing in ranks on the forecastle. At this range, the stadimeter was ineffective, and Willy Kim ceased his range reports. It was all seaman's eye now. Judging the lateral separation as well as the overtaking speed was a skill acquired through experience. Tanner knew that in addition to *Sara's* CO, Captain Mike Reasoner, Admiral McCall would be on the flag bridge alongside Commodore Vanzant, watching *Dauntless'* performance. Dozens of other staff officers and ship's company would be spectating as well, each judging for themselves how well or how poorly *Dauntless* performed this routine seamanship evolution. Some, like spectators at a NASCAR event, wanting to be witnesses if some catastrophe occurred. Tanner couldn't help himself and placed his right hand on Gardner's shoulder, but still said nothing. Risking a quick glance backward, Gardner saw his captain staring intently as the bow came even with the carrier's stern. He turned toward the pilothouse door as if to issue an order, but stopped when he felt Tanner give his shoulder a squeeze.

"Not yet," whispered Tanner.

Normally, crossing the stern on an oiler was a good time to cut speed to slide forward into station, but *Saratoga* was 1,000 feet long, and there was more distance to cover. The lateral separation looked good. As Dauntless moved forward at speed, Gardner felt two quick squeezes on his shoulder.

"All engines ahead standard, indicate turns for 13 knots!"

Dauntless began slowing as she moved forward, the massive aircraft carrier looming high overhead. They passed the after refueling sponson, the *Saratoga* rig crew standing casually on station, the large black refueling hose hanging limply from the outrigger kingpost. As they began to come abreast of the island, Tanner nodded to Morton who gave Reinhart a thumb's up.

Reinhart pressed the 1MC mike button and gave two tweets on the whistle on a lanyard around his neck. "Attention to port," he announced. Everybody but Tanner and Gardner came to attention.

"Drop two turns," ordered Gardner without prompting. Tanner smiled, *good call*, he thought. The ship was drawing into position but needed to slow just a little so as not to overshoot.

One whistle from Reinhart, "Hand salute."

In rapid fire, from *Saratoga* came first one whistle, calling the crew to attention to starboard. Nobody moved on the carrier. Then another whistle for hand salute. A few people standing on the flight deck rendered a haphazard salute, most dropping it immediately. Two more whistles, ordering the salutes dropped. Then three quick whistles signaling carry-on.

Tanner looked at Morton and shook his head ruefully. Morton smiled and signaled Reinhart to answer the whistle signals with their own 'ready, two and carry on.'

"They're aviators, Captain," said Morton.

The two ships were now riding smoothly alongside at about 175 feet. From *Saratoga* came the announcement over the topside speakers, "On the *USS Dauntless*, stand by to receive shotlines forward and aft!"

A gunner's mate at each station, dressed out in a red float-coat and red hard hat style helmet, raised an M-14 rifle to his shoulder with a beer can-like device at the end of the barrel. On the forecastle, Tanner watched his phone and distance team of six sailors take shelter on the starboard side of Mount 51. A whistle blew, followed quickly by two shots from the gunner's mates at *Saratoga's* forward and after refueling stations. The canisters flew across the distance between the two ships, arcing through the sky and trailing a thin orange line. One landed on the forecastle, bounced twice and then hung up on the lifeline. A sailor ran out and grabbed the line and began hauling it in hand over hand with the help of his shipmates. On the O-1 level aft, the same thing happened. Connected to the orange shotline was a larger manila line and connected to that was an even larger nylon line. These were the messenger lines that would eventually lead to the inhaul lines which would bring over the one-inch wire rope spanwire. On the forecastle, the phone and distance line was sent back across to the aircraft carrier, the colored flags spaced every twenty feet. Once connected, the phone and distance line gave the conning officer an indication of the distance between the ships while also permitting sound-powered conversation between the two ship's bridges.

Tanner watched as the spanwire began its trip across the 150 feet now separating the two ships. The water between the ships roiled violently as the two wakes collided and the water raced between the two hulls as if in a narrow slipway.

"Bridge-to-bridge comms established," announced Seaman Jeremy Collins, his phone talker. Still watching the line-up and lateral distance as Pete Gardner ordered periodic minor course and speed changes to hold position, Tanner grabbed his handset.

"CO *Dauntless* here," he announced.

"Yeah, hey skipper, CO *Sara*. Welcome alongside."

"Thanks, sir, appreciate the gas."

"No problem, we're getting used to this. I'll be glad when that French oiler shows up."

"I bet. What do you hear about Iraq?"

"Well, it doesn't look like anything is going to happen soon. The force build-up is continuing, and the striped suit crowd is still talking. How are things up north?"

"Besides the one Iraqi ship that wouldn't stop and the guy carrying cars that *Montgomery* sent back, it's been pretty much routine, no real trouble. Appreciate your docs taking care of my electrician's mate who broke his hip. That was a bad one."

"Yeah, too bad about that. He was flown off by COD to Hurghada day before yesterday for a medevac flight to Landstuhl, Germany. Doc said he really crushed the hip. Gonna take a couple of surgeries at least to patch him up. Hang on, Commodore Vanzant is here, wants to talk to you."

Tanner waited for his boss to come on the line.

"Vanzant, here."

Very formal, thought Tanner to himself.

"Afternoon Commodore, Will Tanner here sir."

"Tanner, saw that intel report on the suspicious fishing boat up north. What's your assessment? And do you have the film?"

"Sir, the film went over on the T and D line, addressed to COMDESRON Two Four."

Tanner wanted to add, *you better send someone down there to look for it*. Things had a way of getting lost on an aircraft carrier.

"OK. What about your thoughts."

"Sir, as I reported, he had been hanging around for several days and didn't appear to my watch officers to be doing any fishing. When I asked a few simple questions on bridge-to-bridge, his answers sounded fishy. No pun intended. Like he was making it up as he went. He was still there yesterday, but *Montgomery's* helo reported that he was streaming his nets."

"Doesn't sound too suspicious to me."

"Well sir, he hadn't been using the nets before we questioned him. And the water is pretty deep there. He can't be dragging the bottom."

"OK. We'll let the intel types look at it."

Like that, the commodore was gone. No good bye. No comment on future operations or compliments on anything that had been accomplished. No 'nice approach on the carrier.' Just gone.

Tanner held the handset out and looked at it quizzically, then realized he could be seen from the carrier's bridge. He pulled it back to his ear.

In a moment, Captain Reasoner came back on. They discussed break away procedures and then signed off. Tanner turned his full attention back to the replenishment.

After an hour alongside, Pete Gardner and Willy Kim traded places, so Willy could get some alongside time and make the break away. When the conn had turned over, Tanner complimented Gardner on his performance.

"Any questions, Pete?"

"No sir, thanks for letting me drive. Guess I was gonna take the speed off too soon, huh?"

"A little. *Sara* is about 250 feet longer than *Detroit,* so you have to factor that in."

Andy Morton came out. "Five-minute standby Captain."

When the signalmen at the forward and after stations gave the signal to stop pumping, *Saratoga* shut off the pumps, and both ships got ready to initiate a practice emergency break away.

Tanner coached Willy Kim, "No different than the regular break away for you Willy. The rig crews will work faster, and you might open the distance a little, but don't do anything drastic until the rigs are clear."

"Yessir, understood."

Suddenly *Saratoga* sounded five short blasts from the ships whistle; the danger signal. *Dauntless* answered with five of her own. Tanner watched the forward station under the direction of Boatswain Mate First Class Butt break down the rig and trip the probe receiver handle. The probe backed out, dripping a gallon of fuel oil on deck, and began swiftly moving across the expanse between the two ships. Tanner looked aft and saw that the after probe had not yet disengaged. As the forward probe approached the side of the carrier, the carrier rig crew de-tensioned the spanwire. Suddenly, 2,000 pounds of pressure pulling the forward half of the ship toward *Saratoga* was gone. Looking aft quickly, Tanner saw that the after rig was still under tension.

"Get ready Willy, the after rig is going to pull the stern into *Sara*. You'll need left rudder. Ops! What's the problem back aft?"

"Checking Captain!" shouted Morton.

The pull, back aft, combined with the lack of tension forward began drawing the stern toward *Saratoga*. Before he could say anything, the forward rig crew tripped the pelican hook and started paying out line to send the spanwire back. *Shit, too late to ask for re-tension*, he thought.

"Captain, Chief Wise says the release handle's jammed, the probe won't unseat," called out Morton.

"Willy put on five degrees left rudder," ordered Tanner.

Tanner considered his options. Left rudder might temporarily hold the stern off, but it would drive the bow into

Saratoga. He looked forward and saw the phone and distance line being hauled aboard. No flags for reference and no way for him to talk to Captain Reasoner.

The XO called out from inside the pilothouse, "CO *Sara* on bridge-to-bridge Captain, wants to know what the problem is."

"Tell him the probe is stuck, ask if he can de-tension aft. Willy, rudder amidships, now!"

McKnight spoke into the bridge-to-bridge hand set," Captain, can you de-tension? We can't unseat the probe."

Aboard *Saratoga* Reasoner turned and shouted to one of his officers, directing the after refueling station to de-tension the spanwire. The distance between the two ships was now only about 75 feet, the stern even closer.

Tanner realized he couldn't keep relaying orders through Willy Kim.

"This is the Captain, I have the conn, belay reports!"

Andy Morton leaned out, "Still jammed, sir, they're trying to beat it loose with a hammer. Can't trip the pelican hook with the wire under tension."

Tanner realized it would take time for the rig crew on *Sara* to get the word to de-tension with the probe still seated. It was unorthodox; against procedures. They might waste a minute questioning the order.

"All ahead full, indicate turns for 18 knots," he ordered. *Maybe a little power, pull ahead, change the physics of whatever was going on at the after station.*

Reasoner was back on the bridge-to-bridge radio, "Told them to de-tension. You're getting close. Any progress?"

"Adding power, trying to power ahead," replied McKnight

Tanner was really multi-tasking now, conning the ship, relaying orders to McKnight, taking status reports from Morton, and watching his ship being pulled closer and closer to the side of the aircraft carrier. The ships were now only fifty feet apart back aft. Tanner kept the rudder amidships and the additional speed on. The combination moved the bow away but did nothing to improve the situation aft. It did seem to stop the progress toward the carrier.

"Ops, tell them to stand clear of the after station, just get out of the way."

Morton relayed the order via walkie-talkie to Vince DeVito who had taken over at the after station.

As *Dauntless* began moving ahead of *Saratoga*, the spanwire and hose began tending aft. With the pull from the tensioned wire cocking the stern toward *Saratoga's* side at the after station and the rudder amidships, the bow was now pointing away from *Saratoga's* side forward.

At the after refueling station, Vince DeVito, walkie-talkie in hand, shouted to Chief Wise, "Boats! Get everybody away from the rig forward, go forward!"

As the after refueling rig crew scrambled forward away from the receiving probe and connected hose and spanwire, DeVito watched the receiver begin to swivel aft as *Dauntless* moved forward. Looking across at the *Saratoga* rig crew he saw the signalman frantically giving the disconnect signal with his wooden paddles. The spanwire paid out to accommodate the now opening distance as *Dauntless* moved forward. The refueling hose began to tighten, losing its catenary as the distance increased from point to point.

With a sudden splash of dark black fuel oil, the probe pulled free of the receiver and slid back along the spanwire until it met the resistance of the re-mating line which was still made up to the cleat. Immediately, the spanwire was slackened by the *Saratoga* rig crew. Chief Wise raced underneath the rig and ordered his rig crew into position to begin sending the rig back.

On the bridge, Tanner saw the probe jerk free, and the spanwire slacken. Immediately he slowed the ship to ten knots and adjusted course back to parallel to fall back into position. *Dauntless* was far from safe, as the two ships rode side by side only 50 feet apart.

"Ops, tell the rig crew to trip the wire and cut the outhaul line if they have to, we need to get out of here!"

Tanner had been involved in tight spots before, but never as the captain of the ship. He knew two ships riding close together can be drawn into a collision by the low-pressure area between the hulls created by the Venturi effect as the water is forced between the hulls and gains velocity.

Looking up at the large sides of the carrier, Tanner realized his ship was in extremis. Aboard *Saratoga,* the collision alarm was sounded. He craned his neck upward to see Captain Reasoner looking anxiously down at what appeared to be an imminent collision.

"All engines ahead flank, indicate turns for 25 knots!" he shouted through the open bridge door. There was no room to turn away from the carrier, that would only throw the stern to port, against *Saratoga's* hull. He had to power straight out ahead of the carrier as fast as possible.

At the after station, Vince DeVito relayed the order to trip the spanwire to Boatswain Mate Chief Orville Wise. He heard the forced draft blowers wind up and felt *Dauntless* squat as the screws dug in and the ship began to accelerate.

"Chief, cut it now, get everybody out of there! Now!"

"Get the fuck out of here! Everybody! Go!" shouted Wise, pushing anyone he could reach forward of the rig. Chief Wise shoved Petty Officer O'Dell out of the way and grabbed a large pair of pliers out of his hand. Reaching up, he yanked the cotter pin out of the pelican hook and shoved the u-bolt away from the hook with his right hand, violently releasing the spanwire which jerked clear of the side of the ship, stopping abruptly as the inhaul-outhaul line held. Reaching down to his left ankle Wise pulled a large pocket knife out of his ankle holster. Working quickly, he sawed through the inhaul-outhaul line. The entire rig jerked free, crashing down on the main deck lifeline and then falling into the sea. The lifeline stanchions on either end bent with the force of the impact. The entire rig; probe, hose, spanwire, saddle whips, and saddles, dragged through the water, falling against the side of the carrier as the rig crew hauled the whole mess in as fast as they could. 600 feet of *Saratoga's* inhaul-outhaul line remained on *Dauntless'* O-1 level deck.

Tanner, seeing that the connection to the carrier was broken, concentrated on getting clear of *Saratoga's* side. *Dauntless* was rapidly accelerating as the engineers answered the flank bell, but 300 feet of aircraft carrier remained to be cleared. As *Dauntless'* fantail drew even with the carrier's island, Captain Reasoner ordered left five degrees rudder to try to move his bow away from *Dauntless*.

"Come right steady one-eight-one," ordered Tanner.

Standing behind the helmsman, Pete Gardner could see only gray hull out the bridge door. Nobody spoke except to acknowledge orders. On the port bridge wing, Willy Kim unconsciously backed away from the splinter shield, his back against the bridge bulkhead. Seaman Collins had stepped inside the pilothouse, next to the chart table. Tanner's mind was racing, *nothing to do but press ahead and hope to clear Sara's bow.* He was afraid to order any more courses to the right, as that would move the stern left. Reasoner's five-degree left rudder order was slowly taking effect, but not yet apparent aboard *Dauntless*.

From *Saratoga's* flag bridge, one deck below the navigation bridge, Admiral McCall, and Commodore Vanzant looked down as *Dauntless* accelerated forward almost directly below. Neither spoke, watching as this near tragedy unfolded. As *Dauntless* continued forward, the bridge now almost even with the forward edge of the flight deck, McCall muttered, "Go. Fly you son of a bitch."

Vanzant gave him a funny look but said nothing, a frown clouding his face.

As Tanner watched the forward edge of the flight deck pass almost overhead, he turned his attention aft. If there were to be a collision, it would happen there.

"Sound the collision alarm," he shouted to Morton.

Boatswain Mate of the Watch Reinhart needed no further encouragement. Hitting the collision alarm, he grabbed the 1MC mike and announced, "All hands stand by for collision, port side. Seek shelter on the starboard side!"

He repeated the order and then looked back at Morton for further instructions. Quartermaster Third Class Aquilino was diligently recording everything in the ship's log, his pencil flying across the page.

Now at almost 23 knots and still accelerating, *Dauntless* moved inexorably ahead. Tanner, almost a spectator now at his own funeral, watched as the distance between the two hulls slowly opened.

From Vince DeVito on the O-1 level aft next to the refueling station came a report over the walkie-talkie, "We're gonna make it, stern is almost clear."

"Bridge aye," replied Morton, relaying the report to Tanner.

For the first time in what seemed minutes, Tanner allowed himself a breath.

"Roger, tell Weps to report when we're clear."

Aboard *Saratoga*, Mike Reasoner also breathed a sigh of relief.

"Slow to five knots," he ordered his OOD. *Should have thought of that earlier,* he thought to himself.

"Get a report of damage from the after rig."

On the flag bridge, Admiral McCall gave a little fist pump. "Made it," he said, turning to Vanzant with a smile.

Commodore Vanzant did not share the admiral's enthusiasm.

"That was one of the most fucked up unreps I've ever seen," he said.

"Some damned good ship handling to get out of it," said McCall, fixing Vanzant with a quizzical look.

"That may be sir, but something is wrong on *Dauntless*. I'll find out what happened. Conduct an investigation."

McCall hesitated before responding, "Very well Al. Keep in mind that this is dangerous business. Shit happens. Appears to me the only damage is a cut line and some bent stanchions."

"There's a pattern here sir," replied Vanzant after a pause, "Commander Tanner has already been involved in one collision. He left station without signal during a storm, and he acted recklessly during the incident with the Iraqi merchant. I'm just concerned, that's all."

"He's under your tactical command Al, so do what you think is necessary. But keep in mind that his ship was the only one that avoided damage during that storm, and his actions solved the problem with the Iraqi ship. And a second collision just *didn't* happen. Be fair."

"Yes sir," replied Vanzant.

As *Dauntless* cleared the carrier's bow, Tanner put the rudder right and opened away to the west. He turned to Willy Kim, "Willy take the conn back, slow to 15, and head north until we get a signal from either Alpha Sierra or *Biddle*."

He went to his chair on the starboard side of the bridge and picked up the bridge-to-bridge radio handset.

"*Saratoga*, this is Dauntless Charlie Oscar for Charlie Oscar, Channel one-six, over."

Reasoner came on the circuit immediately, "*Sara* Charlie Oscar, roger, over."

"Captain, Will Tanner here, sir. Sorry about the close call. We'll find out what happened with the probe. I'll get your line over to you as well, sorry about having to cut it. Thanks for whatever you did over there to help, over."

After a pause, Reasoner came back, "Roger skipper, not to worry, any landing you walk away from and all that. I'll send a helo over to pick up the line later. We've got another unrep scheduled in two days, over."

"Roger sir, thanks, we'll have it ready for pick up, over."

"Roger, out."

Tanner looked over at *Saratoga*, beginning a slow turn to port to start heading back north. The tactical circuit crackled and then came a tactical signal from *Biddle* directing *Dauntless* to proceed independently north to Fenway. *Biddle* would remain in company with *Saratoga* until *Philippine Sea* returned.

Vince DeVito came to the bridge with Chief Wise. Wise, still dressed out in his white hard hat and kapok life jacket was rubbing his hand.

"Anybody hurt back there Chief?" asked Tanner, looking pointedly at the chief's hand.

"This is nothing Captain, just bruised. Everybody else is OK."

"Any idea why the probe got hung up?"

"No sir, not yet. We'll take a good look at the receiver, make sure it's not fu... uh, screwed up sir."

"OK Chief, good work back there. Vinny, dig into it and figure out what went wrong. I'm going to get some questions from over on the carrier."

As if it were scripted, Lieutenant Wilson's voice came over the bitch box, "Captain, CIC, Commodore is on the secure admin circuit for you."

Tanner hustled aft into CIC and picked up the red hand set, "Alpha Sierra, *Dauntless* actual, over."

The speaker hissed and then synched, "Commander Tanner, Commodore here, send me a P-4 report on today's foul up. Report any damage at your end. Include the qualifications of your refueling rig captain and PQS status of the rig team, over."

Keeping his poker face, Tanner replied, "Roger sir, will do. Also, nobody was hurt over here, over." *Thanks for asking*, he didn't say.

"Roger, out."

Tanner replaced the hand set and returned to the bridge. As he climbed into his chair, he felt his right knee begin shaking uncontrollably. *That was close,* he thought to himself. *I am off to a shitty start with Commodore Vanzant. What has that guy got against me*, he wondered.

THIRTEEN

Damascus International Airport, Syria

Major Abdul Tikriti studied the intelligence report that had been delivered to him at Damascus International Airport by his liaison officer, Major Muhammed Bandari. The Mukhabarat had placed an agent on a fishing boat in the northern Red Sea to report on the American naval activity. At present, the Americans had only a few ships in the area to enforce the illegal embargo against Iraqi shipping. That would soon change. The stupid Americans announced every military move they were making, revealing their plans for the whole world to see. CNN was reporting that additional American ships were on their way to the Persian Gulf and the Red Sea. Ships from other countries, lackeys of America, were also coming. The window of opportunity to execute Operation Birds of Prey was rapidly closing. Once the full armada was assembled, it would be that much harder to launch their attack on the aircraft carrier, this *Saratoga*. The Mukhabarat had determined that only one ship now guarding the aircraft carrier was judged effective in defeating the Exocet missile. This *Philippine Sea,* described as an Aegis cruiser. He did not know why this was so, perhaps it was more modern. He thought Aegis meant "shield" or "protection," perhaps that had something to do with it.

The Mukhabarat had reported that periodically this *Philippine Sea* would leave the aircraft carrier's side and move north while another, less capable ship, took its place. It was during this window that they would launch Operation Birds of Prey. His commander, Colonel Bashir Mohamed, had told him that even if only one Exocet penetrated the defenses and struck the American aircraft carrier, the mission would be a success. The Americans thought their aircraft carriers to be invincible. It would be a crushing blow to have a missile explode in the carrier, killing American sailors and embarrassing the so-called superpower.

The Mukhabarat agent had reported that when a certain ship, the one numbered 34, left the area south of the Sinai Peninsula, this *Philippine Sea,* would appear the next day and stay at least 24 hours, sometimes more. They had to be ready as soon they saw number 34 leave the area. From then they would have no more than a day to strike. It had to be the next time. Otherwise, additional American ships would arrive. Some, no doubt, would have this Aegis. Their chances of success would go down with time.

Tikriti shuffled the pages of the intelligence report and stuffed them into the red folder. Reaching below the desk in his small bunkroom, he shoved the folder into a small safe and spun the dial, locking it. Reaching for his telephone, he dialed a four-digit number.

"This is Major Tikriti, send my car, I will be outside."

Stepping out into the scorching sunlight on the military side of Damascus International Airport, he donned his imitation Ray-Ban aviator style sunglasses and went down the steps to the curb. Five years ago he had bought the sunglasses from a stall on Straight Street, in Damascus, after seeing the American movie *Top Gun.* Stretching to his left, he saw the revetments which housed the Syrian Air Force fighter squadron jets based at DIA. Mig-21's for the most part, older, almost ancient, single seat jets provided to the Syrians by the Soviet Union. *The soon to be no more Soviet Union*, he mused. The Soviet Union was in the process of splintering, collapsing. Client states like Syria and Iraq, even the Egyptians, would have to look elsewhere for modern military hardware. His supreme leader, the great General Saddam Hussein, had been smart, buying the Mirage jets from the unscrupulous French. They would sell anything to anyone if the price were right. With the Mirage jets came the deadly Exocet missiles.

An older Mercedes Benz approached from the direction of the revetments, three of which housed his Mirage jets, awaiting the signal to attack the Americans. As coordinated with Baghdad, the Syrians had announced that the three jets and their pilots had defected across the border to Syria. The jets had been impounded and their pilots arrested. The three pilots had reportedly requested political asylum in Syria, fearing for their lives if they were sent back to Iraq. In keeping with the charade, the Syrian government had announced that it was in negotiations with Baghdad to decide the fate of the pilots. Nobody had any doubt that if the three traitorous cowards were returned to Baghdad, they would be hanged within hours of setting foot on Iraqi soil.

The Mercedes wheezed to a stop, a young Syrian sergeant at the wheel. Tikriti hopped in the back seat, and the car wheeled around and headed south alongside the runways toward the revetments. Tikriti got out, thanked the sergeant and strode into the center of the three revetments housing the Iraqi jets. Major Dawud El-Amin and Captain Falah Al-Tawfeek, his wingmen, were leaned over a table, studying a technical manual. El-Amin's fighter occupied this revetment.

Seeing Tikriti approach, Captain Tawfeek stood and saluted. El-Amin remained concentrated on the manual.

"At ease Captain," said Tikriti dismissively. He did not stand on formality during a special mission like this. Tawfeek however, could not bring himself to act casually around the two more senior and combat veteran pilots.

"Is there a problem?" he asked El-Amin.

Looking up, El-Amin quickly closed the manual and straightened, "No my brother, we have been studying the sequence of switches to arm and fire the missiles."

Tikriti understood. He and El-Amin were experienced in air-to-air combat, having eight Iranian kills between them. Tawfeek, though not combat-tested, had been trained for the air-to-air role. Although all three pilots had received training on the anti-surface ship mission with the Exocet missile, it had not been their primary purpose.

"That is good. We may be going soon."

Both pilots exchanged glances and looked back at Tikriti expectantly.

"Relax," he said, "I think we have two, maybe three days before we strike."

"Why is this?" asked El-Amin.

"There is a particular ship guarding the aircraft carrier. An Aegis. Every four or five days it leaves the aircraft carrier's side and is replaced by another ship. A different ship, perhaps older and not as capable."

"How do we know this?" asked Tawfeek, speaking for the first time.

"That is not your concern. But we are aware. When it is reported, we will arm the jets and make final preparations to launch. It will be in the daytime, that cannot be helped. We must be sure that the particular ship is far away from the aircraft carrier and unable to help defend against our missiles. We can only be certain if this Aegis ship is known to be away."

The Iraqi's had discussed this element of the plan. A nighttime attack would be preferable, the darkness adding to the confusion of the Americans who believed that their ships were safe, beyond reach, in the Red Sea.

"Come," Tikriti ordered, "let us review the plan in my office."

The trio walked across the tarmac to the northernmost revetment which housed Tikriti's aircraft. Opening the door to his office, he startled a dozing Major Muhammed Bandari, the liaison officer assigned to the mission by Baghdad. Quickly jumping to his feet and straightening his tunic, Bandari reached for a stack of intelligence reports which lay on the desk.

Tikriti fixed the intelligence officer with a glare. Except for being the conduit for information from Baghdad, he considered Bandari worthless. A bureaucrat, Bandari had never seen combat. He was a rear area officer, a staff officer, one who participated in sending real warriors to fight but stayed safely behind himself. But he needed Bandari for this mission, so he tolerated the overweight officer.

Attempting to conceal his disgust, he summoned Bandari to join them at the chart table.

"What is the latest from Baghdad?" he asked.

"There is nothing new. The last report had the American ships in their usual positions, continuing to illegally interfere with trade in the Arab world."

"Is there a projection on when the special ship, what is it, Aegis?... will be away from the target?"

Relishing the opportunity to demonstrate his worth, Bandari began to lecture, "Yes, they call it Aegis, but it has a name. *Philippine Sea*. It is a cruiser."

"What does that mean? Cruiser."

"It is like a destroyer or frigate, but bigger. It is the American's newest fighting ship."

"And why is it better than the others?"

"I do not know, exactly," admitted Bandari, "but because it is new, it must have the most advanced equipment."

"Can our missiles penetrate its defenses?"

"Perhaps. Firing six missiles at once will create problems. But, if we attack when this ship is away, our odds are much better. I do not know the details, but the older ships will have great difficulty shooting down our missiles."

"What about the aircraft carrier itself," pressed Tikriti, "it has many fighters on deck, no?"

"Yes, and the aircraft carrier also has defensive missiles of its own. There will be CAP protecting the carrier. That is why the element of surprise is so important."

Tikriti had long been concerned about the American combat air patrol. They had to get the aircraft carrier on the Cyrano IV radar and launch their missiles before they were intercepted by the CAP. He moved to the table containing the map of the attack route and target area.

"We have discussed the route many times, but now I want to focus on the terminal phase," he announced.

All four officers gathered around the table. Tawfeek and El-Amin at each side and Bandari across from the three pilots.

Tikriti pulled an extendable pointer from his flight suit. "We have discussed the route from Damascus and over the Iraqi desert east of the Jordanian border," he began, tracing the path with the pointer.

"We will fly in close formation to appear as one large aircraft on radar. Your transponders will be off," he said, looking pointedly at his two wingmen. "I will transmit a commercial code indicating a routine flight from Damascus to Arar, in the western Saudi desert."

Both pilots nodded their acknowledgment, they had been over all this many times. Tikriti sensed their impatience.

Sharply rapping the map with his pointer, he said, "Until we approach the American aircraft carrier this will be the most dangerous part of the flight. If the Americans become suspicious, they will send their jets flying CAP over Saudi Arabia to intercept and investigate. We will be defenseless with only the Exocet missiles and our guns."

Both pilots nodded their understanding.

Continuing, Tikriti traced the route due south, away from Arar and toward the mountain range in the Al Jowf region of Saudi Arabia. "When we turn south, I will silence my transponder, and we will descend to 1,000 feet. It will be approximately 600 kilometers to the coast at Duba."

Again, the pilots nodded, mentally calculating the fuel consumption at low altitude for the 375-mile flight to the coast.

"We will be shielded from the American CAP far to the north and from the aircraft carrier CAP and ship radars by the Tabuk mountains until we emerge over the coast near Duba. As we cross the coast, we will pop-up to acquire the American aircraft carrier on radar. They have been operating in an area due west of Duba, only about 90 kilometers from the coast. Our missiles will be in range almost as soon as we are over water."

"What is the firing plan brother Abdul?" asked El-Amin.

"Two scenarios. I will order a spread formation as we approach the coast. It is best that we all fire at once after each of us has confirmed lock-on to the target. If that becomes impossible, I will signal that each of us is to shoot as soon as lock-on is achieved. Firing all together will complicate the defense of the enemy ships."

"And after that?" asked El-Amin pointedly.

Tikriti fixed him with a long stare, "We are to disperse and attempt to land in Egypt, at the Hurghada airport."

Both El-Amin and Tawfeek looked skeptical. Finally, Tikriti broke the silence.

"As for me, if the Americans have fighters in the air, they will certainly shoot us down. I will become the seventh missile rather than bail out. What each of you does is your decision."

"Praise be to Allah," said El-Amin, "If that be the case, I too will follow my missiles into the target."

Tikriti turned to his left, fixing the younger officer with a questioning look.

"Allahu Ahkbar," responded Tawfeek, "together we will destroy the Americans."

Satisfied, Tikriti turned to Bandari, "Major, alert Baghdad that all is ready. We must know immediately when this, what is it, cruiser, is no longer guarding the enemy aircraft carrier."

He again turned to his wingmen, "Beginning this afternoon we will do twice daily engine and system tests on all three fighters. They are to be kept completely filled with fuel, and the missiles are to be attached to the pylons and ready for arming. Is that understood?"

Turning again to Bandari he said, "Tell Colonel Asmeh of our requirements. I want no interference from the Syrian technicians. When we ask for clearance for takeoff, it must be granted without hesitation. Understood?"

Nervously, Bandari nodded his acquiescence, "Yes Major, I understand."

FOURTEEN

Northern Red Sea

Lieutenant Commander Ricky McKnight sat in his stateroom and stared at the letter in his hand. After a month gone and several opportunities to receive mail, Theresa had finally written. Only it was not what he wanted to hear. A Dear John letter in the classic sense of the genre:

> *Dear Rick,*
> *This is the hardest thing I have ever done. I hope you can appreciate that. I am not cut out to be a Navy wife. I hate it. I hate everything about it. I hate that you have no time for me when you are home, and I hate that you are <u>never</u> home! You are always gone, even when that stupid ship stays tied up to the pier. Now you are gone again, and I don't know when you will be back.*
> *Please try to understand. When we got married, I loved you. I thought I knew what I was getting into marrying a Navy man. I loved you in your uniform, and I loved the thought of what you did - but I didn't really know what you did. I am so sorry.*
> *I am filing for a divorce. It really isn't your fault. You didn't know, and I didn't know that we just couldn't live this way. I hate doing this to you now while you are out there somewhere doing whatever it is you are doing. I watch the news every night, so I know you are somehow involved in everything that is going on. It scares me. Please try to understand and don't hate me. Please don't fight me on this. I am so sorry. I hope you will be safe and that you will do good for our country.*

Fondly, Theresa
P.S. The papers will come in the mail - please just sign
them - let's don't fight.

McKnight reread the letter, and then a third time. *Fuck me purple*, he thought to himself, *I am now and totally fucked.* Not only was his XO tour not going swimmingly, but he was also now about to become one of many divorced lieutenant commanders who had put their job before their personal lives and paid the price. The Navy expected its leaders to be balanced. It was an impossible combination of expectations. First, you had to excel at your profession. You had to take on the tough jobs, work your ass off, sacrifice everything for the almighty fucking United States Navy: your personal life, your family, everything. Then they expected you to be the perfect fucking husband, married to a beautiful, supportive, Navy wife, who attended all the wardroom functions, never got drunk, knew all the right things to say to kiss up to the old biddies whose husbands ran the Navy, and be happy when you were gone from home 70% of the time. And then, after demanding all this, the Navy looked askance at the perpetual bachelor or the divorced schmuck. Was the bachelor queer? What was wrong with the divorced asshole? Had his wife seen some flaw in him that rendered him unsuitable to lead sailors? A divorced officer was damaged goods, someone who fell short of the standard. Someone with a character flaw somewhere, otherwise why would he have gotten into this marriage in the first place. Or, what had his wife discovered about him that the Navy hadn't?

It was 23:45. The mail had come over during the fucked up unrep with *Sara*. McKnight hadn't had the chance to look at it until now. First, there had been the unrep itself, a fouled up refueling at the after station, a near collision that the captain had somehow managed to avoid. Then the accusatory exchange

236

between Tanner and the commodore. Now the captain had asked him to do an investigation and find out what had gone wrong. As Tanner had explained it, both Weps and Ops were too close to the event to be assigned to impartially investigate. The Suppo, Lieutenant Logan, wasn't qualified. And Cheng was up to his ass in alligators just keeping the steam plant operating. So, it fell to McKnight. He looked at the overflowing in-box. *Motherfucker, how was he going to get all this done?*

Even at almost midnight, it was sweltering hot in the XO's stateroom, sitting above the fire room. McKnight hesitated, and then stood up and closed his stateroom door, locking it as he did. He knelt down to the drawer beneath his combination bed and couch and pulled it out. Reaching behind the folded sweaters, underwear, socks, and civilian trousers and shirts, he fumbled around until his hand rested on the bottle of Beefeater's Gin. He pulled it out from underneath the clothes and looked at it. *Why had he even sneaked it aboard* he wondered to himself? This was why. Emergencies. Beefeater's was the perfect stowaway booze, packaged in square bottles, it wouldn't roll around and give away the game when the ship worked in a heavy seaway.

McKnight stuck the bottle back in the drawer and left his stateroom for the mess decks. The night shift was serving midrats to the off-going watch teams. Sailors who had been on watch from 20:00 to midnight were grabbing sandwiches, bug juice, cookies, whatever the cooks had put out for the watch-standers. A half hour earlier all those going on for the midwatch had eaten the same food. A ship underway never sleeps.

Mess Specialist Third Class Rolando Guiterrez greeted his executive officer, "XO, welcome to midrats. We never see you down here."

McKnight glanced down at the stencil on the petty officer's right breast and then replied, "Working late tonight Guiterrez, got any orange juice down here?"

"No sir, all we got's bug juice - red. All tastes the same, know what I mean?"

"OK, thanks, red bug juice it is, I guess. See you later."

McKnight went to the bubbler and drew himself a large plastic cup of red kool-aid with ice and headed back to his stateroom.

Once inside, he locked the door and mixed a strong red bug juice and gin. He took a big gulp and then added more gin to once again fill the cup. He sat back and thought about his future. Maybe he should just hang it up like he was thinking before. Before the Dear John letter. Maybe not. If Theresa was out of the picture, he could concentrate on his job. He wouldn't be torn between trying to keep her happy and the fucking Navy at the same time. But, he thought as he added some more gin, was Tanner going to take care of him or not? An XO who received a mediocre fitrep from his CO was toast. Damned by faint praise. A selection board would see through that in a New York minute. There had been that talk on the bridge wing before the Suez Canal transit. And then Tanner ragging on him about the POD and late reports. If all that was any indication, Tanner was not going to make him a water walker unless things changed.

Looking down, McKnight realized he had finished the drink. He stuck the bottle of Beefeater's under his pillow and got up to head for the mess decks for another glass of bug juice.

Arriving, he saw Gutierrez swabbing the deck, cleaning up after midrats.

"XO, back already? We're securing for the night."

"Just another glass of red, Gutierrez. Working late," he slurred.

"Sir, I just shut down and cleaned the bubbler til breakfast. Reload it with OJ in the morning. I might have a pitcher of iced tea in the cooler left over from chow in the Chief's Mess."

"OK, that'll do, just pour it in this cup."

Gutierrez took the cup and headed into the galley. He thought he smelled a funny odor as he reached into the cooler, pulled out the steel pitcher, and filled the cup with iced tea.

"Thanks, uh, Gutierrez, any ice left?"

"Yessir, right there next to the bubbler, have a good one XO."

McKnight went to the ice machine and sloshed iced tea on the freshly mopped deck as he pulled it away.

"Sorry shipmate," he grinned crookedly as he headed for his stateroom.

Returning to his stateroom, McKnight stripped down to a pair of running shorts and a tee shirt for sleeping and poured a generous amount of gin into the iced tea, stirring it with his finger. What to do next, he pondered as he drank the gin and iced tea, what to do next? When the iced tea was down about a quarter, he added yet more gin. As he sat drinking the gin and contemplating his future, the growler phone buzzed next to his rack.

"XO."

"XO, Weps here sir. TAO. We've got a ship coming out of the Gulf of Aqaba that Alpha Sierra wants us to board."

"After fucking midnight?" he almost shouted.

"Yessir, bridge is querying him now. Alpha Sierra says this one should be easy, he was boarded on the way in three days ago. No issues. Captain's on the bridge. Told me to let you know."

"OK, thanks."

McKnight took another swallow of his drink. They don't need me up there he thought to himself as he took another swallow and added more gin.

He heard the 1MC announcement calling away Boarding Team Alpha and heard the pounding of feet and shouted voices from outside and above his stateroom as the boatswain mates prepared the motor whale boat for lowering.

A few minutes later, the growler phone howled again. McKnight grabbed it, "What now, Weps?"

"XO, Captain here," A pause while Tanner considered the XO's response. "How about going to the boat deck and watching things for me, it's a little rough tonight."

"Oh, uh, sorry Captain, thought it was Weps. Yeshir, I'll be there in a minute."

Reluctantly, McKnight began dressing while finishing his drink. He casually stuck the half empty bottle of Beefeater's back in the under-rack drawer and pushed it shut with his foot. The latch did not catch.

Leaving his stateroom, McKnight left after-officer's country through the port side weather decks watertight door onto the main deck. Looking up, he saw the motor whale boat swinging from the davits. A sailor forward and a sailor aft held steadying lines as *Dauntless* rolled in the four-foot seas. Staggering aft on the main deck he saw the boarding team gathering on the fantail in the reddish gloom of the after underway replenishment lights, the red lenses intended to preserve night-vision while taking on fuel at night. Clumsily, McKnight climbed the ladder to the O-1 level and walked forward to the boat deck. Chief Wise was supervising the lowering of the boat, walkie-talkie in hand.

Weaving a little as the ship rolled, he approached the Chief Boatswain Mate and reached for the walkie-talkie, "Lemme have that Chief."

Chief Wise was engaged in conversation with the bridge, "Boat deck, aye."

He waved off the XO and shouted, "Lower away, fenders over!"

"XO, I'm in the middle of this. Got the OOD on the other end."

"Gimmee the walkie-talkie Chief. Captain sent me back here."

Giving McKnight a quizzical look, the Chief reluctantly handed him the walkie-talkie, "You taking over sir?"

Ignoring Wise, McKnight keyed the mike, "OOD, XO, let the Captain know I'm on the boat deck."

Just then the ship took a roll to port. McKnight lost his balance and stumbled against the lifeline, bumping into Seaman Moncrief who was handling the after steadying line. The walkie-talkie fell on deck, took one bounce over the side and landed on the main deck below. Moncrief, grabbing the XO's arm to steady him, lost his grip on the steadying line. Chief Wise leaped forward to grab McKnight and looked down to the main deck to see what had happened to the walkie-talkie. He heard it crackle as something was said from the bridge.

"You okay XO?"

"Fuck," muttered McKnight.

With the after steadying line no longer held, the after end of the motor whale boat swung out to port as the ship rolled. The boat falls were cockeyed as another seaman struggled with the forward, steadying line. Boatswain Mate Third Class O'Dell, the coxswain, lost his balance on the coxswain flat and began to fall out of the boat. Grabbing the monkey line with both hands, he hung over the side as the ship rolled back to starboard and the motor whale boat swung back in over the boat deck. O'Dell managed to lever himself back in just before the boat slammed into the davit chocks.

"Get a hold of that line Moncrief!" bellowed Wise, letting go of the XO. Turning to the 1JV phone talker, he shouted, "Tell the bridge to stand by, we've got a problem here." On the main deck below, the walkie-talkie slid to port as the ship rolled again, found a scupper, and went over the side.

"Motherfucker," said Chief Wise, looking wildly at the XO who was leaning over, both hands on his knees. Suddenly,

McKnight retched and vomited all over his shoes, trousers, and the O-1 level deck.

Moncrief regained control of the steadying line, and the crew got the motor whale boat under control. The 1JV phone talker looked at his Chief and his XO and said, "Bridge wants to know what the hold-up is."

"Tell 'em we're lowering now," said the Chief. He looked at the XO, grimacing in pain and dry heaving.

The boat was lowered, and O'Dell started the engine as they hit the water. They tripped the falls, cast off the steadying lines and the sea painter, and the motor whale boat headed aft to the fantail to pick up the boarding team. With a backward glance at the XO, Chief Wise headed down the ladder to the fantail to supervise the loading of the boarding team.

McKnight leaned against the after deckhouse as the boat lowering detail stood easy on station, coiling lines and readying the davits for when the boat returned. Unsteadily, he went down the ladder to the main deck and re-entered after-officer's country. Pushing open his stateroom door, he flopped onto his rack and closed his eyes, one leg over the side, a foot on the deck.

On the port bridge wing, Tanner watched as the motor whale boat loaded the boarding team and headed for the small coastal freighter which had stopped and was lying to some 400 yards downwind. He turned to the OOD, Lieutenant John Woodson, "Still no comms with the XO?"

"No sir, phone talker says the walkie-talkie fell overboard and sank."

"What the hell happened back there?" muttered Tanner to himself.

He turned to the 1JV talker, "See if the XO is back on the fantail and ask him to come up to the bridge."

"Chief Wise said the XO is not there. Says he got sick. Probably went to his stateroom."

Tanner watched as the motor whale boat approached the freighter and made its side without difficulty. The boarding team climbed the pilot ladder and began the inspection, reporting all conditions normal.

"Hold her right here Woody, I'll be back in a moment. Pass the word for me if you need me back in a hurry."

Tanner headed aft to the fantail before checking on McKnight. When he arrived, Chief Wise was supervising his deck seamen as they re-stowed fenders and lines until it was time to bring the boarding team back aboard.

"Chief, what happened with the boat launch?"

Chief Wise looked uncomfortable, "We lost control of the after steadying line. The boat swung out on a roll, and BM3 O'Dell almost fell out. He's okay, grabbed a monkey line and hung on."

Tanner sensed the Chief was holding back.

"What happened to the walkie-talkie?"

Wise, didn't reply immediately. It was obvious he was thinking his response over, considering how much to say.

"XO dropped it when we took a roll. It landed on the main deck. Before I could get anyone down there to get it, it slipped over the side through a scupper. We were busy wrestling with the boat."

It was obvious to Tanner that Chief Wise wanted to say more.

"Go on," he urged.

"Skipper, the XO was acting strangely. He wasn't too steady. Slurring his words. He lost his balance and banged into Moncrief who let go of the steadying line to catch the XO. Then he puked."

Tanner paused a few beats, "You think he was drunk?"

Chief Wise squirmed. He looked over at the ship being boarded and then back at Tanner.

"I can't say, sir, it's dark up there, the ship was rolling in the swells. I couldn't say."

Tanner frowned, "OK Chief, thanks, good work. Hopefully, this won't take too long, and your guys can get some sack time."

Tanner headed forward up the port side, glancing at the davits hanging out over the water, the monkey lines swinging as the ship rolled, ready for the motor whale boat when it returned. After a glance across the expanse of water at the freighter, he opened the door to after-officers country, passed through the light locker, and entered the dimly lit passageway. Turning left, he saw that the XO's stateroom door was open, swinging back and forth with the roll of the ship. Sticking his head around the corner, he saw McKnight lying on top of his rack in his uniform. He smelled an overpowering odor of vomit. Below the bunk, the clothing drawer swung slightly open and then almost closed as the ship moved.

Tanner stepped inside, intending to shake the XO awake when the drawer slid open, and he saw the half full gin bottle in the light from the XO's desk lamp. He kicked the drawer shut with a bang. McKnight, startled into semi-wakefulness, peered at his captain through half open eyes. He reeked of vomit and gin.

"Uhh, ah, Cap'n...," he began, attempting to sit up. Tanner put a hand on his shoulder and pushed him back down.

"XO, you're relieved. Get up, get in the shower and get cleaned up. You're confined to your stateroom. We'll talk tomorrow. Sober up."

Tanner turned and walked out, slamming the stateroom door behind him and returned to the bridge, fuming.

"Captain's on the bridge," announced the Boatswain Mate of the Watch.

"Lieutenant Nicholson says they're just about done Captain," reported John Woodson. Jimmy Nicholson, the R Division Officer, was the leader for Boarding Team Alpha.

"Very well, thanks, Woody."

Tanner climbed into his port bridge wing chair, lost in thought. It was almost two in the morning, and he was tired from a full day; this was their third boarding since morning.

He listened as the JOOD ordered a small backing bell to keep *Dauntless* in position abeam the small freighter. How long had this been going on he wondered? He had never detected alcohol on the XO's breath, nor had he acted drunk. What to do now, he wondered. This was the last thing he needed, to have to shit-can his XO now while they were deployed on this operation.

As the motor whale boat left the side of the ship and headed toward *Dauntless,* he put the XO out of his mind and focused on the always dangerous business of handling small boats in the middle of the night. He listened as Lieutenant Woodson raised the master of the freighter on bridge-to-bridge radio, thanked him for his cooperation, and granted permission for him to continue his voyage.

The boarding team clambered aboard via the pilot ladder and began stowing their gear and weapons. *Dauntless* maneuvered in the seas to provide a lee for the motor whale boat, and the boat crew hoisted it clear of the water and secured it in the davits. Turning to John Woodson, Tanner said, "John, I'm hitting the sack, patrol our sector at five knots and have the OOD give me a wake-up call at oh-seven-hundred."

Hesitating, he continued, "In fact, push reveille back to oh-seven-hundred, been a long day for the crew."

* * *

"Bzzt!" Tanner grabbed the growler phone next to his rack and acknowledged the OOD's morning report. Reluctantly hauling himself out of his bunk, he dropped to the deck for his 50 pushups before heading in to shower and shave. As he dragged the razor over his face he contemplated the events of the previous night - *this morning actually*, he thought to himself. What next with the

XO? He had confined him to his stateroom and summarily relieved him of his duties. He wondered if McKnight had fully comprehended what had happened. He would have to have a sit down with the XO and formally reprimand him. He'd also have to make Andy Morton, the next senior line officer in the ship, the acting executive officer. Finally, he'd have to report this up the chain of command, both to Commodore Vanzant and Admiral McCall and to Commodore Nordstrom back in Mayport. Then there was the question of discipline. Court martial? Captain's Mast? For sure a punitive letter of reprimand and relief for cause, but some type of judicial hearing would need to precede that. The XO would have to be given the opportunity to explain himself. *What a fucking mess.*

First things first, a trip through CIC and the Bridge to get a grip on the tactical situation. Then go through the message traffic. He checked his tuck and then climbed the ladder to the O-2 level and turned right through the door into the Combat Information Center. Lieutenant Commander Vince DeVito had the morning TAO watch.

"Morning Vinny, what's the latest?"

"Morning Captain, nothing significant to report. All the MIO ships are on station, *Spruance* is getting ready to board a northbound bulk cargo carrier down in Three Rivers. No business for us yet. *Sara* and *Phil Sea* are about 120 miles south. One section of CAP up. We're at Condition Three with Mount 52 the ready mount."

"OK, anything hot in the traffic overnight?"

"Got the unrep schedule for the next week. We go south in two days to refuel again from *Sara*. Looks like the same deal as before, we go south with *Biddle,* and *Phil Sea* comes north for MIO."

"All right, thanks, I'll be on the bridge, have radio send up my traffic."

Arriving on the bridge, Tanner went through the same ritual with Lieutenant Walt Wilson, the OOD, and hopped into his chair. Boatswain Mate Third Class Reinhart came over to offer Tanner a cup of coffee. It was another beautiful day in the northern Red Sea. The swells from earlier had subsided, and the ocean was almost like a lake.

As he sat in his chair sipping the chart house coffee and looking over the message traffic, he considered how to handle the situation with the XO as far as the crew was concerned. This would be delicate. First, he'd deal with the XO in the light of day, then inform Ops he was acting. He decided illness might be the best cover story. Nobody would believe it, especially after Chief Wise told his version of events in the Chief's Mess.

Almost on signal Master Chief Derwood King walked onto the bridge through the starboard side bridge wing door. The ever-present coffee mug welded to his hand.

"Mornin' Cap'n," he said, "looks like another fine Navy day in paradise."

Tanner returned the greeting and fixed King with a meaningful look. He knew what this visit was about.

"Let's go out on the bridge wing Master Chief and enjoy the morning sunshine."

As they stepped out on the starboard bridge wing, King looked up, caught the eye of the forward lookout, and with a shake of his head sent him over to the port side.

"Cap'n, understand we had some excitement on the boat deck last night," began the Master Chief.

"Let's don't kid ourselves Master Chief, what are you hearing?"

King gave Tanner an appraising look, glanced around to make sure there were no unauthorized ears in range, and replied, "Word is the XO was acting weird. Chief Boats mentioned it at breakfast this morning. Petty Officer Guitierrez says the XO paid him a visit after midrats, had a big glass of bug juice followed by an iced tea. First time he ever saw the XO at midrats." King cocked an eyebrow, leaving the rest unsaid.

"This all over the ship?" asked Tanner.

"I think so, Cap'n, crew's gonna talk."

"All right Master Chief. Yes, we have a problem, and I'm going to handle it this morning. Once I figure out what I'm gonna do, I'll need your support – and that of the rest of the chiefs. Impossible as it may be, I'd like to tamp this down, quietly send the XO home with as little fanfare as possible. I'll think of something, and then I need you to back me up with the crew."

King looked skeptical. "Cap'n, I told you I'd never bullshit you, and I'm not gonna start now. By lunchtime, every swingin' dick on this ship will know the XO was drunk last night. Sooner you get him off the ship the better. I'll back up whatever story you come up with, but trust me, ain't nobody gonna buy it."

Tanner smiled ruefully, "Thanks, Master Chief, you're right of course, it's on me to handle this as best I can. I appreciate your honesty. Keep your ear to the ground and let me know how this is playing with the crew."

"Aye, aye, Cap'n, by your leave sir, time for a little walk around."

King gave a little salute, spun on his heel and head aft toward the ASROC deck. Tanner took a few minutes to think and then returned to his chair in the pilothouse.

He grabbed the growler phone and with a quick twist of the hand crank he growled the XO's stateroom, "XO, Captain, you up?"

"Yessir. Captain, I--"

Tanner cut him off, "Save it. Meet me in my cabin in fifteen minutes."

Climbing out of his chair he told Lieutenant Wilson he'd be in his cabin and went below.

With a knock on the door, Lieutenant Commander Ricky McKnight entered the cabin and stood before Tanner who was sitting at his desk. Tanner motioned him to the couch. McKnight looked terrible, his face puffy and his eyes bloodshot. He looked utterly humiliated and chagrined. He clutched a piece of paper in his left hand.

"XO, what the hell happened last night?"

"Sir, I have no excuse. I'm sorry. I got this in the mail yesterday."

He handed the Dear John letter to Tanner who took it and quickly scanned it, handing it back.

"I saw the gin in your drawer. What was that even doing on the ship?"

"I'm sorry sir, I don't know what I was thinking. Maybe take it ashore if we set up an admin somewhere," he lamely explained. "I never touched it before last night, I swear."

"Why don't I believe you?" said Tanner, looking McKnight directly in the eye.

"I don't blame you, Captain," replied McKnight, nervously rolling the letter in his hands and looking at his shoes.

He looked up, tears welling up in his eyes, "What now, sir?"

"XO, I have no choice, I'm relieving you of your duties. The boat handling detail saw what happened last night. Chief Wise suspects that you were drunk. I have to report this up the chain. I also have to decide on punishment. I can't treat you any differently than one of the crew caught doing the same thing."

"I understand sir."

"I'm going to have Ops take over as acting XO. Give him all the pending actions sitting in your in-box. I'm going to tell the crew that you are sick, but I doubt they will believe it. Stay in your stateroom, I'll have Suppo set it up to bring you your meals. When I figure out the logistics, you'll be transferred to *Sara* and sent back to the squadron to await disposition."

With a stricken look, McKnight acknowledged the decision, "Aye, aye sir."

He got up to leave.

"Ricky, I know this is tough, I'm sorry about Theresa, but you leave me no choice."

"I understand sir."

When McKnight had gone, Tanner called the wardroom. Andy Morton picked up the phone.

"Ops, come up to my cabin, I've got something for you."

Morton knocked on the door and entered.

"Sit down Ops."

Morton sat on the edge of the couch and looked expectantly at his captain.

"Andy, I'm designating you acting XO." He waited expectantly for Morton's reaction. When there was none, he knew that the word about the XO's behavior was already around the wardroom.

"You were expecting this?"

Morton shifted uncomfortably, "There's rumors Captain. The XO didn't show for Officer's Call this morning. I dismissed everybody and told them to execute the Plan of the Day."

"All right. The story is that the XO is sick. He's going to stay in his stateroom and take his meals there. Get down there and get any turnover you can; clean out his in-box and out box."

"Aye, aye Captain," he paused, "I think I need to stay on the watch bill, we don't have enough qualified TAOs without me."

"You're right. Take your admin work on watch with you, the CIC watch officers can handle the routine stuff."

When Morton left, Tanner began composing a P4 to Commodore Vanzant and Commodore Nordstrom, with a copy to Rear Admiral McCall, outlining the relief of his executive officer and recommending transfer to Destroyer Squadron 12. As he wrote, he considered how this would reflect on him. Already he sensed that Vanzant was unhappy with his performance in command. He had been extremely cold and abrupt with Tanner from the beginning. How much about Tanner and *Dauntless* had been relayed back to Commodore Nordstrom in Mayport, he wondered. *No turning back now* he mused, what had happened last night could not be ignored. Turning to his desk, he mentally began drafting the message to the Bureau of Naval Personnel, officially removing McKnight as executive officer in *Dauntless*.

FIFTEEN

Northern Red Sea

Will Tanner stepped onto the bridge and was greeted by the OOD, Lieutenant (junior grade) Paul Nelson.

"Afternoon Captain, all quiet this afternoon. Currently no boardings in progress and right now, nobody on the horizon. *Spruance* has a helo airborne conducting triple-SC. *Sara* and *Phil Sea* are 130 miles south conducting unrep. One section of CAP and the E-2 airborne down south."

"Thanks, Paul, what's the latest on *Aphrodite*?"

"*Spruance* sent her helo by to take a look about an hour ago. Reported that she was steaming south of the Sinai, nets in the water."

Tanner looked over at the status board. Since *Aphrodite* had been designated a contact of interest by Alpha Sierra, *Dauntless* had stopped tracking her with a 'skunk' designator, instead showing her position by name. The last time the status board had been updated, *Aphrodite* was located to the northwest at about 11 miles.

Tanner stepped over to the chart table to take a look at *Dauntless'* position relative to *Aphrodite*.

"Petty Officer Aquilino, let me have the dividers for a second."

QM3 Aquilino handed over his dividers and watched as Tanner measured out eleven miles on the latitude scale at the chart edge and then drew an arc on the chart to the northwest of *Dauntless'* current position.

He frowned, the water depths dropped off very sharply from the Sinai Peninsula to depths more than 1,000 fathoms; over a mile. Unless *Aphrodite* was dragging nets at random, hoping to snag fish swimming within 100, perhaps 200, feet of the surface, they were not conducting serious fishing activity. The water was simply too deep for bottom fishing or trawling.

Handing the dividers back to the Quartermaster of the Watch, Tanner turned to Paul Nelson, "Paul, have you got a visual on *Aphrodite*?"

"Not really Captain, too far to see anything but the top of the outrigger booms and sometimes a little bit of superstructure. She's pretty small."

Tanner moved over to his chair and thought about the fishing vessel that he had initially reported as suspicious to the chain of command. Alpha Sierra had ordered that the MIO ships keep an eye out for her and report any suspicious activity, but Commodore Vanzant had seemed skeptical when discussing the report with Tanner. There had been no further intelligence reporting as to the identity and nationality of *Aphrodite*. That suggested that the pictures *Dauntless* had sent over had not aroused any suspicion or provided any other clues. Occupying Fenway, *Dauntless* was the MIO ship closest to the Strait of Tiran and therefore closest to where *Aphrodite* typically operated. *Biddle*, in Yankee, was almost due south of the tip of the Sinai Peninsula but had evidenced no particular interest in *Aphrodite*.

Putting the fishing vessel out of his mind, Tanner sat contemplating the reaction to his sacking of Ricky McKnight. His "eyes only" P4 message had been met without emotion, either on *Saratoga* or back in Mayport. Commodore Vanzant had acknowledged the report in a come-back P4, directing Tanner to conduct non-judicial punishment, an Article 15 hearing, and report results. Commodore Nordstrom, in Mayport, had not been as directive as Vanzant but had acknowledged the need to remove McKnight from the ship and transfer him back to the destroyer squadron in a temporary duty status until his ultimate fate was decided. He had further advised that accounting data was being provided to arrange military air transport to Jacksonville once McKnight was transferred to *Saratoga* for a carrier onboard delivery, or COD, flight ashore in Egypt at Hurghada. Tanner had considered the meeting the next morning in his cabin as sufficient to qualify as non-judicial punishment. He would formalize McKnight's confession in a punitive letter of reprimand and notify the Bureau of Naval Personnel of his relief for cause in formal correspondence. He was not going to subject his executive officer to the humiliation of a formal Captain's Mast, complete with the presence of the collateral duty legal officer, the Chief Master-at-Arms, and witnesses, such as Chief Wise. McKnight had confessed and acknowledged Tanner's decision; that was enough.

He had stayed attuned to the reaction of the crew, knowing that the illness cover story had no legs. Master Chief King had been a loyal and trustworthy advisor, keeping Tanner fully apprised of the shipboard scuttlebutt and mood of the crew. Sadly, he was learning that the disappearance of McKnight from day-to-day activities was being accepted with happiness more than with suspicion. In a small way that made him glad – but at what cost to one man's life? He knew that the illness story was a sad charade; he knew Chief Wise had described the XO's actions that night on the boat deck to his fellow chief petty officers. The wardroom mess attendants had been delivering three meals a day to the XO; they knew he wasn't sick. Tanner had had a private conversation with Chief Wise after appointing Morton as acting XO.

"Chief, I would appreciate it if you dropped any further discussions about the XO in the Chief's Mess. At least until he's off the ship."

"Roger Captain, understood, Master Chief and I have already talked. I'm zip lip, sir." had been Wise's response.

* * *

Akram Najaf turned nervously as the after-door to the pilothouse opened and Mahmod Da'wud approached. Da'wud seemed to be in a perpetually bad mood.

"Any further interest from the Americans?" he asked.

"No Excellency, not since the helicopter flew by."

"It will be dark soon. Tonight, we will move further west, closer to number three-four."

Najaf nodded nervously, accepting the directive without question.

Da'wud continued, "I calculate that very soon the Aegis ship will come north and the two-five and three-four ships will depart the area. If the pattern holds."

Again, Najaf merely nodded, fearing to make any comment that might somehow be misinterpreted, bringing on the wrath of the Mukhabarat official.

"Begin moving west now. Pay attention to the movements of two-five and three-four. Track them carefully on radar. Call me if they leave station."

With that, Da'wud abruptly turned on his heel and disappeared down the ladder to the below decks area.

Having survived another encounter with his most unwelcome passenger, Najaf moved to the Furuno radar repeater and noted the positions of the two American ships of interest. As directed, he had been keeping track of their positions, marking each with a grease pencil every ten or fifteen minutes so as not to lose track of which of the yellow-green blips on his repeater represented the two ships. His first mate had been doing the same when it was his turn to man the small pilothouse.

* * *

"Whiskey Three Echo, this is Golf Bravo Two, immediate execute, Tango Alpha Eight Eight Tack One, desig Whiskey Three Echo, I say again, immediate execute, Tango Alpha Eight Eight Tack One, desig Whiskey Three Echo,...Standby, execute, over."

Lieutenant Walt Wilson reached for the tactical radio circuit handset and responded, "This is Whiskey Three Echo, roger, out."

From the 21MC speaker came the voice of Lieutenant (junior grade), Willy Kim, the CIC watch officer, "Bridge, Combat, *Biddle* just took tactical control."

"Bridge aye, bridge concurs," answered Wilson. He reached for the growler phone handle, dialed up the CO's cabin, and twisted the crank.

"Captain."

"Captain, Lieutenant Wilson sir, OOD. *Biddle* just took us under tactical control. Station assignment should be coming in a minute."

"OK, thanks, Walt. What's range and bearing to Biddle?"

"She's in Yankee, two five zero at 20,000 yards."

"OK, start heading over there at 20 knots, refine the course to station when you get it."

Putting down his pen and setting aside the letter he was writing to Karen, Tanner switched off his desk light and got up to go to the bridge. He glanced at his watch: 2100. He'd been expecting this, they were due to be down south in the morning to once again refuel from *Saratoga*. He knew they'd be able to get mail off the ship during the underway replenishment. He'd finish the letter later, once *Dauntless* had safely arrived in whatever station Roger Welsh assigned for the trip south.

As he left his stateroom, he heard the growler phone behind him. He ignored it, that would be LT Wilson with the station assignment and a recommended course to station. He'd be on the bridge in less than a minute. Getting no answer, Wilson would know he was on the way.

Arriving on the bridge, he was met by Lieutenant Wilson. His JOOD, Ensign Wilt Grimmage had his head buried in the SPA-25 radar repeater rubber light shield. Spinning the dials, he was calling out ranges and bearings to *Biddle* as they headed southwest at 20 knots.

"Got it, Walt," he said before Wilson could begin the scripted litany that was a tradition each time the captain arrived on the bridge.

"Same station as before?"

"Yessir, one-eight-zero relative, 2,000 yards. Base speed one-six."

"OK, kick it up to 25 knots, let's get over there."

Tanner climbed into the familiar starboard side chair and picked up his binoculars. Just off the bow, he saw a single white light. That would be *Biddle's* stern light he thought to himself. He settled in to watch while the watch team took station. This was a low-threat maneuver, but he enjoyed the ship handling and watching the officers at work gave him a better sense of which ones were good, and which ones bore watching.

* * *

Akram Najaf sidled over to his Furuno display and noted that the blips representing the two American ships had moved a greater distance relative to *Basra* than had been the case ten minutes earlier. Mumbling a curse, he updated the positions with the grease pencil and wrote in the hull numbers next to each blip. He had to be sure before he called Da'wud and made his report. As he watched the scope, he noted that the distance separating the two blips was narrowing. The ships were coming together, as they had done before. Looking up, he raised his binoculars but could not make out the ship's lights. *Too far away*, he said to himself. Still, he waited. It would not do to raise a false alarm and call Da'wud to the bridge if they were not actually heading out of the area.

Gradually the range opened, soon the two blips would disappear from the radar scope. His Furuno antenna was only about four meters above the water and had a limited radar horizon.

Nervously he leaned into the voice tube that led to the small galley dining area one deck below. That was where Da'wud stayed when he was not sleeping or working in the cramped space containing the special radio equipment.

"Excellency, Captain Najaf here," he tentatively called into the tube.

"What is it?" came the instant reply.

"The American ships, it appears they are departing."

"Are you sure?" growled Da'wud.

"Almost certain, Excellency, I have been closely tracking their positions by radar."

There was no reply. One minute later the pilothouse door pushed open, and Da'wud entered the bridge. He stared at the Furuno display but did not understand what he was seeing. He was no sailor. He had to rely on this halfwit Najaf.

"Show me," he demanded.

Nervously, Najaf indicated the two radar blips at the edge of the display. A series of small grease pencil dots, connected by unsteady lines, traced the relative movement of the two radar blips as they moved away to the south and gradually drew together.

"You are sure?" he repeated.

"It is the same as they have done before when leaving the area."

"Any sign of the special ship, the Aegis?"

Najaf considered his answer carefully, not wanting to offend Da'wud.

"There is no way to know for sure. This radar cannot identify ships. They all look the same, just a dot of light. We will have to wait until the sun is up to know if that ship is here."

Da'wud considered this information. The sun would not be up for at least ten hours. Time wasted if the Americans were doing what they had done before. He made a decision.

"I am going below. Notify me immediately if the Americans return."

"Yes Excellency," replied Najaf. He did not dare tell the Mukhabarat agent that once he lost track of these two, there would be no way to know for sure if they returned until morning.

Da'wud went below to the cramped hold containing the encrypted high-frequency radio set. He would send a preliminary report, alerting Baghdad and then Damascus that the Americans appeared to be leaving the aircraft carrier unprotected. Better to put them on alert now rather than wait until morning.

Damascus International Airport, Syria

Major Abdul Tikriti rubbed his eyes and glanced at his watch. Someone was banging on the door to his sleeping quarters. Four-fifteen in the morning.

"Yes, what?" he shouted at the door.

The voice of Major Muhammad Bandari came faintly from the other side, "I have a report from Baghdad. Today may be the day."

Springing out of bed, Tikriti crossed the room in two steps and jerked open the door. Bandari stood there in full uniform, holding out a piece of paper.

"You are up early Major," said Tikriti.

"I was called at midnight by Colonel Mohamed, I have been waiting for this message to come in. It did not arrive until three o'clock. It took some time to decode. I came as quickly as I could."

Tikriti snatched the paper from Bandari's hand and quickly scanned it. He frowned. It was only a warning, based on uncertain information. He considered his options. Better to prepare now... rather than delay.

"Wake the others," he ordered Bandari. "Meet in my operations room on the flight line as soon as dressed. Flight suits," he added.

Northern Red Sea

Aboard *USS Saratoga*, Captain Alexander Vanzant sat at the small fold out desk in his stateroom in the blue-tiled flag-country area. He sipped at a cup of coffee as he reread the draft letter that had been brought to him by the squadron Chief Yeoman. Picking up his red pen he made some minor edits before crossing through one complete sentence. Drawing a red arrow to the bottom of the page, he hand-wrote a revised sentence and then handed the page back to the Chief.

"One more cut Chief. Again, you type it up, I don't want anyone else reading it."

"Aye, Commodore, okay if I bring it back in the morning?"

Vanzant glanced at the brass chronometer mounted on his cabin bulkhead on a glossily stained wood plaque. Just then seven tiny bells sounded from the device, two bells, two bells, two bells, one bell. 23:30. It was almost midnight. Time to turn in after a pass through flag plot to see what was going on operationally.

"Sure Chief, see you in the morning."

Standing and arching backward to stretch his back and rolling his shoulders, Vanzant left his stateroom and headed forward, high stepping over knee knockers every twenty feet as he passed by structural frames and watertight doors. Commissioned in 1956, *Saratoga* was old, over 30 years old, her service life extended in the early 80's during a complex overhaul period in the Philadelphia Naval Shipyard.

Entering flag plot, he surprised his staff watch officer, a lieutenant commander wearing the pin of a surface warfare officer.

"Evening Commodore."

"Evening, what's the situation?"

Just then a loud crash sounded on the flight deck one level above, the scream of a jet engine audible through the steel deck. Glancing at the PLAT camera mounted on the bulkhead, he watched as an F-14 Tomcat coasted slightly backward, raised its tail hook, and dropped the arresting cable that had brought it to a stop on the flight deck. Lights blinking, the jet taxied out of the landing area to make room for his wingman, on final approach two miles behind the carrier.

"That's the CAP coming in Commodore. One more and then the E-2. No more flight ops tonight and tomorrow is a no-fly day."

Vanzant frowned, although it would be easier to sleep without the aircraft taking off and landing all night long, he did not agree with Admiral McCall, Captain Reasoner, and CAG, that securing flight ops at midnight was smart. He felt that they were becoming complacent, secure in the knowledge that the Iraqis would not fly at night and, in any case, did not have the reach to threaten the Red Sea ships. He could understand CAG and the CO wanting a no-fly day, the aircraft needed routine maintenance, and the flight deck crews had been working day and night since the carrier arrived in the Red Sea. Still, he felt Admiral McCall had given in too quickly. *Seen it before*, he thought to himself, a surface warfare admiral felt pressure to accede to the professional opinions of his aviator subordinates when it came to the operation of the air wing. Still, sometimes you have to assert yourself. *McCall is a little too accommodating*.

"How about MIO?"

"No customers right now sir. *Biddle* and *Dauntless* have left station and are 50 miles north on the way here to refuel tomorrow.

When they get to 20 miles, *Biddle* will pick up Alpha Whiskey from *Phil Sea,* and she'll head north."

"What's the latest on the French?"

"Left Djibouti this morning sir and on the way north; should get here day after tomorrow. *Sara* should be done playing gas station after tomorrow's unrep."

"All right, I'm turning in. Give me a call when Alpha Whiskey shifts to *Biddle* and when they report in to shotgun *Sara.*"

Vanzant headed back to his stateroom, thinking and re-thinking the letter of instruction that he had been drafting for Commander Will Tanner. Once he was satisfied in the morning, he'd have it sent over with the pallets of mail that would be delivered to both *Biddle* and *Dauntless* during the underway replenishment. The letter was designed to officially advise Tanner of his shortcomings in command. It was a formal counseling tool which was not supposed to be part of Tanner's official record. Presumably, it was just between Tanner and Vanzant. He had not informed Admiral McCall of his intent to write the letter, partly because he felt McCall would disapprove. Besides, as the admiral had noted, Tanner was under his tactical command, how he dealt with a subordinate was his business and his alone. For some reason the admiral had been protective of Tanner, excusing his transgressions. Vanzant was under no obligation beyond professional courtesy to tell McCall what he was doing. If at some future date Tanner did something so egregious that he had to be relieved or formally reprimanded, the letter of instruction would serve as proof that Vanzant had given him every chance to improve his performance.

* * *

Seven frames forward of flag-country, Lieutenant Commander Chuck 'Boomer' Schoonhower, made a notation on the VF-74 flight schedule and handed it back to the duty yeoman, "Go smooth and then post it," he directed the young petty officer. Schoonhower was the Operations Officer for the *Be-Devilers* of VF-74, an F-14 Tomcat squadron assigned to Carrier Air Wing 7. The E-2 had just recovered on the flight deck one level above his head. He could hear the twin propellers churning up on deck as the pilot taxied the Hawkeye into position just aft of the island where it would sit for the night. Flight ops were over for the night and tomorrow was a no-fly day. Glancing at the ready room status board, he made a note of the line-up for his Alert 15 air crews for the next 36 hours. He had assigned himself to the afternoon Alert 15 along with his radar intercept officer, or RIO, Lieutenant Kevin "Snake" Gardner. His Alert 15 wingmen in Devil Two would be pilot Lieutenant Mike "Wilbur" Wright and RIO Lieutenant Steve "Suds" Brewer.

Schoonhower reflected on the operations up to this point; pretty boring he thought to himself. All the real work was being done by the black shoes, stopping and boarding the ships going into and out of Aqaba. The air wing had been flying CAP missions and once in a while supporting a boarding when no helicopter was available to circle the ship, count crewmembers on deck, and keep an eye out for an ambush. They had conducted some exercises, war at sea strikes and air-to-air engagements, but so far Operation Desert Shield was pretty boring. CAG had told them the CAP was necessary just in case some kind of air attack happened, but everybody knew it was highly improbable. Every day that went by the Air Force build-up in Saudi Arabia continued, and the chance of the Iraqis trying something in the Red Sea grew more and more unlikely. The real deal would begin if and when Saddam Hussein refused to leave Kuwait and the coalition moved forward to forcibly liberate that country. Then things would get interesting. *If* that happened.

He decided to get some sleep, the *Jolly Rogers* of VF-103 would man the Alert 15 CAP through the night, his squadron would pick it up at 0800 tomorrow morning. Alert 15 meant that aircraft were positioned on the catapults, ready for a quick launch, but the pilots could sit in the ready room, suited up, awaiting the call. When it came, they would sprint to the flight deck, climb into their aircraft with the assistance of the crew chief, and be ready to launch, all within 15 minutes. It was a pain in the ass, but better than alert five, which meant sitting in the airplane in the hot sun.

* * *

Commander Will Tanner took a last look at the radar picture on the SPA-25 repeater and then glanced forward through the bridge window. Ahead at one nautical mile was the glow of *Biddle's* stern light. No other lights were visible. *Dauntless* was sailing south on a calm sea in *Biddle's* wake at 16 knots. One other contact was visible on the radar scope, Skunk Tango, 18,000 yards to the east, heading north at 14 knots. Alpha Sierra hadn't designated a ship to query this one yet. Judging from the other ship's position, course, and speed, it would probably be assigned to *Spruance* in Three Rivers.

He turned to Lieutenant Chris Palmer who had just taken over for the midwatch from Walt Wilson, "Chris, I'm going below, give me a wake-up call at 0600. Let me know if anything changes."

"Aye Captain, good night."

Passing through CIC, he saw that Andy Morton had taken the watch as TAO. A stack of message folders, service records, and correspondence folders sat on the desk in front of him. Morton sat facing aft, surrounded by sailors monitoring consoles and wearing sound-powered phone headsets. The CIC Officer, Lieutenant (junior grade) Willy Kim hovered over the Dead Reckoning

Tracer, watching two operations specialists plot the positions of *Dauntless*, *Biddle*, and Skunk Tango. *Montgomery* and *Spruance* were no longer in radar range to the north, and they had not yet closed *Saratoga* and *Philippine Sea* enough for them to appear. It was shaping up to be a quiet watch.

"How's it going Ops?" he said, approaching the table.

Morton put down the report he had been editing and turned to his captain.

"All quiet, sir. Flight ops are secured on *Sara*, only one contact, Tango, at 18,000 yards, headed north. We're on station astern of *Biddle*. Mount 51 is the ready mount."

"OK, thanks, Ops, er, XO, I'm headed down to get some shuteye. Who's your relief in the morning?"

"Weps, sir."

"OK, good, tell him I want to conduct a PACFIRE in the morning, both mounts. We'll do it around nine before the unrep starts. Let *Biddle* and Alpha Sierra know."

"Got it, sir, same as before, use the RF and VT?"

"Yes, I want the fire control team to get used to that set up. Might as well offload through the barrel, that much less to do when this is over."

Morton grinned and nodded. Whenever this Desert Shield operation ended, *Dauntless* would head back to Mayport and begin preparations for decommissioning. That would include a trip up the Cooper River to the Naval Weapons Station in Charleston, South Carolina to offload all the ammunition. Everything would have to go, five-inch rounds, missiles, torpedoes, ASROCs and small arms. The less they had in the magazines, the quicker it would go. Tanner could justify the expenditure as necessary to train his crew and ensure the five-inch guns were ready for action. PACFIRE stood for pre-action calibration, a way to warm up the gun barrels and assess how tight the fire control system was.

"Roger sir, I'll make sure everyone knows."

Turning to leave, Tanner reconsidered, turning back he signaled for Morton to follow him out of CIC. Pausing in the passageway between CIC and the Bridge, he said, "You talk to Commander McKnight lately?"

"Yessir, earlier today. I had a question on that Golden Anchor input I sent you this evening." Tanner nodded, the Golden Anchor was a competition between ships that had achieved good sailor retention statistics. It required a glowing write-up to augment the statistics themselves, explaining all the initiatives that the ship had undertaken to encourage its crew to re-enlist. The fact that *Dauntless* was not scheduled to deploy and would be decommissioning the following year had, ironically, motivated some sailors who were on the fence to re-enlist.

"How's he doing?"

"He's ready to go, sir. We didn't talk much."

"OK, thanks, see you in the morning."

SIXTEEN

Northern Red Sea

The sun rose bright and hot as Will Tanner walked out to the bridge, a fresh cup of wardroom coffee in his hand, and took the report from his OOD, Lieutenant John Woodson.

"Morning Captain, we're on course one-six-zero at thirteen knots. *Biddle* up ahead at 2,000 yards, *Saratoga* ahead of them at 4,000 yards. This will be Romeo Corpen and speed. *Biddle* goes alongside first at eleven-hundred. We're next. After the unrep, we head back to Fenway just like last week."

Captain Roger Welsh in *Biddle* had put *Dauntless* in a loose column astern at 2,000 yards as they transited south for the underway replenishment. Earlier that morning they had passed *Philippine Sea* headed north for the MIO station. *Biddle* had assumed duties as Alpha Whiskey.

"No change to the carrier flight plan?"

"No sir, today is a no-fly day. They've got two CAP at Alert Fifteen."

Tanner hopped into his port bridge wing chair to read the morning message traffic and soak up the warm rays of the morning sun. It was shaping up to be another beautiful, early September day in the Red Sea. The transit south from Fenway in company with *Biddle* had been uneventful. He was glad that Roger Welsh in *Biddle* was assigning *Dauntless* a station for these transits as it was good station-keeping training for the junior officers standing watch.

He paused a few moments to enjoy the view from the port bridge wing. The sea was like a lake, incredibly calm. The sun, low in the eastern sky, colored the water a bronze-like hue. Looking over the port bow, he watched as three flying fish sped away from the ship, their tails creating a small wake as they stroked away from the ship and then glided clear.

Andy Morton walked through the bridge and joined Tanner on the port bridge wing.

"Morning Captain, I've been relieved as TAO, Weps has the morning watch." The three tactical action officers had been standing six-hour watches, six on in CIC and twelve off to sleep, eat, and attend to their other duties. Morton had been on since midnight.

"Thanks, Ops, anything hot in the traffic?"

"No, sir. Best news is that the French left Djibouti and are on the way north. Should get here tomorrow. *Durance* will stay south in the vicinity of *Saratoga*, but *Cassard* will join the MIO forces up north. Alpha Sierra is setting up a new box for them, Stade Velodrome," he said, grinning.

Tanner smiled, "Clever of them." Stade Velodrome was the French football stadium in Marseille.

Morton put on his acting XO hat, "Schedule calls for *Biddle* to go alongside at eleven-hundred. We'll set lifeguard detail then and unrep detail about an hour into *Biddle's* unrep. Weps says the rigs are all set. After station checks out. Weps has the word on the PACFIRE, and he's getting his people ready."

In the disruption over McKnight's relief, the refueling probe investigation he was to spearhead had fallen by the wayside. Vinny DeVito had taken over and between himself, Chief Wise, and Wilton Grimmage, they had discovered a damaged flange where the probe collar rested against the inside of the receiving horn. It had caused the probe collar to get trapped on the inside of the bent portion, preventing it from unseating normally when the handle was tripped.

"Good. Who's driving for this one?"

"Willy Kim. He hasn't made an approach yet, and he really didn't get to do the breakaway last time," said Morton with a sly look at his captain.

Tanner just nodded, a smile playing at the corners of his mouth, "No he didn't, did he. Probably just as happy."

Morton laughed, "Sir, I'm going below, get some breakfast."

"Before you go, Andy, everything set for Commander McKnight to leave?"

"Yessir, Sara will send a helo over once we break away and head north."

* * *

In his stateroom, Ricky McKnight thanked the young seaman who had delivered his scrambled eggs, toast and bacon from the wardroom. The past three days had been pure hell. He was all packed up, ready to leave the ship. Those items too bulky to carry were boxed up to be shipped back to Mayport. He had remained in his stateroom, leaving only to use the head down the passageway and delaying his daily shower until mid-morning when the other officers in after-officer's country would be out and about, standing watches or administering to their assigned duties.

The Captain had come down to see him once, to inform him that arrangements were being made to transfer him home to be "stashed" at DESRON 12 while his future in the Navy was decided. Tanner had handed him his copy of the formal letter of reprimand that would become a permanent part of his service record. He had also delivered an unsatisfactory report of fitness coincident with his relief from duties, recommending that he not be promoted to commander and that he not be screened for ship command. He had taken the letter of reprimand, not reading it until the captain had left. He had signed the fitness report after glancing at the marks and reading the damning words which would surely end his career.

He both dreaded and eagerly awaited the time when he was to leave *Dauntless*. First would be the humiliating walk to the flight deck while he awaited the helicopter. Then, arriving on the *Saratoga* flight deck, he was sure that everyone he encountered would know why he was there, what had happened. Finally, would come the arrival in Jacksonville and check in to the squadron. He would be assigned a desk, maybe given some trivial duties to keep him busy. Again, everyone would know he had been fired, kicked off the ship. Part of him wanted to blame Theresa for this; her unhappiness with the Navy, the Dear John letter. How would he explain this to his parents? His father had served a full career in the Navy, retiring as a captain and having commanded two ships. He would be hard to bullshit. He would know something was wrong no matter what McKnight told him. Ships didn't just send their XO home without a full tour and in the middle of an important deployment. He would try convince his father that he had tired of the Navy and had asked to leave in order to try save his marriage. He had yet to write them and tell them about the impending divorce. That was going to be messy too. He would play the two off each other, the divorce over Theresa's unhappiness with the life of a Navy wife, his decision a noble gesture to put his marriage ahead of a promising career. He shook his head, no way this would fool the old man. He was too savvy, he would smell a rat. He might even have some of his contacts from active duty days dig into the real reason he was leaving the ship and the Navy. It seemed hopeless, but he would stick to his story, power through. McKnight picked at his breakfast. How much longer? He reread the POD, signed by Andy Morton. Unrep around 12:30, followed by flight quarters for "personnel transfer." Probably be around 14:30 he thought to himself. *Can't come too soon.*

* * *

As the sun rose over the rugged coast of Saudi Arabia to the east, Akram Najaf eagerly scanned the horizon with his binoculars. He had not slept. He did not trust his first mate with the responsibility of identifying the Aegis. He had carefully monitored the radar, and acting on his own initiative he had positioned *Basra* even further to the east, directly south of the Strait of Tiran. He had also moved further south, away from the strait and closer to the direction from which the American ship would come. If it came. He had studied the photograph taped to the bulkhead at the rear of the pilothouse. He had seen the Aegis the last time. It was easy to identify. With a big, boxy superstructure, it looked nothing like the other American ships. Still, he must be sure. Earlier he had seen a radar contact appear at the outer edge of his Furuno scope. It was moving north and should come into view soon. Straining his eyes, he focused the binoculars in the direction of this new contact. Over the bridge-to-bridge radio, he heard an American voice calling out the familiar words of a challenge to some innocent merchant ship, minding its own business. *The sons of camels.*

Re-checking the radar picture, he saw that the ship number 963 was near the blip he had seen earlier. So, that was not the special ship. It still had not appeared. But the other two were gone, they had not reappeared after sailing out of radar range last night. He would stay alert; the special ship must be coming north later today. He would be sure before he called Da'wud.

Damascus International Airport, Syria

The same sun rose over the desert to the east of Damascus International Airport, dancing in the hazy heat as it climbed above the horizon. Major Abdul Tikriti smoked a cigarette as he watched the sun rise. If he had been more devout, he would have placed his prayer rug in the appropriate position and said his morning prayers. In the far distance, on the opposite side of the runways, on the civilian side, he heard the morning call to prayer carrying across.

His flight had gathered in the revetment housing his Mirage jet at five in the morning. His wingmen, El-Amin and Tawfeek, were wide awake, alert, sensing that action was close. Bandari, on the other hand, had been drowsy, nodding off. He was not used to staying up all night. At six, Tikriti dispatched him to Colonel Asmeh's offices to await the next missive from Baghdad. The next one was all-important, it would either confirm that the aircraft carrier was vulnerable and the mission was a go, or it would order a stand down to await the right time.

He turned and for the umpteenth time that morning and asked the Syrian crew chief if his Mirage jet was fully ready to fly. He was assured it was. He once again circled the aircraft, looking for discrepancies and patting the two five-meter long, 670-kilogram Exocet missiles, one hanging under each wing. He glanced with disapproval at the centerline auxiliary fuel tank suspended under the fuselage. After calculating and re-calculating the attack route, they had reluctantly concluded that without the drop tank, they were in danger of flaming out before reaching their target. His squadron commander, Colonel Mohamed, had dispatched the three fuel tanks by truck to Damascus. They would burn the fuel in the auxiliary tanks first, and then jettison them over the Saudi desert. This would ensure adequate fuel for the attack and also enhance their chances of evading and recovering in Egypt. Satisfied that his aircraft was ready, he headed to the adjoining revetments to once again assure himself of the readiness of his wingmen. His stomach churned, something told him that today would be the day. Operation Birds of Prey would soon launch.

Entering the adjacent revetment, he saw El-Amin and Tawfeek studying the aviation charts and reviewing the intelligence reports which had been arriving daily from Baghdad.

They looked up expectantly as Tikriti entered. Tikriti looked pointedly at El-Amin's jet.

"All is ready?" he inquired.

"Yes brother," answered El-Amin, "we are reviewing the route. Also studying the latest intelligence. It appears the Americans have increased their operations in Saudi Arabia."

Tikriti sensed that his wingmen were uncomfortable.

"Yes," he looked from face to face, sensing that El-Amin was holding back, "go on," he urged.

El-Amin, cleared his throat, shifting on his feet. Looking first at Tawfeek he fixed Tikriti with a hard stare.

"Brother, I am concerned that the American air activity is too intense. They will see our flight and investigate. We will be intercepted at the Saudi border." He looked imploringly at Tikriti and then continued, "without air-to-air weapons we are defenseless."

Tikriti held up a hand, "Stop. Do you not think that we have considered this? General Saddam Hussein has planned a diversion."

Both pilots exchanged a glance and looked expectantly at Tikriti. El-Amin spoke for them both, "What is this diversion?"

"Do not worry," replied Tikriti, "the details are not important but have faith, the Americans will have no time to worry about our flight once the diversion begins."

Northern Red Sea

Leaning against the pilothouse window sill, Akram Najaf, jerked awake as his head dipped toward his chest. Catching himself, he opened his eyes into bright sunlight. He was so tired he had fallen asleep on his feet. Praise be to Allah, Da'wud had not found him dozing. He looked at the chronometer bolted to the bulkhead above the chart table; 7:40 AM. He turned once again to the

Furuno radar picture. Suddenly, he was wide awake. A new blip appeared on the scope only 15 kilometers distant. How long had he dozed? He looked at the grease pencil marks on the American ships 963 and 1082. Nine six three had not moved, it was near the other ship he had seen earlier, the one they were boarding. But 1082 was a significant distance from his last mark. He must have been dozing for at least half an hour.

Quickly raising his binoculars, he looked in the direction that the radar told him the new ship should be. He saw it, the unmistakable top mast of a warship. But was it the Aegis, or one of the others from last night returning? He looked at the pictures taped to the bulkhead. The masts were too similar to tell at this range.

He heard the pilothouse door open and turned as Da'wud entered.

"Excellency, I was just about to call you," lied Najaf.

"What is it?" demanded Da'wud.

"I see a warship approaching, at this distance I cannot identify it."

"You fool, turn toward it, close the distance. We cannot afford to waste time if it is the Aegis ship."

"Yes, Excellency, immediately."

Grabbing the wheel, Najaf turned *Basra* in the direction of the approaching ship and pushed the throttle forward. The ship shuddered as the diesel engine roared and a cloud of black smoke poured from the single stack rising above the small superstructure. A loud cracking noise came from the after deck as *Basra* struggled to gain speed.

"The nets," exclaimed Najaf. In his haste he had not considered the large seine net dragging uselessly behind the boat, acting as a giant sea anchor, and impeding progress.

Da'wud grabbed the binoculars from Najaf's hands. "Release them, now!" he demanded.

Najaf hesitated only a second. Leaning into the voice tube, he shouted for his first mate to release the nets.

Da'wud was peering intently at the approaching ship. It was not moving swiftly, but gradually more of the mast came into view followed by a large dome-like structure and the beginning of the superstructure itself. He looked back at the pictures. Yes, it appeared to be the Aegis. Turning back to the window he focused intently on the approaching ship. Gradually more superstructure came into view and then he was sure; it was the Aegis.

Turning to Najaf, he shouted, "Turn away now, we must not arouse suspicion. Head for the coast. I need time to radio Baghdad!"

As Da'wud hurried from the pilothouse, Najaf spun the wheel hard-left and began to turn *Basra* back to the north, away from the approaching cruiser. He felt the boat lurch unusually and then start to gain speed. Moments later the first mate stuck his head inside the pilothouse door on the port side.

"It is done," he said, "the net and all the wire from the drums, all gone. Now what?"

Najaf merely shook his head. "Take the wheel, steer for the strait at best speed. Pray for us."

In the cramped space below decks, Mahmod Da'wud transmitted his coded message on the prescribed high-frequency band. *Praise be to Allah*; Operation Birds of Prey had begun.

* * *

One-hundred and twenty miles to the south *USS Dauntless* sailed on a southeasterly heading, trailing *USS Biddle* at one nautical mile. *Biddle*, in turn, trailed *USS Saratoga*, again at one nautical mile.

Will Tanner leaned into the 21MC and selected the TAO station, "TAO, Captain, report when manned and ready for PACFIRE."

"TAO, aye," answered Lieutenant Commander Vinny DeVito, "getting the OK from Alpha Sierra now, all stations manned and ready, planning five rounds each from Mounts 51 and 52. Two rounds single fire from each mount, followed by three rounds rapid continuous, both mounts. All rounds alternating, HE-RF and HE-VT."

Andy Morton, standing next to Tanner, lowered his binoculars, "Biddle has her mount out to starboard," he reported.

Once *Dauntless* had requested permission to conduct a PACFIRE while awaiting time for the underway replenishment, Captain Roger Welsh in *Biddle* had decided he would do the same. Although *Biddle* was a more capable missile ship than *Dauntless* with her extended range SM-2 Terrier missile system, she had only one five-inch gun mount, located on the fantail.

DeVito called out from CIC, "Green range from Alpha Sierra."

"Captain aye, batteries released, five rounds Mounts 51 and 52, HE-RF and VT."

They watched as Mount 51 swung out to starboard, the train warning bell ringing. Tanner and Morton stayed inside the pilothouse with the starboard bridge wing door closed, the experience from the first test round of the barrage fire tactic fresh in their minds.

Ahead, they saw a puff of smoke from *Biddle's* gun mount and a second later, heard the dull thud as the sound carried across the distance between the two ships. Morton looked off to starboard and saw the splash about four miles to the west.

"Looks like they're shooting BL and P," he announced.

A telltale clanking sound came from Mount 51 as the breech block slammed shut, followed a split-second later by a loud bang as the mount fired. Two seconds later a black airburst exploded just above the ocean surface a mile away.

"Airburst," announced Morton into the 21MC.

"That was RF," reported DeVito.

A second later Mount 52 fired. Another airburst at approximately one mile.

"VT," came the report from the TAO.

Up ahead, *Biddle* continued firing her gun mount in slow fire mode using the inert BL and P training rounds.

Tanner leaned into the 21MC bitch box, "TAO, Captain, shift to rapid continuous."

"TAO, aye."

Five seconds later both gun mounts opened up, the rounds exiting the barrels at three second intervals. Paint flecks flew off the overhead and bulkheads from the shock and vibration. A mile to the west, six airbursts, and two surface hits shredded the water in rapid succession.

"Ten rounds expended, Mounts 51 and 52, bores clear, no casualties," announced DeVito over the 21MC.

"Captain, aye, cease fire," replied the Captain, "looks like we got six airbursts and two on the surface. Can you figure out which rounds didn't get an airburst?"

"Standby, checking with Sky One."

Sky One was the Mark 37 director officer, Ensign Wally Sloan. Sloan had been prepared to count rounds and using a check sheet with the load sequence from each mount, figure out which shots hit the water without fuzing.

"Best as Guns can tell, Captain, both rounds that failed to fuze were VT. Hard to say in rapid fire mode."

"Captain, aye," he turned to Morton, "Not surprised, the fuze setter has to work fast in rapid fire mode."

"Big splash of water may be just as good as an airburst against a low-flying missile like Exocet," replied Morton.

"Good point," said Tanner, "secure from PACFIRE, I'm headed below until we set lifeguard detail."

* * *

On *Saratoga's* flag bridge Captain Alexander Vanzant lowered his binoculars and turned to Admiral McCall, "There he goes again," he frowned.

McCall frowned back, "How so?"

"All they asked for was permission to PACFIRE the five-inch, not put on a fire power demonstration."

"I liked it," replied McCall, "You can see what he's doing. That was a pretty impressive wall of flak they put up."

"That's not the point Admiral," fumed Vanzant, "he should have made it clear what his intent was when he made the request, to begin with. It's part of a pattern. I'm never sure what I'm gonna get with this guy."

Rear Admiral McCall fixed Vanzant with a frustrated look, "Al, I like his initiative. He's thinking out of the box. Figuring out ways to deal with potential threats. Isn't that what you want from your commanding officers?"

Vanzant looked at his feet and then back at the admiral, "Sure, but he owes his chain of command the courtesy of advising us of his intentions, not springing surprises all the time."

McCall paused and looking Vanzant directly in the eye, vented, "Al, you've had a hard-on for Commander Tanner ever since we sailed. As far as I can see he's doing a fine job in command. What's your beef?"

"He's damaged goods, Admiral. You know about the collision on *Wade*. I don't know who his sea daddy is, but he should have been censured over the collision and never screened for command."

"But he wasn't," answered McCall, "the board of inquiry did not find him at fault. And a duly chartered selection board promoted him to commander. Another board screened him for command. He's been vetted by the system and given command."

McCall paused, considering his next words.

"Al, you may not agree with all that, but there he is," pointing aft vaguely in the direction of the two ships trailing *Saratoga*, "Time for you to exercise some positive leadership. Work with Tanner. Let him know your concerns in a measured way. Give him the chance to measure up."

Vanzant nodded, thinking about the letter of instruction sitting on his desk, ready for his signature. He decided not to mention it to McCall.

"Aye, aye Admiral. I'll handle it."

"And while you're at it," added McCall, "find out how they put up that wall of flak. Seems to me that's something to be shared with the other ships, especially those without a missile system."

SEVENTEEN

Damascus International Airport, Syria

Major Muhammed Bandari ripped the coded message off the teletype machine in the secure communications office of Colonel Bashir Asmeh, Damascus Military Airfield Commander. Hurrying past the sergeant manning the office he almost ran to the small cubicle which had been set aside for his use by the Syrians. The message was thankfully brief, only a few characters. Fumbling with the dial on the small safe next to the desk, he opened the door and withdrew a red envelope containing the decoding template. Working feverishly, he began decoding the message. Before he was halfway finished, he knew, Operation Birds of Prey was a go.

Finishing the decoding, he reread the entire message. It was on. Time was of the essence. The Aegis ship was no longer with the carrier. For how long, nobody knew. At least a day, maybe two, if past experience was any indicator. Bandari knew, however, that they could not count on anything. They must launch as soon as possible.

Racing to Colonel Asmeh's office he burst in, waving the decoded message in his right hand. The sergeant at his desk in the outer office rose as if to stop him but was too late. Without knocking, Bandari, pushed open the door, startling the colonel who was gently dipping his tea bag in a delicate blue and white China tea cup.

"Eminence, sir," exclaimed Bandari, "it is time. Please clear our jets for launch. I must talk to Major Tikriti immediately."

Asmeh, raised his hand as if to fend off the excited Iraqi major, "Calm down Major. Let me see that."

"Please," beseeched Bandari, "I must get word to Major Tikriti immediately. I need a car."

Asmeh stood and took the paper from Bandari's hand. Glancing quickly at the text, he gave it back to the major and shouted to the sergeant, now standing helplessly in the doorway, "Get me the Iraqi pilot, now, and order a car to take Major Bandari to the hangars."

Turning to Bandari, he said, "Go, I will tell the major you are on the way."

As Bandari hurried out of the room, the light on Asmeh's phone flashed on, blinking. Picking up the receiver, he announced, "Colonel Asmeh."

"Major Tikriti, sir."

"Ahh, Major. Your assistant is on the way with the message you have been waiting for. I will make the necessary arrangements with the tower."

"Praise be to Allah, thank you, Colonel," said Tikriti.

"Good luck and good hunting," replied Asmeh, setting the receiver back in the cradle. Worriedly, he considered the events about to unfold. No doubt the Americans would figure out that the attack had been facilitated by the Syrians. The defection cover story would not withstand scrutiny. What then? This would be a major betrayal of the coalition, especially if the attack succeeded and Americans were killed, the carrier sunk or damaged. He began considering his options, perhaps a trip to Paris was in order.

Tikriti replaced the handset and crossed the tarmac to the center of the three revetments. El-Amin was under the starboard wing of his jet, inspecting the Exocet missile slung underneath.

"Get Tawfeek, come to my office," he ordered.

When the three pilots were gathered, Tikriti informed them that Operation Birds of Prey was about to launch. They waited for Bandari with the decoded message.

An old staff car screeched to a halt on the tarmac outside. Major Bandari scrambled out of the back seat and rushed into the revetment.

"Here it is sir, the conditions are set for the attack."

Without a word, Tikriti snatched the paper from Bandari's hand. Skimming it, he looked up and met his fellow pilot's eyes.

"Man your jets, we attack today. You are ready, execute the plan as we have briefed it."

Without hesitation, the two wingmen grinned and sprinted to their jets. Handing the message back to Bandari along with a slip of paper pulled from his flight suit shoulder pocket, Tikriti instructed the portly staff officer, "Go to my office and telephone Baghdad at this number. Inform them as soon as the last jet has left the ground. This is very important. Do not fail me."

With that, Tikriti turned on his heel and went to the ladder on the port side of his Mirage jet. He had not told Bandari why the phone call was important. The fool knew too much already. If the diversion were to be effective, the timing had to be right. Mounting the ladder, he settled into the cockpit as his Syrian plane captain handed him his helmet and double checked his harness, oxygen, ejection seat, and communications connections.

When the technician had the start cart properly configured, he fired up the engine and waited while the air compressor built pressure. With his cockpit raised, Tikriti heard El-Amin's turbojet engine cough once and then begin to spin up.

At the technician's signal, he pushed the starter and felt his Atar 9k-50 engine come to life. Checking his instruments, he saw all systems in the green. With a thumb's up, he signaled his crew chief to disconnect the starter power. Releasing the brakes, he taxied forward once all exterior connections were clear. The crew chief held up the red flags which indicated that the two Exocet missiles were no longer locked into the safe position. His jet was armed and ready.

Taxiing onto the tarmac, he turned left past the revetment containing El-Amin's jet. With a gesture, El-Amin indicated his readiness to launch. Once Tikriti's aircraft had passed, El-Amin taxied his plane onto the tarmac with a salute to his crew chief. The same sequence was repeated as first Tikriti, and then El-Amin passed the revetment housing Tawfeek's jet.

Taxiing to the southern end of runway zero two, he received clearance for takeoff from the dual use Damascus International Airport tower. Colonel Asmeh had been true to his word.

With one last check of his instruments, Tikriti cycled his control surfaces, powered up his engine and released his brakes. As he raced down the runway and rotated his jet into the air, he felt the exhilaration of flight once again after too long on the ground. Clearing out to the northeast, he looked over his shoulder and saw his wingmen lifting off and rapidly closing on his jet.

As his wingmen closed into close trail formation, Tikriti checked out of Damascus departure control and switched on his Identification, Friend or Foe, or IFF, transponder which he had disabled for takeoff. Activating Mode 3A, he spun the finger wheels to 4387, a deliberately false identifier, which identified his jet as a commercial airliner to anyone with an IFF transponder; most importantly, the American Air Force over Saudi Arabia.

Climbing to 30,000 feet, the three jets flew in close formation for 30 minutes before exiting Syrian airspace and entering Iraqi airspace. Turning southeast, the flight paralleled the Jordanian border, remaining inside Iraq. Unlike the night they had simulated defecting Iraqi pilots, this time no Jordanian air defense systems lit them up, the commercial air IFF code emanating from Tikriti's jet satisfying the operators that they were seeing a commercial flight crossing far western Iraq and heading somewhere in Saudi Arabia.

Northeastern Saudi Arabia

Twenty thousand feet over the western Saudi desert, Captain Erick "Jeb" Stewart studied his display as he sat sideways in the tubular fuselage of his E3A Sentry AWACS airborne warning and control surveillance aircraft. Pressing his intercom button, he transmitted on the internal coordination circuit, "Major, got what looks like commair over western Iraq. Mode 3, headed southeast."

"Roger," replied Major Paul 'Bwana' Breedlove, his surveillance supervisor and mission commander for this flight, "got skin?"

"Negative, no skin, too far away. Angels 30, speed three-five-zero."

"Rog, keep an eye on him. On a commair route?"

Stewart consulted his chart overlay.

"Not really. Guess he could have come from up north, Aleppo, maybe Turkey. There's a route across from Damascus to Arar and then on to Riyadh, but he's north of that. Heading looks like Arar."

Breedlove considered the report. It was mid-morning, nothing going on, maybe he'd send a section of CAP down there to investigate. He had two sections of F-16 and two sections of F-15 up and patrolling along the border between Iraq and Saudi Arabia. Had to watch the fuel though. Burn up a bunch on a wild goose chase and the CAP would have to go off station to tank.

"OK, Jeb, watch him a little longer, see if he continues toward the Saudi border. Probably just some raghead pilot doesn't know how to follow the air routes."

Stewart chuckled, the major was probably right. He'd be able to get some radar return pretty soon if they continued to close the border. He shifted his scan away from the unknown aircraft and checked the positions of his CAP and the two sections of Iraqi CAP up over eastern Iraq. All looked routine.

Shifting back to the unknown aircraft he saw that he was beginning to get intermittent radar return as it approached the Saudi border. He squinted at the screen, leaning in and adjusting his glasses.

"Sir, starting to get paint on four three eight seven," he reported, "about to cross over into Saudi airspace."

Breedlove acknowledged the report. Their guidance was to intercept any aircraft crossing into Saudi airspace from Iraq or Kuwait, but their focus was much further east, south of Baghdad, around Kuwait. There was nothing of importance way out in western Saudi Arabia, just empty desert and Bedouins. He focused his own display on track 4387.

Stewart's voice came over the intercom, "Bwana, maybe it's the range, but 4387 is breaking up, getting more than one return."

"I'm looking at it," responded Breedlove. Making up his mind he said, "Take control of Viper Four and send them down to take a look."

Switching to another intercom channel Breedlove called the cockpit, "Hoser, Bwana, take us some more to the east, I've got a contact squawking commair just crossing into Saudi airspace, need to get a closer look."

"Roger," responded Captain Kevin 'Hoser' Mueller, the aircraft commander.

Breedlove refocused on the unknown track, listening as Stewart broke off the westernmost section of two F-16s, Viper 4, and sent them on an intercept course toward 4387.

* * *

Two-hundred and fifty miles west, Major Abdul Tikriti checked his charts and then his watch. He was over the border into Saudi airspace on a heading toward the western Saudi city of Arar. He scanned the sky for enemy aircraft. Flying without radar so as not to give away his identity he was reliant on his eagle sharp eyes. The morning sun was directly in the direction the Americans were most likely to come from if they detected him. If that fool Bandari had done his job correctly, General Saddam would soon give the Americans something more important to worry about. Glancing over his shoulder, he saw that El-Amin had drifted back, spreading out the formation too much. Sending the pre-arranged signal so as not to break radio silence, he dipped his left wing twice, the signal to close up the formation.

* * *

Watching his display and listening on the fighter control circuit, Breedlove saw the section of F-16s depart their lazy orbit and go buster, full afterburner, off to the west to intercept 4387.

"Seven minutes to intercept," came Stewart's voice over the intercom.

Breedlove acknowledged, hooking the two fighters on his display and checking their fuel state. Afterburner would eat it up in a hurry.

Turning his attention back to the bigger picture, he was taken aback. Eight contacts were climbing out of Al-Asad Air Base, west of Baghdad, heading southeast toward Kuwait and the Saudi border. He hesitated, watching the tracks continue to climb out and head south-east. Hooking the closest target, he saw it was at 550 knots.

"Eagle, Winston, Single Group, BRAA 300 for 140, hot bogey."

The track numbers were fed to the fighters via the Link-16 data link. He watched as the Iraqi aircraft rapidly sped southeast toward the border. It appeared that the two sections of Iraqi airborne CAP were maneuvering to intercept the eight aircraft that had launched from Al-Asad. *Shit*, he thought to himself, *this could be it*! Now a dozen Iraqi aircraft, undoubtedly fighters, were streaking toward the Saudi border.

"Jeb, break off Viper 4! Vector to intercept track number 3356!"

Stewart was following the action on his display, "Roger, WILCO!"

At a closing speed of 1,400 knots, the American and Iraqi aircraft raced toward each other. It looked like the fight was on at last. But only if the Iraqis crossed the border. His rules of engagement, or ROE, forbade the American aircraft from crossing into Iraqi airspace and forbade attacking an aircraft until it had penetrated into Saudi airspace.

* * *

Checking his watch, Tikriti wagged his wings, once to starboard, once to port, and then again to starboard. He turned due south and began to descend. El-Amin and Tawfeek followed him around and down to the new course. Dropping steadily, he switched off his IFF transponder when they reached 5,000 feet. Fuel consumption would be much greater in the heavier air at 5,000 feet, but they were still on the drop tanks. When that supply was exhausted, they'd jettison them and rely on internal fuel for the rest of the mission. He checked his chart once again. The rugged mountain range which defined the border between Jordan and Saudi Arabia was just off his nose to the west. They would soon pass over the Al Jowf region and then Tabuk. Duba, on the Red Sea coast, was 300 miles ahead. One hour at this speed.

* * *

Major Paul Breedlove worriedly watched the two groups of fighters approach each other as he radioed his report to the Combined Air Operations Center at Al-Kharj.

"Chariot, Winston, am vectoring CAP to intercept multiple bogeys, heading one five zero, Mach point eight. Range one eight five. Recommend launch alerts. Bogeys remain inside Iraq airspace, over."

"Winston, Chariot, roger all, we see em' in the link. Remain inside Saudi airspace, weapons tight, confirm, over."

"Chariot, Winston, roger, weapons tight, copy all, out."

Breedlove watched his display and listened on the tactical net as Stewart vectored Eagle Flight and Viper Flight to intercept the incoming bogeys. "Weapons tight," he reminded the younger officer. If these guys kept coming it would be weapons free for sure, but he didn't want to be the one to start the war. Iraqi aircraft would soon be in range of his fighter's AIM-7 Sparrow missiles, but the rules of engagement would not allow a shot without positive visual identification. Too bad, he mused, the weapon was capable of engagements beyond visual range.

Jeb Stewart nervously studied his display, transmitting intercept orders to his eight fighters streaking toward the border with Iraq. Hooking the lead Iraqi jet, he saw a course change to the east. Within seconds it became apparent that the Iraqis were no longer approaching the border, rather, all twelve aircraft had turned east, paralleling the border some 20 miles inside Iraqi airspace.

"Eagle, Viper, Winston. Hold bogeys turning east and paralleling the border. Hold position and loiter, over," he transmitted.

As the flight leads acknowledged the new orders, he could hear the disappointment in their voices. The Air Force had not engaged in aerial combat since the Vietnam war. Almost nobody on active duty had a combat kill to their credit. The Navy had splashed Libyan MiGs over the Gulf of Sidra, but the Air Force had not had the opportunity.

"Jeb, let's keep them orbiting where they are until we figure out what's going on. Looks like it was just a test. We've got alerts coming up to join from Chariot."

"Roger," acknowledged Stewart, disappointment in his voice as well. His heart was pounding, the AWACS had never seen combat despite thousands of Cold War missions. He had been on the brink of becoming the first AWACS air combat controller to direct an enemy kill. As he watched, the Iraqi jets turned northwest, away from the border. Two sections hung back, re-filling the vacated CAP stations. It looked like the action was over.

Breedlove radioed the CAOC, updating the situation and recommending the alert fighters launched out of Al-Kharj continue to fill the CAP stations. His aircraft had consumed a lot of fuel during the fruitless high-speed intercept run.

As the Iraqi aircraft continued to open the range, apparently heading to Al-Asad, it appeared that the excitement was over. He turned his attention back to track 4387. It no longer appeared on his display.

"Jeb, still got 4387?" he asked Stewart.

"Ahh, just a second... negative, no squawk, no skin. Might have landed at Arar."

"Roger, keep an eye out but focus on the Iraqi fighters. I'll check the international flight listing."

Checking the document listing all the regularly scheduled international flights and flight routes, he found nothing matching 4387. *Might have been a charter. When did all the ragheads travel to Mecca?* He'd look it up when he got back to base.

* * *

Cruising south-southwest steadily at 300 knots and 5,000 feet, Major Abdul Tikriti checked his fuel status. The drop tank was almost dry, time to unload it. He glanced left and right at his wingmen, flying loose formation on either wing at a comfortable 500 meters. The plan called for each pilot to exercise his own judgment as to when to jettison the auxiliary fuel tank and begin drawing down his internal tanks. Looking to his right, he saw the Al Jowf mountains rising above the light brown sands of the Saudi western desert. Below him stretched nothingness. Perfect, he thought, as he shifted fuel sources and flipped the switch to jettison the tank. With a soft bang and a slight jerk, he felt his jet leap forward and pitch nose up as the drag lessened. Adjusting trim and throttles, he settled back to 300 knots and 5,000 feet. Ahead stretched more nothingness. Soon, he thought to himself, we will unleash hell on the infidel Americans. As they crossed the coast he would activate the Cyrano IV radar, acquire the American ships, launch his missiles and descend to wave top level, following the missiles to target. What El-Amin and Tawfeek did after launching their missiles was up to them.

EIGHTEEN

Northern Red Sea

Bzzt! The growler phone jolted Will Tanner as he sat at his desk poring over a stack of chief petty officer evaluations. *Dauntless* rolled gently in a calm sea as he sat facing aft, the one-foot diameter porthole above his left shoulder.

"Captain."

"Captain, OOD sir, Lieutenant Nicholson. Ops said to call you before we set lifeguard detail. *Biddle* is moving up into waiting station. I'll close up to a thousand yards when she does."

"OK, thanks, Jimmy, be up in a minute." Tanner put down his pen and leaned back in his chair. The admin never ended, no matter what was going on in the real world. But, he reasoned, chief petty officer evaluations were important, and he meant to give them his full attention. He had decided that he would sign all of the chief petty officer evaluations, it would have more impact that way he reasoned, better for the chief than an eval signed by a lieutenant or lieutenant commander department head.

As was his habit, Tanner stopped in CIC on his way to the bridge. Lieutenant Commander Vince DeVito was still on watch.

"How we doing Weps?" asked Tanner.

"Good sir, *Biddle* is getting ready to go alongside, just manned the lifeguard detail. The forward and after unrep stations are ready to go. *Spruance* is still boarding a large container ship up north, and Alpha Sierra is going to hand the next one to *Phil Sea*. Hope it's a sheep carrier," grinned DeVito.

Tanner smiled. Rightly or wrongly, there was an unspoken resentment when it came to the Aegis cruisers. They were considered prima donnas by those assigned to older ships. Some of that reputation was well earned, thought Tanner. The Aegis combat system was the most advanced in the world, and Aegis cruiser assignments were the most highly sought among surface officers of all ranks. Some of that arrogance was justified he thought, the Aegis system made older systems, like that in *Dauntless*, seem antique by comparison.

"Good job on the PACFIRE this morning," he continued, "the settings seemed to work except on a couple of rounds."

"Yessir, we went back and looked at it, and the two that hit the water were both VT-Frag. Guns is having the guys take a look at the fuze setter. Both came out of Mount 52."

"OK, good," said Tanner, "let me know if they find a problem. I'll be on the bridge. What's our setup now?"

"Mount 51 is the ready mount, the missile system is Condition Three manned, sonar is manned, but the tubes are not. The gunner's mates are in Mount 52 checking the fuze setter."

Tanner entered the bridge to the usual flurry of standard announcements and reports. Jimmy Nicholson was coaching Willy Kim into station 1,000 yards astern of *Biddle*. Up ahead, *Saratoga* steamed through a calm sea, the Romeo flag at the dip on her starboard side.

Tanner went to the port bridge wing and climbed into his chair, settling in to enjoy the mild weather, the joy of being at sea, and to watch his crew operate the ship.

Western Saudi Arabia

Passing just south of Tabuk, Major Abdul Tikriti studied the rising terrain ahead. To the north lay the low-lying mountains jutting sharply skyward to the north of the city of Duba. Ahead were the taller coastal mountains that ran sharply down to the water's edge on the eastern banks of the Red Sea. The terrain was perfect for a surprise attack on the unsuspecting Americans. Once they crested the coastal mountain range, they would drop down to 1,000 feet and accelerate to the west, toward the presumed position of the American aircraft carrier. The mountain range behind them would confuse the American radars, masking their approach as they tried to pick out the low-flying incoming aircraft against the mountainous backdrop. The low altitude would limit the effectiveness of his Cyrano IV radar, but that was a risk worth taking. The variable was the actual location of the carrier. It was unlikely to be due east of where they crossed the coastline so some adjustment would be necessary once they picked up radar contacts.

He scanned his gauges. Everything was within limits. Glancing first left, he caught El-Amin's eye 200 meters on his wing. As agreed, they had tightened up the formation as they passed south of Tabuk. Imperceptibly, El-Amin nodded, confirming all was good with his jet. He looked right toward Tawfeek's jet. The young pilot's head was down, scanning his own instruments. Tikriti wondered how the untested captain would perform when the action became hot and heavy. Thus far he had seemed a cool customer, quiet but efficient, living up to the reputation he had earned in training.

The coastal mountains were only thirty miles ahead. It would not be long now.

Northern Red Sea

"Romeo closed up on *Sara*," announced Jimmy Nicholson. Tanner glanced up from the stack of message traffic he was pouring through while sitting in the port bridge wing chair to see *Biddle's* wake suddenly grow, foaming a snowy white as she began her run into station. The Romeo flag on *Biddle's* port yardarm fluttered to the top. He checked his watch, 11:30, a little behind schedule. Probably best to have lunch sent up from the wardroom, stay on the bridge. He watched as Willy Kim increased speed to assume position 1,000 yards behind the cruiser and the carrier while they refueled. Looking over his shoulder, he saw the motor whaleboat crew standing easy on station, ready to launch in the event some unfortunate sailor from *Saratoga* or *Biddle* fell overboard while the two ships were connected for refueling.

* * *

Dressed out in his flight suit, Lieutenant Commander Chuck 'Boomer' Schoonhower stood on the starboard side of the flight deck and watched the *Leahy* class cruiser make its approach on *Saratoga*. He had to admit it was a good-looking ship. The twin armed Terrier missile launcher on the sloping forecastle, raked bow, good lines, the missile fire control directors sitting formidably above the bridge forward, the large rectangular air search radar on the mast above the directors, a bone in her teeth as she charged into station. It was no Tomcat, but still an impressive ship. Schoonhower reflected on how he had almost become a surface officer himself. The Navy recruiters on campus at the University of Georgia were steering him in that direction to make a quota. Fortunately, an upper classman who was already enrolled in the Aviation Reserve Officer Candidate program found out he had 20/20 vision and steered him into the aviation program. *Dodged a bullet,* he said to himself. SWOs worked their asses off, getting no sleep and little recognition. Fighter pilots, on the other hand, were glamorized, especially since the movie *Top Gun.* Flying was challenging and fun, despite the terror of landing on the carrier on a dark night.

Shaking himself out of his reverie, he watched *Biddle* slide smoothly into station alongside the carrier. A series of whistles blew, the meanings of which he had no clue. Two shots sounded in rapid succession, and he watched as two can shaped devices, each trailing a small orange line, arced through the air between the two ships. He turned and headed for the island and the *Be-*

Deviler's ready room. It was about time to begin sitting the Alert Fifteen.

Western Saudi Arabia

Climbing to 5,000 feet, Tikriti led his flight of three Mirages up and over the coastal mountain range. They were now only five miles from the coast as they crested the peaks. Stretching out before him was the azure blue water of the Red Sea. Somewhere out there was the American aircraft carrier. *His prey*, he thought to himself. As his flight cleared the mountains, he activated his Cyrano IV radar for a 30-second sweep. It took several seconds to warm up and begin painting a picture. When it did, several yellow blips appeared on the twenty-centimeter diameter green scope. Quickly he analyzed what he saw, regretting every second that the radar remained active. A single blip at two o'clock off the nose. Too far north, he calculated. On the next sweep, a large blip at 11 o'clock, and another, closer in, only 20 kilometers, on the nose, also large. He raised his head. There, on the horizon, a single ship with a white superstructure. Not an aircraft carrier. He turned his attention back to the radar scope. On the next sweep, he assessed that the target at 11 o'clock was really two targets, close together. Range 77 kilometers. That could be it he thought. Wasn't he told there would be three ships, the carrier, and two others? Still, this contact looked the most promising. He switched off the radar and, signaling his two wingmen, gently banked his jet ten degrees left while descending to 1,000 feet. The coastal mountains behind him would make his flight of three difficult to detect.

Northern Red Sea

Electronic Warfare Specialist Second Class Paul Dalton returned his attention to his AN/SLQ-32 Electronic Warfare System

Console. A high-toned beep in his headset had taken his attention away from Operations Specialist Seaman Dewey Whitley who had been extolling the virtues of the University of Miami Hurricanes football team, the preseason number one ranked college team. Studying the screen in the dim light of the *Dauntless* Combat Information Center, he noted a symbol indicating a Cyrano IV radar in search mode bearing zero-four-zero. Then it was gone. He waited before reporting anything. *See if it comes back.* The SLQ-32 was notorious for false alarming on all kinds of spurious electronic signals. Its performance relied on a library of emitters that were loaded into the system based upon the likely threat emitters in the area of the world where the ship was operating. A frequency close to one of the threat frequencies could trigger an alert. Probably a commercial ship radar side lobe that triggered the false alarm he guessed. Turning back to Seaman Whitley he said, "No fucking way man, the Noles are gonna kick their ass this year."

Reconsidering his assessment, he keyed his headset mike, "Air, EW, got anything bearing zero-four-zero?"

Operations Specialist Third Class Demetrious Washington checked his console display and replied, "Negat, bearing clear."

Dalton turned back to Whitley, "Amp Lee is gonna run the ball right up their sorry asses."

TAO Vince DeVito had been monitoring the air defense intercom net.

"EW, TAO, what was that about?"

Forgetting the football discussion, Dalton sounded embarrassed as he replied, "Uh, TAO, EW, had a spurious signal, probably nothing." *Damn, never knew when the fuckin' TAO was monitoring your net.*

"What was it?" asked DeVito.

"System id'd as Cyrano IV, but I think it was a false alarm. Gone now."

DeVito considered the report. Cyrano IV was an F-1 Mirage radar. He also knew the limitations of the SLQ-32.

"Roger EW, keep an eye out. Report it to me if it comes up again." Turning his attention to the air defense operator, DeVito queried Petty Officer Washington, "Air, TAO, what's the air picture?"

"All clear sir, got nothing," replied Washington.

* * *

Will Tanner climbed out of his port side bridge wing chair and entered the pilothouse, dropping a stack of messages into the burn bag next to the XO's chair. He held six in his hand, marked up for routing to the appropriate department head to take for action. Glancing forward he watched as *Saratoga* and *Biddle* sailed alongside each other, the large black refueling hoses connected forward and aft, pumping the life-giving fuel into *Biddle's* tanks. Willy Kim stood at the centerline pelorus, the stadimeter in his left hand, issuing minor course and speed change orders to keep *Dauntless* solidly in *Biddle's* wake.

Andy Morton walked into the pilothouse through the starboard bridge wing door.

"We're all set Captain, how much longer you think?"

Tanner had seen *Biddle's* nightly report in his morning traffic and knew Roger Welsh had reported his fuel at seventy-six percent the night prior.

"Probably another 45 minutes, maybe an hour."

"All right sir, recommend we set the detail in 15 minutes."

"Make it so," he said, turning to look at the navigation chart on the chart table against the rear bridge bulkhead.

Northern Red Sea

At 400 knots and 1,000 feet above the surface of the Red Sea, Tikriti made his decision as the three-jet formation sped in the direction of the radar contact he had guessed might be the American aircraft carrier. One more sweep in search mode, acquire the target, switch to targeting mode, program the missiles, and then launch. He blinked his navigation lights three times, the signal to arm the missiles and prepare to activate the radars. El-Amin and Tawfeek would each have to acquire the target with their own radars to launch their missiles. *Were they close enough to acquire the target at this altitude?* He calculated that they were. He felt a surge of adrenalin and his neck hairs tingle. He blinked his navigation lights four times and flipped the toggle switch to activate his radar. One sweep of warm-up, no contacts. On the second sweep, he detected two targets, five degrees to the left of his nose at 51 kilometers. One painted larger the than the other, but as close as they were together, it was possible that his missiles could home on the smaller target. Once the weapon shifted to active homing, it was on its own, he had no control over what it hit.

Out of his peripheral vision, he saw a single flash of navigation lights from the port wingtip of Tawfeek's jet. He had acquired the target. He glanced left at El-Amin's aircraft, a moment later his starboard wingtip navigation light blinked once. As they had briefed the mission, each pilot was now on his own to launch when he was satisfied he had a valid target.

Tikriti shifted his Cyrano IV radar to targeting mode. It was now communicating with the two Exocet missiles slung under his wings.

* * *

In *Saratoga's* Combat Direction Center, Electronic Warfare Technician First Class Ronaldo Cabayang suddenly jerked up in his chair. A high-pitched beep sounded in his headset, and an alert appeared on his SLQ-32 scope. He hesitated, giving the system a chance to decide if the signal was false. The display held steady.

"TAO, EW," he shouted into his intercom mike, "Cyrano Four, bearing zero three seven. Targeting mode!"

Lieutenant Commander John "Cooter" Cotswall jerked upright and stared at his console which was in surface mode. Switching to air mode, he pressed his mike button, "Air, TAO, any tracks at zero three seven?"

"Negative sir," came the reply from Operations Specialist Second Class Doug Fentress.

* * *

In *Dauntless'* CIC, EW2 Dalton quickly leaned forward, staring at his console as the high-pitched alarm again sounded in his headset. The hair on his neck stood up, and a sinking feeling invaded his stomach.

"TAO, EW, Cyrano Four, bearing zero-three-eight! Targeting mode!"

DeVito double checked his scope, *nothing*.

"Air, TAO, any correlating air tracks?"

"Negative, sir," came the reply from OS3 Washington.

DeVito pressed the 21MC button for the Captain's chair on the bridge.

"Captain, TAO, got EW on a Cyrano radar bearing zero-three-eight. Targeting mode. No air tracks."

Jimmy Nicholson pressed the 21MC lever, looking over at Will Tanner at the chart table, "OOD aye, Captain copies."

Tanner rushed across the bridge and pushed the 21MC TAO lever, "Anything from *Sara*?"

"Negative sir."

Tanner considered his next move. The SLQ-32 and air search radars on *Saratoga* were at least a hundred feet higher on the carrier than on *Dauntless*, they would have a better look over the horizon.

"Report it to Alpha Whiskey. Set General Quarters!"

The "bong, bong, bong" of the General Quarters alarm sounded throughout the ship. Startled by the unexpected alarm, sailors throughout *Dauntless* first hesitated and then began scrambling to their GQ stations. Those on the underway replenishment rigs looked first toward the bridge as if questioning the alarm. Did some knucklehead lean on the alarm lever? The alarm continued, and then an excited voice came over the 1MC, "General Quarters, General Quarters, all hands man your battle stations, this is not a drill!" As they dropped their equipment and ran to their stations the announcement was repeated.

Tanner hesitated a second and then announced, "This is the Captain, I have the conn! All engines ahead flank, indicate turns for twenty-seven knots! Left five degrees rudder, belay your reports!"

This could be a false alarm, he thought. *But if it isn't...*

The helmsman and lee helmsman acknowledged the orders and *Dauntless* squatted in the calm seas as the engineers opened the valves and went to maximum available speed with two boilers on the line. General Quarters doctrine called for lighting fires in the two offline boilers, and they gave the orders to the firerooms.

Dauntless crossed *Saratoga's* wake and began moving up to overtake the carrier on its port side, the side exposed to this electronic radar signal.

* * *

On the port bridge wing of *USS Biddle*, Captain Roger Welsh stood behind his conning officer as the cruiser sailed smoothly 150 feet alongside the carrier. His OOD, a lieutenant, leaned out the bridge wing door, "Captain, TAO says *Dauntless* reports a Cyrano radar bearing zero three seven."

"What?" exclaimed Welsh, "Tell the TAO to get confirmation, check with *Saratoga!*"

Welsh considered his options. He was blind in that direction, his radars and ESM gear blocked by the carrier. He grabbed the phone and distance line handset.

"*Saratoga, Biddle* Charlie Oscar for your Charlie Oscar, quick!"

Captain Mike Reasoner answered, "Reasoner here, what's up Roger?"

"Just got a report that *Dauntless* picked up a Cyrano radar. Mirage. You getting anything over there?" he asked.

"I'll check, stand by."

Fuck, thought Welsh, *were there any French aircraft around?* Their ships were on the way.

***

Thirty miles to the north, Major Abdul Tikriti programmed his two Exocet missiles to activate their homing radars at 20 kilometers from the target. Once launched, they would descend to 100 meters above the ocean surface and cruise under inertial guidance at Mach .8, roughly 500 miles per hour. When the active homing radars came alive, they would guide the missiles to the most attractive target they acquired, most likely the much larger aircraft carrier. Then the missiles would descend further, to three to five meters above the surface. If there were more than one target in the scan, they would most likely home on the most inviting target, that providing the best radar return. Undoubtedly that would be the much larger aircraft carrier, not the smaller second target.

A flash of light to his right told him that Tawfeek had launched. This was followed an instant later by a second flash as Tawfeek's second missile dropped from its hardpoint beneath the wing, and its solid rocket propellant turbojet engine kicked in.

Both missiles streaked ahead of the three aircraft. Tikriti fired his two missiles at the same time as El-Amin launched. As Tikriti watched, one of El-Amin's missiles failed to transition to powered flight and dropped harmlessly into the Red Sea. Five Exocet missiles descended to 300 feet above the ocean and powered away from the formation. With a look to his left and right, Tikriti pointed down with his left hand and lowered the nose of his jet. He would follow the missiles toward the target, further complicating the American's defenses. Tawfeek followed suit. El-Amin hesitated and then turned up and right, away from the line of attack, heading northwest toward the Egyptian coastline. Tikriti twisted his neck and looked over his right shoulder, watching as El-Amin passed above and behind him. *So be it*, he said to himself. He had issued the guidance that permitted each pilot to decide for himself what to do once the missiles had been delivered. It had taken courage to come this far on this one-way mission. Although somewhat disappointed, he harbored no ill will toward his former squadron-mate.

* * *

Fourteen miles from Saratoga, Tawfeek's first missile activated its active homing radar and began scanning in a thirty-degree arc across it's heading. He had chosen to enable his missile seeker further from the target than had Tikriti. At first, there was no return. As it continued on course at almost ten miles a minute, the scan received an electronic return. The missile seeker head stopped its slew and focused on the bearing of the signal. Receiving a solid return signal, it achieved lock-on, shifted to terminal mode and began descending to terminal altitude. It's internal homing logics would keep the missile above the target horizon until the final terminal phase when it would come in at wave top height.

* * *

Aboard *Saratoga* and *Dauntless* a flurry of activity coincided as the electronic warfare operators on both ships detected the incoming missiles. *Biddle* was out of the loop, her own sensors blinded. Neither *Dauntless* nor *Saratoga* had yet picked up the incoming missiles on radar; they were too small, just above the horizon and masked by the coastal mountain range behind.

"Vampire, Vampire, Vampire, missiles inbound, bearing zero-three-nine true!" blared over the tactical circuit in the clear from *Saratoga's* TAO, Lieutenant Commander Cotswall. The role of the air defense commander, *Biddle*, had been superseded by necessity.

Simultaneously aboard *Dauntless*, EW2 Dalton screamed, "Missile inbound, zero-three-eight true, evaluate Exocet!"

Vince DeVito shouted out to the bridge on the 21MC, "bridge, TAO, missile inbound, engaging with guns and missiles when able! Id'd Exocet! No track!"

Will Tanner nodded to BM3 Reinhart who grabbed the 1MC microphone and announced, "Missile inbound, port side! All hands brace for impact!"

Tanner shouted into the pilothouse, "Launch chaff, port and starboard side."

Tanner heard whistle signals from *Saratoga* and knew *Biddle* was beginning to execute an emergency breakaway. It would take several minutes; all lines were still across between the two ships. He watched as the bow came even with *Saratoga's* stern. *Dauntless* had raced across Saratoga's wake, gaining speed and rapidly overtaking the aircraft carrier, still tethered to *Biddle* by the refueling hoses. As they crossed the carrier's wake, Tanner eye-balled the relative motion. He needed to put *Dauntless* between *Saratoga* and the incoming missile. *How many*, he wondered. "Come right, steady course one-eight-zero," he ordered. *Dauntless* continued to move up *Saratoga's* side, 300 yards to the port side of the carrier and in the direction from which the reported missiles would come. *If they came.*

"Steady one-eight-zero, aye," answered the helmsman.

Lieutenant Jimmy Nicholson was fumbling with the latch on the Super-Rapid-Blooming Off-board Chaff console mounted under the bridge window.

DeVito's voice came over the 21MC, "Bridge, TAO, launch chaff."

Warning bells sounded as both Mount 51, and Mount 52 swung out to port, the barrels lowering to the barrage fire elevation. Within seconds, they began firing, pumping out five-inch rounds at the rate of one round per gun every three seconds. Empty powder cases, ejected onto the deck, rolled around.

* * *

In after-officer's country, Lieutenant Commander Ricky McKnight jolted awake as the GQ alarm sounded. He had been napping, waiting until it was time to leave the ship. He felt the ship accelerate and heel to starboard as the rudder went over. *What the fuck*, he thought to himself. He got off his rack where he had been lying, fully clothed, and pulled on his shoes. What should he do? He no longer had a GQ station, now merely a passenger in *Dauntless. Missile inbound port side*? That's where he was. Then he heard the guns begin firing, mainly Mount 52 which was closest. He raced out of his stateroom and into the passageway and headed for the mess decks. Repair 5 gathered there. As good a place as any, and it put more ship between him and the incoming missile.

* * *

As *Dauntless* pulled even with *Saratoga's* island, Tanner moved to the starboard bridge wing to better judge his position relative to the massive aircraft carrier. He adjusted speed to remain in position, riding even with the carrier at thirteen knots. He could envision *Saratoga* and *Biddle* rapidly breaking down the refueling rigs to free *Biddle* to engage any incoming missiles. He shouted into the bridge, "Ops, tell TAO, barrage fire, two-seven-zero relative, both mounts!" In the excitement of the moment, he forgot Andy Morton's new status as acting XO. Both mounts were already firing, but he thought he should issue the order anyway. Make it official.

* * *

In CIC, Vince DeVito was rapidly issuing orders to his missile and gunnery personnel. He still did not have radar contact on the incoming missile.

"White bird on the rail," announced Lieutenant Chris Palmer.

"Directors two and three in sector scan, bearing zero-four-zero true!" ordered DeVito. He remembered the SWDG guidance advising *Adams*-class DDGs not to try to engage the Exocet with SM-1. *Fuck that*, he thought, the carrier is a bigger target than we'll ever be and the captain has put us between the missile and the carrier.

"Guns, TAO, Mounts 51 and 52, barrage fire bearing..." he glanced at the gyro repeater above his head, they were on 180 true. He did some quick math, "Bearing two-six-zero relative, batteries released!" They were already firing, but his order changed the lay of the guns to the direction from which the missiles had been detected on the SLQ-32. He paused, gathering his thoughts. What was the captain doing on the bridge? Pressing the 21MC lever, he called out, "Captain, TAO, commencing barrage fire bearing two-six-zero relative. No tracks."

Tanner nodded from the starboard bridge wing, and Nicholson acknowledged the report, "Captain concurs, batteries released!" The excitement of the attack had everyone repeating themselves, unnecessarily. "Captain's positioning us on *Sara's* port beam," added Nicholson.

Standing on the starboard bridge wing, Tanner heard the exchange between his OOD and TAO. He took off speed and coasted into position 300 yards on *Saratoga's* port beam, his bridge even with the island. Both gun mounts were blasting away, squinting across the pilothouse through the portside door, he saw the black airbursts of the first several rounds setting up the barrage of flack. Things were happening fast. *Stay calm*, he told himself, *everybody's doing their job.*

"Multiple air contacts bearing zero-four-zero true," shouted OS3 Washington in CIC as the five Exocet missiles popped over the horizon 9 miles away.

"Got 'em Chris?" shouted DeVito at Chris Palmer, the Fire Control Officer.

"Not yet sir," called Palmer. He was standing over his two TSTC operators as they tried desperately to generate a track for the fire control system to guide his SPG-51 missile fire control directors onto the low-flying missiles.

* * *

Aboard *Saratoga*, Rear Admiral McCall and Captain Vanzant had watched helplessly from the flag bridge as *Dauntless* pulled alongside the carrier, gun mounts trained off to port and a live missile, painted white, up on the single-armed Mark 13 guided-missile launcher. The weapon sat vertically on the rail, pointing straight up, awaiting the signal from the fire control system to slew into launch position. On the starboard side the lines between *Saratoga* and *Biddle* fell into the water and *Biddle* began accelerating out of station, her GQ alarm sounding. They felt *Saratoga* begin to accelerate as Captain Reasoner, one deck above on the navigation bridge, ordered a flank bell. On the flight deck, two crews had clambered into the cockpits of the Alert 15 F-14

Tomcats, sitting on the bow catapults, waiting to launch. *Saratoga's* GQ alarm sounded incessantly, adding to the sense of crisis permeating the ship. *Dauntless* began firing in rapid fire mode from Mount 51. Seconds later Mount 52 started firing. Just below the flight deck aft of the LSO platform, they watched as a NATO Sea Sparrow mount trained out to port. *Dauntless* began launching chaff from the port and starboard side launchers. They watched the three-foot-long gray canisters float up and toward the carrier. Just as it looked like they would reach apogee 400 feet above the water and fall back on the flight deck or into the water, a loud pop was heard, and hundreds of strips of Mylar chaff exploded from the canister and began drifting behind the ship on the wind, gently fluttering toward the ocean surface. There was nothing either of them could do, survival now depended on the training of the men under their command.

* * *

Shifting his attention between the aircraft carrier close aboard to starboard and the engagement to port, Tanner watched through the port side bridge door as the five-inch rounds began to create airbursts a mile away. With both mounts firing in rapid continuous mode, *Dauntless* was putting 40 rounds per minute in the direction of the incoming missiles. Some rounds failed to explode over the water, impacting instead and throwing up a huge splash of seawater. Each air burst created an ugly black cloud, the shrapnel peppering the water's surface. He moved to the center of the bridge, alternately watching their position relative to *Saratoga* and searching the sky to port, looking for the inbound missiles. *How many,* he wondered. *Saratoga* was accelerating, and Tanner kept increasing speed to keep pace.

* * *

On catapult number one, Lieutenant Commander 'Boomer' Schoonhower cycled through his control surfaces and powered up his two Pratt and Whitney TF-30 turbofan engines. At maximum power, those engines generated 40,000 pounds of thrust, capable of achieving speeds in excess of Mach 2. He looked across at Cat 2 to see his wingman, Lieutenant 'Wilbur' Wright doing the same. The yellow jacketed catapult officer signaled that winds were not yet sufficient for launch. It was a calm day in the Red Sea, *Saratoga* would have to make her own wind, and that would take time as she slowly accelerated. Ahead he watched as *Biddle* powered away in front of the carrier and began angling left across the bow. Two white SM-2 extended range Terrier missiles sat on the rails of her Mark 10 guided-missile launcher. On the fantail, her five-inch gun mount trained out to port but did not fire.

Hearing a loud explosion, he looked left over his shoulder past the angled flight deck to see *Dauntless*, riding close aboard, begin firing her five-inch guns off to port. *You go you sons a bitches*, he thought to himself, silently cheering the little destroyer as it fought to protect the aircraft carrier. He was itching to launch and join the fight. He was in the dark as to the actual threat. Not until he was airborne and checked in with Alfa Whiskey would he know what he had been launched to deal with.

* * *

Twenty miles northeast of the American ships, Major Abdul Tikriti and Captain Fatah Al-Tawfeek, streaked across the surface of the ocean at 500 feet and 450 knots. The five Exocets were no longer in sight ahead, only the remaining exhaust smoke from their turbojet engines as it streaked by their cockpits. Tikriti was not sure what he would do when the carrier came into view. He knew his aircraft would occupy the American defenses, increasing the chances of the missiles getting through, but then what? A suicide attack like the Japanese Kamikazes, or try to evade and escape, follow El-Amin into Egypt? Glancing to his right, he saw Tawfeek, grimly staring straight ahead and staying on his wing. It appeared that Tawfeek had decided.

* * *

Lieutenant Commander Ricky McKnight stood next to Damage Controlman Chief Johnny Ray Hatcher, team leader for Repair 5, the damage control team responsible for fighting fires and damage in the engineering spaces aboard *Dauntless*. Hatcher was issuing orders and checking equipment as his team, made up of petty officers, seamen, and firemen from all departments, dressed out in their gear. The ship vibrated each time the guns fired, chips of paint and dust, flying out of the overhead cabling and piping.

"Anything I can do, Chief?" he asked.

Hatcher eyed the lieutenant commander, "Sir, just help me check the gear and maybe stay next to Hamilton on the sound-powered phones, help relay the word from DC Central or the bridge."

"You got it, Chief."

* * *

"TAO, Air, two more inbound, zero-four-zero true, 15 miles," shouted OS3 Washington at his console. "I'm losing the picture, too much return from the gunfire."

DeVito, rogered, acknowledging the report. The airbursts were creating too much radar return, obscuring any chance they had to acquire the incoming missiles. He could only keep firing down the bearing and hope the tactic worked. The guided-missile system had still not acquired the incoming missiles, they were too low and now being obscured by the wall of flak and water one mile off the beam.

* * *

Fatah Al-Tawfeek's first missile had achieved a solid lock on *Saratoga* at nine miles from the ship. Dropping to ten feet above the smooth surface of the Red Sea, it streaked toward its target at 500 mph. It would cover those nine miles in less than 60 seconds. Four additional Exocet missiles followed the first, each slightly offset from the first, with three to ten seconds separating their projected time of arrival at the target. The radar seeker in the first missile began to experience milliseconds of lost track as the five-inch airbursts, and 20-foot-high splashes of impacting rounds interfered with the solid return from the aircraft carrier. As each of the trailing four missiles acquired the target, they too descended to sea skimming level, likewise experiencing intermittent disruption, preventing solid target acquisition.

* * *

With a salute to the catapult officer, 'Boomer' Schoonhower's F-14 shot down the catapult toward the bow of the carrier. Within two seconds, the steam-powered catapult had accelerated his jet to 165 miles an hour. With a jolt, he cleared the edge of the flight deck and began climbing out to the left, in the direction of the incoming missiles. Seconds later, 'Wilbur' Wright left the deck and climbed out to take position on his flight leader's wing. Schoonhower checked in with the air controller in *Biddle*, "Red Crown, Devil One and Devil Two outbound, checking in with 2/2/0 each, request BRAA to threat. "

Lacking a firm target, the air controller, a first class petty officer, vectored the two fighters to zero-nine-zero true, east, the direction from which the hostile emissions had originated.

* * *

Aboard *Dauntless*, OS3 Washington detected the two Iraqi Mirage F-1 at 12 miles, on the deck in trail of the inbound missiles. Passing the range and bearing to the TSTC operator's, he assigned a track number and broadcast the warning to DeVito.

DeVito directed the Fire Control Officer, Lieutenant Chris Palmer, "Take tracks 4165, 4166, with birds!"

Palmer stared at the TSTC consoles, willing the two Fire Controlmen to generate a track. Suddenly a light glowed brightly on the right-hand console. Above the after superstructure, SPG-51 illuminator number two ceased sector scan mode and slewed swiftly to port, locking on to Tikriti's F-1.

"Got a lock! Track 4166!" shouted Palmer.

"DeVito repeated his order, "Take track 4166 with birds, shoot, shoot, look, shoot!"

Palmer squeezed the trigger. From back on the after O-1 level a loud whoosh sounded as the missile left the rail. Within seconds the RIM-66 Standard missile was at Mach 3.5, streaking toward Tikriti's jet. Immediately the Mark 13 launcher slewed back to the centerline position, the arm going vertical, and another white missile slid smoothly onto the rail. The launcher slewed back to port and the second missile screamed off the rail. Once again, the launcher slewed to the load position, and a third warshot slid up the rail, ready for the next firing order.

* * *

Tawfeek's first missile flew directly into an explosive cloud of shrapnel from a five-inch gun airburst one mile from *Dauntless* and disintegrated. The destruction of the missile could not be discerned by the naked eye, lost in the violence of the exploding projectile. None of the missiles could be reliably tracked on radar, lost in the return of the exploding five-inch rounds and the towering sprays of water as rounds which failed to fuze impacted the water. On the bridge, Tanner watched as both of his gun mounts continuously pumped out five-inch rounds, unaware that the first attacking missile had been destroyed. *Dauntless* was at 25 knots now, keeping pace with *Saratoga* 300 yards to starboard. A loud pop sounded as Jimmy Nicholson launched yet another round of chaff.

Three seconds later, Tawfeek's second missile found an opening in the barrage of five-inch and achieved a solid lock on the combined radar return of *Dauntless* and *Saratoga*.

* * *

Five miles behind the flight of Exocet missiles, a loud alarm sounded in Tikriti's cockpit as the radar warning receiver detected the continuous wave illumination from *Dauntless'* SPG-51 illuminator number two. Reacting instantly, Tikriti jinked left, away from Tawfeek's jet. Instinctively he pulled back on the stick to climb away from the surface of the water. It was a fatal mistake. A split-second later, the directed fragmentation warhead exploded into the underbelly of the Mirage in a ball of fire. The jet broke in two and tumbled violently into the sea. Tikriti died almost instantly, barely having the time to register the explosion and his imminent death. The second missile passed through the debris and exploded on the surface of the ocean.

Glancing at his flight leader's violent maneuver and then the more violent explosion and fireball, Captain Fatah Al-Tawfeek, jerked his stick to the right and peeled off his attack, turning north and going to afterburner. He checked his fuel. He was in the red, he could not remain in afterburner and hope to make the Egyptian coast. If necessary, he would eject and take his chances in the water.

* * *

Aboard *Dauntless*, a shout went up in CIC as the kill was observed and track 4166 disappeared.

"Splash one!" called out Vince DeVito on the 21MC. Tanner had seen the explosion, but also the leaker, Tawfeek's second missile, now only a half mile from the ship.

"Prepare for impact! Port side! All hands brace for shock!" shouted BM3 Reinhart into the 1MC, dropping the microphone and ducking behind the chart table.

Ordering 27 knots, Tanner saw a second leaker come into view, having avoided the barrage fire. Inside the wall of shrapnel, both missiles homed relentlessly on the two ships. A second later, a third missile appeared, flying straight and true toward its target.

A loud whoosh sounded, and a NATO Sea Sparrow missile from *Saratoga's* after launcher streaked outbound, crossing over *Dauntless'* fantail, homing on the third leaker, now less than a mile away.

* * *

Tawfeek's second Exocet slammed into *Dauntless'* port side, just below the main deck forward of the Mark 13 missile launcher. A split-second later the 365-pound warhead exploded in a tremendous ball of fire, shredding piping, cabling, and bulkheads. The 1,500-pound missile and remaining fuel created an even more violent explosion as it tore through the ship. The entire area burst into flame, isolating the after-section of the ship and trapping Machinist Mate Third Class Victor Valencia and Electricians Mate Fireman Apprentice Henry Busch in after-steering. The O-1 level deck buckled from the force of the blast, knocking Mount 52 out of alignment and out of commission. The armored sides of the missile magazine withstood the explosion, but all power in the after-part of the ship was lost. The lights went out below decks, to be replaced in seconds by the dim glow of battle lanterns, programmed to activate upon a loss of electrical power. Some failed to light, their batteries dead. Repair Three, under the supervision of BMC Orville Wise, was stationed in the passageway fifty feet forward of the explosion. A violent surge of flame and debris rocketed through the passageway but was diminished in force as it blew out a watertight door which had been closed and dogged tightly shut as GQ was set. The door blew through the dogs and off its hinges and flames struck three hose men crouching in the passageway. Miraculously, nobody was killed. Immediately, Chief Wise organized his fire party to begin fighting the fire as the passageway quickly filled with toxic smoke.

On the bridge, the helmsman shouted out, "Lost steering control!" as he noticed the ship failing to respond as he made minor movements of the helm to hold the ship steady on course 180 true. Tanner ran to the port bridge wing. Looking aft, he saw large clouds of oily black smoke pouring from the side of the ship.

In Director 1, above the bridge, Gunnery Officer Ensign Walter Sloan, reported a loss of power and communications with Mount 52. In CIC, Lieutenant Chris Palmer turned to Vince DeVito and reported a loss of power to the missile launcher. On the forecastle, Mount 51 continued to fire. Over 40 empty powder cases rolled around on the forecastle, a fresh one being ejected every three seconds.

* * *

Tikriti's first missile continued in unengaged, passing just astern of *Dauntless* and slammed into *Saratoga's* port side, ten feet above the waterline. It exploded into a large, unmanned machinery space containing the air conditioning plant for the after-part of the ship. As with *Dauntless*, a firestorm followed fueled more by the remaining solid propellant fuel in the body of the missile than by the explosive in the warhead.

* * *

Still on the port bridge wing, Will Tanner watched as this third missile passed just astern of *Dauntless*. A second later he heard the explosion as the missile slammed into *Saratoga*. Looking out to port, he saw Saratoga's RIM-7 NATO Sea Sparrow missile splash the third Exocet as its 90-pound annular blast fragmentation warhead detonated just above the incoming missile, knocking it into the water 400 yards from *Dauntless*. He turned into the pilothouse, "Indicate nine nine nine! Port engine ahead full, starboard engine ahead flank!"

The lee helmsman spun the dials on the Engine Order Telegraph until the numbers nine nine nine appeared in the window. He then pulled the handle for the port engine back to the full position; the starboard handle was already in the flank position.

"Nine nine nine indicated! Port engine answers ahead full, starboard engine answers ahead flank!" he reported.

With no control over the rudder, the ship started to drift slowly to port, opening the distance to the aircraft carrier as the starboard engine began overpowering the port. Tanner glanced at the rudder angle indicator. If it was accurate, they had lost steering control with about two degrees of right rudder applied. He turned to his JA talker, Seaman Collins, "Got comms with after-steering?" he asked.

"No sir," replied Collins, "can't get an answer."

* * *

As Tanner moved to the 21MC to call DC Central, the one remaining Exocet, the only functioning missile fired from El-Amin's aircraft, flew into a solid wall of seawater created by a round from Mount 51 which had failed to fuze. The missile tumbled, hitting the water 1,500 yards from *Dauntless* and failed to explode. Mount 51 continued to fire. Before Tanner could press the lever for DC Central, the bitch box clicked, and Vince DeVito's voice came over, "Captain, TAO, we lost power aft when the missile hit. Missile system is down, so is Mount 52. Continuing rapid continuous from Mount 51 and launching chaff, one round left in the portside super-r-boc launcher."

"Captain aye. Any air contacts?"

"Sir, we've got two, both opening. One's at twenty miles north of us, headed west, fast. The other is forty miles north of us, also headed west. *Sara* has two Tomcats up under *Biddle* control."

Tanner looked out the port side bridge door as another five-inch round detonated a mile from the ship, creating a large black flak cloud. He did some mental math, he had seen two missiles hit their targets, one into *Dauntless*, the other into *Saratoga*, one had been splashed by the NATO Sea Sparrow system. A fourth might have gone into the water. One jet had been splashed by *Dauntless*. Two escaping. He still did not know that the first missile had been taken out by barrage fire.

"Vinny, I think this is over. Cease fire Mount 51."

He turned his attention to damage control, "Central, Captain, give me a damage report."

Ensign Pete Gardner, the DCA, replied, "Captain, we've got a major conflagration at frame one-eight-zero. Lost power aft. Lost steering. Repair three is fighting the fire."

"What about casualties?"

"Don't know yet Captain, Repair 3 says three men are down, being moved to the mess decks for medical evaluation. No word from after-steering."

Tanner next called main control, "Cheng, Captain, how's the plant?"

"Two boilers on the line, fires lit in One Bravo and Two Alfa, building up steam pressure, no problems there. We've lost electrical power aft. Electricians are investigating, but the fire is pretty intense, looks like the firemain piping is ruptured back around frame one-eighty." responded Ken Carpenter.

Tanner thought for a second, "What about the magazines?"

"DC Central reports high temp alarms from the missile launcher, so far Mount 52 magazine is okay but without power."

"Alright, keep me posted. I'm steering with engines, we'll try to stay with *Sara* as long as we can." The carrier had now reached full speed, more than 30 knots, and was gradually pulling ahead of *Dauntless*.

Switching to DC Central, Tanner ordered Ensign Gardner to be prepared to flood the missile magazine and watch the temperatures in Mount 52.

"Central aye, looks like we'll need to jumper firemain aft. The lines are ruptured. No pressure to the magazine sprinkler system."

* * *

Rear Admiral Nick McCall turned to Commodore Alexander Vanzant, "We were damn lucky only two missiles got through. How those bastards got down here is anybody's guess."

Vanzant nodded, still staring out the portside bridge window as *Dauntless* slowly opened the distance to the carrier and fell behind, enormous clouds of black smoke pouring out of both sides of the ship just forward of the missile launcher. The fantail was completely obscured by the smoke.

"Admiral, I'm headed down to CDC, said Vanzant, turning to leave.

"I'll be right behind you," said the admiral. The action had only lasted two minutes. Neither officer had had time to depart the flag bridge, transfixed by the barrage fire from *Dauntless*, the Alert 15 jets launching, the incoming missiles, *Dauntless* downing the enemy aircraftt, *Biddle* charging out ahead of the carrier and crossing the bow to the port side; it had all happened so fast. It was over before either of them could have arrived to provide any guidance to the warriors fighting to save the carrier. McCall looked back at *Dauntless*, her forecastle littered with empty five-inch powder cans and smoke blanketing the after-quarter of the ship. They had put up a valiant fight.

* * *

"Tally ho, Mirage F-1," announced 'Boomer' Schoonhower as Tawfeek's jet came into view six miles ahead. *Biddle's* air controller had vectored him in hot pursuit once Tawfeek had climbed out to make a run for it. Going to full afterburner, Schoonhower and Wright had rapidly overtaken Tawfeek, who had come out of afterburner, hoping to make the Egyptian coast with his remaining fuel. A tweedling tone sounded in Schoonhower's headset as the AWG-9 radar achieved lock on Tawfeek's jet.

"Got a tone, solid lock," reported his RIO, 'Snake' Gardner.

"I got this one," Schoonhower announced to his wingman.

Flipping up the safety latch, he punched the firing key, "Fox one."

With a burst of flame, the 12-foot, 500-pound missile sped away from the Tomcat at Mach 2.5.

Tawfeek's radar warning gear announced the lock-on as soon as the AWG-9 radar acquired his jet. He began jinking, hoping to throw the missile off, but it was hopeless. A semi-active homer, the Sparrow missile stayed glued to his tail, following the reflected energy of the AWG-9 radar. It disappeared up the Mirage tailpipe, and the 88-pound warhead exploded, blowing his jet apart. Tawfeek was knocked briefly unconscious from the blast, but came to as the forward part of the plane plummeted toward the ocean 6,000 feet below. Tawfeek reached between his legs to pull the ejection handle, and then hesitated.

"Allahu Ahkbar," he muttered, releasing the handle. Inverted, he watched as the water rushed at him. They were his last words, his last thoughts, as his crippled jet smashed into the water.

"Splash one F-1," announced Schoonhower over the fighter control circuit.

"Roger Devil flight, got another 30 miles at your 10 o'clock, declared hostile. Turn left, three zero zero, buster," replied the *Biddle* Air Intercept Controller.

"This one's yours," transmitted Schoonhower as he and Wright banked their jets to the west and firewalled the throttles.

* * *

Major Dawud El-Amin glanced at his fuel gauge and waited for the inevitable. He was on fumes, he wasn't going to make it. Ahead he could see the flat, dusty brown coastline and barrier islands of the coast of Egypt. Hurghada International airport was only about 30 kilometers ahead. He had throttled back to 200 knots and climbed to 10,000 feet to milk every kilometer he could out of his dying jet, but it was not going to be enough. As he looked down again at his instruments, his engine flamed out. He nosed the jet over, hoping to gain as much distance as he could before he had to eject. He looked down at the water, it looked calm, no whitecaps. As the jet descended through 4,000 feet, he felt the controls becoming difficult to manipulate. *Time to get out.* Reaching between his legs, he grasped the red handle with both hands, straightened his back, pushed his helmet against the headrest, tucked in his knees, and pulled.

His cockpit canopy blasted away with a small bang, and a second later he felt a tremendous pressure on his spine as his seat pan rocketed away from his dying aircraft. He momentarily lost all sense of perspective as the rockets carried him up and away from the jet. As he began to tumble, his chute popped open, and with a jerk he found himself floating toward the water below, a good chute billowing above his head.

* * *

Checking his radar sweep, Lieutenant Steve 'Suds' Brewer gained contact on Tawfeek's jet as it passed through 2,000 feet on the way to the water.

"Got him," he announced to "Wilbur" Wright." Eleven o'clock, nine miles." Wright squinted through his canopy." Got a chute, we're too late. Musta run outta gas. Either that or he didn't want a fight."

Both fighters descended and closed on the parachute, now clearly visible as it approached the water.

Arriving overhead, they dirtied up their jets and slowly circled as El-Amin escaped from his parachute and clambered into a small, yellow, one-man life raft.

Schoonhower reported the situation to his air intercept controller in *Biddle*. After a brief delay, they were ordered to return to the carrier and take up a defensive CAP station. One of the MIO ships was being diverted to pick up the downed pilot, soon to be a prisoner.

NINETEEN

Northern Red Sea

Aboard *Dauntless,* one petty officer third class and one fireman apprentice manned their General Quarters station in after-steering all the way aft in the ship, above the twin rudders. The senior man was Machinist Mate Third Class Victor Valencia. He was accompanied by Electricians Mate Fireman Apprentice Henry Busch. In the event of an emergency, these two sailors could steer the ship, acting on orders relayed from the bridge. They had been assigned to after-steering for the refueling evolution for the same reason. When the General Quarters alarm sounded, they were already at their designated station.

When the missile hit *Dauntless* thirty feet forward, and just above their level, both men reeled from the shock as all lights in their cramped space suddenly went dark. Automatically, the two battery powered battle lanterns mounted on the forward bulkhead came to life, emitting a weak light into the compartment. Shaking off the shock of the missile hit, MM3 Valencia climbed to his feet and helped Busch to his.

He looked at the twin rudder posts, connected to the steering motors by a drive arm that moved both rudders simultaneously in response to the helm on the bridge. They were not moving.

"Busch, call the bridge, find out what's going on!"

EMFA Busch, pressed the button on his sound-powered phone mouthpiece, "bridge, after-steering, what just happened?"

There was no response. He pressed again, "Any station, after-steering, phone check."

Still nothing. Busch turned to Valencia, "Nobody on the line, it's dead. Let's get the fuck outta here."

Valencia thought for a second and then moved to the forward end of the compartment and tried to open the watertight door leading out of after-steering. He could not move the handle. Something was wrong, the hatch door looked out of alignment, slightly bulging inward.

He turned to Busch, "Try the scuttle," pointing to the five ladder rungs on the starboard side bulkhead which led to a water tight scuttle which opened onto the fantail at the main deck level.

Removing his sound-powered phones, Busch climbed two steps up the ladder and grasped the scuttle wheel with both hands. It would not move.

"It's stuck," he said, a panicked look on his face.

* * *

LCDR Ricky McKnight stood next to Ship's Serviceman Third Class Jimmy Hamilton on the messdecks as the phone talker relayed damage reports to Chief Hatcher, Repair 5 Team Leader. Thin wisps of increasingly denser smoke crept forward into the messdecks up the first deck passageway, curling along the overhead. McKnight had been following the action through Hamilton 's reports and knew that a serious fire was raging in the after-part of the ship, that much of the ship's electrical power in the after-section of the ship had been knocked out, and that they had lost control of the rudders.

"DC Central says send help to Repair 3, they need more OBAs!" shouted Hamilton.

Chief Hatcher dispatched nine men dressed out in the bulky firefighting ensembles with the oxygen breathing apparatus, or OBAs, strapped to their backs.

At Repair 3, Chief Wise backed his team up as the fires raged, spreading and forcing the fire fighters away from the inferno. Exhausted fire team members staggered his way, faces dripping sweat, their OBAs expended, to be replaced by new fire fighters to take their places on the hoses. With no power to fire pumps five and six, the hoses had been coupled together to provide the seawater from the remaining four fire pumps, positioned further forward in the ship and still provided with electrical power. The ruptured firemain piping had been isolated by securing valves further forward in the ship. Electricians were busy rigging emergency power to restore electrical power to the after-third of the ship, but it was taking time, and the crew was dealing with increasingly more smoke below the main deck. The combination of firefighting water and ruptured piping resulted in six inches of water sloshing around the first deck passageways, making the electrician's job that much more dangerous.

* * *

In after-steering, MM3 Valencia tried the hand wheel on the scuttle leading to the fantail and fresh air above. It was still jammed. The force of the Exocet hit had buckled the main deck, jamming the scuttle. EMFA Busch pulled his hand away from the watertight door leading forward, the only other escape route from after-steering. It was hot to the touch. He looked anxiously at Valencia. The heat in after-steering was increasing, and small wisps of gray smoke seeped into the cramped space through wire runs that penetrated the forward bulkhead. It appeared they could not escape forward; the fire was somewhere on the other side of the watertight door. Their only escape seemed to be through the jammed scuttle to the fantail above.

* * *

On the bridge, Will Tanner ordered *Dauntless* slowed as *Saratoga* and *Biddle* pulled away to the south. He needed to concentrate on fighting the fire and damage in his own ship. *Biddle* would protect *Saratoga* from any further attacks. No doubt the air wing was springing into action; no-fly day was officially over. As *Dauntless* slowed, he looked aft again. Huge clouds of oily black smoke poured out of both sides of the ship, obscuring his view of anything aft of Mount 52.

He turned to his OOD, LT Jimmy Nicholson, "What's true wind?"

Nicholson worked it out on maneuvering board, "Three-five-zero at seven knots."

Tanner turned the conn back over to Willy Kim, "Slow to five knots," he ordered. Turning to the 21MC he pressed the lever for DC Central and DCA Ensign Pete Gardner, the young officer suddenly confronted with the most challenging damage control situation imaginable.

"DCA, Captain, I'm going to try position the ship, so the smoke gets blown to one side of the ship, check with Repair 3, which side do they want clear?"

After a pause, Gardner came back, "Captain, DCA, they say blow the smoke off the starboard side. They need to get back to the fantail and check on the after-steering crew, still unaccounted for."

The secure radio on the bridge crackled as it synchronized and the voice of Captain Alex Vanzant came over, "*Dauntless*, this is Alpha Sierra Actual for your Charlie Oscar, over."

Tanner grabbed the handset, "Roger Commodore, Tanner here, over."

"What's your situation Will?" Suddenly Vanzant sounded friendlier than he had since they had sailed out of Mayport.

"I've got a major conflagration back aft around the missile magazine. Took one missile back there. We're fighting the fire. We're watching the temps in the missile magazine, and in Mount 52. They're kind of high in the missile mag and climbing in Mount 52 magazine. We're watching it. No casualty count yet. We've still got propulsion, but I've lost electrical power in the after-third of the ship and have no steering control, over."

There was a pause, while Vanzant mulled over the report, "You need help fighting the fire? I can send *Biddle* back, over."

"Not yet, sir, I'll let you know if we don't think we can get it under control, over."

The voice of Admiral McCall interrupted the conversation, "Will, I've been following the conversation, that was some nice work back there, screening the carrier."

"Thanks, sir, I guess one got through though, over."

"That's right, but it hit an unmanned space above the waterline. We'll be OK, over."

"Sir, I need to get back to work, we've slowed and turned to let the wind blow the smoke over the side, I'll get back to you with a progress report and damage assessment, over."

"Alpha Bravo, roger out."

Tanner stepped to the port bridge wing and looked aft. Willy Kim had twisted the ship using the engines. Without rudder control, it was a slow process, but gradually the bow turned into the wind until it was almost broadside, coming from the port side of the ship. The maneuver seemed to be working, thick black clouds of oily smoke poured over the starboard side. He leaned out over the splinter shield and looked at Mount 52, still trained out port. He could see flames aft of the gun mount penetrating the O-1 level deck and the main deck, blocking access to the fantail.

He returned to the 21MC next to his chair, "DC Central, Captain, what are the temps in the missile mag?"

"200 and climbing Captain," replied Pete Gardner.

"Flood it," he replied.

"Sir, we can't. With fire pumps five and six down and the firemain piping ruptured, we'll have to rig jumper hoses and flood from the topside hatch or the access hatch. We can't get to either one until the fire is out."

Tanner considered this disturbing report, "How about Mount 52?"

"Temps are rising there too, at one-eighty, we're rigging jumpers to the system, but the major fire is further aft, around the missile launcher."

Tanner knew that if the missile solid rocket propellants cooked off in the launcher, he could lose the ship. Thirty-three SM-1 Standard missiles, four Harpoon missiles, and the inert, maintenance missile remained after the engagement, one still on the launcher rail in the load position. It had not been fired when the first two had successfully splashed the Mirage. With no power to the launcher, it was stuck on the rail.

"Pete, get all three damage control teams back to fight the fire. You're going to need to fight it from the O-1 level as well as below decks. Put as much water as you can on the missile launcher. Try to keep it cool."

He turned to Andy Morton who had been helping coordinate damage control and ship handling efforts while passing information to Vince DeVito in CIC who was keeping Alpha Sierra and Alpha Bravo informed. All the while he had been coaching Willy Kim on the engines to keep the wind off the port beam.

"Andy, get down to Repair 5 and help Chief Hatcher and Chief Wise."

"Aye, aye Captain." Morton headed down the ladder to the messdecks. Despite their best efforts, smoke was creeping throughout the ship, following passageways, wire runs, piping pass-throughs, and any ventilation that allowed it to move. If they didn't get it under control soon, the interior of the ship would become uninhabitable. There weren't enough OBAs for everybody.

* * *

Ricky McKnight turned to see Andy Morton enter the messdecks from the forward first deck hatch, passing the serving line. BM1

Octavious Butt, Repair 2 Team Leader, was conferring with Chief Hatcher as they doled out assignments to the combined Repair Locker teams.

"Andy," said McKnight, "we need to get somebody back to the fantail to check the guys in after-steering. Everyone else is accounted for."

"Right XO," said Morton, forgetting the true status of McKnight.

He turned to Hatcher, "What's the plan Chief?"

Hatcher dispatched two more men in firefighting ensembles and OBAs back to Repair 3. Turning to Morton, he said, "We're sending Butt and his team from Repair 2 up to the O-1 level via the boat deck ladders to get water on the fire from above and on the missile launcher if we can. Got hoses running from all the way forward. Four fire pumps on line."

As Morton took this report, McKnight stepped forward, "I'm going topside with Butt, give him a hand." Morton started to object, but McKnight cut him off, "Forget it Ops, I'm going, live with it."

Morton nodded his acquiescence, next to the Captain, McKnight was the most experienced officer on the ship. Butt was an experienced first class petty officer, but he could use all the help he could get. This was no time to stand on protocol.

* * *

Repair 2 had run fire hoses forward on both sides of the main deck and up the motor whale boat and gig boat deck ladders to the O-1 level on either side of Mount 52. McKnight watched as BM1 Butt directed his two fire teams toward the flames penetrating the deck just forward of the missile launcher. They put as much water as they could on the flames licking through the O-1 level deck from below. Fire main pressure was an issue. With only four of six pumps available and teams fighting the fires below decks and on the O-1 level, the system was struggling to keep up. Repair 3 had rigged a P-250 portable fire pump on the port side and was attempting to apply water in the vicinity of the Paint Locker. With the ship moving slowly through the water, the pump was having difficulty maintaining suction through the hose hanging over the side.

With the light wind blowing from the port side, most of the smoke was rolling off the ship to starboard, but the view aft was still almost entirely obscured. McKnight turned to Butt, "Boats, try concentrate on the port side aft. If you can beat the smoke and flames down enough, I'll try to get to the fantail and check on after-steering."

The after superstructure featured a vertical ladder which ran next to the missile magazine on the port side between the main deck and the O-1 level. With the main deck still in flames above where the missile hit, it was the only way to get to the fantail.

"You sure, sir? It's pretty hot there. Ladder will be scorching."

"Just do it Boats, that's an order."

"Aye, aye sir, but I don't think this a good idea, not yet."

BM1 Butt directed the efforts of both of his hose teams to concentrate the hose streams on the area at the port corner of the O-1 level. The deck was so hot that as the water struck it, it flashed to steam. Gradually the flames diminished in that corner of the deck. Tying a handkerchief around his mouth and nose, McKnight grabbed a pair of heavy-duty firefighting gloves from one of the team members and made a dash for the edge of the deck, timing his move for that moment when the flames seemed diminished. A tongue of flame singed his khaki trousers as he leaped over the fire and skidded to the edge of the wet deck. Without hesitating, he scrambled down the ladder to the main deck. Batting at his burning trousers with the gloves, he put out the fire on his pants leg, but it hurt like hell. The trouser fire out, he ran aft to the transom, escaping the intense heat. As he looked forward, the magnitude of the blaze was overwhelming. He looked at the missile sitting on the launcher rail; orange and yellow flames licked at the base of the missile. Now that he was on the fantail, it appeared he had no way forward until the fire was out. But for the moment, he felt he was safe. He looked down at the deck level scuttle which led to after-steering. At a glance, he could see that the deck was misshapen, buckled slightly along the centerline of the fantail. The scuttle wheel sat at an angle over the scuttle.

He walked over, limping slightly from the burn to his left leg, and grabbed the scuttle wheel. It moved about an inch, but no further. He tried it back the other direction, the tightening direction. Again, about an inch of play and then nothing. Once again, he tried to loosen the scuttle. It moved the same inch.

One deck below, MM3 Victor Valencia felt the scuttle wheel move. He added his strength to the effort, but the wheel would not budge. He had been using a dogging wrench, a one-foot length of one-inch diameter pipe, as a lever in the scuttle wheel but had been unable to move it.

"Somebody's up there!" he shouted to Electrician's Mate Fireman Apprentice Henry Busch.

"Shit hot!" exclaimed Busch. He was sweating profusely. Both men had been struggling with the scuttle wheel ever since the space began to heat up and the smoke began creeping in. They had been out of voice contact with anyone since the missile hit.

Valencia banged on the scuttle with the dogging wrench.

McKnight heard the banging. Somebody was still down there, trapped. He looked around for something to give him some leverage. A lifeline stanchion maybe? At the corner of the fantail, the corner stanchion had a small three-foot-long bracing strut angling down to a padeye on the deck to give it extra support. The strut was held in place by two cotter pins. McKnight struggled with the seizing wire, cutting his fingers as he freed the strut from the stanchion. Hobbling back to the scuttle, he wedged the strut into the spokes of the scuttle wheel and put his weight on it. The three-quarter-inch aluminum pipe simply bent in half. The wheel did not move.

From down below he heard frantic banging on the scuttle.

"Hang on, I'll get you!" he shouted over the roar of the fire, banging back on the scuttle with the bent strut. It was useless, so he tossed it over the side and turned his attention to the lifeline stanchion itself.

He picked a likely looking stanchion and began struggling with the cotter pin and seizing wire connecting it to the deck. The lifeline consisted of a quarter inch diameter wire at the top and two additional strands below. Three sections of wire to remove from the ladyfinger hooks through which it was strung to free the steel stanchion.

In after-steering, Valencia turned to Busch, "I don't hear them anymore. Fuck, I hope they didn't leave."

After-steering was becoming progressively hotter, and the smoke was thicker, hovering almost a foot deep against the overhead. Valencia had to stick his head into the smoke layer and hold his breath to struggle with the scuttle wheel. He had only the vertical ladder welded into the bulkhead to stand on and could get no real leverage on the wheel. There was not room for both men to get a firm footing to try and turn the scuttle wheel.

A shift in the wind blew flames aft along with a cloud of thick black smoke. McKnight was forced to abandon his position and move to the port side to avoid being burned. He felt the ship shudder as the bridge team reversed the port engine and increased power on the starboard to twist the ship and once again move the ship to place the wind off the port beam. It was slow going, but gradually working. When the smoke and flame had abated, he returned to the stanchion and began loosening turnbuckles to slack the lifelines and break the stanchion loose. It was difficult and time consuming. Each turnbuckle had holes at either end into which a marlin spike could be inserted to provide leverage to back off the threaded turnbuckles. McKnight had no marlin spike, only his bare hands.

On the O-1 level, BM1 Butt advanced his team as the wind shifted the flames further aft. They had almost reached the edge of the circular missile magazine when the twist began to take effect and turn the smoke and fire back over the starboard side. In the brief time he had been able to approach the launcher and magazine, he was alarmed to see flames licking the base of the launcher, burning the non-skid and ablative coating atop the magazine, and rising dangerously close to the bottom of the missile sitting vertically on the launcher arm.

"Get water on the missile," he shouted at the hose team on the port side. *Shit*, he thought to himself, *if that thing blows, we're dead.*

The starboard side hose team was working to beat down the flames and pour hundreds of gallons of seawater on the missile magazine deck in an attempt to diminish the heat. They could not get close enough to open the magazine scuttle and pour water directly on to the missiles within.

As Butt and the team were forced away from the magazine by the shifting flames and smoke, his phone talker shouted, "Central says they've jumpered the magazine sprinklers and are flooding!"

Butt acknowledged the report. This was good news, the missiles in the magazine were being by soaked with fire main water, significantly reducing the chance of the missiles cooking off. Gradually the magazine would fill with water, ruining 37 million dollars' worth of surface-to-air and Harpoon missiles and the associated electronics inside the launcher system. A small price to pay to save the ship.

In after-steering, Petty Officer Victor Valencia dropped to the deck coughing, unable to breathe in the vicinity of the scuttle. The smoke in the space was increasing, and both he and Busch sought shelter low in the space. The heat was becoming unbearable. If they didn't get out soon, they would both die. There were no more noises from the deck above. Perhaps their rescuers had had to vacate the area due to the fire. The two men exchanged worried looks and watched as the space continued to fill with smoke.

Ricky McKnight glanced up at the Standard missile on the rail and saw flames licking the bottom, exhaust section, of the missile. He knew that 300 pounds of solid rocket fuel was just above the fire. Ignoring the pain, he succeeded in loosening the last of three turnbuckles, slacking the lifelines and taking the pressure off the stanchion. His hands bleeding, he removed the locking pin and pulled the stanchion out of the deck socket. He now had a three-foot steel pipe to use as a lever in the scuttle wheel.

Moving to the scuttle wheel, he wedged the pipe between a section of the wheel spokes and put his full weight against the stanchion. He felt it move slightly. Adjusting his feet against another stanchion, he pressed with all his strength. The wheel gave a little more.

MM3 Valencia saw the wheel move through the smoke, "They're back! Come on!"

Holding his breath, he grasped the wheel and added his strength to the effort. Busch climbed up and despite having no good purchase, did what he could to assist. As the wheel began to slowly turn, they saw the spider arms start to retract from the dogs. Once the spider arms were clear, the scuttle could be opened as long as the hinges functioned.

McKnight sensed the effort from below and watched as the scuttle slowly loosened. With a jolt, he felt the spider arms come clear. He fell as the scuttle popped up two inches and stopped. Crawling to the gap, he shouted down, "Who's down there?"

"Valencia and Busch!" shouted Valencia. He coughed and continued, "Get us outta here, place is full of smoke!" Indeed, smoke began escaping through the partially open scuttle hatch.

From below, Valencia pressed on the scuttle hatch while McKnight pulled from above. The hatch came up about six inches but would go no further. Not enough to allow the men to escape. The buckled deck, resulting from the impact of the Exocet missile, had knocked the hinges out of alignment. McKnight climbed to his feet and jammed the stanchion into the opening and began pressing upward to lever open the hatch.

With the stanchion lodged between the hatch coaming and the hatch, McKnight put his full weight on the bar and strained to pry it open. With a sudden popping sound, the hatch jerked open. McKnight fell back, hitting his head on a deck padeye and landing hard on his right shoulder. A cloud of gray smoke escaped through the suddenly open scuttle, followed immediately by Valencia and Busch, coughing and hacking. Both men moved to the port side, gulping big breaths of fresh air as they leaned, hands on knees, and tried to recover from the horror of being trapped in after-steering. Looking forward, they realized that they were trapped on the fantail by the roaring fire. But at least now they were out of the smoke-filled compartment and in fresh air. Valencia looked down at McKnight, "XO, you alright? Thanks for getting us out of there."

McKnight shook his head to clear it. Gradually his vision refocused, and he looked at the two men he had rescued, trying to recall their names. He felt the back of his head and looked as his hand came back, bloody.

"Aaagh, uh.... no problem," he muttered, "glad you're okay."

Glancing forward, he sized up the situation. Flames continued to lick at the missile on the rail. Large clouds of black smoke streamed off the starboard side, and tall flames were visible on the main deck on both sides of the missile magazine and launcher, blocking the way forward on the main deck. Looking forward on the port side, he saw streams of water from the fire party attempting to beat down the flames. It appeared he and the two sailors were trapped on the fantail.

On the O1 level, BM1 Butt directed the efforts of his two hose teams while carefully watching the fire on top of the magazine and below the missile on the rail. It seemed to be growing, and his efforts to beat back the fire that raged across the rest of the O1 level and deck below had not yet yielded positive results. The fire continued to block access to the fantail. His training told him that in addition to the explosion of the warhead, they were fighting a fire fueled by the unexpended fuel in the Exocet missile itself which spread inside the ship as the missile body disintegrated upon impact.

As he carefully studied the RIM-66B Standard missile, he noted what appeared to be some kind of fluid leaking out of the exhaust of the missile. *Shit*, he thought, *the solid fuel is melting from the heat. It could flash to fire any second.*

"Everybody back!" he shouted, "back away, keep the water on the missile!"

Both hose teams backed toward the deckhouse, seeking cover on the forward side of Mount 52, placing the gun mount between themselves and the missile launcher while still playing the stream of salt water from the hoses on the flames. But the distance was too great and the water pressure too weak. From the safety of Mount 52, they could not get adequate water on the missile and launcher.

Turning to his phone talker, he reported the situation to Damage Control Central and Ensign Gardner.

On the bridge, Will Tanner took the report. The Mark 13 guided-missile launcher had a hydraulic device for kicking a dud missile off the rail, over the side, and into the water. But, it would not work with the rail in the vertical position, and without power, the launcher could not be moved to the eject position.

With the firemain now jumpered to the magazine sprinkler system, and slowly flooding the missile magazine, it was becoming increasingly unlikely that the missiles in the magazine would cook off. But the missile on the rail could blow if the solid rocket fuel ignited.

Pressing the bitch box lever, he directed the DCA to have all topside fire teams pull forward away from the missile launcher. As he gave this order, he saw an SH-3 Sea King helicopter from *Saratoga* approaching the ship.

Pressing another lever, he ordered, "TAO, Captain, keep the *Sara* helo away from the area around the missile launcher, it's in danger of exploding."

"TAO, aye," replied Lieutenant Commander Vince DeVito.

On the fantail, Ricky McKnight could not see the leaking rocket fuel from his vantage point, but he could see the flames licking at the bottom of the missile.

Over the 1MC ship's announcing system, he heard the announcement, "All hands topside remain clear of the missile launcher, danger of explosion, I say again, all hands topside stay clear of the missile launcher, danger of explosion."

McKnight looked around, there was no cover on the fantail and no way to escape the flames forward. He looked at the open scuttle to after-steering. Thick gray smoke poured out. *No going back there.* He then saw the *Saratoga* helicopter hovering off the port side of the ship, upwind of the smoke and even with the bridge. Turning to Valencia and Busch, he pointed to the helicopter and said, "Let's go, over the side!"

Both sailors hesitated, looking at McKnight then over at the hovering helicopter. Valencia began waving his arms to attract the attention of the crew. Then Busch took a running start and dove over the port side lifeline, barely clearing the screw guard. Valencia was more careful as he and McKnight moved to the port corner of the fantail, where the port side ended, and the transom began, McKnight limping noticeably. The ship was slowly moving forward as the bridge team maneuvered the ship to keep the wind on the port beam. Valencia swung his legs over the lifeline with McKnight steadying him, hesitated on the deck edge, and jumped into the water, holding his nose.

McKnight swung his burned left leg over the lifeline and began to climb over. At that moment, the puddle of solid rocket fuel under the missile ignited and climbed the stream of dripping, melting fuel into the body of the missile. A fraction of a second later, the remaining solid rocket fuel in the missile exploded in a huge ball of flame. The missile body shattered into countless pieces, sending a three-hundred and sixty-degree blossom of deadly shrapnel flying in all directions. The shrapnel peppered the after deckhouse, Mount 52, and the fantail. The water on three sides of the ship was instantly boiling with the impact of thousands of fragments of the destroyed missile.

Lieutenant Commander Ricky McKnight never knew what hit him. For a thousandth of a second, he was conscious of the flash of the explosion as his body was torn apart by the pieces of the missile body, the rocket motor, and the guidance section. He was blown clear of the side, tumbling into the water in a red mist of pieces. What was left of him sank into the depths of the Red Sea.

Valencia and Busch were sheltered from the deadly storm of shrapnel by the side of the ship, the pieces flying over their heads into the water. Instinctively, they both ducked under the water to avoid the blast. When they surfaced, it was over; nothing but a column of smoke floating off the starboard side of the ship. There was no sign of the XO. Looking forward as the ship moved away, they trod water and began waving at the helicopter hovering off the port bow of *Dauntless*.

TWENTY

Northern Red Sea

Major Dawud El-Amin watched nervously from his life raft as the two F-14 Tomcats, landing gear extended and flaps down, slowly circled 500 feet above. *Would they come in and strafe him*, he wondered. He knew that if he had been an Iranian pilot shot down over the Persian Gulf during that war, his fellow Iraqi pilots would not have hesitated to do so. He decided the Americans would not do the same, they were notoriously conscious of public opinion and notions of high minded concepts like the rule of lawful warfare. They lacked true killer instincts. Were it not for their technical superiority they would be an easy enemy to defeat.

While descending beneath his chute, he had nervously watched the two jets approach. Scanning the waters around him for witnesses he had seen the gray masts and superstructure of another Navy ship on the distant horizon to the north. Undoubtedly another American ship, he guessed correctly. Too far away to witness his murder if it were to happen. He hoped to spot a fishing boat or commercial freighter that would pick him up and deliver him safely ashore somewhere before the Americans came for him.

Rather than sit idly in his raft, he decided to begin paddling west. He guessed he was 25 or 30 kilometers from the coast of Egypt. It was something to do, and if the American pilots did not kill him, they could do little else but watch until they ran low on fuel and had to leave. He was sure that the ship he had seen on the horizon would be sent to pick him up and about that he was also correct. But it wouldn't hurt to paddle west, put some distance, no matter how little, between his current position and however far he could get.

While gently paddling, he scanned the smooth ocean surface for signs of sharks. He knew the Red Sea was notoriously full of the dangerous creatures and his flimsy little raft offered little protection against a large and determined shark. He reflected on the mission, Operation Birds of Prey as Tikriti had called it. He had no idea of the level of success. He was disappointed in the fact that one of his own missiles had failed to ignite and had fallen harmlessly into the ocean. But he had seen both Tikriti and Tawfeek launch and have their missiles transition to powered flight. That meant five Exocet missiles headed toward the American aircraft carrier. He had also watched as Tikriti and Tawfeek had dropped their noses and continued on toward their targets. He felt a pang of guilt at not pressing the attack. He dismissed that thought; if they had both continued in, there was no way they would both survive. No one need know that he alone had elected to try to escape to Egypt. He had been running away to the northwest when the surface-to-air missiles from *Dauntless* had splashed Tikriti's jet. He had not seen what happened. Likewise, he was 20 miles ahead of Tawfeek when the Americans had shot him out of the sky. He was unaware of that as well.

* * *

Mahmod Da'wud sat in the cramped compartment containing his radio equipment. He was sweating profusely in the oppressive heat of the tiny space. The air was still, and stifling. Around him, everything vibrated as the fishing vessel *Basra* ran at full power toward the Sinai Peninsula of Egypt. The smell of diesel exhaust and fuel oil contributed to the oppressive atmosphere below decks. But he dare not leave the radio set. He was expecting a signal confirming that the attack on the American aircraft carrier had occurred. If it had not, for whatever reason, he and Najaf would have to remain in the area to once again report on the movements of the American ships. This possibility worried him.

Already the Americans, especially the number twenty-five ship, had shown too much interest in the *Basra*. It seemed that every day since the first encounter a helicopter had flown by to take a look at the little fishing boat. It was only a matter of time before one of the ships decided to board and inspect. Especially now, after the nets had been let go, the façade that they were merely fisherman would not hold up. He was sure that that idiot Najaf would fall to pieces and ruin everything if an American boarding team came aboard. He prayed for the report from Baghdad that the attack had been successful and that the Americans had suffered a massive blow. In the meantime, he would head for Sharm-el-Sheikh and seek shelter there. He would tell the Egyptian authorities that they had lost their nets and needed to make repairs. The Mukhabarat would work with Egyptian intelligence and arrange for his escape. He might have to kill Najaf and his first mate so that they would not talk. *Inshallah*, so be it.

* * *

Aboard *USS Spruance*, Commander Chris Winters took a call in his cabin from his TAO, "Captain."

"Captain, TAO, just got word that *Saratoga*, *Biddle,* and *Dauntless* have come under missile attack down south. No more details, but Alpha Sierra has just ordered Warning Red, Weapons Tight. Recommend setting GQ."

"Roger, set GQ. Any unknown air or surface contacts?"

"One merchant, southeast of us, *Montgomery* has been ordered to board her."

"I'm on the way."

As the General Quarters alarm sounded, Chris Winters hurried to the Combat Information Center and sat next to his TAO in the chair designated for the commanding officer. Slipping on his headset, he listened as manned and ready reports came in from battle stations throughout the ship. He knew his executive officer was gathering the reports out on the bridge. Slipping off one ear of his headset he leaned in to his TAO.

"What do we know?"

"Near as I can tell from the reports coming in, it was an air attack coming off the coast of Saudi Arabia. Appears to be several Exocets. Both *Sara* and *Dauntless* were hit. No idea yet on the extent of damage or casualties."

Just then the voice of the ATAC, the air tactical controller came over the headset,

"TAO, Air, got two unknown, non-squawkers, 179 at 86 and 175 at 110, headed northwest."

"Roger Air, are they closing our position?"

"Negat sir, appear to be headed toward the Egyptian coast... Wait, two more, squawking. F-14's from *Sara*. In pursuit."

Chris Winters considered all this information and got his head into defending his own ship, if necessary.

"Any other friendly air in the area?"

"Negat sir, *Montgomery's* helo is on deck."

"Roger, TAO, Captain, CIWS to full-auto."

Setting the Vulcan Phalanx Close-in-Weapons System, or CIWS, to full-auto, meant the system would automatically detect and engage any aircraft or missile flying at the ship with 2,000 rounds per minute of 20-millimeter depleted uranium bullets. It was the last line of defense system designed specifically with the Exocet missile, or others like it, in mind. The system had no way to discriminate a friendly aircraft from an enemy. Therefore full-auto was only set for training under very controlled conditions, or in a real-world high threat environment.

"Holy shit," came over the air control circuit, "the F-14's just splashed the second bogey, the one at 181 and 103 miles. Looks like they are continuing after the other."

Chris Winters shifted his console from surface-to-air mode so he could watch the action himself. It did not appear that there were any threatening surface contacts. He hooked the non-squawking bogey and saw that it had slowed and the two F-14's were rapidly gaining. His SPS-40 air search radar could give him range and bearing to the aircraft but not altitude. As he watched the distance between the unknown aircraft and the section of fighters quickly closing, the unknown disappeared from his display.

"Air, Captain, any report of missile firing by the fighters?"

"Negat, sir, he either dove for the deck, flamed out... who knows sir. Should get something from the fighters. Wait... yessir, they have a chute. Looks like he bailed out."

"Captain aye, plot the lat and long. Surface, Captain, I think we're going to be the closest ship. Any other surface contacts out there?"

"Negat sir, gate guard ships and the one merchie that *Montgomery* was going to board."

Switching channels, Winters called the bridge, "XO, Captain, we'll stay at GQ but head for the downed pilot. Alert the rescue detail."

Turning to his TAO, he said, "Notify Alpha Sierra and prep the helo for launch, I'm going to the bridge."

As Winters left CIC, his watch officers began setting his orders into motion.

* * *

Forty miles southwest of *Spruance*, El-Amin continued to slowly paddle his small raft in the direction of the Egyptian coast. The two American fighters had departed the area. For the time being, he was alone. *Could I really make it to shore,* he wondered?

The unmistakable beat of an approaching helicopter quickly abused him of this notion. Looking over his right shoulder, he saw the small helicopter approaching from the northeast. He had no doubt it was American and had come from the ship he had seen while floating down in his parachute. Accepting his fate, he pulled a flare from the pocket of his survival vest, held it up, and pulled the activating ring. A cloud of bright pink smoke rose quickly from the flare as he began waving his arm. Within seconds he saw the helicopter bank right and head directly toward him. Whatever the future held between the Americans and his country would not involve him.

* * *

On the flag bridge aboard *USS Saratoga*, Rear Admiral Nicholas McCall and Captain Alexander Vanzant watched as the SH-2 helicopter grew slowly larger as it approached the aircraft carrier. A steady stream of staff officers had been coming and going with draft operational reports for approval and release to higher authority. Likewise, Captain Mike Reasoner, *Sara's* CO, had been providing a steady stream of updates on the damage suffered when the Exocet missile had struck the carrier. There had been no casualties, the missile hitting an unmanned space above the waterline containing air conditioning and other ventilation equipment. The fire had been significant, on a scale with that being fought on *Dauntless*, but the damage control team had managed to get it under control and then extinguished. The ship was in no real danger and was fully capable of executing its mission. To that end, the Alert 15 aircraft that had been scrambled during the attack had recovered, and two sections of CAP launched to protect the ship from further attack. *USS Biddle* was riding shotgun five miles to the east, the direction from which the attack had come. They had positioned *Saratoga* further toward the western edge of the Red Sea, providing more stand-off from the coast of Saudi Arabia and therefore allowing more warning time in the event of another attack. *Philippine Sea* had been ordered to steam south at best speed and resume duties as the air warfare commander. All the ships in the *Saratoga* Battle Group had been ordered to battle stations in the event a follow-on attack was planned. Lieutenant Commander 'Boomer' Schoonhower and Lieutenant 'Snake' Gardner were in the carrier intelligence center, CVIC, being debriefed by CAG and the flag intelligence officer, Lieutenant Commander Steve Reilly.

Setting down an internal communications handset, Vanzant turned to Admiral McCall, "Admiral, that was my watch, *Spruance* reports that the pilot was completely cooperative when they plucked him out of the water."

McCall nodded, then shifted his gaze to the approaching helicopter. He had given specific instructions to Mike Reasoner that the prisoner was to be handled strictly in accordance with the Geneva Convention. He would be taken under armed guard to the ship's sick bay where he would be examined for injuries and treated if necessary. From there he would be taken to the brig to be held until higher authority decided what to do with him. McCall fully intended to have his intelligence officer question him while he remained in custody to learn what they could about the attack. He had no doubt that he was in for a blizzard of questions from Washington.

The two officers watched as the SH-2 Seasprite helicopter approached the carrier, hovering off the port side briefly before sliding sideways over the flight deck and gently settling down. Immediately a team of armed Marines sprinted from the island to the helicopter and stood ready to receive the prisoner as he climbed out.

El-Amin stepped out of the helicopter with the assistance of the aircrewman who had entered the water and helped him out of the raft and into the horse-collar to be hoisted into the hovering helicopter. Ducking his head, he moved out from under the spinning blades and took in his surroundings. He was immediately surrounded by the Marines, one stepping behind him and handcuffing his hands behind his back. El-Amin hardly noticed; he was looking in awe at the sheer size of the aircraft carrier and at the number of jets spotted on deck. As he was guided toward the island, he continued to look at his surroundings, his jaw slack with amazement. At that moment he knew that his country was doomed if the Americans decided to go to war over Kuwait. Then all went black as a hood was placed over his head, and he was guided toward the island.

McCall turned to Vanzant, "Well, he doesn't look injured. I'm going below."

TWENTY-ONE

Central Red Sea

Exhausted, Commander Will Tanner walked forward through the first deck passageway, followed by Lieutenant Commander Andy Morton, his acting Executive Officer. It was almost midnight. Together they had inspected the damage throughout the ship. Aboard the flagship, *Saratoga*, Admiral McCall, and Commodore Vanzant were awaiting a detailed damage report. After a four-hour battle, the *Dauntless* damage control teams had put out the fire resulting from the Exocet missile attack. Emergency power had been restored to the after-part of the ship and steering control had been regained. Because the missile had struck above the waterline, the ship was in no danger of sinking. Thousands of gallons of firefighting water had been pumped over the side. *Dauntless* steamed slowly south, their orders were to proceed to the Saudi port of Jeddah. There a team from Commander, Middle East Force, and the Naval Sea Systems Command would survey the damage and determine the extent of voyage repairs that would be necessary for the ship to return home. Whatever the future held for the confrontation with Iraq, *Dauntless* would not be part of it. In all likelihood, de-commissioning would be moved forward, the cost of repairs not worth the limited service life remaining. The ship was no longer an effective fighting machine. Mount 51 and the anti-submarine weapons systems were the only major weapons still available. The missile system was completely out of commission, the launcher damaged, the magazine flooded, the remaining missiles rendered useless. Mount 52 was unusable, knocked out of alignment by the Exocet strike. It remained trained out to port where it had fired its last round before the missile hit. Inside the ship, the Engineering Department berthing compartment had been completely consumed by fire. Those that could sleep were on blankets and pillows on the mess decks or in unoccupied racks in other berthing compartments.

Miraculously there were few serious injuries. The Repair Three firefighters burned in the initial blast had been flown to *Saratoga* by helicopter for treatment by the medical staff and eventual evacuation to the military hospital in Landstuhl, Germany, if necessary. Lieutenant Commander McKnight was missing, and several crewmembers had been overcome by smoke. They too had been flown to the carrier. Several had suffered minor contusions and one a broken ankle. Those requiring more complex treatment had been lifted off the ship by helicopters from *Saratoga* and taken to the carrier where the medical department doctors would examine them. There they had joined MM3 Valencia and EMFA Busch who had been plucked out of the water with the aid of the rescue swimmer in the Sea King helicopter. Another helicopter had taken the wounded off, hovering over the forecastle because of the damage to the flight deck on the fantail and the interference of the disabled missile launcher. Valencia, Busch and the other injured crewmembers were being questioned by Admiral McCall's Intelligence Officer.

Nobody had witnessed McKnight's death. When Valencia and Busch had surfaced, he was gone. The helicopter crew had not seen him get blown off the lifeline aft, their attention had been drawn to the exploding missile. Their last sighting of McKnight had been of the last man on the fantail, dressed in a khaki uniform, about to join the other two in the water.

Wearily, Tanner climbed the ladder to the 0-2 level and turned into CIC. The CIC Officer, Lieutenant (junior grade) Willy Kim, had the watch. There was no department head level Tactical Action Officer on watch, they were otherwise occupied. Weapons Officer Vince DeVito was conducting his own assessment of the damage to his department, as was Chief Engineer Ken Carpenter.

With the ship sailing slowly south toward Jeddah, there was little in the way of operations left to conduct, merely safe navigation.

"Willy, what's the latest?" said Tanner.

"Sir, *Saratoga* is back on station north of here being screened by *Philippine Sea* and *Biddle*. She's got CAP up twenty-four seven now. The French have joined up. *Durance* is in company with *Sara,* and *Cassard* is in gate guard station. They're in our old station in Fenway."

Consulting his notes, Tanner sat in his CO chair and reached for the red radio hand set to make his latest report to Admiral McCall. He keyed the microphone button and waited for the encrypted signal to synchronize with the system on the carrier.

"Alpha Bravo this is *Dauntless* actual for Alpha Bravo actual, over."

Admiral McCall answered himself, "Go ahead Will, Admiral here, over."

"Admiral, I'll get you a complete written report in the morning. We're putting it together now. To summarize, I have only one killed in action, the XO, and several minor injuries. Those requiring treatment are aboard *Sara.* I appreciate *Sara's* support in medevacing the injured. Fires are out. We have full propulsion capability and have restored the steering system. My missile system is out of commission as is Mount 52. We're pumping out the flooded magazines. We have extensive fire damage in the after-part of the ship. Engineering Department berthing is unlivable, and several storerooms were damaged, over."

"Roger, Will," answered McCall, "What do you know about the XO's loss? Over."

"Sir, he was apparently still on the fantail when the missile on the rail exploded. Nobody actually saw what happened. My guess is he was blown over the side and drowned if he wasn't already dead from the blast. He saved the lives of the two men in after-steering. They would have been overcome by smoke, over."

There was a pause before the admiral responded, "Have you thought about how you want to handle the earlier situation given what happened today? Over."

Tanner also paused before responding. He looked around CIC. Heads were down at consoles, but he knew everyone within earshot was listening. The bridge would have the circuit dialed in as well.

"Admiral, I'd like to come over to the carrier and discuss it with you and the Commodore, tomorrow if possible. I'll hand carry the report, over."

"Roger Will, we'll send a helo down in the morning. Get some sleep tonight. Alpha Bravo, out."

Wearily Tanner turned to Kim, "Willy, I'll be on the bridge for a bit and then hit the rack. Follow the night orders and call me if you need to."

Tanner walked out into the darkened bridge, took the standard reports and climbed into his chair. *Dauntless* rode easily in a gently rolling sea. A bright three-quarter moon cast a yellow light on the ocean surface, running from the east, in the direction of Saudi Arabia, and ending at the ship, as it always did.

Tanner thought about Ricky McKnight. What he had done was nothing short of heroic. He had started the casualty notification process with a message to Commodore Nordstrom back in Mayport. The squadron would assign an officer to travel to the home of Theresa McKnight's parents and personally deliver the news. That same officer would be responsible for rendering all the assistance necessary for Theresa McKnight to receive the benefits due her following her husband's death. Typically that would include assisting with the burial arrangements, but in this case, there was no body.

He reflected on the surrounding circumstances. There was no undoing what had been done. He had fired McKnight, notified the chain of command, and notified the Bureau of Naval

Personnel. There was no walking that back. But McKnight had risked his life, ultimately losing it, to save the lives of Valencia and Busch.

For an hour Tanner sat in his chair, lost in thought. Periodically one of the department heads would enter the bridge and update him on their assessment of the damage in their respective areas of responsibility. Andy Morton consulted with him several times to review the official report which was slowly coming together. The bridge team quietly went about their business, speaking in low tones when necessary, acutely aware of the burden borne by their captain.

* * *

Ding, ding, ding, ding "*Dauntless*, departing," blared over the ship's announcing system as Commander Will Tanner slipped into the yellow horse-collar dangling beneath the SH-3 Sea King helicopter hovering over the forecastle. Lieutenant Commander Andy Morton, temporarily in command, watched from the bridge. Mount 51 was trained out to starboard, the barrel depressed, to clear enough room to use the forecastle as an emergency flight deck.

As the aircrewman grabbed the cable and pulled Tanner into a sitting position in the helicopter door, the CO gave a quick salute to Morton on the bridge. He scooted out of the open doorway and scrambled into a canvas seat on the opposite side of the helicopter, releasing the horse-collar and giving the young petty officer a thumb's up. Tanner settled in for the 100-mile flight north to where *Saratoga* was operating. Stuffed inside his khaki uniform shirt was a twenty-page report which outlined all of the events of the previous 24 hours as best as he, Morton, and the other department heads could reconstruct them. Morton had stayed up all night, taking statements from Vinny DeVito who had been the TAO, from the DCA and Chief Engineer, and from the three fire team leaders. Key among those was the statement of BM1 Octavious Butt, team leader for Repair Two. Missing from the report were the details of what had taken place in after-steering and on the fantail. Valencia and Busch remained aboard *Saratoga*, being treated for smoke inhalation. They had broken the report into two parts. The first covered the engagement with the Iraqi jets and Exocet missiles. The second section described the damage control efforts and summarized the extent of damage to *Dauntless*.

Tanner had gotten little sleep the previous night, assisting Morton with the report and sleeping fitfully when he could. Drafting the report had given him the opportunity to reflect on all the actions he had taken to fight off the attack, protect the carrier, and defend *Dauntless*. He had tossed and turned, playing and re-playing events in his head. Was there more he could have done? What could he have done differently? Weighing most heavily on his mind was Ricky McKnight. According to Petty Officer Butt, McKnight had been determined to get to the fantail and to the two men trapped in after-steering. Little was known about what had taken place on the fantail as the smoke and flames had blocked the view of Petty Officer Butt and his fire teams. They had been sheltering behind Mount 52 when the missile on the rail had exploded. They probably knew more on the carrier about what happened after interviewing Valencia and Busch.

Forty-five minutes later, the Sea King slowed and Tanner saw the white, foaming wake of the carrier as it churned through the Red Sea at 25 knots, launching and recovering aircraft. They paralleled the movement of the huge ship until the final aircraft of the cycle recovered and then the helicopter moved into a hover over the deck and gently settled in to land. As Tanner hopped out onto the flight deck, he smelled the familiar odor of jet fuel and sensed the heat and activity as the flight deck crew re-spotted the deck. Ducking his head, he jogged to the island where Saratoga's

Executive Officer, Captain Ben "Saint" Nicholson, awaited his arrival.

"Welcome aboard, Skipper," said Nicholson. "The admiral and everyone is waiting in the flag mess."

"Thanks, sir," shouted Tanner over the noise of jet engines. "Take me to sick bay first."

Nicholson gave Tanner a peculiar look, "The admiral, Commodore Vanzant, Captain Reasoner, CAG, they're all waiting for you."

Tanner fixed the more senior officer with a determined look, "I need to see my men first."

"Follow me," said Nicholson, raising his walkie-talkie to report the change in plans to the admiral's aide.

As he followed the XO, high stepping over knee knockers, Tanner marveled at the maze that was an aircraft carrier. *Have to give the XO credit for knowing where he's going* he thought to himself.

Entering Sick Bay, he immediately spotted his crew members, gathered around the bed holding Fireman William Cottrell, his broken ankle in a cast.

"Attention on deck," shouted MM3 Valencia, coughing slightly.

"At ease, carry on," said Tanner, holding out his hands palms down. "How's everybody doing?"

EMFA Busch spoke for the group, "They're taking good care of us, Captain. Good chow too. We can get ice cream anytime we want. And this thing doesn't move at all."

Tanner smiled. Destroyer sailors were always surprised and thrown a little off balance when they set foot on an aircraft carrier. After the rocking and rolling of a tin can, riding an aircraft carrier was like being on land.

Tanner motioned to MM3 Valencia, "Step over here and tell me what happened in after-steering. What did Commander McKnight do? And what happened to him?"

"Sir, he saved our lives. The hatch was jammed, and the space was filling up with smoke. The XO broke off a stanchion and pried the hatch open. Me and Busch would be fuckin'... oh, sorry sir... anyway, the place was filling up with smoke, and we couldn't get out."

Tanner nodded, what he expected, just not the details. "How'd you end up in the water?"

"There were flames all around the missile on the launcher. We heard the word passed about the missile maybe exploding. We saw a helicopter, and the XO told us to jump and swim for it."

"Did the XO jump too?"

"Captain, I don't know. Busch went first. Fuckin' dived in head first." Valencia blushed again. "Sorry, sir."

"Don't worry. Keep going."

"Anyway, I jumped in after Busch. I figured the XO would be right behind me. When I came up for air, there was an explosion, so I ducked under water again. So did Busch-man."

Tanner urged him on, "So you didn't see the XO jump?"

"No sir, when I came up again shit was flying everywhere, splashing into the water. But I never saw the XO again. I told all this to some lieutenant commander last night."

Tanner patted the sailor on the shoulder, "OK, Petty Officer Valencia, glad you're all right."

They rejoined the rest, "Fireman Cottrell looks like you're gonna be here for a while. I'll check with the Doc on the rest of you. As soon as you're ready, we need you back on *Dauntless*."

As a group, they saluted as Tanner headed for the door. "Thanks, XO," he said, "let's go see the admiral."

Escorted by Captain Nicholson, Tanner walked into the flag mess. Seated on the stuffed leather couch and adjoining chairs were Admiral McCall, Commodore Vanzant, Chief of Staff Captain Campbell, Captain Reasoner, and CAG, Commander Jim Herlong.

McCall waved Tanner to an empty chair, "Sit down Will, take a load off. How about some coffee?"

"Thanks, sir, that'd be great," answered Tanner. As he sat in an empty chair around the coffee table, he pulled his report out of his uniform shirt.

"Guess I should give this to the Commodore first," he said with a questioning look at Admiral McCall.

Commodore Vanzant grabbed it, "I'll have copies made," he said, motioning to his Chief Staff Officer and handing him the report.

A mess attendant handed Tanner a porcelain mug of steaming black coffee embossed with a two-star flag.

Admiral McCall began, "Will, I'm sorry to hear about Commander McKnight. Sounds like he acted heroically after the missile hit. We'll get to him in a minute. That was some great headwork yesterday, placing *Dauntless* between the attackers and *Saratoga* and using the five-inch like that. Near as we can tell, you knocked down two missiles with gunfire and one of the attacking jets with your SAMs."

Tanner nodded, he had not been sure about a second missile.

McCall continued, "*Sara* got a third missile with Sea Sparrow. As you know, two got through. CAG's guys bagged a second Mirage, and the third one ran out of gas. He punched out and was picked up by *Spruance* and brought here. He's been talking, so we know that there were three jets and six missiles were fired. Only five launched successfully, so that's what you were dealing with. As it turns out, the one that failed to transition to powered flight was launched by the pilot we picked up."

When McCall paused, Tanner interjected, "What happens now? That was an act of war against the United States."

McCall nodded, "It absolutely was. Higher authority is trying to figure out how to respond. We're still building up force in the region. Might not be ready just yet to strike back."

Before replying, Tanner looked at the other, more senior, officers. Nobody said anything.

"A few Tomahawks in to Baghdad would seem to be in order. Maybe hit the air base."

Admiral McCall smiled, "One would think so. Actually, it gets more complicated than that. These guys launched from Damascus, so the Syrians are involved at some level. Washington has a real mess on its hands, the Syrians are supposedly joining the coalition against Iraq. This calls all that into question. At any rate, that was great work yesterday. Now, as to *Dauntless*, Middle East Force will send a team to Jeddah to survey the damage. They'll be joined by some naval architect types from NAVSEA, my guess is as soon as you're deemed seaworthy, you'll be headed home to Mayport."

Tanner nodded, he had expected as much. They would want to put a patch in the side where the missile went in so the ship would be safe to steam across the Atlantic. So far, the admiral had done all the talking. He looked at Commodore Vanzant, still his direct operational boss.

With a nod to the admiral, Vanzant said, "Will, I'll be making a full report of your actions yesterday. I think a Presidential Unit Citation will be in order for *Dauntless*."

Mentally, Captain Alexander Vanzant had already thrown the letter of instruction he had drafted into the trash can.

He continued, "I'll be recommending you for a personal award and anyone else on *Dauntless* you want to recognize for their actions yesterday. Send me a write-up on each along with a recommended award."

"Yes sir, will do," said Tanner, and then he paused. "What... what about Commander McKnight?"

The admiral interjected, turning to the carrier commanding officer, XO, and CAG, he said, "Skipper, would you, XO, and CAG mind giving us some alone time to discuss a sensitive issue?"

As the three officers departed, McCall turned to Tanner, "Where do you stand on McKnight's relief... with regard to the Bureau?"

Tanner replied, "I had already notified the Bureau and requested a relief. Of course, Commodore Nordstrom knows back at DESRON 12, but I don't think anything official has happened yet. Haven't heard back from BUPERS. As you know, they cut the accounting data at the squadron to fly him home."

McCall and Vanzant exchanged glances. "He was married, right?" asked McCall.

"Yes sir, but they were having problems. I think his wife left town to be with her parents somewhere. Ricky showed me a Dear John letter the morning after he got drunk."

McCall considered this news. "How much does Commodore Nordstrom know about everything that happened yesterday?"

"He was on the OPREP-3 Navy Blue we got out last night. And your OPREP-3. Whatever is on the news back home, I guess."

McCall leaned forward, having decided how to proceed. "OK, first things first. Get the casualty assistance thing going through Commodore Nordstrom. We've got to get word to Mrs. McKnight. Do it right."

"Already done sir, DESRON 12 is assigning a CACO."

Turning to his Chief of Staff he said, "John, send out a follow-up to the OPREP-3 Navy Blue we sent last night. ASAP. Fold in additional details from Will's report, including casualties. Report that the CACO process is underway in the case of the XO. Make it clear he was the XO. No mention of the other problem."

"Yes sir," said Captain John Campbell, "on it."

Turning back to Tanner, McCall continued, "Will, in view of what happened yesterday, I think we ought to forget McKnight's transgression the other night. Of course, it's your call, he was your XO, but...," he trailed off.

"Sir, I was hoping you'd say that. I agree completely."

"You've got some missionary work to do back on *Dauntless*. I assume what happened is known by the crew," he said with a raised eyebrow.

"I can handle that sir," replied Tanner, "everyone knows what he did to save the two men in after-steering. I don't think it will be a problem."

Admiral McCall turned to Commodore Vanzant, "Commodore, anything else?"

Vanzant nodded at the admiral, "Yessir, Will and I have a couple of things to go over. We'll do it in my cabin."

Admiral McCall stood up and extended his hand, "Captain, great job yesterday. I want to come to the ship and talk to the crew when you get to Jeddah. Bravo Zulu."

As Vanzant and Tanner exited the flag mess, McCall considered his options. *Perhaps a call to his flag officer contacts at BUPERS might help erase any record of McKnight's earlier transgressions.*

* * *

Will Tanner followed Commodore Vanzant through the blue-tiled passageway to his stateroom, high stepping the knee knockers and watching as sailors going about their business flattened against the bulkhead as the commodore passed.

Pushing his stateroom door open, Vanzant motioned Tanner to take a seat on his couch as he plopped into his chair and swiveled around to face Tanner.

"How's the crew doing?" he asked.

This was a side of Vanzant that Tanner had not seen in their brief relationship. "They're tired. But otherwise doing great. To tell the truth, I think some of them are glad to know we're heading home. Some are pissed. Everybody is proud that we splashed one of the jets and knocked down a missile. They don't know about the second one... yet."

Vanzant nodded, "They have good reason to be proud. You did good yesterday Will."

Tanner nodded, waiting for the "but."

Vanzant noted the expectant look, smiled slightly, and went on, "Relax Will, all else is forgotten. You know I was initially unhappy with some of your actions in command. Yesterday changed all that. I'm going to recommend to Admiral McCall that he put you in for a Silver Star. You earned it. I'll also endorse any awards you recommend for your crew. I imagine there will be a lot."

Tanner nodded, "Silver Star seems kinda... extreme."

"It's not," responded Vanzant quickly, "let me worry about that."

Tanner looked down, then directly at Vanzant, "Roger sir, whatever you say. I'll get to work on the other awards. Anything else, sir?"

"No Will, you need to get back to your ship. Keep me informed on progress. Repairs, NAVCENT assessment, etcetera."

"Roger sir, will do." He stood, turned to leave, then turned back with his hand on the doorknob.

"Commodore, I want you to know that everything I've done in command of *Dauntless* has been done with the best of intentions. Taking care of my ship and crew, accomplishing the mission... everything. I was never trying to showboat or usurp your authority."

Vanzant fixed Tanner with an appraising look, then smiled slightly, "I know that Will, like I said, all is forgotten. Now get back to your ship."

Sharm-El-Sheikh, Egypt

The fishing vessel *Basra* motored northwest through the night, headed in the general direction of the Sinai Peninsula. Akram Najaf stayed in the pilothouse nervously considering all the possibilities that lay ahead. Da'wud had said nothing about the success or failure of the attack on the American aircraft carrier, remaining below in the small space containing his radio equipment. Ahead he saw the light on Ras Mohammed, at the very southern tip of the peninsula. A thousand thoughts raced through his mind, *what would happen next*? Could they sail into an Egyptian harbor and claim the need for voyage repairs to replace the lost nets? How would the Egyptian authorities react? Their passports identified he and the first mate as Iraqi, would that get them arrested perhaps? If the aircraft carrier had been attacked, might the *Basra* be viewed with more suspicion? Da'wud looked nothing like a fisherman, his hands were too soft, his skin not hardened by the sun and salt spray. He didn't dress like a fisherman.

He felt a presence behind him, turned and saw a figure silhouetted in the doorway by the light coming from below.

"Wake the mate, I need his help," ordered Da'wud from the doorway.

"Yes excellency, at once. What do you need?"

"The radio equipment, we must remove it before making port. Show me where we are heading."

After a quick scan of the horizon and a look at the radar to be sure no other ships were in the vicinity, Najaf secured the helm and walked to his chart table, pulling a flashlight out of the drawer.

"We are here," he said, jabbing a finger in the general area south and east of Ras Mohammed, "we can make Sharm El-Sheikh by mid-morning."

Da'wud studied the chart, not fully understanding what he was seeing.

"Have you been there before?"

"Never Excellency, I have never been this far north in the Red Sea."

Da'wud studied the chart, noting the city roughly indicated by a grid representing streets. It looked substantial as compared to some other towns both north and south along the coast. It would likely have a more vigilant harbor organization and a police force, perhaps also a military presence.

"I do not like it," he said, "where else can we go?"

Najaf studied the chart. The sooner he was rid of this man, the better.

"There are two smaller harbors to the south. Perhaps we would attract less attention there. I can anchor the boat and take you ashore in the Zodiac."

Najaf was savoring the possibility of being rid of the Mukhabarat officer, perhaps before the noon prayers.

"Head for the smaller of the two harbors," he said, jabbing his finger at the one labeled Ofira, "send the mate to the radio room."

Da'wud turned and disappeared down the small ladder to the messing area below. He had one more call to make on the radio before it went over the side.

* * *

It was past midnight when Da'wud and the mate finished disconnecting the radio equipment and tossing it over the side along with the special high-frequency antenna that had been mounted on the roof of the pilothouse. As the mate leaned over the transom, feeding the last of the antenna wiring into the wake, Da'would crept up behind him, a slender knife with a very long and very sharp blade in his right hand. The mate sensed the movement and began to turn forward, but Da'wud was too fast. He grabbed the mate under the chin from behind and jerked his head to the side. With a slashing motion, he cut the man's throat, pushing him against the transom as he did. The mate registered a wide-eyed look of shock as the blood sprayed out of his neck, the Carotid artery completely severed. Releasing the knife to fall on deck, Da'wud leaned down and grabbed an ankle with one hand and levered the mate over the transom into the wake.

He picked up the knife and looked for a rag to wipe it clean. *The blood will attract sharks, by morning there will be nothing left to find.* He inspected himself in the dim light provided by the moon, his shirt was bloodstained. He would have to hide it until it was time to deal with Najaf.

* * *

As the sun rose over the Saudi Arabian mainland, a very tired Akram Najaf steered the Basra into a small harbor just south of Ofira, Egypt. Next to him in the pilothouse stood Mahmoud Da'wud, silently watching as Najaf called down to the mess deck for his first mate, getting no response. The harbor featured nothing more than a small fishing village with a few commercial dive boats to cater to the European tourists eager to explore the reefs and crystal-clear waters off the Sinai Peninsula. A small peninsula jutted into the Red Sea, separating the harbor from the larger Egyptian town of Ofira.

"Where is that oaf?" muttered Najaf.

"Never mind him, he is no doubt asleep, we were up all night."

So was I, but best not to irritate this man.

"Anchor the boat and take me ashore in the Zodiac."

Afraid to argue, Najaf slowed the *Basra*, consulted his chart and depth finder and headed for an open area some 100 meters from a small pier on the south side of the bay. Stopping the fishing boat, he scrambled to the forecastle to lower the anchor, cursing his absent first mate as he did. Da'wud remained in the pilothouse, studying the shoreline through the binoculars.

As Najaf re-entered the pilothouse and gently backed the engine to set the anchor, he looked worriedly at Da'wud. *Now what, something is not right here, the mate would have awakened as the chain rattled over the side and the engine stopped.*

He looked sideways at Da'wud and was suddenly facing a pistol. In Da'wud's other hand was a small briefcase.

"Now take me ashore in the Zodiac. To that beach over there."

"What has happened to my mate?" said a suddenly emboldened Najaf. He feared he would be killed himself once he delivered Da'wud to the deserted stretch of beach.

"Do not worry about him, do as I say, now!"

Najaf and Da'wud went to the fantail where Najaf began to prepare the Zodiac to be swung over the side. He saw the bloodstained deck at the transom and knew that the first mate was gone.

Da'wud nervously scanned the shore and the surrounding water for signs that someone in authority was interested in the newly arrived fishing vessel. There was no activity. Turning his attention to Najaf, he kept the pistol pointed while the fisherman lowered the inflatable boat over the side.

"Now go down and start it."

Najaf climbed over the rail into the Zodiac and started the engine. He considered making a run for it, but Da'wud hovered at the rail, his gun aimed at the fisherman. He climbed back aboard, expecting his life would end at any moment. Thoughts of his family raced through his mind. Da'wud simply signaled him to the opposite side of the deck and climbed over the side. Casting off the line, he revved the engine and sped off toward an empty stretch of beach. Akram Najaf could not believe his luck; it was over. He cursed the bad luck that had placed his fishing boat in Sudan when all of this trouble started. Watching as the Zodiac made landfall, he saw Da'wud climb out into knee deep water and make his way ashore carrying the briefcase. Resignedly, he turned to go below decks to look for his first mate. In his heart, he knew he would not find him.

TWENTY-TWO

Epilogue

Jeddah, Saudi Arabia

USS Dauntless sat at a decrepit commercial pier in the busy Saudi Arabian Red Sea port of Jeddah, halfway down the Red Sea, 600 miles south of the area where the Exocet attack had occurred. She was a shadow of her former self, her "greyhound of the sea" lines marred by the actions taken by the Naval Sea Systems Command engineers and Saudi yard workers under contract to the U.S. Navy. Tied up to the starboard side of the ship was a large floating barge upon which rested Mount 52 and the single arm Mark 13 guided-missile launcher. Both had been disconnected from all power and hydraulic fittings and lifted off the ship by floating crane. The engineers had determined that stability would be improved by removing their combined topside weight. They were now strapped to the barge with a series of sturdy wires and straps in preparation for a contracted ocean-going tug to deliver them to the naval shipyard in Philadelphia. The after-part of the ship looked naked, the gun mount gone and the missile launcher removed, leaving only the cylindrical missile magazine aft of the deckhouse. A temporary patch had been welded over the hole in the port side where the Exocet missile had entered the ship. Some cosmetic touch-up painting had been applied, but the port side hull and the after deckhouse were marred by black smoke smudges and burned areas where the fire had raged. Below decks the after-part of the ship was unlivable. Passageways and bulkheads were scarred with the evidence of fire, much lagging and insulation, badly burned, had been ripped out and discarded. Many electrical cables had also been pulled, no longer functional or no longer needed to

363

deliver electrical power to the badly damaged spaces they once served. Much torn and ripped aluminum and steel had been cut away, and an attempt made to smooth rough edges. Still, crewmembers and yard workers were scurrying about the ship, cleaning up after the repair work and making her ready to go to sea. There was little thought given to a more thorough refurbishment. A decision had been made to send the ship directly to Philadelphia to be decommissioned and then probably scrapped. With the help of Commodore Nordstrom and Admiral McCall, Tanner had successfully fought this decision. *Dauntless* would sail home to Mayport where a proper decommissioning ceremony would be conducted; then the ship would go to Philadelphia Naval Shipyard. Tanner had argued that the ship had finished a distinguished thirty-year career with the heroic action in the Red Sea – the crew deserved a proper send-off.

It had been two frenzied weeks since the attack. Will Tanner had been fully engrossed in the recovery of his ship, the myriad reports which were required, monitoring the progress of repairs, and dealing with personnel issues. While he had kept abreast of the operational reports emanating from the *Saratoga* Battle Group, he knew that he was out of the picture, no longer part of the team. In the weeks following the attack, much activity had occurred on the diplomatic as well as the military front. There were now a much larger group of ships in the Red Sea, enforcing the United Nations sanctions on Iraq. American ships were now sailing in company with destroyers and frigates from France, Great Britain, Italy, Spain, and Greece. A second U.S. carrier, *USS America (CV-66),* was underway in the Mediterranean and would soon transit Suez and join *Saratoga*. Inside the Persian Gulf, an even larger flotilla was assembling and a second aircraft carrier was on the way to join *USS Independence.*

Ashore, the force build-up of Army, Marine and Air Force units continued. The Air Force, smarting from the embarrassment of having been outwitted by Tikriti's strike, had increased combat air patrols and extended the coverage further west. The odds of a second air attack in the Red Sea were infinitesimal.

Despite all this, no retaliatory strikes had been ordered. Tanner was dismayed by this fact. Having been on the receiving end, he could not understand the hesitancy on the part of the U.S. to punish Iraq for the attack. The Iraqi government under Saddam Hussein had claimed that the attack was unauthorized, planned and executed by a group of rogue pilots who had faked their defection to escape with the jets and missiles. In an attempt to convince the world of this fact, Saddam had publicly hanged four senior air force officers, claiming that they had facilitated the plot. In captivity, Major Dawud El-Amin told a different story, alleging that he had been ordered to participate in the attack or face his own trip to the gallows. He was talking freely, maintaining that the attack was backed by the Iraqi government, even disclosing the code name Tikriti had chosen: Operation Birds of Prey. Regardless, his voice was drowned out by the higher-level diplomatic squabbling. In Syria, President Assad had likewise claimed that the attack had been enabled by a small group of traitors who were all now under arrest. Neither of these claims was believed by clear thinking leaders in any capital. But the United Nations had urged restraint until the claims could be further investigated and either proven or disproven. President Bush, in the process of building an international coalition to force Iraq from Kuwait, had demurred, not wanting to risk the collapse of the coalition by conducting a unilateral retaliatory strike. The involvement of Syria further complicated things. *So, there you have it*, thought Tanner, *inaction*.

Aboard *Dauntless*, they had been visited by Rear Admiral McCall the day before. The crew had been assembled on the forecastle, and the admiral had pinned awards on many of the crew. The higher-level awards requiring approval in Washington, including Tanner's Silver Star, were not yet ready, but many deserving crewmembers who had performed heroically during the tragedy were recognized with lesser awards. Will had put Ricky McKnight in for a posthumous Bronze Star, but that too would take more time. They planned a memorial service for the former exec when the ship was back in Mayport, and Theresa McKnight could attend.

His own future, beyond returning *Dauntless* to the United States, was less certain. Depending on the timing of the transit and decommissioning, he would be leaving *Dauntless* with less than six months in command, hardly a full tour. A second destroyer command would seem to be in order but that all depended on the mysterious workings of the Navy personnel system. Walking forward on the starboard side main deck, Tanner entered the ship by a water tight hatch just aft of the starboard break. Passing through the light locker curtains, he turned forward and headed for the wardroom. It was time for that day's planning meeting with the officers and key chief petty officers.

"Attention on deck," announced Andy Morton as Tanner pushed through the wardroom door. Chairs scraped as those officers sitting around the table leaped to their feet.

"At ease, seats everybody," he said, taking his own seat at the head of the table. "Let's go over the status of repairs and readiness for sea, then we'll talk about the transit. Cheng, you first."

Each of the department heads ran down his own list of equipment casualties and status of repairs. Vince DeVito had the most mission degrading report with the loss of the after-gun mount and the missile launcher. Ken Carpenter reported the engineering plant in good condition and ready for the trip home. Supply Officer Larry Logan updated Tanner on stores and his department's ability to issue spare parts and feed the crew.

Finally, Andy Morton, as acting Executive Officer and also Operations Officer ran down the schedule.

"Captain, we're scheduled underway tomorrow with the Suez transit north in two days. We'll anchor at Port Suez the night before and be the first ship in the convoy north the next day around oh-six-hundred. We're scheduled into Naples to refuel and take on stores on the fifteenth, and we'll do a BSF in Rota on the nineteenth. Should be back in Mayport on the twenty-sixth. So far the weather looks good all the way."

Tanner interrupted the brief to add his own input.

"Ops, got a P4 in from the admiral a little while ago, seems we are to join up with *Sara* day after tomorrow for a sail-by. Looks like they want to say goodbye before we go through the ditch and head home. Although there are no details, let's plan on manning the rail in summer white uniform. Fly the battle ensign. If nothing else, it'll be good practice for pulling in to Mayport."

Andy Morton paused, then added, "Not everybody has whites Captain, particularly the snipes. A lot got destroyed in the fire."

Tanner smiled, "You department heads figure it out. Do the best you can. If an electrician is wearing a gunner's mate crow, nobody on the carrier will notice."

Everyone nodded their understanding. Some uniform swapping was in order.

Tanner nodded, "Okay everybody, good work getting the ship ready to head home. Cheng, keep an eye on the soft patch, especially if we hit any weather. Let's make all preparations to get underway."

Northern Red Sea

Commander Will Tanner lowered his binoculars and turned to the Officer of the Deck, Lieutenant John Woodson, "All stations ready?" he asked.

"Yes sir, restricted maneuvering is set, we're ready to go alongside."

Tanner looked over the port side bridge wing at the forecastle and then aft along the port side main deck and ASROC deck. *Dauntless'* crew was manning the rails, a sailor in summer white uniform spaced every five feet along the port side main deck and O-1 level decks. They looked sharp, standing at parade rest.

He tapped the conning officer, Ensign Walter Sloan, on the shoulder, "Okay Wally, bring her alongside."

In his P4 message, Admiral McCall had ordered *Dauntless* to pass in review of *Saratoga* as they made their way north to the Gulf of Suez. Admiral McCall had not directed the dress uniform, but Tanner thought it appropriate. He glanced up at the port yardarm to see the over-sized American flag, the battle ensign, fluttering in the breeze.

As they had briefed, *Dauntless* made a more leisurely approach up the aircraft carrier's starboard side; at fifteen knots instead of twenty-five. Tanner did not want a high-speed approach to soak the crew manning the rail. Besides he recognized this for what it was, a chance for his crew to be recognized for what they had done to protect the carrier. As they drew abeam of the carrier, he saw that the flight deck was lined with *Saratoga* officers and crew, watching the approach of the gritty little destroyer which had fought so valiantly.

As *Dauntless* drew even with the carrier's island, Tanner nodded to John Woodson while Sloan slowed to match the carrier's speed.

"*Tweet, tweet*, attention to port!" sounded over *Dauntless'* announcing system. Tanner watched proudly as his crew snapped to attention, the giant aircraft carrier looming overhead 300 feet away.

Saratoga responded with one whistle blast and those manning the decks also snapped to attention. Before Tanner could give the order for his crew to salute in the direction of the carrier, one whistle sounded from *Saratoga,* and all hands on deck saluted *Dauntless.* This was a reversal of protocol with the admiral and a more senior commanding officer in *Saratoga,* but the meaning was not lost on Tanner or his crew. As they returned the salute, a loud roar sounded overhead. Tanner looked up to see a flight of two F-14 Tomcats roar overhead. As they passed forward of the bow, both fighters waggled their wings in salute and then climbed vertically in full afterburner.

As the two jets climbed almost out of sight, Tanner looked at the island to see Rear Admiral McCall and Commodore Vanzant waving from the bridge, standing next to Captain Mike Reasoner. He waved back.

Over Saratoga's loudspeakers came, "Aboard *USS Dauntless*, welcome alongside *USS Saratoga!*" then, "Hip, hip, hooray, hip, hip, hooray, hip, hip hooray!"

As they watched from *Dauntless*, they saw that every person on the flight deck was joining in the cheer.

As *Saratoga* tweeted the carry-on signal, Tanner turned to Ensign Sloan, "All right Wally, take us out of here, twenty knots."

As *Dauntless* powered away from the carrier's side, Andy Morton secured the crew from manning the rail. Once clear, Tanner stepped into the pilothouse and grabbed the 1MC microphone.

"Bombers, this is the Captain. Let's go home."

# # #

USS DAUNTLESS (DDG-25)

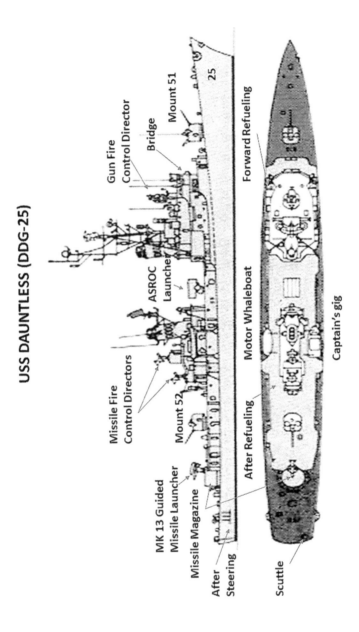

Gun Fire Control Director

Bridge

Mount 51

Forward Refueling

Missile Fire Control Directors

Mount 52

ASROC Launcher

Motor Whaleboat

Captain's gig

MK 13 Guided Missile Launcher

Missile Magazine

After Refueling

After Steering

Scuttle

25

GLOSSARY OF TERMS

1MC	The ship's general announcing system.
21MC	A system for communicating between various locations on a Navy ship. Often called the "bitch box."
530F	French-made short to medium range air-to-air missile. Widely exported.
A-6	A two-seat attack jet aircraft launched from an aircraft carrier designed to attack ground targets or enemy ships. Named *Intruder*. Introduced in 1963, retired in 1997.
A-7	A single seat attack jet aircraft designed to attack ground targets or enemy ships. Named *Corsair*. Introduced in 1967, retired in 1991.
AAWC	Anti-Air Warfare Commander. Responsible for air defense in the Composite Warfare Commander concept.
AD	NATO designation for a destroyer tender. A repair ship.
AIM-9	U.S. made short range air-to-air missile using infrared homing.
Alidade	A magnified scope mounted on a pelorus and gyro repeater with a mirror system to determine the bearing to other ships or objects.
Alpha Bravo	The Battle Group Commander in the Composite Warfare Commander concept.

Alpha Sierra	The Screen Commander in the Composite Warfare Commander concept.
AOE	Abbreviation for an auxiliary ship capable of delivering fuel oil, ammunition, and stores to Navy ships at sea.
ASROC	Anti-Submarine Rocket. A rocket mounted with an anti-submarine torpedo. Allows an attack on an enemy submarine from a safer distance.
AWACS	Airborne Warning and Control System. A modified Boeing 707 airframe with a large rotating radome radar for detecting aircraft and controlling fighters for intercepts.
BRAA	Fighter control voice call abbreviation for Bearing, Range, Altitude, Aspect
BRAVO ZULU	Navy Signal Book code for "Well Done."
CACO	Casualty Assistance Control Officer.
CAP	Abbreviation for Combat Air Patrol, a section of fighters airborne to protect the battle group from attack.
CASREP	Casualty Report. For reporting equipment degradations.
CDO	Command Duty Officer. The officer responsible for the ship while in port or at anchor.
CG	NATO designation for a guided-missile cruiser.
Chaff	Mylar strips launched to decoy an incoming missile away from a ship.
CHENG	Slang for Chief Engineer.

CIC	Combat Information Center. The nerve center of a Navy ship containing all the displays and weapons control consoles necessary to fight the ship.
CIWS	Close-in-Weapons System. A 20 mm Gatling gun designed to provide basic point defense against an incoming missile.
CO	Abbreviation for Commanding Officer.
Commair	Commercial aircraft
Commodore	An officer in overall charge of a group of Navy ships. Normally holds the rank of captain.
Conn	To drive the ship. The officer driving the ship is said to have the conn; the conning officer.
CPA	Closest Point of Approach.
Cru-Des	Slang for cruiser, destroyer, and frigate class Navy ships
CRUDESGRU	Abbreviation for Cruiser-Destroyer Group.
CTF	Navy designation, followed by a number, for Commander Task Force.
CTG	Navy designation, followed by a number, for Commander Task Group.
CV	NATO designation for an aircraft carrier not powered by a nuclear reactor.
CWC	Composite Warfare Commander. Overall in charge of subordinate warfare commanders.
DD	NATO designation for a destroyer, not carrying anti-air missiles.
DDG	NATO designation for a guided-missile destroyer.

DESRON	Abbreviation for Destroyer Squadron.
E-2C	A propeller driven airborne command and control aircraft launched from aircraft carriers. Named *Hawkeye*. Introduced in 1964.
EA-6B	A four -seat Electronic Warfare jet aircraft launched from aircraft carriers. Named *Prowler*. Capable of detecting and jamming enemy radars or communications and of launching anti-radar missiles. Introduced in 1971, retired in 2015.
ELINT	Electronics Intelligence.
EMCON	Emission Control. Specifies which electronic transmission equipment may be used.
EVAL	An enlisted performance evaluation report.
Exocet	A French-made (Exocet is "flying fish" in French) missile capable of attacking surface ships which can be launched from aircraft, ships, submarines, and helicopters.
F-14	A multi-role fighter. Named the *Tomcat*. Introduced in 1974, retired in 2006.
Fantail	The after portion of the main deck on a Navy ship.
FF	NATO designation for a frigate.
FFG	NATO designation for a guided-missile frigate.
FITREP	Fitness Report. For reporting on the performance of officers.
Forecastle	The forward-most portion of the main deck on a Navy ship.

Growler A communication device on a Navy ship. The desired station is selected and then a hand crank spun to "ring" the phone at the other end.

Harpoon A surface-to-surface or air-to-surface missile for attacking enemy ships.

JOOD Junior Officer of the Deck. Assistant to the OOD on the bridge. Generally, under instruction and not yet qualified as OOD.

LORAN A low frequency hyperbolic radio signal used as an aid to navigation.

Mirage F-1 A French built single seat fighter and attack aircraft. Widely exported.

Mo-Board Maneuvering Board. A circular plot on paper for converting relative motion as seen on a ship radar to true motion.

Mukhabarat The Iraqi Intelligence Service under Saddam Hussein.

Knot A unit of speed equal to the distance travelled in nautical miles in one hour.

Nautical Mile 2,000 yards or 6,000 feet.

NTDS Naval Tactical Data System.

O-1 Level One deck above the main deck on a Navy ship, each successive deck above numbered O-2, etc.

Omega An electronic aid to navigation using high-frequency radio signals from different transmitting stations.

OOD Officer of the Deck. Officer in charge on the bridge.

Ops	Slang for Operations Officer.
Pelorus	A stand mounting a gyro repeater which indicates the ship's course. Also used to determine the bearing of other ships or objects when fitted with an alidade.
PRITAC	Primary Tactical radio circuit between ships at sea.
POD	Plan of the Day.
Red Phone	Encrypted radio system for communications between ships at Sea.
REFTRA	Refresher training. Determines a ship's basic readiness to proceed to more advanced training.
S-3	A four seat anti-submarine and anti-surface jet launched from aircraft carriers. Named Viking. Introduced in 1974, retired in 2016.
SAM	Surface-to-Air Missile.
SH-2	An anti-submarine helicopter launched from Navy cruisers, destroyers and frigates. Named *Seasprite*. Introduced in 1962, retired in 1993.
SH-3	An anti-submarine helicopter launched from aircraft carriers and large deck amphibious ships. Named *Sea King*. Introduced in1961, retired in 2006.
Skunk	An unidentified radar contact held on surface search radar.
SOE	Schedule of Events.
SPA-25	Radar repeater showing the input from a Navy surface search radar.

Stadimeter A hand held device for measuring the range to ships close by when radars are not effective.

Suppo Slang for Supply Officer.

SWDG Surface Warfare Development Group.

SWO Surface Warfare officer. An officer trained in surface ship operations.

TAO Tactical Action Officer. Stationed in CIC with authority to employ weapons in an emergency.

Taps End of the working day, normally 2200 or 10:00PM. Only emergency announcements permitted until morning reveille.

TG Task group. Followed by a number. Denotes the ships assigned to a Task Group Commander (CTG).

UNREP Underway replenishment. Ships go alongside while underway to transfer fuel, supplies, ammunition and personnel.

VAMPIRE Navy code word transmitted over voice circuits to report an incoming missile.

VERTREP Vertical replenishment by helicopter.

VHF Very High-Frequency, 30MHZ to 300MHZ.

Weps Slang for Weapons Officer.

XO Abbreviation for Executive Officer, the second in command on a Navy ship.

CPSIA information can be obtained
at www.ICGtesting.com
Printed in the USA
BVHW04s2128250518
517470BV00001B/102/P